BARCELONA FLING WITH A SECRET PRINCE

ELLA HAYES

BILLIONAIRE'S SNOWBOUND MARRIAGE REUNION

JUSTINE LEWIS

MILLS & BOON

First published in Great Britain 2023
by Mills & Boon, an imprint of HarperCollins*Publishers* Ltd,
1 London Bridge Street, London, SE1 9GF

www.harpercollins.co.uk

HarperCollins*Publishers*
Macken House, 39/40 Mayor Street Upper,
Dublin 1, D01 C9W8, Ireland

ISBN: 978-0-263-30639-2

02/23

MIX
Paper | Supporting
responsible forestry
FSC™ C007454

BARCELONA FLING WITH A SECRET PRINCE

ELLA HAYES

MILLS & BOON

For my mother-in-law, Gill.

PROLOGUE

Breaking: Dralk crash kills three Brostovenian Royals!

KING CARLOS MUNOZ of Brostovenia and his youngest son Prince Hugo died when the racing car driven by heir apparent Prince Gustav swerved to avoid a collision then ploughed into the VIP stand at Dralk this afternoon.

All three royals and a handful of other spectators were pronounced dead at the scene.

Too stunned to make an official statement, the royal family has requested that its privacy be respected at this time.

Prince Gustav's passion for motor racing has long been criticised by the establishment in Brostovenia, but the thirty-three-year-old Prince would not be dissuaded from competing—encouraged, it seems, by both King Carlos and Prince Hugo, who were both enthusiastic motor-racing fans and regularly attended his races.

Prince Gustav's fiancée, Analiese Mercia, was not, on this occasion, at the trackside on account of illness. She is said to be inconsolable.

This triple tragedy is a devastating blow to the Brostovenian royal family and to the country. Floral tributes are already mounting along the perimeter walls of the Grand Palace at Nyardgat, where a grief-stricken populace is congregating.

King Carlos Munoz was well loved, as were the Princes. Prince Gustav in particular had an easy, approachable quality that, together with his good looks and unquestionable skill behind the wheel, won the hearts and minds of Brostovenians from all walks of life.

The question now is who will accede? King Carlos's younger brother, Prince Bassel, is next in line, but Bassel underwent heart surgery last year and, although it has been reported that the sixty-year-old Prince is recovering well, Bassel's reign may prove to be a short one if his son, Prince Raffiel, is drafted in by the royal household.

How that is going to suit the hitherto independent thirty-one-year-old architect Prince remains to be seen.

CHAPTER ONE

Six months later...

'IT'S GOOD OF you to have come, Your Highness.'

Arlo's smile was tightly framed, hesitant.

Raffiel felt a corresponding tightness notching along his jaw. Is this how things were going to be now, tension twitching behind the eyes of beloved associates who would have previously seized his hand in a vigorous smiling hand-shake, asking him how his flight had been or if he'd seen the match last night? Not Arlo's fault, of course. Formal condolences might have been made months ago but there was still a gaping black hole where normal life had been and everyone was trying to adjust, himself included.

He felt his gaze sliding, as it so often did these days, to the window and the freedom beyond it. Today's freedom was blue. Blue sea. Blue sky. High sun. A perfect Barcelona day, day one of the seven precious days he had left. This week, attending the annual International Conference of Architecture and Interior Design, the conference he'd founded and of which he was the patron, was going to be his last ever week of normal, his last chance to move through the world without a security detail at his shoulder, without everyone around him tripping over themselves to be correct and courteous. He felt his airways starting to constrict, something snapping inside. If this was his last week of freedom, then he absolutely wasn't going to spend it breathing stilted air with Arlo or anyone else. He needed to be himself, for his own sake, and for Arlo's.

He met his friend's gaze. 'Thanks, but I was hardly going to miss it after all the work we put in.' He held out his hand, felt a smile coming as Arlo pumped it warmly. 'And please, don't call me "Your Highness". It feels seriously weird.'

'It does…' Arlo's smile was wider now, but his eyes were sad. 'Especially after all these years…'

Four years specifically, working together on the conference programme, each year aiming for better, brainstorming ideas, ideas such as moving the whole thing to the World Trade Centre, adding the exhibition element. He'd never concealed his royal status, but he'd never invoked it either because it was irrelevant. He'd always styled himself Raffiel Munoz because that was who he was, and it was who he'd always been with Arlo, just another architect with a passion for design in all its forms, an architect who wanted to bring creatives together once a year in Gaudí's city. An ache coiled in his chest. But now he was on a new path, which meant handing over to Arlo. It was why he was here in Arlo's suite at the Barcelona Regal, to bang another nail into the coffin of his old life.

'So…' Arlo was bouncing his palms together in that way he did when he was keen to move things along. 'How about a beer?'

'Sounds good.' Raffiel felt his limbs loosening. This was more like it, more like them. Except he wasn't following Arlo over to the fridge, was he, asking him about his latest project, or about his family? He wanted to but he didn't seem to have it in him to make small talk.

He crossed to the sofa and sank down, letting the weariness rinse through. It was how he felt all the time now—

weary—how he'd been feeling ever since Dralk. That was what grief did to you. Drained you to the last drop. Even the small jumping elation of being in a hotel suite that actually felt like an interesting space wasn't enough to lift him.

'I really am so sorry, Raff.' Arlo was coming back with two beers. He handed one over then dropped onto the opposite sofa, elbows on his knees. 'I can't even begin to imagine…'

Everyone's words ran out like this, but it didn't matter because words didn't help anyway. Words didn't take away the pain. The wall of grief was towering, impenetrable, but curiously the grief itself was athletic, twisting and writhing inside, surfacing then deep diving. Impossible to contain or explain.

He forced out a smile. 'It's fine. I don't need a speech. The beer's enough.' He put the bottle to his lips and drank, which was easier than holding Arlo's gaze. That was another thing about grief. The people who cared about you were always trying to take the measure of it, out of concern, naturally, but still, it was hard to bear sometimes. He went for another mouthful then turned the bottle around in his hands, wiping off the condensation, keeping his eyes down,

Papa wouldn't approve of him drinking in the middle of the day, but then Papa didn't have a say in what he did this week. That was the deal they'd made. This week he was to honour his obligations in Barcelona, hand over the conference reins to Arlo Ferranti, then return home to a schedule of increasingly high-profile royal duties.

'The people don't know you, Raff. You need to be seen, build a public profile, otherwise when the time comes…'

Papa's way of reminding him that the time for him to ascend was coming sooner rather than later. Time for him to step up, fill three pairs of shoes he didn't have a clue how to fill. His whole life he'd been fourth in line with the only expectation being an ever-increasing distance from the throne. Fourth in line hadn't felt like being in line at all. Fourth in line had meant freedom, a career he loved, a life that had in no way prepared him for the top job.

And now poor Papa was blaming himself for not having raised him to be more 'royal', for not equipping him, but it wasn't Papa's fault. No one could have foreseen this, and no one could change it, any more than they could fix Papa's heart. Fact was, in spite of the surgery, Papa's heart wasn't strong. If it had been, Papa would never have been handing him this burden so soon. He knew it—he did—and the part of him that was a loving, loyal son wanted to rise nobly to the challenge, rescue Papa from everything, but the other part of him, the part that had only ever known freedom, was screaming angry, full of bitterness and resentment.

But no amount of screaming could change fate. The royal household was hushing up the real state of Papa's health but beneath the surface feet were paddling hard. Plans were being laid and provisional timetables were being proposed for the abdication of King Bassel and for his own coronation.

He felt the coiling ache in his chest twisting itself into a hard knot. That meant dismantling Raff Munoz piece by piece, his architecture business, his homes in New York and Paris. He had decisions to make about which of his patronages he could maintain but the rest was out of his hands, in the name of duty. How much he wanted to be dutiful, for Papa's sake, but losing control didn't sit well, and neither did being told what to do…how he must filter into active royal life, how he must smile to order, endear himself to the nation.

He felt a prickle along his hairline, sweat breaking. Bad enough, but there was also pressure mounting for him to find a suitable bride, a bride with the right pedigree, and glamorous, of course, someone able to lift the mood of the people, divert them, because obviously diverting and up-lifting the people was way more important than his own happiness!

He felt his fingers tightening around the beer bottle. As if he could even think about someone new when Brianne's sting was still lodged and throbbing beneath his skin. Five years together, thrown away just like that. They were stale, she'd said, past their sell-by date. Funny how he hadn't no-ticed! Funny how he'd been on the verge of proposing, liter-ally had the ring in his pocket, the romantic date lined up...

And now proposing was exactly what the powers behind the throne wanted him to do after, what, a few months of courtship with some picked-out princess? God help him, candidates were already being earmarked. Even poor Analiese's name had been tendered in the name of tidiness. Tidy it might be, but Analiese wasn't his type—whatever that was—and he most definitely wasn't *hers*. Gus was... *Had been.* She'd been crazy for Gus, handsome, laid-back Gus... That dazzling smile of his, that ability he'd had to make everyone feel important, even *him*, the geeky cousin obsessed with buildings and art and design. Gus had al-ways had time for him. It's why he'd loved him so much...

He felt a hot ache filling his throat. He wasn't a worthy successor. He didn't have a quarter of his cousin's charisma, not that charisma had done Gus any good in the end, had it? Charisma wasn't Teflon. He felt the ache spreading, his sinuses burning. Why did Gus have to have been hell-bent on racing no matter what? Why couldn't Uncle Carlos have been less indulgent, said no to Gus for once in his life? He'd been the King after all!

Had been...

He inhaled, swallowing hard. *Selfish, Raffiel!* Who was he to rail at his cousin? Gus had only wanted a little of what he'd always taken for granted: freedom to pursue his passion, freedom to be himself. He couldn't blame Gus for wanting that, and in his heart he didn't. But the fact remained, whether it was ignoble to think it or not, because of Gus, they were all ruined.

And now here he was wandering around inside his own head when he was supposed to be thrashing out details, handing over reins. Arlo was being kind, not hurrying him, but he needed to push himself along. He drained his beer and put the bottle down. Handing over a piece of his life, even to Arlo, was a wrench, but letting the minutes tick past was only prolonging the agony. Better to get it over with then he could hit the streets, lose himself in the crowds, maybe sink a few more beers and forget about everything, at least for a while.

Dulcie dragged her eyes away from the sparkling view and looked at both of her cousins in turn. Tilly was pretzeled in a chair, applying livid purple polish to her toenails, earbuds in, tuned out. Georgina was propped against the wide padded headboard of her king-size, tapping and scrolling on her phone, one silk chemise strap hanging off her shoulder.

'So you don't want to come?'

'Sorry, Dulce, I can't.' Georgina looked up briefly, then went back to her phone. 'I've got a raging bloody hangover.'

Which clearly wasn't affecting her vision, or her coordination. She still seemed to be able to tap and swipe at lightning speed. Dulcie felt a sigh gathering. What was this endless fascination with phones? She didn't get it, meanwhile 'online' seemed to have become Georgie's default setting. Social media, celebrity gossip, this one and that one, doing whatever to whomever, but if this was how Georgie wanted to spend her hen week then who was she to judge? Each to her own and all that.

She bit her lips together. It was just that *she* wasn't hungover herself, and she didn't want to be sitting twiddling her thumbs waiting for Georgie to perk up and for all the other girls to emerge only to be then left dangling at the edges of things as usual.

She slid her gaze back to the view. Not Georgie's fault that she was on the outside. It was where she'd planted herself years ago, wasn't it, deliberately, because of Charlie? Charlie Prentice, the great golden pretender. *The great liar!* She swallowed hard, pushing the thought away. But in any case, she probably wouldn't have fitted in with Georgie's friends. They were light and breezy, always laughing and teasing each other, whereas she was serious, arty, singular. Bridesmaid number five, the one Georgie had had to ask because she was family, because Lady Georgina Rayner was bound over by etiquette whether she was prepared to admit it or not, and etiquette demanded that sisters, cousins and the groom's sisters had to be invited to be attendants even if they weren't an obvious fit.

She felt a little tug inside. So maybe she hadn't always been so insular, and maybe she and Georgie *had* been close once, but in a million years she hadn't imagined that Georgie would actually *want* her to be a bridesmaid. Wrong! At Christmas, just after presents, Georgie had cornered her.

'Look, Dulce, I know you hate all this stuff, but you've got to be there for me... You're my cousin! And I know we don't see each other a lot these days, but that's totally your fault because you never come up to London. You're always buried in that studio of yours in darkest Devon. And, while I admire your work ethic, you really do need to get out more. Circulate! Think about it. If you're a bridesmaid, you'll be noticed by everyone. You might even meet someone...someone nice...'

Which meant someone 'suitable'. Suitable was a big

thing in Georgie's world which was—admit it—her own world too. It was just that she didn't like that world very much, certainly not enough to take an active part in it, and she definitely wasn't looking for someone 'nice' who hailed from it, because 'nice' didn't mean a thing, did it? Charlie had been 'nice' after all. On the outside.

Nice lesson to have learned at fifteen, that charm could mask a wealth of ugliness, that it could blind a crowd, carry a crowd, turn a crowd! She'd seen the way nastiness could hide in the corners of polite smiles, seen the way it spread like ink on blotting paper. It had cut her so deep, changed her, led her to Tommy, and that had driven a wedge right in, hadn't it? Hurt her family, which had cut her all over again, taught her that whatever demons she was battling, hurting family wasn't right, ever.

Looking into Georgie's face on Christmas Day, all she could think was that this was her beloved cousin, the one she'd shared so much of her childhood with, and that she didn't want to be the cause of any more hurt. Disappointment. So she'd caved, agreed to be a bridesmaid, and then Georgie had hit her with this whole hen-week scenario, a week with Georgie and Tilly, and Peter the groom's three sisters—whose names she kept muddling up—and a bunch of Georgie's friends who seemed to have a never-ending supply of tiresome in jokes.

They'd only been here a day, and already it was purgatory. The thought of spending another afternoon trying to find a toehold in the conversation was making her head throb. She wasn't interested in point-to-point, or hunting, or Henley or Ascot. She didn't want to offend anyone, least of all Georgie, but for her own sanity she *had* to escape. She just needed Georgie's permission.

She picked up her bag, toying with the strap. 'So, George, you're okay with me going out for a bit?'

'Sure.' Georgie's eyes flicked up. 'Where did you say you were going?'

She felt a little skip of excitement. 'I thought I'd try to get into La Sagrada Família, as long as the queues aren't too horrendous.'

Georgie's brow pleated. 'You mean the big warty-looking cathedral thingy?'

She held in a smile. La Sagrada Família was kind of warty-looking, but it was also intricate and captivating. It was giving her goosebumps just thinking about it.

'That's the one.'

'Well, if you think it's any good, then maybe I'll check it out later in the week when my head isn't bouncing.' Georgie pulled a sad hangover face then went back to her phone, smiling at something on the screen. 'Have fun, but please be back by five for drinks on the terrace. Saffy's lined up some jolly games apparently, then we're heading out to Opium.'

Jolly games *and* a nightclub? She bit back an expletive and bolted for the door.

The corridor was plush. Silent. She drew in a deep breath then looped her bag crosswise and set off for the lifts. If Georgie really did have a hangover after last night's champagne, then more drinking seemed sensible—*not*. As for Saffy's jolly games... She shuddered, pressed the thought flat. She wasn't going to think about that, not when Barcelona was calling, not when Gaudí's basilica was barely a mile away, waiting.

She felt a tingle. Such a stroke of luck that Georgina's godfather had recently added the Barcelona Regal to his portfolio of hotels and that he'd gifted Georgie three adjoining terrace suites on the top floor for her 'hen party', and how brilliant that Georgie had actually accepted instead of dragging them all off to Ibiza as per the original plan. Ibiza would have been intolerable, but Barcelona was the bomb. She was going to find inspiration for her ceramics here, she just knew it. Walking the same streets that Antoni Gaudí had walked, floating past Casa Batlló and Casa Milà. Today, it was La Sagrada Família, and tomorrow, if she was lucky, there'd be Parc Güell, and then the next day... But maybe that was a wish too far. Best just to think about now, the glorious, hen-free afternoon ahead.

She rounded the corner and her body jumped. The lift was there, doors wide, a glowing pod of light and mirrors. She started to run, feeling a giggle rising, a flash of childhood memory... Princess Georgie flying ahead of her through the maze, glimpses of gold satin at every turn, escaping...like this lift...golden light...doors imminently closing...

Ridiculous, this thrill of heart-pulsing danger. There was another lift on its way, lights blinking, but she wanted this one because it was here, so close, so tantalising, like Georgie ahead of her, laughing, breathless, ready to take off again. The doors twitched and she lunged, launching herself through, feeling her laughter vibrating, shaking itself free.

'Which floor?'

Her heart stopped dead. How hadn't she noticed that there was someone there? If she had, she'd never have shot into the lift quite so inelegantly. She sucked in her cheeks and pivoted only to feel every scrap of her composure vaporising. The man with his finger poised over the panel was the epitome of tall, dark, and handsome. Broad-shouldered, olive-skinned, slate-eyed. *Sad-eyed.* She felt her heart twisting loose, going out to him, which was weird and completely ridiculous because he was a stranger, a stranger who was looking at her with raised eyebrows, waiting for her to speak.

She swallowed. 'Ground, please. Thank you.'

He nodded with what could have been the hint of a smile, then pressed the button.

She moved back against the rail, trying not to look at him, but not looking didn't mean not seeing. It was impossible not to see him because his recurring reflection was coming at her from every side. Lightly bearded, dark hair curling at his nape, blue and white striped shirt, well pressed. Immaculate navy chinos. Tan brogues, polished to the nth. He knew how to dress all right and yet he didn't exude the confidence that usually went with sartorial know-how. He was staring at the panel, his gaze somewhere else, a nervous muscle twitching just where his jaw hinged.

She looked down at her brogues. Down seemed like the safest direction, except now there was a feeling coming that he was studying her, taking her apart piece by piece. She couldn't bring herself to look up and check, but she wasn't wrong, because why else would she be feeling these little electric darts shooting along her spine, warmth spreading up her throat and into her cheeks? Why else would she be feeling so…naked? Because there was no one else here, was there, making her feel like this? Only him, and her, descending at a snail's pace in a cube just two metres by two metres.

She felt a frown coming. Actually, why was the lift going so slow? Yesterday morning, after they'd checked in, the lift had shot them up to the top floor in seconds. Georgie had even remarked on it, called it the *rocket* lift! But there was no rocket now, only this super-charged tingling awareness of *him*, this pulse-throbbing, electric feeling. What was she supposed to do with it? What could she do? Just because he was making her heart give and her knees buckle didn't mean that she was having the same effect on him, and even if she was…

She clamped her lips together. For goodness' sake, she

didn't even want to be thinking about this. She wanted to be thinking about art and beauty and Gaudí, and La Sagrada Família. She wanted to be jaunting through the streets with her sunglasses on, catching the sweet oily smell of warm *churros*, not riding the slowest lift in the world with the hottest guy she'd ever seen.

And then suddenly the lights flickered, buzzing and crackling. Her heart clutched. This wasn't right. She caught the man's eye momentarily, then gripped the rail, scanning the ceiling without knowing why. It wasn't as if she knew the first thing about lifts, except that they were supposed to zip up and down silently and the lights weren't supposed to be dimming like this. Just a glitch, surely. Any second now the lights were going to brighten, and the lift was going to pick up speed, but no. No… That wasn't happening. More the opposite. She felt her stomach clenching, turning over. Oh, God! The lift was stopping. Stopping… Stopped.

CHAPTER TWO

PERFECT! BAD ENOUGH that the girl was making his head spin, that her last-minute laughing leap into the lift had reminded him of what freedom looked and felt like, but now he was going to have to talk to her, look directly into all that sweet blonde sunshine, not that she was looking sunny at this particular moment. More nervous. The way she was holding the rail, gripping it really, as if, what? As if she thought the lift was about to drop like a stone? He felt the resistance inside relenting, warmth trickling in. At least he could reassure her about that.

He looked over. 'It's all right, you know...' Light eyes snapped to his, grey or blue, he couldn't tell, not in this light, but she was listening. 'We're not about to plummet down the shaft.'

Her chin lifted a little. 'How do you know?'

Because he was an architect. Or was he? Could he still claim to *be* an architect in this crossover period? It suddenly felt like a moral dilemma but maybe he was overthinking it. What he was didn't matter; what did was chasing away her fear.

'Because I know all about buildings and all about elevators.' Her eyes held him for a moment, and then her gaze seemed to open out, urging him on. He felt something clicking inside, as if he was slotting back into the well-worn groove of himself, the only self he knew how to be. He pointed to the logo on the control panel. 'See this name: Otis.'

She stepped closer, peering, then nodded, one eyebrow sliding up.

'Elisha Graves Otis invented the safety elevator in 1853. It's basically a ratchet system.' He felt his hands starting to move, air-drawing the system he could see in his mind. 'So the lift sits in the shaft, but it fits quite tightly against the walls. If a hoist goes slack, a leaf spring triggers that snaps into notches cut into the supporting rails on either side of the car, so the car can't fall.' He drew her back into focus, loading his gaze with reassurance. 'So you don't have to worry. We're not going to drop. It's impossible.'

For a beat she looked bemused and then she smiled, a wide cheeky smile. 'Well, I suppose if I was going to get stuck in a lift with anyone, then I picked the right person to get stuck with.'

He felt his lips twitching, a little glow starting inside. 'Not really. The right person would have been the person who could actually fix it. I'm just a theoretician.'

'But you've put my mind at rest, so, you know, that counts for something.' She pressed her palms together. 'I'm Dulcie, by the way.'

Subtle, that pressing of the palms, signalling that a handshake wasn't necessary. Maybe she thought it was simply too weird a situation for formality, or that it would be weird for them to touch. Either way, it was fine by him. Touching her would undoubtedly trigger a surge of inappropriate heat in a certain part of his anatomy.

He smoothed his own palms together. 'Raffiel, but most people call me Raff.'

'Nice to meet you, Raff the theoretician.' And then her eyes darted to the panel. 'Speaking of which, I also have a theory, which is that we should probably be pressing an emergency button or something, so they know we're stuck.'

'They know already.'

'How?'

'It's a digital system, self-monitoring. They'll be working on it right now. It'll be fixed in no time.' Which, confusingly, was suddenly feeling like a blow because he was enjoying her company. She was intriguing, 'quaint' as the English might say.

She *was* English, definitely. She had one of those mellow, slightly husky voices that seemed to contain a chuckle, and she had that quintessential English complexion, creamy skin, roses in her cheeks. Rosebud lips. He'd studied them earlier through the mirror when she'd been looking away. He'd got the shape down, that Cupid's bow above and the fullness below, a sweet, tantalising pout, but he needed not to be staring at her mouth right now, because he could feel heat stirring in exactly the place that he didn't want to be feeling it.

'So…' She was moving back to the rail. 'I presume you're staying here too…'

'No. Actually I'm not.' Something flickered through her gaze, but he couldn't catch it properly, not in this light. 'I was in a business meeting with an associate who's staying in one of the terrace suites.'

'Ah.' She looked down at her shoes.

Black mannish shoes, with no socks. Cropped black pants. White shirt, fitted, but not tight. Black bag, black choker with a silver hieroglyphic layered over some longer silver necklaces. A sort of urchin look, but classy somehow. Maybe it was her loosely knotted hair or the upright way she held herself that was giving her that edge. God, she was hard to pin down.

He swallowed. Why was he even trying? It wasn't as

if pinning her down were important, as if he were in any kind of a place to let this flicker of interest kindle into anything whatsoever. Maybe it was just that trying to pin her down was more enjoyable than churning away about the handover speech Arlo had asked him to make at the conference's charity ball, the ball he'd inaugurated but didn't even want to attend now because it was just another thing he was losing.

But all this pondering wasn't filling in the silence, was it? The problem was what to say. She'd effectively asked him where he was staying, and he needed to give her something, but what? He wasn't exactly prepared for answering questions about himself, even the simplest ones, because nothing was simple any more.

God, he was overthinking again. It really didn't matter what he said because in a few moments the lift was going to be fixed and then they'd be going their separate ways and he was never going to see her again. He pressed his lips together. Even so, he couldn't bring himself to invent something. The truth would have to do, just not all of it.

'I'm staying at Port Vell Marina.'

'Oh.' She lifted her face, smiling. 'So you're a sailor!'

'No. I'm what you call a freeloader. It's my uncle's yacht...' or had been. Why did he keep forgetting that the royal yacht was Papa's now and that soon it would be his? Some part of him clinging to denial, blocking out the inevitable. He shrugged. 'I don't know the first thing about sailing.'

She tilted her head. 'I do. My father's always been keen on it, drilled a few things into me along the way.' Her fingers went to the hieroglyphic at her neck. 'Jibs and booms, sheets, and spinnakers and suchlike. I'm not saying that I'm ready to sail round the world single-handed or anything but I'm not a total disaster on a boat.'

'I'm sure you're not a total disaster anywhere.'

She blinked, registering faint surprise, and his heart seized. What had possessed him to say that—like that—with a completely inappropriate fondness in his voice? He'd been thinking it, but he hadn't meant to say it out loud, hadn't even noticed the words coming out until they were ricocheting in his ears. As if she had anything to worry about on the disaster front! He was the unmitigated disaster, not her.

He bit back a sigh. It was just that he thought he'd heard a note in her voice, a little dent in it, implying that she felt out of place in the world at large, and he'd wanted to smooth it away with a compliment, with some gentleness because for some reason it had felt that she could do with some, but then what did he know? Nothing at all. He'd simply jumped in with his two left feet and now he was feeling awkward and probably she was too. He needed to take back control, steer the conversation onto level ground.

He flicked a glance at the panel then leaned back against the rail, going for a casual tone. 'So, what about you? Are you here on holiday?'

'Not exactly.' Her lips pressed into a line. 'I'm here for a hen week, you know, like an extended bachelorette party.'

He felt his eyes darting to her left hand, a reaction clearly not lost on her because suddenly she was laughing.

'It's not *my* hen party. It's my cousin Georgie who's getting married. I'm just a bridesmaid.'

The *'just'* felt like a hole he could possibly fall into. He couldn't make any more faux pas. He needed to reach for something light, neutral. What would Gustav have said? He'd have smiled, definitely, all twinkly, then he'd have said something like, Cool.

He smiled. 'Cool.'

'No!' Her eyes flew wide and then she was frowning.

'It isn't cool at all. I don't *want* to be a bridesmaid. All that flouncing about in a frock and high heels, trying not to trip or do anything undainty, being on parade, being noticed all day long, I mean, obviously not as much as the bride— thank God—but even so it's my perfect idea of hell!' She sighed then shrugged. 'But I'm stuck with it so that's that.' She sighed again, and then her gaze was tightening on his. 'You don't mind me ranting, do you?'

How could he mind? He was intrigued. Besides, listening to her bemoaning her fate was better than listening to the bleating voice inside his own head that wouldn't stop banging on about how unfortunate he was.

'Not at all.'

She licked her lips. 'And to top it all, there's this stupid hen week.' She pressed her hands to the sides of her head as if it was hurting. 'A whole week with Georgie's friends! I mean, I don't have that much in common with Georgie, but I've got even less in common with her friends. They're just… I don't know…not my kind of people. I can't think of a single thing to say to them, ever, and to be fair I'm sure they feel the same about me. For Georgie's sake I want to make nice with them, I really do, but every time I try it's as if there's a great big wall in the way.' Her hands fell and then her gaze sharpened. 'Do you ever feel like that with people?'

All the time within the royal household but that was because he wasn't used to dealing with the vast number of royal aides and secretaries and advisers that seemed to swirl about the place. What was harder to bear was the wall that seemed to be growing between him and Papa, the increasing number of conversations that contained more silence than actual words.

He felt a band tightening around his chest. They'd always used to get on so well, talking so easily about architecture and art, engineering, and design. It was Papa who'd first brought him to Barcelona when he was fourteen. He'd just been coming alive then to the idea of a career in architecture, and Papa had been with him every step of the way. They'd done La Sagrada Família, taking the lift up into the towers, marvelling at the light, at the sheer scale and audacity of the building. They'd shared the wonder, but now Papa didn't seem to be able to switch back into that gear.

Papa was preoccupied all the time with royal affairs, and he got that, he did. Papa *had* to concern himself with royal business first because he was King now, working under a weight of grief and a weight of worry about his health.

Grief. Change. So much change. It should have been a unifying force, drawing them closer, but it wasn't. His fault, not Papa's. Papa was getting on with things, embracing his new role to the best of his ability, and what was he doing? Languishing in the doldrums, feeling loss on all sides, and, yes, feeling sorry for himself. Papa needed him to be better, stronger, more courageous, but he couldn't seem to find any strength inside. If only he could make himself feel positive about the future, find the good in it somehow, convey to Papa that he was happily reconciled to the new life that was coming, then maybe things would smooth out between them, but he wasn't in that place yet, didn't know how to get there.

The sting lodged under his skin lanced him afresh. And Brianne, the one person who could have supported him through all of this, had ditched him two months before Dralk. He'd dared to hope that the tragedy would bring her running back, but it hadn't. She'd sent a tribute and a letter full of warm words but that was all. So, she really must have fallen out of love with him, or maybe it was that the new sovereign landscape around him was too much for her to even contemplate and if that was it, then how could he blame her when he was struggling with it too?

He blinked, reconnecting with Dulcie's gaze. So yes, he knew exactly what she meant, but he couldn't explain to her the nuts and bolts of how he knew, even if talking about it might give him some relief, because if he got into all the royalty stuff then a fresh wall would start growing right here in this lift and he didn't want that. Right now Dulcie thought he was a regular guy who knew about buildings and elevators, and he liked being that guy. Divulging his situation for the sake of a little mutual commiseration wasn't an option. All he could offer was a palliative.

'I think we all feel like that sometimes.'

Her eyes narrowed momentarily and then she was folding her arms, leaning back against the rail again. 'Well, that feeling is why I was escaping so gleefully.' Her eyes slid around the mirrored walls then back to his. 'Didn't get very far, did I?'

She looked so sweetly despondent that he couldn't help smiling. 'You haven't yet, but you will, very soon. I promise.'

Her gaze deepened into his, mischief gleaming behind it. 'Are you in the habit of making promises to strangers, Raff?'

'No, but you're not a stranger. You're Dulcie, which is a lovely name by the way.'

Her face stiffened slightly, and he felt his heart sinking. Why had he said that? It had sounded like a cheap chat-up line, even though he'd meant it and even though he definitely wasn't chatting her up. What was wrong with him? Why was it that the moment he wasn't focusing hard on what he was saying to her, he was saying all the wrong things, inappropriate things, things that seemed too familiar? He was going to have to work at the whole tact thing because two left feet weren't exactly desirable attributes in a future king. Meanwhile, this time at least, maybe he was going to get away with it. Her face seemed to be softening again and there was a smile tilting at the corners of her mouth.

'Actually, Dulcie's the cute version. The unabridged version is…' she squeezed her eyes shut, faking a wince '… Dulcibella.'

He said it in his head, rolling it around, liking it. Maybe he could cover his first mistake by amplifying it, going for broke. He smiled. 'Also lovely.'

Her eyes popped wide and then she was turning, giving him the side-eye. 'Are you for real or just very well brought up?'

He felt relief winding through, laughter shaking free. 'Both, I hope.'

She gave him a dubious look. 'No one thinks that Dulcibella is a lovely name, except my parents obviously, and I think even they sometimes experience moments of acute regret.'

He felt delight spangling. She had such a lovely way of talking, her voice shading from seriousness into wryness just like that, always with that spark of mischief behind her eyes, primed to ignite. It was impossible not to smile around her, impossible not to feel drawn to her. But he couldn't let himself get sucked in. A few enjoyable moments in a lift. That's all this was. Nothing more.

He arched his eyebrows. 'Going back to the reasons why you're not a stranger…'

'Oh, yes.' She folded her arms again, her eyes merry. 'Go on, then.'

'I know that you're an expert sailor—'

Frowning. 'I did not say that.'

'A reluctant bridesmaid.'

Sighing. 'Yes.'

'And I know that the last thing you wanted today was to get stuck in a lift.'

Her mouth opened and then she rocked away from the

rail and moved to the opposite corner, frowning a bit, her reflection doubling, tripling, multiplying ad infinitum. Dulcie from every angle, every one of them perfect.

'Okay, so maybe you do know me pretty well.' Her eyes caught his through the mirror and then she was turning to face him, her smile suddenly hesitant. 'But you should know that while you're right about the whole getting stuck in a lift thing, it actually hasn't been the worst experience in the world…'

His heart stumbled. Those eyes. Those words. Was she trying to say that she liked being stuck with him? It seemed like it. Her expression was open, guileless. Plain speaking in the wake of his two—or was it three?—compliments, compliments that had fallen from his mouth spontaneously, also without guile.

But now, what was he supposed to say back to her? If he said that he was enjoying it too, which was the truth, then the moment would swell with expectation, demand some kind of follow through and he couldn't follow through, could he? He couldn't even ask her to go for coffee because he'd only end up liking her more than he did already and what would be the point of that? There was no mileage in this, nothing he could offer her that she would want.

For pity's sake, she didn't even want to be a bridesmaid at her cousin's wedding, so princess was out. *Queen!* His stomach clenched. And to be even having *that* thought was ridiculous! How could he, even in the most tenuous way possible, be projecting scenarios onto a girl he'd known for five minutes, a girl who, in spite of all his talk, he didn't know at all?

He felt the tightness in his stomach shifting to his chest. Because that was what he must always do now, project himself, and anyone he wanted to be close to, into a future that was inescapable. It meant being doubly mindful about actions and consequences, meant accepting that, even in this last precious week of freedom, he wasn't free at all.

He inhaled, steadying himself. Of course, there was also the possibility that he was being a massive idiot, reading meaning into her words where there wasn't any. Maybe all she was saying was that sharing a broken lift with him hadn't been so bad, which was entirely different from saying that it had been good! Maybe she was simply being polite. Yes. That had to be it. She was being polite, and he'd latched onto her words, reading into them, because, even though he couldn't do anything about it, part of him wanted to believe that she was feeling the same tug of attraction that he was feeling, that same flowing out of the spirit that was warming and uplifting. He'd grabbed at it because he was morose, and she was a breath of fresh air.

He ran his eyes over her face. So lovely. Beautiful really. And if he could see it, feel it all the way to his bones, then why not every other man on the planet? She wasn't wearing a ring, but it didn't mean she was single. *Stupid, Raffiel!* Getting all tangled up in the thought of her for nothing. The only reason she was on her own right now was because she was on a hen week, or rather she was escaping from it, but back in England there was bound to be someone in her life. *In her bed!* So, time to get a grip and breeze on through as Gustav would have done.

He looked at each wall in turn. 'You're right. It could have been so much worse. Imagine if there'd been ten of us crammed in here!'

Something changed in her face and then her fingers went to her hair. 'Oh, God, yeah. That would have been super grim, shuffling about in here, trying not to bump shoulders.' She shuddered then smiled a smile that for once didn't quite reach her eyes. 'Doesn't bear thinking about.'

CHAPTER THREE

DULCIE STOPPED WALKING and forced herself to savour the sight of the western bell towers reaching skywards in the company of a bright yellow crane. Ridiculous having to consciously make herself look, when looking, *seeing* Gaudí's basilica for herself was the only thing that had kept her going all morning, through all that waiting for Georgie to stir so she could ask for permission to escape.

Her heart contracted. If only she hadn't been quite so keen on escaping. If she'd been just a little less excited, a fraction less overjoyed, she'd never have leapt headlong into Raffiel's lift, would never have met him, and she wouldn't have been in this state now. Distracted. Fluttery. Giddy. And all for nothing because he hadn't seemed to register the massive hint that she'd dropped about how being stuck with him hadn't been that bad an experience. Clear enough, she'd thought, short of actually saying, Raff, I like you and I'd like to see you again, but evidently not clear enough for him. And then suddenly, before she'd had the chance to devise a different line of attack, the lights had been surging back to brightness and in a matter of seconds the doors had been opening to a pink-faced, apologetic concierge.

And then it had been goodbye, Raffiel smiling and saying that it had been nice to meet her, her saying something similar all the while screaming inside for him not to walk away, but he did walk away, striding out, not looking back, which she knew because she'd watched him until he was out of sight.

She sighed and walked on, crossing into the Plaça de la Sagrada Família. So unfair. How long was it since she'd met anyone she actually liked, more than liked? A pang unleashed itself, transforming into a deep tugging ache. This was bonkers. It felt like…like pining, as if a hole were opening up inside.

She sank down onto a vacant bench, letting the feelings resolve. She was missing him, a man she didn't even know. And yet to some inside part of herself that small detail didn't seem to matter. Even if all she knew about him was that he understood buildings and didn't know how to sail, she could feel him still, the sadness inside him, and the light too…

The problem was they'd said goodbye too quickly. No time for extricating herself from the tangle of him, for drawing a line under him in a clean, sensible way, so now it was this elastic tug straining, this wanting to be where he was, wanting to see what they could be…

She felt a frown coming. She was going mad, clearly. How could she even be thinking along those lines…*what they could be*? Raff might have said some unexpected things, some nice, complimentary sorts of things, but that didn't mean he liked her, that they could *be* anything. Obviously not, because he'd taken himself off pretty purposefully, hadn't he, without a backwards glance? That was the writing on the wall, right there. Big letters. Bold. Unequivocal. Raffiel was not interested in Dulcie.

She chewed the edge of her lip, letting the fact harden. Perhaps she'd simply fallen into the trap of easy alliance because of the situation, because when the lift had stopped and the lights had dimmed, she'd felt scared. And he'd taken her fear and wiped it all away with his glorious explanation of how lifts worked, his hands going, long fingers describing shapes in the air, his intelligent gaze all warm and intent. Reassuring. Maybe that was why she'd poured things out about herself so comfortably, because she'd felt safe with him, because Raff made her feel safe.

Poor man, having to listen to her ranting about Georgie's friends. Captive audience, literally, but he hadn't seemed to mind, and it had felt good letting it all out, admitting to her own otherness, that feeling of not belonging. She hadn't confided in anyone like that for a long time, not since Tommy, and feeling that she could, with Raff, must just have ignited something inside her, got her hoping again…

She closed her eyes. So maybe things hadn't gone the way she'd wanted them to go with Raff but if he'd been able to bring her to life, then perhaps it was a sign that she was ready to put herself out there again, *circulate*, find someone 'nice'. Someone 'suitable'.

She felt a sudden throb of nausea. Suitable like Charlie… Exuding all that well-practised charm in front of people who mattered: parents; teachers; the tennis club captain. Thrown together at the tennis club's six-week summer tuition camp, she could hardly believe it when Charlie had started talking to her, properly talking, and smiling. *Flirting!* Tow-haired Charlie, easy on the eye, brimming with confidence and athleticism.

God, how she'd been reeled in, and not only her. Her parents had adored him for years, the dashing son of their friends, Camilla and Simon Prentice. They'd been as thrilled as she was when he invited her to the Hemphill Summer Ball. At fifteen, she'd been too young to go, strictly speaking, but because it was Charlie, seventeen and 'responsible', she'd been allowed. It had meant a flouncy dress, and a corsage, shoes she could barely walk in. Sliding into the Prentices' Bentley that night she'd felt like a princess, as if she were really something...

She bit her lips hard, pushing the memory down, crushing the other trailing memories before they could loosen.

Tommy hadn't been suitable. At. All. It was why she'd liked him, why she'd pursued him so relentlessly at St Martin's, because his background was the polar opposite of her own, because he was refreshingly open, brutally frank. Yeah, he fancied her, yeah, he'd love to give her a whirl in the sack...

Tommy wasn't into etiquette and so-called propriety. What was propriety anyway? Sham and show. It had been music to her twenty-year-old ears. This was a better way to be, surely, being upfront. Honest! For all his dark, unkempt hair, tattoos and tragus piercings, Tommy was pure gold. Golden! That's what she'd thought, what she'd seen in him. She'd loved the effortless way he flung paint on canvas and created magic, and she'd loved that he didn't fall over himself trying to impress her parents.

Not like Charlie! No, Tommy wasn't a suck up. He was her badge of rebellion, a way of giving the finger to her own class and all the things she hated about it, but being with him came at a price. A long night in the cells after Tommy had got them both busted for possession at a Fulham party had shocked her parents, then alienated them.

Never mind that she'd thought the little bag Tommy had given her to *'mind'* was his habitual weed. Never mind that she'd been let off as a naïve accessory. That had been it as far as her family was concerned. Tommy was no longer welcome at Fendlesham. She'd had to pick a side then and God help her she'd picked Tommy's because he'd said he loved her, and she'd wanted to believe it.

But it got harder and harder seeing the hurt and incomprehension in her parents' eyes, because they were good people. It wasn't their fault they didn't know where her anger was coming from, wasn't their fault she'd never been able to bring herself to tell them about Charlie, about what he'd tried to do, what he'd told everyone about her afterwards. They didn't know what she'd had to live with at her smart school, why she'd 'suddenly' decided that she wanted to go to sixth form college to do A levels instead of staying on there.

They'd put it down to a teenage whim, indulged her, thank God, so she'd been able to get away with locking all the anger and resentment inside. But five years on, listening to Tommy ranting about entitlement and the landed classes, the screw that had been tightening inside ever since the night of the Hemphill Ball started reverse turning.

A year after graduating, she'd had enough of being his moll. She ditched him and moved to Devon because it was a long way from home, a long way from everything. She found a small studio space in a quiet village. The stated plan was to *focus* on her work. The private plan was to *find* herself, decide who she wanted to be. She stamped *Dulcie Brown* on the underside of her ceramic creations because Dulcie Brown was who she was in that safe little backwoods' world. But at Georgie's wedding she was going to have to be Lady Dulcibella Davenport-Brown again. She was going to have to smile and shake hands with the ones who'd passed Charlie's lies around behind their whispering hands all those years ago...

She drew Gaudí's towers back into focus. Why was she even thinking about all this? Something to do with Raffiel, feeling that connection humming again, as it had with Tommy, except that the Dulcie who'd connected with Tommy had been an angry Dulcie, a hurt Dulcie, a contrary Dulcie. The Dulcie who'd flowed out to Raff had felt real. Softer, warmer. No point to prove, no axe to grind. Just pure being.

But pure being was no good if it didn't cut both ways,

and even though it had felt as if it was, it couldn't have been, could it? Because she was here, and he wasn't. She'd deluded herself, got herself in a fizz for nothing. But that was ending right now.

She pushed up off the bench, straightening her bag. She wasn't going to think about Raffiel or Charlie or Tommy any more, and she definitely wasn't going to think about the horror show that was going to be Georgie's wedding. She'd come here for Antoni Gaudí, and she was damn well going to enjoy every second of him.

She stepped out of the push and flow, lowering herself onto one of the stone benches that ran beneath the blazing stained-glass windows. She could feel a sob lodging in her chest, wanting to rise, tears budding, wanting to fall. Not what she'd been expecting, this feeling of being overwhelmed, but the light inside the basilica was divine, appropriately enough, bright white punching through glittering oval portholes, green, gold and orange pouring in, flooding the floor, splashing the mighty tree-trunk pillars.

I am the light of the world.

She wasn't religious but the line had been circling through her mind from the moment she'd stepped inside and felt the breath leaving her lungs. Light of the world! Was that what Gaudí had been going for when he conceived this? It felt like it, felt as if he'd been aiming to bring God right in, stage a show not a tell.

I am the light...

She ran her eyes around the vast vaulted space, shutting out the crowds, focusing on the structures and the feeling,

that feeling of being on a forest floor with sunlight dappling through. Organic shapes. Textures. Striated bark,
leafy fronds, and the light. Always the light. It was impossible not to look up, impossible not to feel humbled. Gaudí's
vision, his accomplishment, even in this unfinished state
was almost too moving to bear.

'Mesmerising, isn't it?'

It took a split second to register the deep velvet voice,
another split second to register its familiarity, and two more
split seconds for her heart to leap clear of her body. Somehow—*how?*—Raffiel was sitting at the other end of her
bench, his chin lifted, his eyes trained on the ceiling as if
this wasn't a great big deal. Or maybe it was just a great
big deal for her, just *her* blood that was pumping warm and
fast, *her* wits that were busy scattering, *her* tongue tying
itself into knots.

She slid her eyes over his handsome profile, feeling her
limbs unstringing. How could that even happen just by
looking at someone? She bit her lips together. She couldn't
let him see the effect he was having on her because he
wasn't showing anything, was he? He was simply here,
happily, impossibly, but cool and casual as you like, staring upwards, his broad shoulders loose, a small smile hanging on his lips.

He hadn't been this relaxed in the lift. Oh, no. He'd been
kind and warm and sweet, but also a bit reined in. But of
course they'd been confined then, small space, first meeting, no escape. This was different. Huge space, second
meeting, plenty of exits. *Second meeting.* She felt a tingle.
By chance or design?

'It is mesmerising, yes.' She took a careful breath, reaching for a casual tone. 'So, I'm sorry but…are you stalking me?'

His eyes snapped to hers. 'Last time I checked I wasn't,

but it seems not to have made any difference.' And then he was angling himself towards her, smiling a smile that melted her bones. 'I wasn't sure if I should come over or not, but it seemed rude not to, after the lift, I mean.' Hesitation flickered through his gaze. 'But if you want to be alone, I'll leave you in peace, no hard feelings.'

'No! It's fine. Really.' More perfect than fine, but she wasn't going to say that to his face. She nodded towards the milling tourists. 'What I mean is that you're hardly disturbing me. Besides…' Her belly knotted. Crunch time. Did she dare spell it out for him, risk embarrassing them both? If she didn't, she'd only regret it. Maybe the thing to hold onto was that he was here, sitting on her bench. He'd made the first move, effectively, so maybe it wasn't that much of a risk. She felt a smile coming. 'Besides…it's nice to see you.'

A light came into his eyes that drew a sudden unexpected heat through her veins. She looked away quickly, heart drumming, watching a couple smiling into a phone attached to the end of a selfie stick. Was he feeling it too, this insane tug of attraction, this deep liquid ache?

'It's nice to see you too.' His voice broke through, his accent warm and seductive. Russian? German maybe? Or Swedish? European for sure. 'And lucky actually…'

Lucky!

She turned, meeting his gaze, which was shyer now, more like it had been in the lift. 'Lucky why?'

He faltered for a moment. 'Because after I left you, I got to thinking that maybe I should have suggested a coffee or something, instead of dashing off…'

Her heart skipped and then it was fluttering, lifting higher and higher. He was initiating something, taking the lead, leading her exactly where she wanted to go. She could feel the air between them clearing then filling with a low electric hum. Charged air. Charged moment. It was going to be hard keeping her voice level, even harder to keep her smile neatly corralled. She took a breath. 'Coffee would have gone down very well after the trauma.'

His eyebrows slid up. 'Would it still go down well on the basis of better late than never?'

She let her smile loosen a little, felt her heart jumping like a flame as he smiled back. 'If *churros* are included then, absolutely, better late than never works for me.'

Dulcie's shoulders lifted. 'I'm sorry, Raff, but I'm embarrassed to say that I don't know anything about Brostovenia.'

Ideal, given that he didn't want to talk about his country. He wouldn't have mentioned it at all if she hadn't asked him about his accent but since she had, he'd told her the truth, because lying wasn't an option. Talking around the edges of things, on the other hand, was acceptable, at least for now while he was still catching up with himself, with this whole coffee thing. Yes, he'd approached *her*, and yes, he'd suggested it, but that didn't mean he wasn't reeling, didn't mean that, in the corner of his brain he'd dedicated to royal matters, there weren't fur and feathers flying.

'Don't apologise, and please don't be embarrassed.' He picked up his cup. 'It's not as if I'm an expert on England.'

Her eyes rounded into his. 'Oh, I can make you an expert on England in ten seconds.' Cheeky grin. 'Shakespeare, Buckingham Palace, fish and chips, the pound, Guy Fawkes, Covent Garden, Oxford, Cambridge, rain—especially on bank holidays—Blackpool Pier, Brighton Pier, Ascot, Henley, the Grand National, Wimbledon, the Downs and the Dales, Exmoor and Dartmoor, and pubs. Pubs are very important!'

Dulcie. Impossible not to smile when she was going full tilt, impossible not to like her more with every passing second, which was exactly what he'd known would happen if he spent more time with her. It's why he'd hurried away from the hotel just three hours ago, to escape this very fate and the complications that went with it, but it seemed fate had other ideas.

Dulcie had accused him of stalking her, but it was nostalgia pure and simple that had sent him to La Sagrada Família. In the lift, remembering that first time with Papa, how close they'd been, how secure he'd felt, how supported in his big dream to become an architect...

Those warm memories must have triggered something inside because halfway up La Rambla, churning away over Dulcie and his impending loss of freedom, he'd felt a sudden, overwhelming compulsion to go to the basilica, to lose himself in its intricate vastness, in all of its joyous overkill, to let everything it was swamp the torment out of him. And then somehow there Dulcie had been, sitting in a shaft of golden light, staring upwards with glistening eyes. He'd felt his heart bursting out of his chest, a slew of conflicting emotions. To go over, or not, to risk feeding a fire that could burn him, or, worse, that could burn her, or not.

But then watching her, witnessing her emotional connection to a building that he himself held so dear, it had seemed like a chance too. Twice Dulcie had been put in his way. Twice! Was it something he could ignore? It hadn't felt like it in that moment, or maybe he'd just been too weak, too bewitched to make himself walk away a second time. He'd suddenly wanted to know if what he'd felt flowing between them in the lift had been real or simply a flight of desperate fancy. Going over to talk to her had seemed like a neat way to sort it out.

That had been his logic, the last he'd seen or felt of it. Now everything was Dulcie, stealing his breath with her smile, making him smile with a quirk of her eyebrows, making his blood run hot with a finger at the corner of her mouth catching chocolate from the *churros*. He was done for, help-less, and right now he didn't have the strength to care.

'Do you have pubs in Brostovenia?' She was looking at him over the rim of her cup, that mischievous little spark just visible at the edge of her blue gaze.

He sipped and set his own cup down. 'No. We have café-bars.' He dragged his eyes away from hers and looked around, taking in the tables and the red awning over their heads. 'Quite similar to this, but to be honest…' and thank-fully honesty was his golden ticket out of the Brostovenian hole he could feel opening up beneath him '… I don't know much about bars in Brostovenia. I went to university in the States so I'm more familiar with American bars, not that I'm a barfly or anything.'

She put her cup down, smiling. 'That's reassuring.' And then her eyes came to his, all warm and curious. 'So, what did you study, and where?'

He felt his limbs loosening. This he was happy to talk about!

'Architecture. At Cornell.'

'So *that's* how you know all about buildings. And lifts.' Her fingers moved to a stray lock, tucking it behind her ear. 'So the meeting you were having at the hotel, was it a project meeting…?' Her eyes quickened. 'Are you build-ing something here, in Barcelona?'

His heart went limp. Seven years training, six years in practice, all for nothing because there'd be no more de-signing now, no more creating. It was over. He went for his cup again, sipping slowly, searching for a straight, calm line inside.

'No, sadly. It was just tying off some loose ends…to do with a conference.'

'Oh, right.' And then something resolved in her gaze. 'You mean the architecture thing at the World Trade Centre?'

His breath stopped. He'd mentioned the conference because it was the truth, because as far as he could he wanted to be truthful with her, but he hadn't expected her to know about it. He swallowed hard. Too late for back-pedalling now, but he couldn't get into the intricacies of his involvement—the royal patronage thing—because then she'd know who he was and instead of sitting here nice and easy together she was bound to start looking at him differently, treating him differently, and then everything would be ruined.

He felt his jaw tightening. Life was going to be ruined soon enough, so how could it be wrong to want this sweet little piece of normality to last a bit longer? How could it be wrong to want to downplay things when it was only so he could enjoy her company? Where was the harm? He couldn't see any. All he could see was her lovely face, the expectation in her eyes...

'Yes, that's right.' He set his cup down, shrugging, going for casual self-effacement. 'I'm one of the many backstage minions.'

'Ah! Very noble of you.' And then she smiled. 'The conference caught my eye because of the interior design exhibition...'

Interesting. And also perfect, because now he could steer the conversation away from himself. 'So is that your area, then, interior design?'

Her mouth stiffened and then she was giving him that mischievous smile he loved. 'How to put it...? I'm on the outermost fringes, in a sort of oblique way.'

'Which is to say...?'

A blush touched her cheeks. 'I'm into ceramics.'

'Which is to say...?'

Her gaze fell momentarily, then hesitant eyes came back to his. 'I'm a maker. A ceramicist. I make bowls and jugs...

Although actually, no…that implies functionality…' She frowned then shrugged. 'I make wonky vessels.'

He felt a thread of affinity pulling, warmth taking him over. It was all fitting now: that quality of otherness she had, the quirkiness of her style, that independence of spirit that had sent her fleeing from her cousin's bachelorette and, her choice of destination, La Sagrada Família. Through a shifting sea of tourists with phones and selfie sticks, before the bolt of recognition had struck, it had been her stillness that had drawn his eye, her unwavering focus, her state of being totally absorbed.

He knew that feeling well, that feeling of being lost in beauty, line, shape, that clamouring feeling of trying to receive every scrap, that feeling of not being wide enough or deep enough or tall enough to receive it all. He'd seen that in her, felt it in her in that moment, and now he knew, from her own lips. She was a creative, like him. But, unlike him, she seemed to lack confidence in her work. The use of that word 'wonky'…not wonky with intention and attitude, but wonky with a blushing apology.

He shifted his cup and rested his arms on the table, suddenly wanting to be closer to her, wanting her to feel his interest. 'Please, tell me more.'

She pushed her lips out. 'I don't know what else I can tell you.'

Obfuscating.

'Come on, Dulcie, you can't just dangle wonky vessels in front of me and not expand.'

'Expand how?'

There was a stubborn set to her mouth that was new, but he liked it, the different shades of Dulcie. He felt a smile coming. 'Well, you can start by telling me where you learned how to make your wonky vessels.'

She bit her lips. 'St Martin's, in London.'

'Kudos! It's one of the best schools in the UK, isn't it…?'

She nodded and then her fingers went to her cup, twisting it. 'I was lucky to get in—'

'Or…' he held up a finger '…and I'm only postulating wildly here because, you understand, it might have factored, it could be that you got in because you're talented.'

Her eyes held him, registering the words, and then a smile curved on her lips. 'Are you for real or just very well brought up?'

He laughed, liking that she was using the line she'd used before. 'Both, I hope.' He licked his lips, trying not to look at hers. 'Seriously, though, I know you have to be good to get in there, so you need to stop all that "I was lucky to get in" business.'

Her eyebrows ticked up. 'Are you telling me off?'

'No. I'm telling you to believe in yourself because I'm sensing that you don't, fully.'

Her brow puckered. 'It isn't that I don't believe in myself, it's more that I'm not sure who I am.' She blinked. 'Artistically speaking, I mean.'

'Do we ever though? Aren't we always evolving, taking in new influences? I mean look at Gaudí. There's cohesiveness in his work, for sure, but there's also eclecticism. He wasn't afraid to experiment, to let his imagination run wild. I think the moment you *find yourself* artistically is probably the moment you start looking around again for new things to try, things that make your work "better", in inverted commas. So the tail-chasing never ends.'

He felt a throb gripping his temples. Except for him. It was all ending for him, but he wasn't going to think about that now, not when Dulcie's gaze was warm on his, when she seemed to be listening.

He dipped his chin. 'Anyway, now I've given you the

pep talk, I want to see your work. Have you got pictures
on your phone?'

'Sorry, but no.' She was shaking her head. 'I'm not big
on the whole phone thing. I mean, I know phones are brilliant and all that, but I hate the way people are with them,
eyes down all the time, so I haven't allowed myself to get
sucked in. I call people, send the odd text, but aside from
that...' She paused and then the spark in her eyes was back
and glowing. 'But you didn't want a sermon, did you? If
you want to see pictures, then you need to look at the web
gallery Callum set up for me.'

Callum?

His throat went tight. How could he have forgotten that
she probably had a significant someone in England? It had
been uppermost in his mind just before the lift had come
back to life, but for some reason he hadn't thought about
it since. And now here she was, pulling out this name, to
what, gently warn him that this was coffee and coffee only?
He hadn't even got as far as thinking about anything beyond
this moment because this moment was everything. Simply
being with her across a table in Barri Gòtic, with the sun
warming his back, was filling his senses to the brim, but
that didn't mean he wouldn't have got to thinking about it,
because how could he not want more?

He inhaled a slow breath, pushing down the crushing
disappointment. Nothing to do but bear it, pretend he was
fine. Fine. Chilled. Cool. He ground his jaw. Maybe he
should view it as practice for when he assumed his royal
duties. Smiling stoicism and all that.

He swallowed. 'So, Callum's your—'

'Godsend!' She was wide-smiling, her eyes sparkling.
'He is, truly! When I moved into my studio, he set up the
Wi-Fi for me. His mum was the one who volunteered him,
said he was a bit of a whizz...'

He felt a rallying sensation, his spirits picking themselves up. Suddenly this wasn't sounding like—

'She runs the village shop where I live—in a county called Devon, before you ask—and she was so right. Cal's only fifteen but he's brilliant at tech, and he's pretty handy with a camera too so we struck a deal. I paid him to set up a website and gallery for me and now I pay him to update it. Seriously, everyone should have a Callum.'

'Sounds like it.'

He pulled his phone out, trying to keep his smile on the right side of crazy ecstatic. Having a fifteen-year-old web wizard didn't exactly preclude her from having a significant other, but suddenly it was seeming less and less likely.

The way she'd laughed in the lift...*It's not* my *hen party. It's my cousin Georgie who's getting married!'* As if the very idea that she'd be the one getting married was ridiculous. And then there was the fact that she *had* agreed to have coffee with him, readily, and the fact that he could feel electricity shuttling between them constantly. He wasn't imagining it. Wasn't.

He opened the browser. 'So what am I searching for?'

'Dulcie Brown Ceramic Art.' She was blushing again, twisting her cup around in its saucer.

He tapped, keeping his eyes down to spare her.

The site loaded quickly. Crisp, clean, simple. Totally on point, and the pictures were... *Wow!* Her pieces were impressive. Vessels, as she'd said, with a skewed side, a dropped, or sometimes a pushed-up, jagged lip, disrupting the flow, but what he really liked was the way she'd painted asymmetrical blocks of colour onto the buff clay—blues and rust—sometimes inside, sometimes outside, sometimes both, so that it wasn't only shape that arrested the eye, but design, vibrancy.

He looked up. 'These are outstanding.'

She registered the compliment, but then she was shaking her head, giving him that cheeky smile again. 'It's kind of you to say so, but—'

'No buts, please. I'm not being kind, or polite.' Her smile zipped shut. 'I think these are wonderful. I'm getting shades of Gordon Baldwin, tiny nods to Picasso…'

Her eyes narrowed slightly and then she was sighing. 'Well, you certainly know your stuff but see now I'm worried that my work is too derivative.'

His heart sank. He'd been trying to earth his compliment by mentioning Baldwin and Picasso, not throw her into a fit of self-doubt. He tightened his gaze on hers. 'It isn't. I said "shades of" because that's all I'm seeing: shades, echoes. Nothing wrong with that. We're all porous, influenced by something. That's how art works, architecture, literature, film, everything.'

She lifted her chin, challenging. 'So you're saying originality is impossible?'

He felt his senses sitting up. He liked a good debate, and, from the looks of things, she did too, but this wasn't the right time. Rather, he wanted to focus on the derivative thing, put her mind at rest.

'In a way, yes. I mean, unless you've spent your life in a vacuum you can't avoid being influenced-slash-inspired. Maybe the real problem is that we set too much store on originality for originality's sake.' He tapped the screen back to life, scrolling through her work again. 'What I *feel* when I look at your pieces is pleasure. I like your shapes, your colours, the way you've applied the paint to some parts and not others.'

He met her gaze, feeling its warmth reaching in, turning him over. 'Your work might have its roots in Baldwin, say, but it's also wholly the product of *your* decisions… To bend the clay this way or that, to cut a piece out here, or there, and then with the colour, how much blue, how intense, how deep a rust, a black line or not, brushed or dripped.'

A smile was curving onto her lips, which was making him smile too. 'Maybe you thought long and hard about all those things, or maybe you just flew at it in a frenzy. But whatever you did, whatever you do, that's all you.'

'Which sort of defeats your original argument...'

'Does it though?' Her eyebrows slid up. 'What I'm saying is that pure originality might be impossible but that it actually doesn't matter because whatever our inspiration is, we always transform it. Other makers inspire us, but you reach for cobalt today because of the blue sky you can see through *your* window in *your* corner of the world. So what you make is the product of everything that comes together for you in that moment, shades you acknowledge and shades you don't even notice. But the end result is yours, work that's wholly you, so not derivative.'

Her cheeks dimpled. 'You talk a good talk, Raffiel. You've almost got me believing you.'

'Talking a good talk is essential in the architecture business. If you can't instil faith into your client then it doesn't matter how great your plans are, your building isn't going to get built.'

'I can see that.' And then she was reaching up, adjusting her hair, her shirt tightening momentarily across her breasts, revealing the pert outline of her nipples, a suggestion of lace. 'So if I want to look at your work, where must I go?'

He forced his eyes upwards and back to hers, feeling his skin prickling hot beneath his beard. 'New York or Paris. Or you could look at the website: RM Architecture.'

'So that's Raffiel—?'

He felt a beat of indecision. 'Munoz.'

'Raffiel Munoz...' Her head tilted. 'That has a nice ring to it, a *serious* architect kind of ring.'

'Thank you.' The two words sounded dull to his ears. Nothing he could do about it though because bleakness was seizing him again, draining the light inside. The website was still up, just. Even though he'd been turning down approaches from potential clients for the past six months, he hadn't been able to bring himself to pull the plug, in case Papa changed his mind about abdicating, but next week his web people were going to be taking down the site, disconnecting his old life, the only life he knew, the only life he wanted.

'Hey, are you okay?'

Dulcie's face slipped back into focus, concern playing over her features. He felt a tug, words straining at his tongue. Unburdening himself would feel so good, sharing his grief, all the weight he was under, but he couldn't. It would only pop their bubble and he wasn't ready for that, not yet, not when it was shimmering with rainbow colours, all light and airy.

Maybe he was being selfish, but he liked little Dulcie Brown way too much to risk losing her a second before he had to, and the truth of his situation would send her running a million miles in the opposite direction, he just knew it. He only had a few more days to be plain Raff Munoz. If he was lucky, Dulcie might want to spend some of them with him. Even if it couldn't come to anything, he couldn't make himself not want it, not now, couldn't switch off this feeling of wanting to spend time with her. At least he could be truthful about that.

'Yes, I'm fine...' He smiled, drawing in a slow breath. 'I'm just a bit nervous, that's all.'

'Nervous?' Little frown. 'Why?'

'Because I want to ask you for dinner and I'm not sure how to go about it, or if you'd even be interested.'

Her lips pressed together and then she was giving him the glinting side-eye. 'You're a disingenuous devil, aren't you?'

'Only when I'm nervous.' Might as well go for broke. 'See, I don't know if you've got someone who might not

want you to have dinner with me so the whole asking thing
is quite nerve-racking.'

'Hmm…' Her cheeks were dimpling. 'I can see your
problem.' She scraped back a strand of hair that was blowing across her cheek. 'Would it help to know that I wouldn't
have said yes to coffee if I was with someone?' And then
her gaze sharpened. 'I'm assuming that if you had someone, you wouldn't be asking…'

'Correct.'

'Good.' Her expression softened again. 'I'm glad we've
sorted that out.'

'So am I…' A huge, explosive kind of glad, a glad that
was impossible to contain. He felt a smile breaking his face
apart. 'So, about that dinner…'

The light promptly drained from her face. 'I'm sorry but
I can't. It's Georgie's hen week, remember? We've already
got dinner plans and then, apparently, we've got VIP tickets
to Opium.' She rolled her eyes, sighing. 'It's a nightclub—'

'I know. I've seen it.' He felt a tingle . 'It's right on the
beach, barely ten minutes' walk from Port Vell…'

'Where your uncle's yacht is berthed…?'

He nodded, liking the glow that was coming into her
eyes, liking the way that his pulse was gathering.

Her fingers went to her cup, twisting it slowly. 'Georgie knows that nightclubs aren't my scene. She wouldn't
be remotely surprised if I wanted to step out for some air
at some point, maybe take myself off for a walk…'

'Which would be safer with a chaperone.'

'Definitely.' The corner of her mouth ticked up. 'Are
you offering?'

'It would be remiss of me not to.'

'Okay, then.' Her breaking smile knocked the breath
clean out of him. 'In that case, you'd better give me your
number.'

CHAPTER FOUR

'AT GLASTO LAST YEAR, Etienne's set was insane...'

'It *so* was. But then, Etienne's sets are always insane...'

'I'll tell you who else is *beyond* insane... I mean totally *fabulous*...'

Dulcie reached for her glass so her sleeve would ride up giving her sight of her watch. Ten to midnight. Her stomach quivered. Ten minutes to go until Etienne started his set. Ten minutes to go before they'd be abandoning the plush pink booth for the vast club downstairs. Then there'd be an obligatory ten minutes of shuffling and fist-pumping in Georgie's sightline, so that Georgie would know she was making an effort, and then, with a nice clear conscience, she was going to slip out and meet Raffiel.

She took a sip from her glass, trying to quell the fluttering inside. *Raffiel.* Slate-eyed, broad-shouldered, tall, chiselled, utterly gorgeous Raffiel. That slight olive tone to his skin that hinted at some Mediterranean gene...oh, and that accent! She sipped again, hiding her smile in her glass. So much to find out, so many things to ask. When was the last time she'd felt this excited about anyone, this curious, this tingly?

'Dulce?' Georgie was looking over, her eyes sharp. 'You okay?'

'Of course.' She loosened her smile to fit the moment.

'Great place, isn't it…?' Glassy, glitzy, lights and mirrors. Long pale bar with its rows of jewel-bright bottles. The floor beneath her feet was throbbing faintly courtesy of the support act who'd come on earlier, the support act that would be ceding to the enigmatic Etienne in T minus five minutes. Not that she was counting or anything.

'It's the best!' Georgie was smiling back, a touch of what looked like bemusement hiding at the corners of her red, glossy mouth, and then suddenly Tilly was pulling her back into the conversation.

Georgie… Always the life and soul! She looked radiant in her little red dress—*'More fun than black, darling!'*— having the time of her life with her posse, all of whom seemed to have an encyclopaedic knowledge of the club scene. Festivals.

She held in a sigh. Festivals were another topic she couldn't talk about with any degree of confidence. For sure she'd been to Glastonbury, but only once, with Tommy, and Tommy had been into the up-and-comers, the new DJs and the indie bands, and because he was always so adamant about what was worth listening to, and because she'd thought the sun shone out of him back then, she'd gone along with his choices, convincing herself that Zinc-Tube were way superior to the main stage headliners who were, horrors, so commercial, so intolerably mainstream.

She looked down at her black lace-up pumps. She definitely wasn't mainstream. She didn't fit with these chattering sparkling girls in their clingy micro dresses and spiky heels. But right now she couldn't make herself care because of Raff. Because with Raffiel she fitted.

Foolish, probably, to be even thinking that after what, barely ten minutes with him in a lift, then a scant hour with him discussing art and creativity over coffee in the Gothic Quarter. Thinking that was jumping the gun by miles, but her mind wouldn't be told. There was this feeling inside that wouldn't go away…a giddy, tingling feeling, an alive feeling, like a little pilot light burning—a pilot light that must be leaking brightness somehow because when she'd got back to the hotel Georgie had noticed, Georgie who was always glued to her phone yet seemed to have a third all-seeing eye.

'You're looking very glowy, Dulce…' Eyebrows arching up. *'That cathedral must be really something…'*

'Basilica. And yes, it is. It's fantastic. You should go.'

'I will.' Head tilting over, eyes narrowing. *'I could definitely do with a little bit of whatever you've got going on.'*

'What I've got going on is a serious case of Antoni Gaudí. He's everywhere here and he's wonderful…'

'Gaudí, huh?'

She'd felt her cheeks growing warm under Georgie's forensic gaze, but she'd also felt a window of opportunity opening…

'In fact tomorrow, if it's okay with you, I'd like to check out Parc Güell. The structures there are amazing…the pavilions…the walls…the mosaics. I'm thinking that I'll find some inspiration there for my own work.'

'Knock yourself out, sweetie. I don't think I'll even see the light of day tomorrow.' Sudden deep look. *'You are remembering that we're going to Opium tonight, that it's going to be a super-late one…?'*

'Of course I remember. Etienne, right?'

Fake swooning. 'He's a god.'

'I'm sure he is, but…' And here she'd felt another little window opening. *'You know I'll never last the whole night, right?'*

'Dulce…' Exaggerated scowling. *'You're not going to be a party pooper, are you…?'*

'Probably, but I won't spoil your fun. Promise. When

I've had enough, I'll just cut out and come back here. You don't have to worry about me.'

Sighing. 'Honestly, if you weren't my cousin, I'd be putting you on the next plane home.'

'Well, sadly for you I am, so you're stuck with me.'

Georgie had said something sweet then, about loving her to bits even though she was driving her crazy and she'd said something similar back, so they were good, except that now, suddenly, she could feel guilt itching.

She set her glass down. Was it bad of her to be slipping away to meet Raffiel? Was it a bad thing she'd done— sneaky—laying the foundations for another liaison just in case he wanted to meet tomorrow as well? She bit her lips together. It wasn't as if Parc Güell hadn't been on her wish list anyway but for some reason adding Raff to the mix was making the whole thing feel a little bit underhand. On the flipside, what was she supposed to do? Come clean, tell Georgie she'd met someone? She felt a shiver running through. There'd be an inquisition, and she wasn't ready for that. It was too soon, too new. There was nothing to say. *Ergo*, she couldn't say anything.

'Come on, Dulce…' A champagne-happy Tilly was grabbing her arm, pulling her up. 'It's time!'

She made like a rag doll, letting her younger cousin drag her round the table into Georgie's throng and then they were all moving together through the bar, clacking down the stairs until they hit a bottleneck of excited, queuing clubbers.

She glanced at Tilly. If this had been *her* hen week, and if it had been Tilly who didn't want to spend the next four hours clubbing and drinking, if it had been Tilly saying to her that she'd rather spend her time in Barcelona seeing the sights instead of lying in the suite sleeping off the night before, would *she* have minded? If Tilly had been

her bridesmaid, beloved, but patently uncomfortable with
the rest of the group, might she even have felt a tiny bit relieved if Tilly had taken herself off every now and again?
As long as she knew that Tilly was all right, that she was
truly happier going off than staying, then she'd be okay
with it. Of course she would because she'd want Tilly to
be happy, wouldn't she?

The crowd in front suddenly surged, sweeping them
through the doors into the great foggy darkness.

'Look!' Georgie clutched her arm, pointing to the stage.
'It's *him*.'

Bent over the decks, silver light beams arcing and dipping around him, there he was, Etienne, the one they were
all here for. Their god. But not hers. Hers was on his way.
He'd be outside waiting for her in ten minutes.

Ten.

Minutes.

She felt a fresh flutter starting, morphing into the low
driving pulse that was filling the space, thrumming, driving, building. She started moving, finding the rhythm. She
caught Georgie's eye, felt a smile coming, conviction winding through her veins. If she wouldn't think Tilly was bad
for wanting to go off on her own, then why would Georgie
think that about her? It wasn't as if Georgie didn't know
her feelings about this hen week, and it wasn't as if Georgie
didn't know that the saving grace of it, for her, was Barcelona itself, and Gaudí. Georgie just didn't need to know
quite yet that fate seemed to have thrown her an extra saving grace in the form of a seriously hot architect.

Raffiel leaned against the promenade rail, running his eyes
over the crowd queuing to get into Opium. High spirits.
Bright clothes. *Skimpy.* A small knot tightened in his chest.
Would Dulcie appear wearing a dress that was cut away

all over, showing more skin than fabric? For some reason the thought of it didn't sit well, not that it was any of his business how she dressed. He wasn't her keeper. He wasn't her anything. *Yet.*

He turned to look along the busy boardwalk. People, palm trees, starlit sky. *Yet.* Such a small word but pivotal. Crucial. But crucial how? What was he hoping for, what was he after, waiting here outside this club with his heart drumming and tingles shooting through his veins? Company, friendship, love everlasting, or was this about sex?

He drew in a slow breath. Of course it was about sex. Dulcie was gorgeous. He'd have to be a eunuch not to want her, but there was so much more going on than physical attraction. He just couldn't bring it all into proper focus, give it shape, purpose.

He bit back a sigh. It was his modus, wasn't it? Wanting to draw straight lines between things, visualising, seeing the big picture, but there wasn't a big picture here, no straight lines. Randomness seemed to be the order of the day. Dulcie, in the lift, then somehow at the basilica, and he'd decided to jump in, embrace chance, because this was his last ever week of freedom, but still it seemed that he couldn't switch off the side of him that liked neat lines, prescribed shapes.

Ironic! In no time at all his entire life was going to be prescribed, sandwiched between endless straight lines. A timetabled existence. He blew out the sigh he'd been holding in. With that in mind, he needed to stop all this overthinking and force himself to simply be in the moment, to let this thing with Dulcie evolve, or not, according to the rules of randomness.

'There you are!'

His heart jumped, then skipped. She was standing in front of him, clutching a small black bag, smiling that cheeky smile of hers. Her hair was down, grazing the shoulders of her pale soft shirt. Black pants, soft leather pumps, also black. She was clearly a monochrome kind of girl, except for her lips which were red and dewy and perfect for kissing.

He pressed the thought flat and smiled. 'And there *you* are, right on time.'

Her eyes widened into his. 'A miracle, to be honest, because it's heaving in there.' And then she was miming a karate sequence. 'I literally had to fight my way out.'

He chuckled. 'I'm sure you were terrifying.'

She laughed a little and then her gaze slid away. 'I can be if needs be.'

He felt a frown coming. There was a dark shade in her tone, a hard edge along it that he couldn't ignore. 'So you're a self-defence expert?'

'I am.' Her eyes came back to his, a little bit merry but also a little bit steely. 'Does that bother you?'

'Why should it bother me? I think it's great.' Except that it seemed as if she might have learned self-defence because of something that had happened, and he couldn't make himself not be bothered about that. If he were to ask her about it, would it tarnish the mood? Maybe, but then again, she was the one who'd slanted her voice darkly when she needn't have, when she could simply have breezed past it.

He searched her gaze. Was she trying to open a door? Did she *want* to talk about it? He could throw her an opening, just in case, and if she batted it away then he'd leave it. For now. He took a breath. 'The only thing is that I'm sensing you learned for a reason...'

Her eyebrows slid upwards. 'Intuitive Jedi you are.'

Doing a Yoda voice to what, soften the confirmation? Suddenly it didn't feel like a subject to be talking about outside the club. He straightened, motioning for her to walk with him, feeling his belly hardening, his fists wanting to clench. The thought of anyone—*anyone*—trying to hurt Dulcie was making his blood boil.

He swallowed hard. 'Do you want to get a drink somewhere?'

'Maybe, in a while.' She looped her bag over her head, poking her arm through, and then she was lifting up her hair, shaking it out, powdering the air with a little burst of floral scent. 'Right now I'm just glad to be outside...' Cheeky smile. 'And of course it goes without saying that the company is a bonus.'

He felt his heart warming. She was such a treat, so sweet, so funny. Which only made the thought of someone wanting to hurt her even more unbearable. He couldn't let it go.

'So, forgive me if I'm speaking out of turn, but about the self-defence thing, if you don't mind, I want to know what's behind it.'

Her face stiffened a little and then she drew in a short breath. 'It was a long time ago, Raff, and actually, nothing happened.'

'But it left a mark?'

Her shoulders lifted into a shrug. 'I suppose.' And then a funny little smile twitched onto her lips. 'You know, I've never talked about it to anyone before...' The thought seemed to occupy her for a moment and then suddenly she was cutting across him, walking to the edge of the boardwalk, sitting herself down.

His heart sank. Talk about misjudging a situation.

He went after her, dropping down beside her. 'I'm sorry. I didn't mean to pry. It's none of my business...'

'You don't have to apologise...' She scooped up a handful of sand, letting it stream through her fingers and then suddenly her eyes lifted to his, her gaze level. 'I was fifteen when it happened.'

He felt his insides twisting, fury thickening in his throat. Fifteen. It wasn't a stretch to imagine her at that age because there was something endearingly *gamine* about her even now at—what?—twenty-six, twenty-seven? She couldn't be more than that. He drew in a careful breath, trying to keep his tone even. 'What happened…?'

Her mouth drew tight. 'A boy I liked a lot, a *"very nice"* boy whom my parents thoroughly approved of, escorted me to a summer ball, plied me with fizz and then, in a tucked-away little summer house, tried to—' something retreated in her gaze '—you know.'

His heart lurched. 'He tried to rape you?'

Her eyebrows flickered. 'See, that's a grey area because it didn't get that far.' She swallowed. 'I kneed him hard, left him howling.'

Admiration flared. 'Good for you.' And then the thing she'd said before came back. He went cold inside. 'You didn't tell anyone…'

'No.' She dropped her gaze, scooping up sand again.

He searched her downturned face. Why hadn't she? It didn't make sense but asking didn't feel right. It would be putting *her* on the spot when *she* was the victim, the one who'd had to go through it. Best to let her tell it, if she wanted to, which maybe she did, because suddenly she was drawing a breath, rubbing her hands clean…

'I didn't tell anyone because afterwards I started feeling unsure…wondering if maybe I overreacted.' Her eyes came to his. 'The thing is, our parents were good friends and it's such a whopping accusation to make… I wanted to be clear in my mind… So I went over and over it but then the more I did, the more it seemed to me that it was partly my fault…'

He felt words rising and bit them back hard. Interrupting because of his own seething anger wouldn't help Dulcie. What would help was giving her this safe space to talk about it.

She was shaking her head now. 'Charlie was my first proper date. I liked him. I'd been flirting with him for weeks at this tennis coaching thing we were doing. When he asked me to the ball I was over the moon because it meant he liked me too. And, yes, he did give me champagne, but I took it every time, drank it down. And when he suggested going for a walk in the garden, I didn't hesitate, and when he led me into the summer house, I went willingly…gladly. I thought he was going to kiss me, was hoping he would. And he did, and it was nice—completely lovely—until it wasn't…' A frown ghosted over her features. 'But, see, he'd been drinking too, a lot, and what kept running through my mind afterwards was that maybe all he'd intended to do was kiss me but because of the drink, once we started, he couldn't stop—'

'Dulcie!' He didn't mean to cut in but listening to her making excuses for this boy was suddenly too much to bear. 'You weren't overreacting. What he tried to do was wrong, period.'

Her gaze sharpened. 'Oh, I know that now, believe me, but at the time I was full of doubt, scared of causing a ruckus, worried about upsetting our families. Stupid, in light of—' Her lips clamped shut suddenly and then she was turning away, staring at the black shifting sea. 'Anyway, it's ancient history now…'

So was his La Sagrada Família trip with Papa, but the memories were still bright, always would be. Her memories of Charlie would keep burning as well—darkly—unless she could deal with the part she wasn't talking about. He wanted to know about that part, the part that had zipped her into this sudden silence, but pushing her wasn't an option. She was clearly done talking about it.

And then somehow, she was smiling again, turning to him with mischief in her eyes. 'So anyway, that's why I decided to take self-defence classes and the classes are why I can be utterly terrifying if needs be.'

In spite of himself he couldn't hold in a smile. He could picture her sailing through the air, poised to strike, pale hair streaming behind.

She bumped his shoulder. 'Are you laughing at me?'

'I wouldn't dare.'

'Hmm.' She was giving him the side-eye, and then she was getting to her feet. 'So, I'm thinking that I'd quite like to see your yacht now.'

Which was really Papa's and was going to be his soon, none of which he wanted to tell her right now.

He got up, stamping his feet to get the sand off. 'My uncle's yacht, you mean.'

'Oh, right. Of course.' And then her voice dipped. 'Is he actually on board? Because I wouldn't want to intrude or anything.

The valves in his heart constricted sharply. 'No. He isn't. It's just me, and the staff.'

'You mean the crew...?'

And then suddenly the tightness was loosening. In the lift, she'd assumed that his yacht was a sailing yacht, hadn't she? And he hadn't corrected her because it hadn't felt important, but now...now it seemed that there was an opportunity for a little fun.

'Of course, yes.' He slapped his head, shrugged. 'Like I said before, I don't know the first thing about sailing.'

CHAPTER FIVE

SHE LOOKED AHEAD, registering nothing.

'I can be if needs be...'

Why had she framed her response to Raffiel's remark about her being *terrifying* in such a way that he could only have picked up on it? Had she even framed it as such, thought about it? *No.* The words had simply arrived wrapped in a cryptic tone, as if she'd been angling to talk about it, but she hadn't. Why in the world would she want to spend a single second of her time with Raffiel talking about Charlie fricking Prentice? It was like in the lift, suddenly spilling out all that stuff about not being able to talk to Georgie's friends. What was it about Raff that drew out all the things she usually kept locked up? She shot him a glance. Was it simply that he was a stranger from a different country with no connection to her circle?

She looked down, watching their feet striking the salt-bleached planks. *No.* That wasn't it. She met strangers all the time and managed perfectly well not to burden them with her secrets, her innermost thoughts. There was something else at play here, something particular to Raffiel.

'Dulcie!'

His urgent shout split the air.

She froze, barely glimpsing the cyclist barrelling towards her before she was being lassoed sideways into the broad shelter of Raffiel's chest.

The cyclist whipped past, trailing words. *'Ho sento, senyoreta. Ho sento.'*

'I'll give *him* sorry!' Raff's voice was hard-edged, his focus trained on the escaping cyclist, and then he seemed to come back to himself, noticing she was there. 'Are you okay?'

How could she not be, cocooned in his arms like this, breathing in his warm clean scent?

'Yes, thanks to you. I can't believe I didn't see him.'

'I can…' His eyes were moving over her face, a slow study, as if he was trying to satisfy himself that she really was unharmed. 'He was on his phone, weaving about like an idiot. It's why he didn't see you.'

She felt her pulse gathering. She liked the way he was looking at her, the way his gaze was lingering on her mouth. And she liked the quick way he'd pulled her to safety, that whole protective aura he had, that sense of innate strength, not just physical, but of character. It was intoxicating, irresistible…

Her heart missed. That was it! That protective aura he had… *That* was the particular thing about him, the compelling thing that drew her, the thing she wanted to believe in. *Trust*… Was *that* why some inner part of her psyche had engineered a way into the Charlie story, to see Raff's reaction, because his reaction would show her something of the man he was? Maybe…

She searched his face, his eyes. He seemed every inch the gentleman, but so had Charlie. As for Tommy, part of his appeal was that he'd never pretended to be a gentleman, but deep down she'd hoped he'd come through for her sake, for the love of her.

Charlie: fail.

Tommy: epic fail.

Was Raff just another fail waiting to happen? He might be giving her tingles in all the right places, but he was also making her act out of character: a midnight date at Georgie's expense when, admit it, tomorrow would have been more proper, less obvious! Maybe her subconscious was kicking in to protect her, had got her taking Raff to her darkest place to test him, measure him. It was self-defence all over again, just a different kind.

'Ready to walk on?' He was smiling suddenly, putting her away from him with gentle hands.

'Absolutely...' She tugged her bag straight, using the nanosecond it took to collect herself. 'Happily, I'm still fully functional.'

On one level anyway... Walking and talking she could manage, all along the boardwalk and on until they were at the marina, keeping pace with Raff's conversation about Barcelona, how much he loved it, crazy cyclists aside, but her mind was still whirring. If, unwittingly, she'd been testing Raff, then had he passed?

She flicked him a glance, catching his smile, feeling a smile of her own unfurling, warmth running through her veins. *Yes.* With flying colours. Sitting there with him on the boardwalk, feeling the firm warmth of his arm radiating through the fabric of his shirt, she'd felt protectiveness coming off him in huge primal waves.

It was why she'd had to draw a line, stop herself from telling him the rest about Charlie because the rest would only have stirred him up more, would only have made his fury pulse all the harder, and that would have been too much to take. Too intense. Too damn seductive!

It's why she'd forced herself to her feet, to insert some distance between them, and it was why she'd suggested the yacht, to change the subject, to give herself some breathing space, but then the cyclist had arrived, and Raff had filled that space right up, stealing her breath away all over again and very soon, he was saying, they'd be at the yacht, and then what…?

Her heart stumbled. What kind of signal was she sending, meeting him at midnight, suggesting the yacht, asking if his uncle was on board…? On the other hand, it was *Raff* who'd initially mentioned that Port Vell was close to Opium. She'd just picked up the baton, hadn't she, and now they were both running with it, but running where? Towards what?

Gah! Maybe she was overthinking it. They'd only met twelve hours ago, and they liked each other, clearly. Maybe that was the only thing that mattered, the mutual liking, this happy feeling of connection.

'Here we are…' Raff was stopping, sweeping his arm out.

'Here…' She felt the word dying in her mouth, her mouth falling open. The vessel in front of them was vast. Not a sailing yacht for weekend jaunts but a sleek superyacht. Seventy-five metres at least with three decks—or was it four?—brightly lit. This was serious billionaire territory and Raffiel was what? A working architect, successful, clearly, but surely if his family was in the billionaire bracket—so conspicuously so—then he wouldn't be working, wouldn't have to. Unless he wanted to, which maybe he did. She zipped her lips back together. Anything was possible, but… *No!* This had to be a wind-up, Raff having a little fun.

She turned to look at him. Definitely a wind-up. His lips were twitching, and there was a playful gleam in his eye.

She arched her eyebrows at him. 'Really…? This one?'

He nodded, the mischief in his eyes suddenly fading. 'Yes.'

He was serious, *actually* serious. She flicked a glance

at the gleaming hull then met his gaze again, trying to ignore the dark flutter that was starting in her belly. 'What did you say your uncle did?'

He seemed to falter, and then he pushed a hand through his hair. 'I didn't.'

Instantly, uncharitable mafia kind of thoughts flew in, but she couldn't help it. Fact was, it *was* a really huge yacht. Dauntingly expensive.

She drew in a careful breath. 'Raff, is your uncle some sort of oligarch?'

'No!'

Emphatic. Spontaneous. Which had to mean he was telling the truth. She felt relief skipping through her veins.

He turned a little, motioning across the water to the opposite quay. 'Those megayachts over there belong to the oligarchs, or so I've been told.'

'Right.' She ran her eyes over Raffiel's uncle's boat again. 'So what *does* your uncle do?'

For a moment he was silent and then he took an audible breath. 'He's… He worked for the royal household…' A familiar sadness was filling his gaze, the same sadness that had tugged her heart out in the lift. 'He was a high-up.'

'I see.' It seemed like the right thing to say even though she didn't quite see anything. The size of the yacht certainly befitted a high-ranking royal servant but what did 'high-up' actually mean? And what about that 'was' Raff had slipped in? She wanted to ask him about it, but the pain in his eyes seemed to be connected to it and she didn't want to bring it to the surface again, especially now that his expression was softening.

'So, do you want to come aboard?'

She looked past him to the lower aft deck. Open, luxuriously appointed, bathed in golden light. Beyond inviting! And so was he, standing there at the foot of the gangplank in his white linen shirt, his hair lifting in the slight breeze. His stance was open. Relaxed. No expectation in his eyes, only the question he'd asked. She felt warmth rippling through. He'd brought her here because she'd asked him to, but he wasn't assuming she wanted to board. He was *asking* her. She liked that. It felt respectful. Safe.

She looked at the interior again, feeling her curiosity stirring, a smile rising inside. 'Well, since you're twisting my arm…'

It was impossible not to gawp. At everything. Pale sofas. Pale decking. Brushed steel, brilliant chrome. Downlighters, uplighters, inset spots throwing curved yellow pools over the steps. Luxury cabin after luxury cabin, sleek bathrooms, staterooms, cinema, gym, pool, a vast state-of-the-art kitchen that had nothing of the galley about it. Understated elegance bordering on the cool and neutral, but the warmth in Raffiel's amused smile as he'd toured her around had been more than enough to offset that. And now there was this, this view from the upper deck, Barcelona glowing bright against the inky sky.

She pressed herself against the rail. 'If this were my boat, I think I'd spend all my time up here.'

Suddenly he was beside her, rolling his sleeves back, resting thick tanned forearms on the polished wood. 'So you like being high?'

She forced her eyes upwards to meet his. 'I like a nice view.'

'So do I…' His gaze held her fast, glowing, sending an electric tingle up her spine. She could feel a low liquid ache starting, her heart thudding in her throat. He was so handsome it hurt. A proper grown-up man with broad shoulders and unfathomable depths behind his eyes, not like Charlie the grabby-handed boy, or like Tommy, gangly in his skinny jeans and Docs. Raffiel was in a class of his own.

He turned to the view momentarily, and then his eyes came back. 'Would you like a drink?'

Something to crack the tension apart. Probably a good idea, even though alcohol wasn't the thing she was craving.

'That would be lovely, thank you.'

He straightened, motioning to an ice bucket that had somehow appeared on the low table in the seating area. 'We seem to have champagne.' One eyebrow lifted. 'Will that do?'

She couldn't hold in a smile. 'Very nicely.'

She followed him to the sofas, watching his forearms as he twisted the bottle around the cork until it popped. And then he was pouring, laughing as the champagne frothed up over the rims of the flutes.

His eyes flicked up. 'Does it show that I'm more of a beer drinker?'

She felt warmth surging in. He was so natural, so easy to be with. 'It only went pear-shaped at the end there. Your uncorking procedure was totally on point.'

He flattened a hand to his chest. 'That means so much. Thank you.' And then he was chuckling again, handing her a glass. 'Shall we sit?'

'Sure.' She lowered herself onto one of the pale sofas.

He took a spot beside her, but on the adjacent sofa, then raised his glass. 'Here's to faulty lifts.'

She felt heat rising, tingling in her cheeks. His eyes were saying that he was pleased they'd met, pleased she was here. Could he read pleasure in her eyes too, flowing back, because it was what she was feeling, pleasure, and a thrumming anticipation. She touched her glass to his, holding his gaze tight so he'd know. 'To faulty lifts.'

He smiled a slow warm smile, which set off more tingling.

So much for cracking the tension apart. It was back with a vengeance, winding tighter, pulsing through the air. *Too much.*

She broke away from his gaze, heart drumming, and looked around, trying to tune in to the calming lap of the water below. Dark water, dark sky, and in between, this open deck, all pale and perfect. She swallowed a sip of champagne. She'd been on some nice boats in some lovely locations, but this was definitely the grandest. The grandest and the saddest, somehow. It wasn't just that Raffiel was the only occupant but that it was so utterly pristine... *No.* She felt a frown coming. It was more than that. It was denuded. No personal mementoes, no photographs. It was like a ghost ship.

'What are you thinking so hard about, Dulcie Brown?'

She felt the dark velvet accent tugging at more than just her attention.

She took a breath and turned to look at him. His gaze was warm, open, a smile hiding inside it. If she were to tell him what she was thinking, then that smile would undoubtedly fade. Did she want to risk that, risk bringing his sadness back?

He tilted his head over a little, prompting. Her heart thumped a thick beat. Did she have a choice though, because whatever this was that they were doing—*starting*—be it a friendship or a holiday fling or who knew what, skirting around things, avoiding awkward truths was never a good idea.

If she'd told her parents the truth about Charlie instead of telling them that she'd simply 'gone off him' after that first date, then how different might her life have been? She bit the inside of her cheek. But it was more than that even. She liked Raff, liked him far too much not to want

to know everything about him. If something was griev-
ing him, then that thing was as much a part of him as
his handsome face and his thick forearms and his heart-
stopping smile so how could she not want to know what
it was? The problem was how to lead him to it…

She took a sip from her glass, considering, then set it
down. 'I was just thinking that this boat feels very empty.'

'Well, it is. It's just you and me, plus the twenty staff
and crew obviously.' A wry smile curved on his lips. 'It's
practically the *Marie Celeste.*'

She took a breath. 'I didn't quite mean that.'

His eyebrows flickered faintly.

'What I was thinking is that there's nothing here to show
that it belongs to anyone… I mean, it's your uncle's yacht,
right, but there are no family photographs in the cabins, no
personal effects anywhere…'

His expression was altering, solidifying.

She swallowed, not wanting to push, but also wanting
to know, needing to. 'I was just wondering why that was.
Wondering about your uncle really…'

Was she going too far? Raff's face was growing more
and more masklike, but that could only mean that the pain
inside him was on the rise again and that he was trying to
hold it back, keep it inside. Maybe it was wrong, but the
resistance in him was only making it feel all the more im-
perative to break through because the thought of him hurting alone was too much to bear.

In textbook terms he was a stranger, yes, but for some
reason it didn't feel like that. The strangeness was nothing to this deep feeling of connection, this flame of fellow
feeling. Whatever pain he was feeling, she wanted to share
in it, help him, bolster him if she could. But to do that, it
meant pushing him all the way over the line.

She drew in a careful breath, tightening her gaze on his.

'I know it's none of my business, but I just can't help wondering why you look so sad whenever you mention him.'

His pulse was going hard, jack hammering. Could she see it, sense it? Of course she could. He'd felt it in her from the start, from that first moment in the lift. Empathy behind her eyes that had simply flowed out and reached in, laying him bare. For a piece of a second, he hadn't liked that feeling of being exposed but then the lift had stopped, and everything had changed. Her hand on the rail, her wide scared eyes. Impossible not to drop his resistance. Impossible not to succumb.

That was the thing about Dulcie, wasn't it? The irresistible pull of her, and it had nothing to do with her sweet lips and her big eyes and her neat lithe body. It was greater. Deeper. It was the thing that had impelled his feet in her direction at La Sagrada Família, the thing that had impelled him to mention the proximity of Port Vell to Opium, hope beating in his heart for exactly this, a late-night rendezvous, because waiting sensibly for tomorrow hadn't even occurred to him. That's how caught up he was, how beguiled. And now she was bringing that exact quality of gentle empathy and deep warmth to bear, bringing it right up to his crumbling brink.

His breath stopped halfway. Crumbling because he couldn't not be honest with her. Fudging Uncle Carlos's role in the royal household was one thing, a scant lie, whiter than white, but he couldn't fudge Uncle Carlos back to life, pretend that a living, breathing uncle still owned this yacht. Not when, as she'd so rightly observed, there was no proof of life.

He swept up his glass, sipping to buy time. Uncle Carlos's personal possessions, and Gustav's and Hugo's, had been cleared away after the funerals. Photos and books, mementoes and magazines, jackets in cupboards. Gustav's wetsuits... A knot hitched tight in his chest. Because Gus had loved to surf, had been good at it too. Gus had been good at everything physical: climbing, skiing, soccer. Full of life. Full of energy. That had been Gustav. Always shining bright. A star. Incomparable.

'Raffiel…?'

Dulcie's eyes came back into focus, searching, gently pleading. She knew he wasn't comfortable and now him stalling like this was making her uncomfortable too. He wasn't having that, not when she was only trying to reach out, trying to be kind.

He set his glass down and met her gaze. 'I think I must look sad because I *am* sad…' Her eyes narrowed a little, urging him on. He drew in a slow breath, feeling it catch in his throat. This was going to be his first time telling someone about Uncle Carlos, finding the words himself. After the tragedy the royal aides had stepped in, handling it all, and then a few days later Papa had broadcast a statement to the nation.

Now it was just himself, the future King, addressing an audience of one, except he couldn't tell her the King part. Not yet. Too much information. For him, never mind for her. *No.* That part could wait, and everything that came with it. He drew in another slow breath, refocusing. 'My uncle died. A few months ago.'

She blinked, seemingly at a loss, and then her eyes came to his. 'I'm so sorry, Raff.' Her fingers twisted in her lap. 'Were you close…?'

He felt a hole tearing open, hot coals pouring in. Gustav… Hugo… Cousins. Playmates. Friends. *Accomplices!* He'd loved his sister, Victoria, of course, but a younger sister was no match for Gus and Hugo. Being included so thoroughly by them had meant the world. Halcyon days. Precious times. Before their respective paths had diverged. Before Gus and Hugo had had to don serious suits and take a share of the royal duties. Before he'd left Brostovenia for

Cornell and a whole new life, a life of freedom and ano-
nymity that they must have envied. Not that they'd ever
shown it. Too noble by far for that.

Had been...

He felt his chest starting to buckle. No need to go beyond
Uncle Carlos, no need to tell Dulcie about Gus and Hugo,
except...except maybe it would hurt less if he shared the
grief, let their names ring out.

He swallowed, trying to shape his voice into an even
line. 'We were, yes. But the thing is...' *Breathe.* 'It wasn't
only my uncle who died. It was...' His sinuses were suddenly burning, and his throat, and his eyes behind his lids.

And then suddenly her hand closed over his forearm,
warm and soft. 'Who was it, Raff?' Gentleness in her voice.
'Who else?'

Her gaze was steady, reaching in, breaking him all to
pieces, but shoring him up at the same time, giving him
strength.

'My cousins.' His voice wanted to crack but he had to
go on, make himself say their names to honour them. He
swallowed hard. 'Gus and Hugo.'

The light drained from her face. 'I'm so, so sorry.' Tears
were mounting from her lower lids, glistening, and then
suddenly she was taking her hand away, looking down,
shaking her head in what looked like self-admonishment.
'I should never have asked.'

He felt a pang, a new hole tearing open, a hole with Dulcie's name on it. She'd only asked because of the sadness in
him, because it was clearly moving her, concerning her, and
it was concerning her because she was a kind person, warm
and sweet. There wasn't nearly enough kindness in the world
and here she was apologising for it. He wasn't having that.

He squeezed his eyelids shut, gathering his pain into a
manageable bundle. 'It's fine that you asked, really...' Wet

eyes came to his, blinking back, and suddenly the only thing that mattered was putting her mind at rest. 'Please believe me, Dulcie. I don't mind. Asking doesn't change anything. Asking doesn't make what happened worse. It can't.'

And then a fresh thought was unwinding, pulling him into a different room inside his head. Could it be that *this* was rock bottom, that going forward, even though it didn't feel like it right now, things would start to get better, feel better? Hard to imagine, and yet here he was, talking to Dulcie, feeling her empathy wrapping him up all soft and warm, feeling it lifting him. He exhaled, refocusing, feeling his perspective lengthening. 'It is what it is, and, hard as it is to accept, I can't make it not be true.'

Her eyes were moving over his face, trying to separate his pain from the bravado. And then suddenly a frown was lodging between her eyebrows. 'What *did* happen?' Her cheeks pinked a little. 'What I mean is, do you want to talk about it…?'

He bit down on his tongue. Unburdening himself to Dulcie would be cathartic but talking about the horror of Dralk wasn't an option. Brostovenia was a small country, but the freakish nature of the tragedy had created a ripple in the press. Chances were that she'd have seen or heard something, so if he were to mention Dralk then she'd know immediately who his cousins were and exactly what kind of royal 'high up' Uncle Carlos had been, and then she'd know who *he* was too.

His stomach roiled. Being untruthful wasn't his way, but what good would come of revealing everything now? It would mean dealing with, first, her incredulity and then, inevitably, the wariness and the distance that were bound to follow.

Just that morning hadn't he'd felt awkwardness hovering with Arlo, even though Arlo had known him for years? And if that could happen with a long-cherished associate, then it would happen with Dulcie too, send her fleeing, no doubt.

His heart clenched. And he didn't want that. He wanted her *here*, just to *be* with her, breathing in the night air and the tang of the sea. Just breathing. Being. Being the self he knew how to be, not the one he didn't. So no, God forgive him, he couldn't tell her the whole truth. Not now. Not tonight.

He drew in a breath. 'There's not much to talk about.' *Untrue.* 'It was a car accident.' *True.* 'Gus was driving… came off the road.' *Also true.* 'The car flipped over…' *Exploded*, but he couldn't go there. He swallowed hard. 'According to the medics they died instantly.'

Which was something.

The *only* thing to hold onto.

'Oh, Raffiel…' Her voice was close to a whisper, her eyes full. 'I can't even begin to imagine…'

'I know.' He attempted a smile. 'It's heavy…'

Heavy. Sombre. And somehow not quite the evening he'd imagined, as far as he'd allowed himself to imagine anything in this uncharted landscape of randomness, randomness that had conspired to put an oblivious cyclist on a collision course with an equally oblivious Dulcie, necessitating decisive action on his part, a manoeuvre that had given him an all too tantalising taste of how it felt to have her body crushed against his. Warm. Soft. Warmth pulsing through her softness in waves and that gaze, holding him, tugging at him. He hadn't wanted to let her go. And now something in her eyes was tugging at him again…

He felt sweat breaking along his hairline. Eight months lonely, eight months heartbroken. Loss on all sides, from every angle, change bearing down hard and always that endless, miserable, sapping self-pity. He was weak. Selfish. Gritless. He didn't deserve her and yet here she was somehow, fate's gift, a beautiful soul with a beautiful face, her eyes reaching in, inviting him. Definitely inviting him…

He looked at her lips, felt his pulse spiking. God, how he

wanted to accept that invitation, take her beautiful mouth with his, but kissing her would lead to more and no matter how much he wanted more, no matter how much she seemed to want it too, he couldn't push that button. Dulcie didn't know his situation, probably wouldn't much like his situation, so letting things unfold would be unfair, reckless. Disrespectful! Whether he liked it or not he was going to be King of Brostovenia and until he could find it in himself to tell her that fact he wouldn't, *couldn't,* allow himself to—

'Raff...'

Husky. Urgent. *Close.* Her voice broke through and before he could focus her lips were on his, soft and warm and perfect. He tensed, trying to resist, but then his traitorous muscles were loosening, and he was losing, folding, surrendering. He couldn't not take hold of her face, couldn't not pull her closer, taking over the kiss, tasting her, going slow, until her lips were parting, letting him into the tender heat of her mouth. And then it was deep kissing, feeling his senses skewing with every caress of their tongues, feeling desire mounting in relentless, bittersweet waves.

'Oh, God, Raff...' Hunger in her gasp, breathless need, and then suddenly she was moving, sliding onto his lap, hands winding into his hair, her body pressing closer, so close, so warm.

He cupped her buttocks, drawing her in hard until she was right there, inflicting maximum torture, throwing his pulse into overdrive, and then he took her mouth again, kissing deep, feeling her coming back at him, feeling the blood beating harder in his groin with every hot stroke of her tongue. Somewhere inside his head a pale voice was screaming, 'Stop,' but it was too faint, too distant to hear, or maybe it was just that he didn't have the will to listen.

CHAPTER SIX

A GULL SCREECHED and her heart lurched. Just a bird, wheeling overhead. A bird! Hardly a thing to make a heart bolt but that was how jumpy she was, startling and fluttering at the slightest thing because of Raff, because soon he'd be here with that smile of his and those slate-dark eyes and those lips that fitted to hers just so.

Raffiel...

She felt a tug starting, transforming itself into a deep pulsing ache. She wanted more of him, all of him, had been ready to give everything last night, and would have too if he hadn't put a firm hand over hers as she'd been going for his shirt buttons...

'Dulcie, please. Stop...' Dark eyes, dark velvet voice, *ragged around the edges. 'I can't... I mean, I don't think we should...'*

'Why? I want you. Don't you want me?'

'God yes! Can't you tell? But it's too soon. I think it's too soon.'

'Not for me.'

'That's just the heat of the moment talking.' Slate gaze softening. 'Don't you think it'd be better to wait a while?' Small head shake. 'We only just met today. If we go inside now, then afterwards maybe you'll wonder if you did the right thing...'

'I don't think I'd be wondering that.'

Smiling. 'You have very firm opinions, Dulcie Brown, but please, humour me.'

There'd been no choice but to humour him since he'd been putting her away from him, with a lingering kiss admittedly, saying that he'd walk her back to her hotel now, saying that he had to show his face at the conference for an hour in the morning, but that he'd like to spend the rest of the day with her if she could manage to extricate herself from Georgie and her friends.

Not a problem since she'd laid the foundations for a Parc Güell excursion already but, even if she hadn't, escaping would have been easy seeing as Georgie and Tilly and the others hadn't clattered back in until dawn and were unlikely to resurface until late afternoon at the earliest.

So now here she was perched on a low wall in La Plaza of the World Trade Centre, waiting for Raff, startling at the random cries of gulls, too jittery even to have taken in much of what she saw during her walk around the interior design exhibition. Not like her at all. Usually she'd have been captivated, but the only thing captivating her now, *intriguing* her, was Raffiel Munoz, giddying her senses, making her act so out of character, kissing him like that…

She sighed. She wasn't in the habit of making the first move. With Tommy she had but that was different. Before then and since, she never had, in fact since Tommy she'd hardly dated. It was just that Raffiel had looked so bruised last night, so broken, that something inside had simply taken over. She'd *had* to touch him, *had* to kiss him, to take his grief and pain away, so he'd feel all the things she was feeling for him—tenderness, compassion, infinite warmth—so he'd know for certain he wasn't alone.

For a moment he'd seemed shocked but then he'd started kissing back and, oh, God, *how* he'd kissed back, taking over, taking his time, his tongue teasing and stroking hers until every cell in her body had been vibrating. And then before she knew what she was doing she'd been moving onto his lap and he'd been drawing her right in, his hands warm and sure. And then everything had started unravelling, heat and yearning taking over, and she'd felt it in him too but then all of a sudden he'd put the brakes on, delivered his speech about waiting.

She touched her lips, remembering the firm warmth of his. That Raff wanted to wait was admirable perhaps, but it was also frustrating. She was only here for four more days, and he was only here for the conference. Not much time, not many moments to waste.

'That's just the heat of the moment talking.'

She felt an old chill stirring, a cold weight sinking. It was heat of the moment that had taken her over when she'd met Tommy's eye that day, wasn't it? Boldness rising up and, yes, spitefulness, offering herself to him on a plate because it had felt like a statement, a sharp kick at the world she'd come from, which wasn't a bad world, or at least no worse than any other. That was what she'd learned in the end, the hard way.

She inhaled a slow breath. Maybe Raff was right: heat of the moment couldn't be trusted. For sure it could be exhilarating, could feel momentarily powerful, but it could also lead to wrong turns, turns that kept looping on and on, dragging consequences like chains.

She looked up. Another gull was carving across the sky now, its great wings tilting. The thing about Raff, though, was that even with a few hours' thinking time on the clock she still couldn't make herself feel that getting physically closer to him would have been a mistake. They'd only just met, true, and yes, they were both only here for a short time but even so, there was something about this that felt bizarrely, sublimely right. Maybe it was that aura Raff had, that aura of strength and trustworthiness, that made him seem like a fairy-tale hero: a knight in shining armour or a noble prince!

Noble...

That was Raff. Saving her from the cyclist, clamping down on his own all too obvious desires when they'd been on the brink because he was thinking of *her*, imagining himself into her head, imagining next-day regrets. And it wasn't just for show, to extract consent, because she had consented, hadn't she? And still he'd held firm, walked her back to the hotel like a true gentleman. And then he'd kissed her goodnight, a long, slow, tingling kiss that had left her breathless and in no doubt that his having put the brakes on wasn't any kind of rejection. No. This wasn't about rejection, this was something else... She felt a tingle, a slow smile tugging at her lips. Could it be that Raffiel Munoz was simply an old-fashioned romantic?

She felt a fresh sigh filling her lungs. She'd grown up believing in romance, loving the idea of it, imagining how it would feel to be caught up in it, but after Charlie, all that stopped. And now here was Raffiel threatening to kindle that belief back to life, that side of herself that had always loved fairy tales and happy endings, brave knights, and valiant princes—

'Dulcie!'

Her heart bounced, then filled with a tumbling rush of happiness. Raff was coming across La Plaza towards her. Navy chinos. Burgundy and white striped shirt. Smiling, rolling his sleeves back—off duty now—his stride long and easy.

'Have you been waiting long?' His hands cupped her elbows, and then he was pulling her into his arms, warm light playing in his eyes.

He smelt nice, soapy freshness mingling with the light amber musk of his cologne. She wanted to press her lips into the hollow at the base of his throat, breathe him in, taste his skin, but this wasn't the time or the place.

She slid her arms around his neck. 'No, not out here anyway. I took a turn around the exhibition.'

His eyebrows lifted. 'And…?'

Panic rushed in. He wanted her opinion—as if it even counted for anything—but her mind was firing blanks. His fault. He was taking up all of her bandwidth with his eyes to drown in, and his muscular shoulders and his cologne and his total, utter gorgeousness. *Think!* And then names were surfacing, materials and colours and shapes. Thank God! Raff might have been just a backstage minion, but it was clear that this conference meant a lot to him. The last thing she wanted was to seem lukewarm.

'I loved it. Pablo Cossa's workspace designs blew me away, and I loved Kim Goh's chairs.' He was nodding, looking pleased. 'And I really liked the emphasis on sustainability.'

The light in his eyes altered, shading towards the steely. 'It's the only way to be now. With everything. Not just architecture and design. We have to step up, take responsibility, right?'

So serious suddenly. She felt a little protective flame igniting. 'Yes, we do, but, you know, it's not all down to you personally…'

His gaze sharpened and then there was a playful glimmer coming in. 'Are you telling me off?'

The very words she used on him yesterday! She smiled inside. So they were doing this already, leaning into their own private lexicon. It felt nice, like an extra little bond gluing them together.

'No. I just think you need to cut yourself some slack, let the world take care of itself for today.'

He shrugged. 'I'm not trying to take care of the world. I'm stating the facts, that's all, adding my small voice to the chorus. We have to do better across the board, everyone knows that. It's why I—' His lips pressed together tight, and then he smiled. 'It's why the theme of the conference this year is Building Better, Living Better.'

Smiling, but not all the way to his eyes. Instead there were clouds, complications. It was getting easier to separate the different layers. Grief. Sadness. But there'd been something else too, buried in that shrug, something hiding in the far reaches of his gaze. She could always ask him about it, as she had last night, but not here. Not now.

She put a hand to his face. 'Building better *is* taking care of the world. We can discuss at length if you like, but maybe we could do it somewhere else?'

His gaze cleared. 'Did you have somewhere in mind?'

'I was thinking Parc Güell…'

His face lit, looking suddenly irresistibly boyish. 'I'm totally up for that. It's one of my all-time favourite places.'

'If your mother is half Brazilian, then that makes you one quarter Brazilian…' Dulcie was pivoting slowly, taking in the forest of columns that underpinned the Greek Theatre above them, the small scuffs of her sandals echoing slightly as she moved, and then her eyes came back to his, that irresistible little spark jumping at the edge of her gaze. 'So do you speak Portuguese?'

He felt a smile coming. 'Sim.'

'I like that.' She smiled back. 'It must be wonderful to be able to speak so many languages.'

'It's good, but it's not *so* many. I speak my native language, and English, a little Italian and I'm fluent in Portuguese, but obviously I had a head start with that one so…'

'Whatever.' She pushed her lips out, nodding a slow appreciative nod. 'It's very attractive.'

'I'm glad…' Which he was, of course. The sensual glow in Dulcie's eyes was giving him all kinds of tingles, tingles that—*admit it*—he hadn't felt under Brianne's gaze for a very long time. But talking about family felt like walking through a minefield. It wasn't that he'd minded telling her that his mother was half-Brazilian, or that Papa was heavily invested in solar technology or that his clever sister was an actuary. It was just feeling more and more wrong not to be telling her what else they were. What else *he* was. But if he told her, everything would change. All this—whatever *this* was—would disappear, and he couldn't bear that. Not yet.

A sharp pang took his heart. Of all the weeks to have met someone really worth meeting. A standout someone! Smart, creative, a little bit zany. *Funny!* Kind. Warm. Sexy as hell. Bad luck or good luck? Hard to know, hard to even think straight when she was looking at him like this. All he could think about was her lips. Tasting them. Right now.

He flicked a glance around the columned hall—miraculously empty—then took her shoulders in his hands, walking her backwards to one of the Doric pillars. 'The question is though, Ms Brown, how attractive *is very* attractive?' Her eyes were dancing, her lips twitching, which was making it hard to keep his own face straight. 'More importantly, how can we measure its effect?'

She caught her bottom lip between her teeth, eyes twinkling, and then her hands were coming up, her fingers drawing small shapes in the air between them, parodying his own schematic in the lift. 'Attractiveness is difficult to measure empirically, but a good impression of its effect can be gained through, in the first instance, the act of kissing.'

He could feel his insides vibrating, laughter wanting to explode, but he held it in. He had to hear the rest.

She was pressing her fingertips together now, her mouth working furiously at not smiling. 'The sensations released during a kiss, sensations which might include some or all of the following—tingling, swooning, breathlessness, heart palpitations, weightlessness, and temporary loss of cognitive function—are good indicators for the effect of attractiveness. If we go to the current study, we'll call it the one quarter Brazilian study, the evidence is—'

'Stop, please…' She was too much, too funny. Laughter was taking him, breaking him into happy pieces, and she was laughing too, a rich throatiness to it. Irresistible! He took her face into his hands. 'Did I sound that pompous in the lift?'

'No!' Her brow creased. 'You were beyond perfect.' And then her gaze softened. 'So perfect that I wanted to kiss you.'

Not just him then, in those first moments, feeling that tug.

He moved his thumbs, stroking her cheekbones, feeling his pulse quickening, anticipation tingling. 'I wanted to kiss you too.'

Her voice dipped. 'And what about now…?'

He felt his breath catching. 'What do you think?' And then he couldn't hold back, not for another second. He bent his head, brushing his lips over hers, taking her mouth, going slow. Top lip. Bottom lip. An urgent little noise vibrated low down in her throat, and then her body was rising, soft and warm, and her lips were parting, letting him into the sweet wet heat of her mouth. He felt his limbs loosening. This felt so right. So perfect. He deepened his kiss, caressing her tongue, tuning into her rhythm, feeling his pulse heating, ramping. And then her arms were going around his neck, and she was closer still, warmer still, her breasts pressing into him, her perfume winding into his nostrils.

He felt a transition taking place, his body starting to beat around his pulse. Thick, hot pulsing. Temples. Heart. Belly. Groin. He was getting hard, harder, so hard it hurt, and he was spiralling, cycling through endless opposites. He was heavy, and weightless, liquid, and solid, melting and burning. Just a kiss but the way her lips were moulding to his and that strawberry sweetness he could taste were unleashing sensations, feelings, that went beyond anything—

'Raff... Please, I need...' She was pulling away suddenly, breathless, her eyes reaching in, hazy blue, beseeching. 'I want...'

Closer! She wanted it and God help him, he did too, *wanted* to feel her body right up against him, like last night. He moved his hands, going for her rear, exploring its firm round contours for a tantalising moment before lifting her up, pulling her in hard. Instantly her legs wound around him, tightening, and then her hands were in his hair, her lips on his neck. Her tongue was hot, slick on his skin. He felt the faintest nip of her teeth, a gasp struggling its way up his throat. He was unravelling. Desire was King now, the only thing that mattered.

He moved them back against the pillar, felt her using its support to push against him and then her mouth was on his again and her hands were sliding down, finding him, stroking him. He felt his pulse exploding, his senses surging, spiralling out. *This* feeling... This feeling right here was the reason for not blowing this thing apart. Why on earth wouldn't he want to cling to this magic for as long as possible, drowning in her smile and her laughter, and the beautiful irresistible light in her eyes and these sublime mind-blowing kisses, no, not just kisses, *ultra*-kisses...?

'Do you *mind*?'

He froze, heart bucking, felt Dulcie freezing too. The voice was coming from behind. Male. American. Distinctly put out. There was a sense of shuffling footsteps. A multitude. *Oh, God!* Not a tour, surely. He felt his blood simultaneously draining and rushing to his face, a scalding shame curling. What was wrong with him? He was thirty-one years old. He was a king in waiting. This wasn't acceptable behaviour. What would Papa think?

Papa!

'Raff!' Dulcie's hiss snapped him back. Her legs were loosening around him. He moved, letting her go, catching her pointed look, a look that seemed to be saying, Don't move, don't speak. And then she was stepping around him and away, twisting her body a little one way and then the other, as if—

'That's *so* much better, thank you.' Her eyes were on his, but her voice was ringing out, clearly meant for the audience. She lifted her arms, rolling her shoulders gingerly, then with increasing gusto, and then she was rubbing her lower back, catching his eye. 'Jasper. Honest to God, you're a miracle-worker...'

Jasper?

Her focus shifted to the band of people whose eyes he could feel boring into his back, and then her plummy, husky, smiling voice was ringing out again. 'Listen, if anyone else here has sciatica then you totally need my friend Jasper. He's absolutely the best chiropractor in London.'

He felt his belly starting to vibrate. So he was a London chiropractor now? He wasn't going to be able to keep a straight face the way she could, but he couldn't leave her to handle this by herself. She'd cast him a role, trying to save them. He had to step up, play his part. He checked in with the state of his arousal—*vanquished*—then sucked in a slow breath and turned. Immediately a dozen sets of curious, sceptical eyes pinned him. He searched the faces, homing in on a middle-aged woman whose gaze seemed to contain a grain of amusement.

He smiled at her, shrugging, digging for his inner Gustav. 'Sometimes urgent manipulation is the only way to manage an acute spasm.' He could feel Dulcie's silent mirth shaking the air. He mustn't catch her eye. One glance and he'd be finished.

He swallowed hard, shifting his gaze to a tall, stiff-faced man, clearly the one who'd barked at them. 'Apologies for how it must have looked but it *was* an emergency...' He motioned to Dulcie, taking care not to look at her. 'At least poor Jessica can walk again now. Five minutes ago she was doubled up...'

And then somehow, in spite of the situation, mischief was flaring. He shook his head, arranging his features into a frown. 'It was quite terrible to see. She was experiencing breathlessness, tingling, heart palpitations...' He slid his eyes over the faces to measure their engagement, the way he did when he was giving his conference talks. 'And all because of the—' *one quarter Brazilian effect* '—because of the pain, you see.'

'I can imagine...' This from the woman with amused eyes. She was detaching herself from the group, coming towards him with a smile. 'I suffer terribly with sciatica, myself.' Her gaze flicked to Dulcie. 'It can take you that way, out of the blue. I know.' And then her eyes came back to his. 'I'm actually in London next month, so maybe I'll look you up.' Her eyebrows flickered, amusement twitching at the corners of her mouth. 'Do you have a card?'

CHAPTER SEVEN

'Jasper *Júlio*... Harley Street?' Raff's voice was barely audible over the scuff of their fast-escaping feet. And then he let out a low chuckle, his eyes catching hers. 'I'm quite the bigshot, aren't I?'

'Of course! You're the best in London.'

She'd snatched the Júlio out of the air when the woman had asked for his card, because he'd seemed to be on the verge of cracking and because it had seemed like a good name for a chiropractor who was one quarter Brazilian. And, of course, Harley Street was the *only* credible address.

She smiled over. 'If you're a lie, you might as well be a big fancy one...'

Silence.

Her heart clenched. Had she really just said that, and with so much conviction? She felt her stomach hardening, a bitter taste gathering at the back of her throat. Talk about the past muscling in, twisting thoughts. Words. As if she approved of lying. Dishonesty. Was that why Raff's jaw was looking so tight? Did he think she actually believed what she was saying?

She looked away. If he did, he was wrong. Lying wasn't her way but telling big fancy lies worked, didn't it? She'd learned *that* from Charlie Prentice. Lying a big shiny lie to get her back for what she did, lying to save face, to save his miserable pride, a lie that had trapped her, changed her, but that hadn't mattered to butter-wouldn't-melt-in-his-mouth Charlie…oh, no. She bit down hard on her lip. The injustice was what had rankled the most.

Hurt.

The.

Most.

There she'd been that night after the ball, tossing and turning, trying to rationalise, trying to be fair with the blame—he'd been more than a little drunk, her dress had been a little skimpy—not wanting to say anything to her parents until she'd sorted it out in her mind, until she was absolutely certain. And meanwhile he'd been busy putting it about that in the summer house she'd confessed she was in love with him, had begged him to let her be his girlfriend, messaging his friends that he'd laughed in her face because how could she have ever got it into her head that he'd want her to be his actual girlfriend?

Fenced her in nicely, hadn't he, so that next day at school everyone had been snickering behind their hands. Dulcibella Davenport-Brown *daring* to profess love for Charlie Prentice, *deluded* enough to imagine that he'd actually be interested. Him a senior; her a junior! On what planet, et cetera? Never mind that he'd been the one who'd asked *her* to the ball, the part they seemed to have conveniently forgotten because somehow the truth always got in the way of a good story, didn't it?

She felt a familiar hot ache starting in her throat and swallowed it down hard. Charlie's lie had been bad enough, but then the whole thing had grown arms and legs, turned personal. Not just a junior, but a *gawky* junior, who'd looked as if she'd raided the dress-up box for her outfit.

'Did you see that silly puffball dress and those shoes? Bright pink! So last year!'

'And what about that hair? Did you see the state of it at the end of the evening? I mean—hello—hasn't she ever heard of hairspray?'

How the rumour mill had ground on, the sly digging, the subtle bullying, but it was bullying all the same. And there'd been no comeback because if she'd tried to put them right, they wouldn't have listened, wouldn't have credited that the magnificent Charlie had been the one begging, begging her to let him 'do it' even as he was pinning her down, pushing sour wet kisses at her mouth, hot damp hands groping for her underwear. Standing up for herself would have meant reliving the whole thing, would have meant telling the teachers and her parents, making everything bigger, wider, deeper.

Worse.

She snatched a bitter breath. Maybe that was why she'd just pulled off the performance of a lifetime in the hall of columns. God, how her nerves had been jangling, but being scrutinised, all those eyes staring, weighing, and measuring, had triggered something. A fightback, no, more than that. Payback, for school, for Charlie, for all the things she hadn't been able to say to the gossips and the stirrers. A chance to tell some great big lies of her own, to protect Raff, who was looking pale and shocked.

Oh, and it had been fun, undeniably, acting a part, creating one for Raff too, wielding power over the tight-faced man who hadn't believed a word of it but couldn't bring himself to say so. None of them could. They knew what they'd seen. Unlike Charlie's friends, they'd been drawing the *right* conclusions, but what a glorious feeling, throwing a spanner in the works. Smoke, and mirrors. Roll up, roll up!

But the adrenaline was fading now, and guilt was prickling. Because what they'd been doing was wrong, not the act itself but the place, the time. They'd been out of control, behaving like kids and there was a feeling that it could come back to bite them, that any second now a hand was going to land—

She shuddered and looked back, scanning the path. No sign of the tour group, just a receding line of vacant benches, mellow light flooding in between the knobbly slanted pillars. Relief washed through, then lightness. She looked over. Maybe Raff was feeling lighter now too. The stiffness around his jaw seemed to have gone anyway. But just in case he believed that she thought lying was okay, she ought to say something, set him straight.

She slowed her pace. 'Raff, for the record, I don't actually approve of dishonesty. I was being ironic.'

'I know that.'

There was a hint of smile in his eyes, but there were also bothersome shadows. She bit back a sigh. Just when they'd been having such a good time too, flirting, and walking, and talking, him all lit up: about the conference theme, and about Gaudí, about the way Gaudí had worked with the slopes of the Parc Güell site instead of levelling it first, about the way he used mundane materials to great effect. Like here, in this very promenade. Slanted rubble walls following the angle of the hill, canted rubble pillars that somehow supported the walkway above, managing at the same time to conjure a sense of the ancient and exotic.

But they hadn't only talked about Gaudí. She'd prodded him about his family too—'prodded' being the operative word since he'd seemed strangely reluctant, but she had uncovered a half-Brazilian mother and a consequent fluency in Portuguese. That was the conversation that had sparked the conflagration. Maybe going back there would chase his shadows away.

She took a breath, slipping a tease into her voice. 'You know, you *could* actually be a chiropractor…'

His eyebrows lifted. 'On account of what, my extensive architectural experience…?'

Playful sarcasm. This was better.

She raised her own eyebrows back at him. *'Obviously…'*

His lips twitched and suddenly she couldn't hold in a smile. 'No, what I *meant* is that you look the part, and, it has to be said, *Jasper Júlio* suits you very well. You're totally credible.'

He let out a wry laugh. 'I didn't fool anyone, least of all the woman who's now got my made-up number.' And then suddenly he was stopping, catching her hands, pulling her in. '*You* on the other hand are completely *in*credible!' Warmth in his gaze, open affection, but then his expression clouded. 'I don't know how you did that, or why really, but I feel terrible. I shouldn't have put you in that position. It was stupid. Thoughtless!' His hands tightened around hers. 'I'm so sorry, Dulcie.'

Taking all the blame. She wasn't having that.

'It's not your fault.' She pulled her hands free, took hold of his shoulders. 'It was me too.'

'But I…' Troubled eyes. 'I shouldn't have—'

'You mean, *we*…'

He pressed his lips together tight and then a narrow smile emerged. 'Okay, if you insist—*we*—but I still feel bad.'

'Well, don't. Not on my account. I *wanted* you to kiss me, *wanted* to be lifted up. I want…'

She felt her focus skewing, arrowing to the smooth swell of his shoulders, to the heat pulsing into her palms, delicious heat, like at the side of his neck, that faint salt taste of his skin before those people— Her belly clenched. How to explain, how to put words to this messy swirl of longing?

She took a breath. 'Truth is, Raff, I want to kiss you all the time, in public, in private...' She felt her hands moving involuntarily, sliding to the back of his neck. 'I want to touch you...taste you. I want to *know* you...all of you...'

A light surfaced, travelling through his gaze, and then his lips were moving, mustering what, some inexplicable obstacle? She didn't want to listen, couldn't, not when more words were rising, demanding air.

'And I know we only just met, that we're only here for a few days, but the thing is—' she could feel her skin beating, her voice trying to crack '—I can't help the way I feel when I'm with you, can't help wanting what I want, and I don't know what it means, or where this can go, or even if you want it to go anywhere but, right now, I only care about *now*.'

His lips stilled, silent.

She swallowed hard. Was she really doing this again, offering herself to a man without asking for anything in return? It could go horribly wrong, but it didn't *feel* wrong because Raffiel wasn't Tommy. Raffiel was noble, respectful, a prince among men, and this time she wasn't trying to score a point, she was just...

His eyes were holding hers, his gaze softening, pulling her in. She felt her breath leaving, her senses tangling. She was just... And then something inside was shifting, opening out, and suddenly she knew.

I'm in love.

She felt her heart filling, tears trying.

Of course...

Love was the sublime problem, and the reason for everything...her bold behaviour, impulsive actions. She was head over heels. Done for. Had been from the very first moment.

Her heart fluttered. But what to say? What to do?

She slipped herself back into the fold of his steady gaze.

Still soft, still deep but shading towards the unfathomable. Was he still taking in what she'd said about wanting him, or was he reading the lines of her heart? Impossible to tell, and…impossible to tell him, because love at first sight was fairy-tale stuff, wasn't it, hardly credible? Too huge to say out loud. Oh, but if he'd only let her show him what was inside, then he'd know, feel it, and maybe she'd feel it coming back too.

Or not.

Oh, God! Maybe she was on a road to heartache, but how to turn back when love and desire were tingling, bright and alive, when the love part was making the desire burn harder, hotter. She wanted him more than ever, more than anything she'd ever wanted. Surely, he could see it. Surely now, after what had just happened in the hall of columns, after what she'd just told him, he'd take her back to the yacht.

Just. One. More. Little. Nudge.

'Raff…' She licked the dryness off her lips, heart drumming. 'Do you understand what I'm saying?'

For a long second his eyes held her and then he nodded. 'Yes. You're giving me a free pass. You're saying you're happy not to think about consequences.'

But *he* had to, more than ever now, because of that confusing light in her eyes. Hazy, reaching right in, making him tingle, making his heart flip and tumble. Had his heart done this with Brianne? It didn't ring a bell. This felt new. Exhilarating. Like danger. That was what he was feeling, danger—tugging—because her fingers were playing with the hair at the back of his neck and his body was responding, hardening, and she was seeing it in him for sure, waiting for him to give in, jump on that invitation and whisk her back to the yacht.

God, how he wanted to, with every frayed fibre of his

being, but he couldn't. *Mustn't!* Because no matter what came out of her mouth there was something about the light in her eyes, about her whole being, that went against the casual, something about her that commanded so much more... more respect, more care, more honesty...

He swallowed hard, willing the fire inside to die. Honesty. The biggest hurdle. The hardest. Things she had to know first, things he wanted to tell her, things he could have told her when she'd been asking about his family but hadn't, hadn't because it had felt too huge, too unwieldy.

His stomach coiled. King of Brostovenia. Twelve months away if he was lucky! He didn't want to waste precious time with Dulcie talking about it, assuming she'd even stick around long enough to listen. He wanted to enjoy her company, her laughter, that spark of mischief in her eyes. He wanted to talk about familiar things, about the things he loved, not about what was coming.

Maybe it was weak, petulant even, to be clinging to comfortable threads—Gaudí, architecture, the conference, all the passions that were burning inside—but he couldn't help it. The future was a wall he didn't have the will to breach, especially now that Dulcie was on this side of it. She was *now* and the second he told her about *next* he'd be letting next in, properly, finally. And undoubtedly it would be the wise thing, but if the wise thing scared her away then he didn't want to be wise. He wanted this, whatever *this* was, wanted to hold onto it, forget the rest...

But he couldn't forget himself, couldn't allow himself to take Dulcie to bed, do all the things he wanted to do to her until she knew the truth, because that wouldn't be right. When—*if*—they got to that stage, he didn't want to be a big fancy lie.

He swallowed hard, letting his focus drift to her mouth, her throat, that little hollow at its base where his lips wanted to go. No point trying to pretend he didn't want her, not after that spectacular public display, but he needed to give her a credible reason for not taking things further, for *rejecting* her as she was bound to see it, something rooted in truth so it would come out easily, something that wouldn't bring hurt to her eyes. Something, or someone...

Brianne!

The pain had been startling, real, cut the feet from under him. Why not use it, put it to work, for Dulcie's sake?

He reached up, removing her hand from the back of his neck but holding onto it so she'd know he wasn't withdrawing. 'Dulce—'

'Yes...?' Hope quickened in her eyes, then faded. 'What's wrong?'

'Nothing.' He squeezed her hand, trying to be reassuring. 'It's just that we need to talk.'

Her chin lifted. 'What about?'

'About why I'm not going to use that free pass.'

The words took a moment to register, and then her eyes were narrowing, and she was shaking her head. 'But you want me...' Her voice fell, close to a whisper. 'I know you do. Don't even think of denying it.'

'I'm not denying it.' He let go of her hand and held both of his up high, hoping to stir a smile out of her. 'Absolutely not trying, okay.' Her expression softened a little and he seized the moment, taking hold of her shoulders. 'I'm crazy for you, Dulcie Brown. Crazy enough to have embarrassed both of us very publicly.'

She frowned. 'So why, then?'

'Because—' *how to put it?* '—you deserve a whole person and I'm not whole right now.'

'Because of your loss?'

A familiar glimmer was igniting in her eyes. Empathy. It was her go-to, wasn't it, kindness, that compulsion she had to find some fellow feeling? It made twisting truths harder, but it was for her protection and on that basis he could feel all right about it.

'Yes, but it's not only that, it's…' He looked down, rowing back, searching for the living pulse of the old pain, a pain that felt strangely distant now. But then it was coming, rising again, that ring, burning a hole in his pocket, that rooftop table booked at Gianelli's—her favourite place— that drumming of the heart, that thrill of anticipation, that getting back to the apartment, to the packed bags lined up and Brianne's cool gaze.

'It's over, Raff. We don't work any more.'

He inhaled and looked up, reconnecting with Dulcie's gaze. 'It's also that I'm still getting over someone, someone I'd planned to be with for ever.'

She blinked, her mouth folding inwards. 'You were engaged?'

'No, but I was set to propose. I had the ring, the fancy date lined up, but when I got home, she—Brianne—was packed and waiting to say goodbye.'

'That same day?' Dulcie's eyes were narrowing. She was imagining the scene, the hurt, pouring herself into the frame in that way she did.

'Yes.' He felt a pulsebeat of unexpectedly ripe bitterness. 'You could call it impeccable timing.' He let go of her shoulders so he could rub the tightness that was suddenly clamping his temples. 'I didn't see it coming. Maybe that was the problem! I was on a different wavelength.'

'Or she was.'

There it was again, that little protective edge on her voice, like in front of those poor shocked people. It was bolstering somehow, made him feel less alone.

He pulled in a breath. 'Two months later the accident happened.'

'Oh, Raff…' She was stepping in, taking his hands in hers. 'You're going through so much.' A soft light filled her gaze. 'I could help you. I want to.'

By sleeping with him, her eyes were saying. He held in a smile. She was nothing if not persistent.

'I know you do but it wouldn't be fair…' She was opening her mouth to speak but he knew what was coming, didn't need to hear it. He freed his hands and put them to her face. 'You're going to tell me you don't care about consequences, but you would because caring is what you do. It's why you're reaching out to me now, but I don't want you to get hurt, Dulcie.' He felt a tingle, a truth flying free. 'I like you far too much to risk that.'

Her eyes held him for a long moment and then she was stepping back, huffing a little stoical sigh. 'Well, that's a very sweet rejection, I must say, but, you know, it isn't a big deal. I wasn't pledging my troth or anything.' The tip of her tongue flicked over her bottom lip. 'So…' Her chin lifted. 'What should we do now?'

He felt his heart seizing. The so-called sweet rejection clearly wasn't tasting sweet. There was something busy retreating in her gaze, and the breezy tone belied the look on her face. She was paddling hard but sinking all the same, trying not to show it. *Damn!* Why was doing the right thing so difficult? Trying not to hurt her was hurting her. Trying to respect her meant rejecting her.

He felt his jaw tightening. This was all his fault. He should never have gone to sit beside her at La Sagrada Família. And yet…if he hadn't, there'd have been a Dulcie-shaped hole in his life and for some reason the thought of that was unbearable.

He broke away from her gaze, looking along the promenade. Random stone bent to Gaudí's vision, made to arch, and slant. Just rubble, really, but transformed into something wondrous. That was what he had to do. Turn this rubble he'd made into something with shape, line, intent. He had to give her something, restore their momentum somehow, their lightness, but what? What did he have that wasn't heavy? *Bleak*. He directed his gaze through one of the archways. Maybe getting back out into the sunshine would help.

'I think we should walk.'

She blinked. 'Okay.'

He held out his hand. She took it, which was something at least.

He struck out, felt her falling in. This was better. Walking along, sunshine dappling through the trees, the soft warmth of her hand, the light sound of her footsteps. This was lovely, close to perfect— He bit back a sigh. Who was he trying to kid? Her hand might have been in his, but her heart wasn't in it and his was hurting. There was a silence straining, a sense of everything upending. Thank God for the fork in the path up ahead. It meant consulting. Talking.

He slowed his pace. 'Which way do you want to go?'

'I don't mind.'

Which sounded a lot like *I don't care*. This wasn't Dulcie. She'd been all lit up about the park earlier. He *had* to get her back there somehow, to that happy place, because seeing her like this was torture.

He turned to the uphill fork. 'Okay, then. I think we'll go this way…'

'It's quite steep.' She was frowning now, managing to look appealing all the same.

He felt the grain of a smile. 'Well, yes, but there's a lovely view from the top, and you like a nice a view.'

Her eyebrows drew in, puzzling.

'It's what you said on the boat…that you like a nice view.'

'Ah.' Her gaze softened. 'You remember.'

'Of course I do.' How could he forget? The slap of the waves on the hull, the warm smell of her perfume, the way she'd been leaning against the rail, smiling. He squeezed her hand. 'Barcelona at night from deck number three…' Her eyes were coming to life again, filling with a smile, filling him with hope. He motioned to the path. 'If we go up here, you'll see the whole city and the sea. I think you'll love it…'

Hair blowing against her neck. Soft black blazer, white tee, loose black jeans turned up, last night's black pumps. She seemed to like black and white, but what else did she like…? And then her fingers moved, squeezing back and suddenly his mind was clearing. *Of course…* He needed to reorientate, put her centre, not in this fretful way, in this not wanting to hurt her way, in this scared to tell the truth about himself way, but in a positive way.

'Come on.' He tugged her hand. She resisted for a blink and then she was coming, switching on her mischievous smile. His heart flew skywards and then suddenly everything seemed to be sharpening, brightening. Tangling green cascading over rough-hewn walls. Green, gold, blue whorls of flowers, clusters of white. He couldn't name them, but he was looking at them, wasn't he, properly looking, properly seeing?

He inhaled, feeling the air reaching into every part of his lungs. How the last few months had changed him, curled him inwards, set him revolving inside a loop of his own misery. But that wasn't *him*! He was no Gustav, not even close, but wasn't he known for being open, outward-looking, interested in technologies and the way things worked? He had qualities: an eye for detail, a curiosity about people and places. Brianne had used to tell him he was sensitive, and kind-hearted. Gustav had said it too, once, although he'd gone with, *'You're a soft sucker, Raff!'*

He felt a smile struggling against the sadness. *Smiling!* That was another thing he'd been quite good at before. Because he *did* have a sense of humour. For sure, it had been lying low for a while, but hadn't it just sprung itself upon him in the hall of columns, that notion to tease Dulcie by referencing heart palpitations and so on in front of those people? That proved it! He was still inside here somewhere, all the best bits of himself that had been buried. All he had to do was dig them up.

He threw Dulcie a glance. Maybe she was feeling thwarted right now, but he could, *would*, make it up to her. He felt a smile loosening. He was going to draw her out, make her laugh, give her a lovely afternoon without taking her clothes off.

CHAPTER EIGHT

'JUST ALONG HERE…' Raff was smiling, bouncing along with happy strides, his hand warm and tight around hers. She felt her lips curving up for the hundredth time. He was so different. Full of questions. About her studio, about life in Devon, about the landscape there. Maybe sharing his pain over Brianne had loosened him somehow. So much heartache, on top of the grief. No wonder he didn't feel whole, able to…

She bit her lip. If he'd only give her a chance, she could make him whole again, make him forget the rest, she just knew it. Her heart clenched. Or did she, actually? Was she galloping so hard along that road to heartache that she wasn't reading the signs? Warm go lights flashing then stopping, always stopping, because of Brianne, the one he'd been going to *marry*, the one he'd wanted to be his *for ever*, the one he couldn't get past, the one who was *in the way*…

She inhaled hard, steadying herself. *In the way*, yes, but still, it was *her* hand he was holding right now, not Brianne's, and it counted for a lot that he was being honest, decent. Ironic, really. The very qualities she most admired in him were the qualities that had almost driven a wedge between them. For a desperate moment it had felt as if it was all slipping away but then he'd mentioned the view, and last night, and his eyes had been full of deep warm light, and hope had sprung up again, just like that.

Resolve too. Not to give up. Not to mess up by pushing too hard. He liked her a lot. She could feel it, and he'd said it, hadn't he? So she just needed to be patient, to enjoy this for what it was because what else was there to do when love was already living inside? If holding hands through the park was all he could offer right now, then that was fine. Romantic actually. And it *was* rather lovely being trapped inside the bright beam of his endless curiosity, seeing herself reflected in the glow of his eyes, like at this very moment.

'Here you are…' He was backstepping, pulling her from the shaded part of the path to a bright, open patch by the railing. He smiled. 'First glimpse of a very nice view.'

She forced her eyes from his and looked, felt her heart swelling. The city was below them, a hazy sweep of mostly low, tightly packed buildings. Pale gold, apricot, cream, punctuated with random clusters of deep terracotta roofs and the occasional white high-rise. Beyond the buildings under the bright blue sky stretched a bright blue ribbon of sea.

'Look…' He was motioning left, his other hand settling on the small of her back. A light touch. Warm. Like his deep velvet accent. 'Do you see it… La Sagrada Família?'

She felt a tingle, a gathering urge to slide her arms around him and pull him in for a kiss, but she pushed it down hard. No more moves, invitations. *Rejections!* Whatever happened between them now was up to him. It was for him to lead. Openly. Explicitly.

She refocused, following the line of his pointing finger and suddenly there was a different kind of tingle starting. There it was, Gaudí's basilica, its magnificent bell towers rising above the rest, a sacred place, even more sacred now because of Raff, because it was where they'd met the second time.

'Wonderful.' She looked up at him. 'It's a very nice view indeed.'

'Worth the trek?'

'Definitely.'

And then his hand fell away and he was moving to the rail, leaning his forearms on it. He seemed to consider for a moment, and then he turned, trapping her in a warm, interested gaze. 'So, what about *your* family then…? What does your father do?'

Her throat closed. Talking about ceramics and improbably high Devonian hedges was easy but talking about family wasn't. Only natural that he was asking—after all, she'd asked him about his family, hadn't she? But the thing was, aside from his uncle, his family seemed like regular people and hers were anything but.

As for herself, Raff thought she was Dulcie Brown, a reclusively inclined ceramicist with artistic identity issues. How was she supposed to tell him that her father was an earl, and that home was Fendlesham Hall, a sixteenth-century Warwickshire mansion set in eight hundred acres of prime parkland? She might have spent the past ten years trying to distance herself from it, but it didn't mean that it wasn't real, or that she wasn't part of it. Living in Devon—*hiding*—going by Dulcie Brown didn't change who she was or what was coming, inheriting Fendlesham and everything that went with it.

She felt a throb threatening her temples. If only she knew how to feel about it, but she didn't. Charlie Prentice had muddied those waters, spoiled the taste of everything she'd ever loved so she'd pushed it away, but now Raff was asking and there was this panic fluttering inside, not only because she didn't want to talk about it, but because the truth was bound to throw him for a loop.

Maybe right now he was upbeat, but he wasn't in a good place generally. If he found out that she was Lady Dulcibella Davenport-Brown of Fendlesham, that she came with eight hundred acres of baggage, then he was bound to jump on the brakes again and then she'd never get herself where she wanted to be, which was up close and personal, filling him to the brim with her love so that he'd forget all about cruel Brianne.

So, no… Maybe it was wrong, *selfish*, but she couldn't tell him, not yet, which left what, lying…? She drew an uncomfortable breath. Not outright. She could never do that, but she *could* live with bending the truth a little for the sake of the greater good…

'My father is the estate manager at Fendlesham Hall.'

Raff's eyebrows ticked up.

'It's a big country house.' She slipped some droll into her voice. 'Very stately. Very English.'

'As English as pubs?'

She felt a smile unfurling. Was it really only yesterday that she'd been giving him that quick crib on England over coffee and *churros*? It seemed longer ago somehow.

'Oh, yes, probably more, actually. It's steeped in history. There's a whole gallery of paintings.' She stiffened her face to make him laugh. 'Grim-faced people with big hair and doilies around their necks.'

His eyes crinkled. 'Sounds amazing.'

'It is…' She felt a little tug inside then warmth flooding in, mingling with nostalgia. 'It's *really* something. Parkland with vast spreading oak trees and tall beeches, and around the house there's a gorgeous formal garden. I mean, *this* is wonderful but at Fendlesham there are deep herbaceous borders full of colour, and a walled kitchen garden, and there's an ancient maze—yew—very dense, a bit scary…but irresistible all the same. I used to love riding my bike in there.'

'You got to play in the gardens?'

Her heart seized. Stupid careless tongue, running on like that. She hadn't meant to put herself in the frame and now it was too late to row back. She swallowed carefully. Too much of a lie to say that she'd got to play in the gardens *sometimes*.

Better pressing close to the truth, then at least she wouldn't have to be watching what she said every second.

'I did, all the time, because we lived in.'

'Ah...' He smiled. 'I see.'

'My parents still do. Estate manager's a twenty-four-seven job so there's no choice really. We do have a lovely apartment...' More of a wing really but she couldn't tell him that. It would sound excessive for an estate manager. 'To give you the full picture, Fendlesham Hall is an absolutely enormous house, a huge responsibility, a...'

'A drain,' her father was fond of saying, but always with a twinkle in his eye.

'It's open to the public six months of the year so it can be a bit of a circus. There are staff to manage, tour schedules to keep, and of course there's a gift shop and a café. My mother handles the events side.'

'Events?'

'Corporate hospitality days mostly, but we also host a classic car show once a year, and a charity garden party, oh, and we're on the books of location scouts worldwide because location fees can really boost revenue. I used to love it when the film crews came, and the movie stars...' She felt a tingle, pleasure unfurling. When was the last the time she'd enjoyed talking about home? Maybe it was the warm, interested look on Raff's face, that half-smile hovering at the corners of his mouth that was drawing it out of her, drawing all the good to the front. Like that most special memory of all...

'I remember when I was seven, Amy Madison came. She was shooting a period drama, and I was completely star struck. She was so beautiful, so elegant in her costumes that I couldn't keep away, even though my parents told me to. I'd sneak down to where the trailers were and hide, to catch a glimpse, but she always seemed to know

I was there because suddenly she'd turn and beam me a great big smile. She beckoned me over one time, invited me to have tea with her in her trailer. I was beside myself, tingling all over, but she was so completely normal, you know. She just sat there in her robe, knitting, of all things, making me laugh. She was completely gorgeous.'

'I'll bet she thought you were gorgeous too.'

Her heart skipped. He really needed to stop looking at her like this if he wasn't ready to make good on the promise that was smouldering in his eyes.

She broke away, focusing on the view, but then suddenly another memory was surfacing, making a giggle come. 'I doubt it. If I remember rightly, at the time I'd just lost my two front teeth. I was all gaps. That's probably why she was always chuckling at me.'

'She sounds nice.' He was straightening, turning to lean his back against the rail. 'And your childhood sounds amazing. That's what's coming through anyway—happiness. Love for Fendlesham…'

Her heart clenched. She did love it, always had, always would. And she could have gone back, couldn't she, set up her studio in one of the outbuildings…? That was what her parents had wanted, what they'd offered her, but after Tommy it had felt too hard. She was the fallen one. Out of step, out of grace. Undeserving. And their kindness had only made her shame burn hotter, her guilt weigh heavier.

Easier to stay away. She needed breathing space, time to reflect, she'd told herself, time to *find* herself, *be* her own person. But who was she, really? Because the person she was in Devon was only one half. The other half belonged to Fendlesham. Putting the two sides back together was the thing she was struggling with.

Putting off.

'You haven't mentioned siblings…'

His voice pulled her back.

'That's because I don't have any.'

'Oh…' He wasn't asking but his eyebrows were lifting all the same, questioning.

'I was a difficult birth, apparently.' And she was still being difficult, wasn't she, keeping her distance, keeping to herself? She breathed through a sudden sharp ache and forced a smile out. 'My mother was advised against getting pregnant again, so that was that.'

'That's…' He seemed at a loss. 'I don't know, a bit sad…?' Warmth in his gaze, empathy. 'I mean, Fendlesham sounds like a very big place for one little girl.'

'That's true but, you know, it was a privilege too…' Such a privilege but in her mind, she'd turned it into something monstrous, hadn't she? Something to despise, because of Charlie. She pushed the thought away. 'When you think that so many kids grow up with nothing, no space inside, no space outside. I had lots of both, and I had school. Friends. And Georgie and Tilly would often come at weekends. We actually spent a lot of time together when we were kids.'

His head tilted. 'So, in spite of all your protests, you're actually quite close to Georgie…?'

'I suppose…' Her heart was thumping suddenly. How were they even talking about this? It was nice seeing interest glowing in Raff's eyes, but he seemed to be prodding all the sore spots and she didn't like the way it was hurting. And yet, maybe the hurt was a good thing. Maybe it was flagging up what mattered, what had used to, what could again if she gave it a chance, gave *herself* a chance.

She licked the dryness off her lips and then unexpectedly she felt a smile coming, tears budding. 'Georgie was always boss; always chose the game we played, but, whatever game it was, it usually involved dressing up. She loved dressing up. Still does! I haven't seen her wedding dress yet, but I know it'll be spectacular!'

'And what about you?' Raff was smiling. 'Did you like dressing up?'

He was taking in her outfit. Safe neutrals. Not pink. Puffy. *Skimpy.*

She drew in a careful breath. 'I did, yes…' Before Charlie, before all the jibing— She pressed the memory flat, forcing her thoughts past the Charlie days to the Georgie and Tilly days, and then there it was, happiness trickling back in, taking over. 'Between us, we had quite the extensive wardrobe. Georgie's best dresses came out during her ballroom-dancing phase.'

'Ballroom?'

He seemed amused—or maybe it was *bemused.*

'Yes. It's because there's a ballroom-dancing programme on the television here that's been going for years. Very popular. Professional dancers partnering celebrities. Every week one couple is eliminated…'

'Okay…'

'So anyway, when Georgie was nine, she was totally addicted, probably because of the dresses, to be honest. She learned the different waltzes and the quickstep and she taught me and Tilly, but Tilly was too short to dance with her, so that left me. We'd rehearse and rehearse, then we'd put on a show for the parents. Tilly was the presenter, and Georgie and I were the dancing couple. She was always the girl.'

Raff's eyebrows shot up. 'So you were always the boy?'

'Yes…' She felt a giggle vibrating. 'I was the ideal candidate because I had short hair back then and a suave manly appeal once my teeth grew back. Georgie would get out the face paints, give me a beard and a moustache.' She let her eyes slide over the contours of his face and felt a fresh giggle rising. 'I actually looked a bit like you.'

'Suave and manly…' He was laughing. 'I'll take that.'

And then suddenly he was folding his arms, and a sweet light was coming into his eyes. 'Did you like the dancing?'

'Yes, I did…' Moving with the music, rising, and falling and whirling, Georgie's face all serious, counting out the beats between tight lips. 'It was great fun, and, you know, we got to be pretty good at it. The only thing is that I'd have liked to be the one wearing the dress sometimes…'

He felt a tingle. It was in his power to give her this, the chance to waltz in a dress, to waltz as the girl. But it would mean attending the charity ball. His chest went tight. And that would mean risking the possibility of someone addressing him as 'Your Highness' in front of her.

Then again, who would actually do that? At dinner they'd be sitting with his inner circle, colleagues and associates who'd known him for years and who wouldn't dream of alluding to his changed situation, or of calling him anything but Raff. As for the other guests, out of the very few who'd ever made his actual acquaintance, none of them were likely to come over because he was in mourning, wasn't he, rendered unapproachable by the grim cloak of Dralk?

If only its folds could save him from having to make that dreaded handover speech Arlo wanted. Handing over to Arlo in private had been bad enough. Infinitely worse doing it in front of two hundred people, pretending he was all right about relinquishing his conference role, but he'd endure it for Dulcie's sake… *Dulcie!* He'd told her he was a backstage minion, hadn't he? He rubbed his jaw. Still, that was a minor hiccup in comparison to the rest. He could always pass it off as acute modesty…

'You're looking very thoughtful.' She was pushing her lips out, giving him the side-eye.

His heart gave. God she was lovely and...an enigma. There was something going on with her that he wanted to get into, pull apart. The way she'd been talking about Fendlesham as if it belonged to her, those comings and goings in her eyes. Love shining out. Clouds coming in. And her voice, up one moment, wistful the next, but almost always threaded through with subtle bravado. It was something he was learning how to do too, controlling his voice, his face. It was what he'd have to do if they attended the ball, but he wasn't going to dwell on that. Far better dwelling on Dulcie, imagining her in a dress, waltzing in his arms. He felt a smile coming. It had to be worth the anxiety just to experience that. But, more importantly, this was something real, something he *could* give her and, God help him, he wanted to give it with every beat of his heart.

He unfolded his arms and pushed his hands into his pockets, going for a tease. 'That's because I'm thinking...'

She waggled her eyebrows at him. 'Funny!' And then she was pinning him with a warm gaze. 'About what?'

'About a black-tie gig I've got to attend tomorrow night...' Her eyes narrowed a little, interested. 'It's a charity ball the conference inaugurated a while back to raise money for housing projects for the homeless.'

'Sounds lovely.' Could she see where he was going with this? If so, it wasn't showing on her face. She smiled. 'And, respect! It's a really good cause.'

'It is, but here's the thing. There's dancing. Waltzing, in fact...' Her eyes lit, cottoning on now. He felt a spark jumping, a smile twitching. 'And since you're an expert, I was wondering if you'd consider coming with me if I promise to let you wear the dress.'

CHAPTER NINE

'YOU'VE MET SOMEONE...' Georgie's eyebrows were climbing to maximum elevation.

Dulcie felt her insides shrinking. Telling Georgie about Raffiel hadn't exactly been at the top of her to do list, but that was before he'd surprised her with his sweet invitation to the ball. Now there was no getting round it. The ball meant abandoning Georgie and the girls for a whole evening and for that she was going to need special dispensation. Also, she was going to need some help on the dress front.

She arched her eyebrows, trying to reclaim at least a little bit of the offensive. 'Could you please try not to look quite so incredulous? I do meet people sometimes.'

'I'm sure. It's just...*here*...this week?' And then Georgie's gaze sharpened. 'Is this someone the reason you left Opium early last night?'

Her insides shrank more. Georgie was too quick by half.

'Sort of.' She lowered herself onto the bed edge, trying to trim the guilt out of her voice. 'But I probably wouldn't have stayed long anyway.'

'Hmm.' And then Georgie was plonking down beside her, crossing her legs like she'd used to when they were kids. 'So spill the goss, Dulcibella-lella. Where did you meet him?'

Her heart gave. When was the last time Georgie had called her that? And when was the last time they'd talked properly, just the two of them, leaning into their old closeness? *Georgie...* She felt a tug, warmth swelling, and then suddenly she couldn't not shuffle over, tucking her own legs up too.

'I met him here in the hotel.'

'Uh-huh...?'

She felt a tingle. 'Well, in the lift actually. And then it broke down, so we were kind of stuck—'

'Romantic!' And then Georgie's eyes narrowed a little. 'So he's a guest?'

'No. He was just visiting a business associate on this floor.'

Georgie's expression was recalibrating. So easy to read her thoughts. A man with a business associate staying in a terrace suite at the Regal was potentially the right sort. *Suitable!* But Georgie wasn't done yet.

'So does he have a name?'

'Raffiel.'

'Raffiel what...?'

Her stomach clenched. If she told Georgie that then everything would stop for a forensic examination of Raff's social media, that was if he even *did* social media! And if he did, then what if there were pictures of Brianne, selfies of him and Brianne—arm's-length smiles, faces pressed close—the girl he'd wanted to marry, the girl who'd cast him off but was still, inexplicably, in the way!

She swallowed hard. No! She couldn't let Georgie loose, raking over Raff, asking her questions she couldn't answer. Right now her heart was on the rise because of the ball, because of the way he'd kissed her when she'd said yes, as if it meant the world, as if she *were* his world. She wanted to hold that thought, keep it warm and alive. Untrammelled.

She licked her lips. 'I'm sorry, George, but I'd rather not say.'

'Why? Is he a spy or something?'

'No. He's an architect.'

Georgie's eyes clouded. It wasn't Raff's profession, it was because of *her*, because she was being secretive.

She touched Georgie's knee. 'I'm not trying to be mean. It's just that it's all so new, you know. Unexpected! I like him—a lot—and I don't want the whole thing being dissected before it's even—'

'Fine.' Georgie's lips pursed and then she flashed her palms, conceding. 'You're right, I totally would have typed his name in but it's only because I care about you.' She sighed. 'You absolutely can't get involved with another Tommy Sinclair, Dulce.'

Her chest went tight. Tommy! Still here, hanging over her even after all this time. Her fault. Because she'd never talked about him afterwards. But she could shake him off now, couldn't she, say the words to Georgie out loud?

'You don't have to worry about that. Tommy was a phase I had to go through, that's all.' Georgie's eyebrows slid up, prompting. 'He was a huge mistake, okay! See, I'm admitting it...'

'But why did you even...?' For once, Georgie's words ran out, but her eyes were reaching in, pleading.

She felt their old closeness tugging, words wanting to come, but explaining Tommy would mean tipping out the contents of the Charlie Prentice box and she couldn't do that, not for Georgie. Georgie and Tilly's school had been three counties away. They didn't know what happened at the ball, didn't know about the bullying. If she had known, Georgie would never have become friends with some of those people at uni, would never have invited them to her wedding. But Georgie had, and now *she* was going to be

a bridesmaid, on parade, defenceless in front of them all
over again…

Her breath slowed. Or was she looking at it the wrong
way? Maybe this wedding was an opportunity to launch an
offensive, a chance to look those people square in the eye
and rise above them, as she had with those people in the
hall of columns! She wouldn't have to say a word because
they'd know, *they'd know* and maybe seeing it registering,
watching them squirm, would feel like payback and she'd
come away stronger. *Maybe…*

But, however she handled it, it was *her* problem. Telling Georgie would only cause an upset and, God help her,
she'd caused enough upset in this family already.

She drew Georgie back into focus. 'I don't know why,
George, but I've learned my lesson and I promise you:
Raffiel is about as far away from Tommy as you could
possibly go. He's the perfect gentleman, polite, respectful,
noble, kind—'

'Good-looking?' Georgie was smiling again, mollified.

'Supremely!' She felt a tingle, a smile escaping. 'He's
asked me to a charity ball at The Imperial tomorrow night.'

Instantly Georgie's face fell. 'But we're doing the sunset cocktail cruise tomorrow, remember, then we're going
to El Toro for tapas…'

Shame ripped through her. How could she have forgotten? The cruise had been an extra gift to Georgie from her
beloved godfather, the highlight of the week. She couldn't
not go, not after Georgie had been so indulgent with her,
letting her off hook after hook. She felt a burn starting behind her lids, a hot ache filling her throat. When had she
got so selfish, so unforgivably self-absorbed? She'd just
gone right ahead, accepting Raff's invitation without even
thinking about—

'Having said that, what's a cocktail cruise to a ball at The Imperial with a supremely handsome architect...?'

Her heart stopped. Was Georgie giving her this? Was that the little spark she was seeing in Georgie's eyes, the little uptick that was affecting the corners of her mouth? And then the uptick was spreading into a wide smile, and Georgie was showering her with imaginary fairy dust. 'You *shall* go to the ball, Dulcibella-lella!'

She felt a bubble of affection exploding, tears and words spilling out. 'Oh, Georgie, thank you, thank you, thank you.' She grabbed Georgie's hands, squeezing so she'd know how much it meant. 'It's going to be proper dancing, George. Waltzing!'

'What?' Georgie's face stiffened, incredulous. 'You've found a man who can waltz?'

'Yes, I have, and apparently he's something of an expert.'

'Well, in that case...' And then Georgie was drifting, disappearing into a cloud of her own thoughts, but it was easy to read them.

She held her breath, tingling. It was coming, any second now—

'You're going to need a dress, Dulce.' Georgie's eyes came to hers, warm and sparkling. 'Something fabulous!'

CHAPTER TEN

'YOU'RE BRINGING SOMEONE...?' The surprise on Arlo's face was quickly eclipsed by a knowing chuckle. 'And is this *someone* the reason for the spring I'm suddenly seeing in your step?'

He couldn't hold in his smile. 'Probably.'

Pointless denying it. His feet did feel lighter today, his heart too, because of Dulcie, because she was coming tonight, had lit up like the Fourth of July when he'd asked her...

'You'd let me wear the dress?' Laughing. 'Are you being polite or are you just very well brought up?'

That line again that was theirs, that he could only answer one way.

'Both, I hope.'

'Well, I'm saying yes. I'd love to go. Thank you.' Small frowning hesitation. 'I'm assuming you can dance...?'

'Of course.'

'Seriously?'

'Can I dance seriously, or seriously, can I dance?'

Fake stern look. 'The second one... Because, you know, not many people can.'

He'd felt a sudden, unexpected stab of national pride.

'Unless they're Brostovenian! Waltzing is a passion in my country. It's in our blood, ingrained in our culture.

Everyone can dance the waltz, from folk to Viennese. We love it!'

Little glinting side-eye. 'And what I'm starting to love is the sound of Brostovenia...'

He'd had to kiss her then because for some reason her warmth for his country had filled him to the brim. And it was still filling him, recharging his spirit somehow. Maybe that was what Arlo was seeing.

'So...?' Arlo's pace was slowing, his brown gaze warm and curious. 'Who is she?'

What to say? What he didn't know about Dulcie far outweighed what he did, and his curiosity about her outweighed the two put together. So much to unravel still. About that Charlie kid, for one thing, the part she'd sealed off. And there was Fendlesham too, stirring questions, and what about all her little contradictions, the deep and obvious affection she had for Georgie that didn't tally with her declaration in the lift that they had nothing in common, and those modest, monochrome clothes she wore that didn't mesh with her wistfulness about never being the one to wear the dress...

It was that irresistible wistfulness that had landed him with a speech to write and this little inquisition. Not that he minded the latter. For months all his conversations with Arlo had been painted over with gloom. It was nice having something new to talk about, even if he was short on actual detail.

'Her name is Dulcie Brown. She's a ceramicist. Very talented.'

'I'm not recognising the name.' Arlo was shaking his head. 'Is she exhibiting...?'

'No. She's here with her cousin, some extended bachelorette thing.' He felt a smile coming. 'I bumped into her at the Regal, right after our meeting, actually.'

'Wow! So now you're dating…?'

His heart pulsed. *Were* they…? They'd been on dates, sort of, but putting a label on it—

'I mean—' Arlo was leaning in, a teasing glow burning in his eyes '—are we talking about a future queen here?'

His heart stopped dead. Now *that* was a question! And yet, hadn't something like it crossed his own mind in the lift barely five minutes after he and Dulcie had met? And yesterday, when he'd asked her about her family, could he hand on heart say that his motivation had had nothing to do with trying to assess—

He swallowed hard. He couldn't think about this now, not when Arlo was busy messing with him, trying reel him in. Teasing was what they did, back and forth. Fine when it was just the two of them, but he couldn't have Arlo saying stuff like this in front of Dulcie.

He strapped on the expected smile. 'Very funny, but do me a favour, would you? When you meet Dulcie tonight, please don't mention the royalty thing.'

'She doesn't know?' Arlo's eyes narrowed into a silent, What the hell, Raff?

He felt a pang, guilt winding tight. The secrecy was gnawing at him too, increasingly, so Arlo wasn't wrong, but Arlo wasn't in his shoes either. He wasn't the one trying to hang onto bliss by his fingernails.

He offered up a shrug. 'It's a lot to lay on someone you just met.'

'I suppose…' Arlo frowned a little, and then a mischievous spark was flaring. 'And I suppose if you're just having a last little fling before—'

'No!' Anger exploded in his chest. Dulcie wasn't any kind of a fling, a girl to play with and throw away. How could his friend even go there, think that? He locked eyes with Arlo, felt his fingers curling into his palms. 'It's not like that, do you hear me? *Nothing* like that!'

Arlo's hands shot up, pushing back. 'Hey, I'm sorry. Calm down, okay. I didn't mean anything by it…'

His heart seized. Of course he didn't. Arlo was only joining obvious dots. He was here for a few days, going back to a life that wouldn't be remotely free. He'd met a girl who was also passing through, had been spending time with her but wasn't filling her in on his situation. It had all the hallmarks of a last desperate fling, didn't it?

He felt his anger draining, shame burning.

'No. *I'm* sorry. Truly.' He pressed his fingers hard into his forehead then met Arlo's gaze. 'I don't know what got into me.'

Arlo looked at him for a long scrutinising moment and then suddenly he smiled. 'Oh, my dear Raffiel, I think I do…' He lifted his chin. 'You're in love.'

'What about this fabulous pink one?' Saffy was holding the satin bodice against herself, swishing the organza skirt.

Dulcie smiled, swallowing the emphatic *No!* that was trying to explode from her mouth. Letting her revulsion hang out, all loose and flapping, wouldn't do at all. It was just a dress, and the revulsion was just a kneejerk, because of Hemphill, and Charlie, because of the past she had to put behind her somehow, but even so, that dress… She met Saffy's hopeful gaze. 'It's adorable, but sadly pink isn't my colour.'

'Okay.' Saffy smiled a little wistfully then turned, heading back for the rails.

She felt a tug, guilt pooling. Saffy didn't need to be combing the rails, none of the girls did, because the two assistants were already hanging the prime contenders in the changing room under Georgie's watchful eye, but still, here they all were, picking things out, making suggestions: 'Dulce, this is *so* in right now...' or, 'Now, Dulce, I know it's cut away everywhere, but you've *totally* got the figure.'

How was she suddenly *Dulce* to these girls, attracting smiles and compliments? How was she sitting here like a queen bee, sipping champagne on a plush chaise longue in an appointment-only boutique on the Passeig de Gràcia, while they were all running around, helping her, *being kind*?

She felt her neck prickling. She hadn't been kind to them in her head, had she? She'd set her face against them from the start, wallowed in her own superior otherness instead of trying to get to know them. Even last night, when Georgie had announced a girls' day out, dress-shopping for Dulcie, she'd felt her toes curling while they'd all been clapping and laughing, being jolly.

She took a little sip from her glass. And they were still being jolly, weren't they, chattering and laughing? Could *she* be like that, fit in with them, being jolly? She sipped again, feeling the buzz starting. Surely, she could, after all, she had a lot to feel jolly about: Raff for one thing, his unexpected invitation, and proper dancing...

A tingle spiralled up her spine. Tonight she'd be waltzing in his arms at The Imperial, and she was going to be wearing a dress, a beautiful, fabulous *dress*! Not that she didn't like her signature style. Monochrome felt right most of the time, but it didn't address that little flamboyant corner of her soul, did it, the side that compelled her to daub colour on her wonky vessels?

She felt a frown coming. When was the last time she'd daubed colour on herself, or even worn a dress? It must have been Tilly's graduation, that black silk sheath with the high neck. Safe. Because safe was her go-to, had been ever since—

She put her glass to her lips again, letting the bubbles loose on her tongue. But safety wasn't an issue where Raff was concerned. He was safe as houses, wasn't he, the king of self-control? She felt something hard sinking, lodging inside. Because of Brianne. The invisible enemy. The one he'd wanted to marry, to be with for ever and ever and ever! She swallowed hard. Had Brianne been glamorous? Could Brianne dance?

She went for another mouthful of champagne. Maybe Brianne was a beauty, and maybe she could dance, but she was gone. Tonight it was *her* chance to show Raff a different future, to slice through those threads that were holding him. She drained her glass, not caring about daintiness. She had Georgie on her side, and, knowing Georgie, she'd have lined up a carnival of colour and flounce, some glitz and sparkle, wanting to shake poor Dulcie up, wanting poor Dulcie not to be boring. Well, that was perfect because she didn't want to be boring either. Not tonight! Tonight she wanted to dazzle, to shine, *no*, outshine everybody and everything. Tonight she wanted to knock Raffiel Munoz clean off his perch, steal his heart.

In love.

Could it be?

He watched Arlo disappearing through the doors of the Word Trade Centre then he turned one-eighty, striking out for Barri Gòtic. He needed some alone time, time to process the thoughts that were swarming in, like the thought that when Arlo had said what he said there'd been no spontaneous denial rearing up. Rather, there'd been a beat of recognition, a slow steady stream of warmth, which could mean, *might* mean—

A bright ping split the air just north of his pocket.

He fumbled his phone out, swiped.

Having fun with the girls. I know, right? Me! Having fun with them! Missing you, of course. Slightly! Can't wait for tonight. D x

He felt a smile straining at his cheeks. *Dulcie!* Of course she was having fun. How could she not when she had so much fun inside? She was, quite simply, funny. That stunt she'd pulled in the hall of columns, the way she'd jumped into the lift giggling, and what about that chuckle in her voice when she'd declared her nine-year-old self *suave and manly*? Not a chance! At any age. Dulcie exuded femininity, beauty, inside and out. She was compelling, kind, smart, mischievous, spirited. A good person, a sweet soul. That was why... He felt his breath slowing, his body tingling. That was why...

I love her.

He felt his lungs emptying, his heart filling. Arlo was right. He was smitten! Delirious. Hopelessly, irrefutably in love with Dulcie Brown.

He shoved his phone back, forcing his feet to move. Replying now was impossible. Shaky hands, shaky heart. Epiphany happening. *In love!* It certainly explained the symptoms. *Symptoms?* Was that the right word? No other word was coming to mind, but then his mind was busy spinning, or was it his head? Both! Which meant using the crossing would be smart.

He waited for the light, then sailed over Passeig de Colom, striding up a narrow lane barely wider than his outstretched arms. Why was he stretching out his arms, not caring? Was that a symptom? *Probably.* Craziness fitted, and all the rest. The heart palpitations that came whenever she sprang to mind, which was all the time by the way, the breathlessness that took hold whenever she was near, and the hole that clanged, echoing, when she wasn't. And then of course there was the headrush that happened every time her eyes lit, the bolt to the heart that happened every time she smiled, and there was the constant craving, the longing that wouldn't leave...

He floated on, past small dim tapas bars with their chalk

boards propped, past outdoor tables pressed tight against grey-gold walls, on and on through the spiderweb streets until suddenly there was brightness arriving, warmth and spangling sunshine. He blinked. Pla de la Seu. And over the square on the other side, the mesmerising Catedral de Barcelona.

He went to the wide plaza steps and sat down, trying, and failing, to steady himself.

I love Dulcie.

Such a feeling! New. Uncharted. Bright, alive, tingling. Miles wider, leagues deeper than anything he'd ever felt before. Was that why his wheels were on fire, why the road ahead was opening up at the speed of light, why there was not a shadow of doubt in his mind or in his heart? This love had only one future: marriage. He wanted to marry Dulcie.

His heart pulsed. But would Dulcie want him? Did she have feelings for him? He felt his wheels cooling, his heart sinking. And if she did care for him, did somehow still want him after he came clean about who he was, then would the royal aides find an estate manager's daughter an acceptable choice?

He dragged his hands down his face. Hell, if they didn't then he'd employ different aides, or he'd table parliament for a change in the law. That was in the future, the least of his problems. The biggest was explaining himself. The omissions, the half-truths.

Would she understand, forgive him?

Maybe. If she cared about him. That was his best hope: that she cared, cared enough.

He closed his eyes, conjuring the warmth in hers, that easy instant connection, that sweet tingle of fellow feeling, her touch, and the way her lips fitted to his, the way she kissed, opened for him, the taste of her...

'I can't help the way I feel when I'm with you...can't help wanting what I want...'

That speech, the little crack in her voice, the passion in

it, her eyes reaching in, taking him all apart. He'd felt his breath leaving, hadn't he, his heart turning over? It was why he'd dug in, resisted taking her back to the yacht, because it had suddenly seemed that making love to her would be playing with her heart, the heart that was…in fact…right there… On. Her. Sleeve.

He blinked his eyes open, felt warmth flooding in. Hope. Could it be? And then his pulse was ramping because she'd said that other thing too…

'I don't know what it means, or where this can go, or even if you want it to go anywhere.'

A leading question, obliquely framed, one she surely wouldn't have even raised if the idea of a relationship, a continuation, wasn't already alive in her mind.

His heart plummeted. But would she still want a relationship once she knew who he was? Because in the lift she'd said that being 'on parade' was her perfect idea of hell—exact words—and yet dancing with Georgie, she'd wanted to be the one wearing the dress, the dress-up-box dress, no doubt a bright, flouncy, attention-grabbing dress! Which one was the real Dulcie?

His throat went tight. He loved them both, but it was beyond important to know, because if she *could* bear to be on parade some of the time and if she *did* care for him, then maybe the future he was already seeing could really happen, the future that, he could see now, had been coming into focus ever since she'd said that thing about starting to love the sound of his country.

A throwaway comment perhaps, but the tantalising thought that Dulcie could come to love Brostovenia had raised him up, reigniting the torch of his own pride. He could feel it glowing even now.

He lifted his gaze to the cathedral, sliding his eyes over the ornate portico. Barcelona was a fine city, but so was

Nyardgat. The domed eighteenth-century palace, the parliament building with its grand neo-classical façade, the soaring gothic cathedral. Modernist galleries and museums, the old quarter with its narrow streets and jostling half-timbered buildings.

He felt a smile coming. Nyardgat was a crazy, paradoxical city and Brostovenia was a crazy, paradoxical country. Yes, there was poverty and there were religious divisions, but what country in the world didn't suffer those? And what country in the world didn't elect disappointing governments from time to time? But there were elections coming, new faces emerging, full of passion and promise. And there was a new king coming too, wasn't there…?

He braced himself for the drop, for the shrinking feeling to start, but there was nothing, just the glow burning inside, a kinetic thrum building. He touched his forehead. No tension. No ache behind the eyes. No grey fog.

He leaned forward, resting his forearms on his thighs. Clarity was good. Logic!

No, he wasn't Gustav. He wasn't handsome, or daring, or charming in that easy, boyish way of Gus's, but that was all right, because he had other qualities. Experience of the wider world, of living in other countries as an ordinary person able to do ordinary things. Laundry, taking out his own trash, buying groceries… He knew how it felt to have a bag split, provisions crashing onto the sidewalk in a liquid splatter, knew how it felt to miss the last train. He understood the small everyday challenges of the ordinary world, which *had* to be a desirable trait in a monarch. And he understood business, more than understood it. He was good at it! Success in the States. Success in Paris. *Awards!* Earned through hard work, not by leaning on his royal connections.

Could he use his passions and experience to good effect when he was King, force improvements in the country, be

more than a face and a title? He felt his pulse quickening.
For one thing Brostovenia was too reliant on coal and the
government wasn't doing enough to change that. Green
energy was the only way forward. Everyone knew that.
He could spearhead the campaign, push hard, be a thorn
in the side, a pain in the ass. He felt a tingle, a smile tugging. Hell, if the state thought that King Raffiel Munoz
was going to keep his mouth shut and his nose out of poli-
tics, then they were very much mistaken!

He blinked. And here was the Raffiel he recognised! Alive,
questing, starting to imagine the challenge, not just imagining it, but relishing it. This was more like him. Papa would
recognise him now. He'd be smiling, thinking, *That's* my son.

Papa... He felt his chest constricting. Poor Papa. Dealing
with everything, looking for support from *him*, for strength,
strength he hadn't been able to find, but it was coming back
now, running through his veins. He was going to step up,
take the weight off Papa's shoulders. He was going to make
everything right, make Papa proud.

He shook himself. But first, and most importantly, he
had to tell Dulcie everything—*tonight*—face up to what
he'd done. His heart stumbled. But telling her before the
ball might ruin everything. She might not come, and he
couldn't risk that. He'd promised her a dance and if a waltz
turned out to be the only thing he could give her, the only
thing they'd both have left, then it had to happen.

Which meant, telling her afterwards. Straight after.

He got to his feet, pressed his hands to his face. That
way, if she didn't like what she was hearing, at least he'd
be able to see her back to the hotel, know that she was safe.
His heart clenched. At least there'd be that.

CHAPTER ELEVEN

SO PINK, THEN, after all. Not bright, and not remotely puff-ball, but still pink…or rather, ashes of roses.

'Like a vintage rose…'

That had been Georgie in the fitting room, looking all pleased with herself.

'I bet you thought I was going to put you in red with diamanté, didn't you?'

'Well…' It was what she'd been hoping for. Something bright. Dazzling. The opposite of monochrome but definitely *not* pink.

Little frown. 'Red with diamanté is me, darling, but you're softer, more romantic. Old rose suits you, and the drape is divine. Twirl for me…'

She'd twirled dutifully, liking the feel of the lifting silk, liking the appreciative little noises Georgie was making.

'That handkerchief hem is going to flare even more when you're dancing, and mid-calf's perfect. It isn't swamping you.' And then Georgie's hand had shot out, stopping her mid-pivot. *'As for this low back…'* Mischievous gleam. *'You'll be able to feel his hand, every little movement.'*

'Georgie!'

'Georgie what? It's what you want to feel, isn't it? I mean, you're clearly besotted—'

'Am I?'

She'd felt peeled back suddenly, involuntarily defensive, but Georgie wasn't having any of it.

'Er...hello? You're all glowy. Dreamy-looking. The last time you looked like this was when you were in love with Amy Madison. I'm just putting two and two together...'

And then Georgie had pulled her round so they were face to face.

'Look, I get that you're not ready to share, but it's obvious you've got the deep feels for this Raffiel fellow. And I don't know if he deserves them or not, but for now I'm on your side and, trust me, so is this dress! Elegant. Romantic. Quietly but seriously sexy. It's you, Dulce! One hundred per cent. Honestly, he's going to die when he sees you.'

Not quite the result she was after, but still, it was a lovely dress, and if Georgie thought it was perfect, then that was endorsement enough.

She reconnected with her reflection, feeling the little seismic shock all over again. It *was* herself looking back, but also not. Impeccable make-up, courtesy of Saffy, a few fine braids plaited into her hair—Tilly's gleeful idea—all of it swept up into a Boho chignon by Georgie, and—she smoothed her hands over the bodice—this beautiful dress.

She touched the straps. Wide. Silky-soft. Such an unexpected day. Getting to know the girls, laughing with them, making them laugh, feeling included. Properly included! They had their in jokes, yes. And, yes, they did love Ascot and Henley, but they loved other things too. Saffy had just run a charity half-marathon—'Ran it like a tortoise, darling!' And Peter's eldest sister, Katherine, was learning how to sign because 'not enough people can'.

Bottom line: the girls were nice. Lovely! And they were her friends now, seemingly, excited for her date with 'the waltzing architect', blowing her air kisses, throwing her little over-the-shoulder winks as they'd filed out, heading off for their sunset cruise.

'If you don't come back tonight, we'll know you where you are...'

Her heart dipped. Would she be back tonight? She didn't want to be. She wanted to be on Raff's yacht, being unwrapped by him, loving him all night long, but there was Brianne, wasn't there? Reining him in for some inexplicable reason, the ex who was supposed to have been his for ever but who'd thought nothing of leaving him just like that. No discussion. No trying to work things out!

How could she have done that, walked out on someone like Raff? More to the point, how could he still be getting over her when she'd treated him that way? It didn't make sense, and it definitely didn't fit with the fond light in his eyes, or with his toe-tingling kisses. Oh, and what about the way he'd kissed her after she'd said yes to the ball? That had been a whole new level of warm and deep, achingly tender, as if he'd been trying to fill every one of her senses up with himself. No reticence. No taste of hurt in his mouth. No trace of Brianne in *that* kiss!

She picked up her clutch, turning it over in her hands. What to make of it, of him? Holding back, not wanting to hurt her, but also not holding back, asking her to the ball, kissing her senseless, with *crazy for you* vibes coming off him in great big waves. It was there in his kiss, in his gaze, in his touch, and if she was feeling it then surely it had to be real, and if it *was* real, then why—?

A sudden bright knock swept the thought away.

Raff! Stubbornly insistent about coming up even though she'd said she could meet him in the lobby. Stubborn. Noble. *Here!*

She drew a quick breath and hurried through the suite, noticing the unfamiliar tap of her heels on the terrazzo, the tremble threatening her knees. Just thinking about him standing on the other side of the door was giving her delicious shivers. Black-tie Raff… He was bound to be the hottest black-tie guy she'd ever seen because there was no one like him. No one. Her belly quivered. Question was, what was he going to think of this new pink Dulcie?

'Hello, Raff!'

'Dulce! You're—' He felt his lungs emptying, his senses scrambling. Where to look when every detail was heartbreakingly perfect? Face, dress, hair. Milky skin, those straps that, by the way, looked as if they'd push off her smooth shoulders without too much encouragement, and that bodice, the pleasing swell of her breasts.

His pulse jumped. He'd felt her breasts pressing into his chest every time they'd kissed, felt his hands straining at the cuffs he'd shackled himself with, wanting to touch, desperate to. But he couldn't go there, couldn't let himself think about what he wanted to unfold, what might happen, or not, depending on how things went later. Hard enough tamping down the rogue thought that she looked every inch a queen: elegant, beautiful, radiant.

'You're stunning, Dulce.'

Doubt, of all things, ghosting through her gaze. How could she not know how perfect she looked when she was incomparable?

'I mean it.' He loaded his voice, so she'd feel how much. 'You're exquisite…'

The words were registering now, drawing her smile out.

'Thank you.' And then her head was tilting with the tiniest frown. 'So are you…'

Was she seeing it? Any second now, surely… She was looking right at him after all. He felt a chuckle agitating under his ribs and dropped his gaze, adjusting his cuff to hide his smile. 'Thanks, but a suit's a suit.'

'Not when it's bespoke, which yours obviously is. You look very…' Small silence. 'Very…' Long silence.

He felt the chuckle agitating more. Surely, she was seeing it now…?

He looked up to check. Still frowning. Unbelievable! She was able to spot a bespoke suit—black, boring—but the most obvious thing of all—*the most obvious thing*—seemed to be eluding her. He couldn't wait. The gift in his pocket was burning a hole. Also, the car was waiting.

'Dulcie.' He jerked his thumbs towards his face. 'I shaved.'

'Oh, my God!' Her hand flew to her mouth. 'That's it! I can't believe I didn't see it straight away. I was thinking you looked brighter somehow, younger—'

'I'll take brighter and younger…' And vital, and happy; all the things he felt around her.

And then suddenly her hand was coming to his cheek, flattening against it all warm and soft. 'So, what did the beard do to deserve its untimely end?'

He felt his breath catching, a sublime but unwelcome heat stirring. 'Nothing, other than that it didn't belong.'

Her eyebrows ticked up.

She wanted him to expand, meanwhile what he wanted was to put his hand over hers, bring it to his lips, then pull her close, kiss the place where that little loose tendril was touching the side of her neck. But he couldn't. Mustn't. Because if he did then they'd never get to the ball. Poor Arlo would be left scratching his head, Dulcie wouldn't get her dance, but, most importantly, he'd be breaking the promise he'd made to himself not to make love to her until she knew who he was. *What* he was. His stomach clenched. A

conversation for later. Right now there was this one to finish, and then the gift…

'The beard was an aberration.' He felt the grief inside
shifting and stretching, trying to storm the air in his lungs.
He swallowed hard. 'I let a lot of things slide after—'

'Of course.' Cutting in so he didn't have to say the words
out loud, caressing his cheek to soothe. She was so tuned
in, so quick to stretch her imagination in his direction. And
then she was removing her hand, stepping back, her gaze
gentle. 'Do you want to come in?'

And talk about it, was what she was really asking, wanting to pull him into her fold, tuck kindness around him.
A beautiful trait. One of so very many. Not that he actually needed kindness. Fact was, in spite of the momentary
dip, he was fine. The beard might have grown out of misery, but shaving had been a joy. Cathartic. Seeing his features emerging. That feeling of: Here I am after all, better,
stronger. *Ready!*

He drew her back into focus. But he *did* need to go in so
he could give her his gift. It was why he'd come up, after all.

He smiled. 'That'd be good, just for a minute.'

The suite was similar to Arlo's. Same lofty sitting-din-
ing-kitchen space, same full-length windows running along.
The view was of darkness now, peppered with a scattering
of distant lights: buoys, boats, a plane winking its descent.

'I know how it feels, Raff…'

Her voice spun him around.

'…walls caving in, soul shrinking, that heaviness inside
that makes doing even the smallest things impossible…'
She was setting her purse down, coming over, her eyes glistening at the edges. 'I know all about it because of Charlie,
or rather, because of what happened afterwards…'

His ribs went tight. The car was waiting, and his gift,
but he couldn't interrupt. This was the bit she'd snipped off

before and now, to make him feel better, she was going to share it, even though it was costing her. He felt his heart contracting. She was trusting him with something she'd never spoken about to anyone before.

Trusting *him*.

He caught her hand, folding it into his. 'What did happen?'

Her gaze drifted then came back. 'After Charlie did what he did I didn't do anything or say anything for the reasons I told you before, but Charlie did.' Her lips pressed together. 'He told everyone that I'd declared undying love for him, that he found it hysterical.'

'Making you the butt of a joke to save his bruised balls and ego?' He felt his gorge rising. 'How fricking mean! How pathetic!'

Her eyes registered acknowledgement. 'And effective. Putting me down made it impossible for me to climb back up. Anything I said to counter, you know, like *the truth*, would have sounded like I was trying to get back at him because he'd spurned me and not the other way round.' And then, unbelievably, she was shrugging. 'Nauseating as it was, I could have coped, but unfortunately at my fine, up-standing school *pathetic* grew arms and legs...'

Her eyes closed for a long moment. When they opened again, they were gleaming wet, tearing at his heart. 'In no time at all I went from sad, lovelorn junior to sad dresser, sad student, all-round sad individual. Sad Dulcie. Droopy Dulcie.' A tear was rolling down. He went to catch it, but she stopped his hand. 'Please, it's fine. I just need to finish.'

Hurting but strong as well, determined. He felt admiration flaring, anger burning a hole in his chest.

'It affected me so badly that after exams I couldn't bear to go back. I persuaded Mummy and Daddy to let me go to sixth form college. Fresh start and all that, but even then,

I couldn't raise myself back up. Not for the longest time.'
And then her gaze sharpened into his. 'You couldn't bring
yourself to shave. I couldn't be bothered to wash my hair.
I'd just throw on a black beanie.' Her eyebrows flickered.
'Black became my go-to. Black everything because it didn't
require an ounce of thought, a single ounce of effort.' She
took a little breath. 'So that's how I know what it feels like
to lose yourself, and I wanted you to know that, to know
that if you want to, you can talk to me...'

Dry-eyed now. Calm. Killing him, making his heart
hurt. *Bullying!* That was what she'd endured. Keeping it
all to herself, working through it alone because she hadn't
wanted to upset her parents, their friendship with Charlie's
parents, putting herself last, thinking, what, that everyone
else was more important?

He reached for her other hand, so he had both of hers, so
he could squeeze love into them. 'I wish you didn't know
it, Dulce; wish you hadn't had to go through that.'

'The point is, I *did* go through it, and guess what? I'm
still here, still standing.' She smiled, and then she was stepping back, tugging his arms full stretch, twisting, swirling
her dress, powdering the air with her perfume. 'You could
even say I'm in the pink...'

Those eyes, reaching in, so full of warmth, so full of...
He felt hope tingling and pushed it down hard. One thing
at once.

'You certainly are, pink, and lovely...' He felt a smile
stirring. 'And too far away.' He pulled on her hands.

She stilled, her eyes sparkling. 'Too far away for what?'

He felt his smile breaking, spreading. 'Come here and
I'll show you.' He pulled again and then she was coming,
letting him tow her in until she was right there.

She cocked an eyebrow. 'You weren't thinking of spoil-
ing my lipstick, were you?'

He'd been thinking about the gift, but now he was totally thinking about her mouth! Dewy. Lush. That sweet strawberry heat inside it. He swallowed hard. But he couldn't go there, couldn't risk letting himself loose inside her kiss.

'I'm thinking about it, but there's a car waiting and also—' he let her go, slid his hand into his pocket '—I've got something to give you.'

She faltered, eyes widening. 'A present?'

'Yes…' His fingers connected with the velvet case. Would she like what was inside it, or would she think it was too much? His heart creased. As if anything could ever be too much for Dulcie. That was the thought that had overtaken him in the Pla de la Seu, the thought that had sent him on a three-hour quest through the city looking for the perfect piece, something she'd love, something to signal at least a portion of what he was feeling if she turned her back on him before he got to declaring it. A cold river ran down his spine. Would she do that?

He drew out the box. No point thinking about it now, not when her eyes were quickening, shining. He licked the dryness off his lips. Maybe downplaying his efforts would be wise though, just in case she hated it.

He sprang the lid, heart thumping. 'It was a whim, okay, but I hope you like it…'

Baroque pearls, multiple strands of them glowing on twisted silver link chains, different lengths, some fine, some bold and chunky. An asymmetrical piece, edgy, Boho, and absolutely one hundred per cent her kind of thing.

She felt her heart giving, her breath struggling to come. 'Oh, Raff…' She looked up, catching a flicker of needless anxiety in his eyes, eyes that seemed so much larger and darker now that he was clean-shaven, gorgeously, smoothly handsome. 'What can I say? It's beautiful. I love it.'

A smile broke his face apart, relief shining through, and then he was lifting the necklace up, making it clack and tinkle. 'It's platinum.'

Her mouth went dry.

'I thought you'd prefer it to gold because you seem to favour silver.'

Silver, yes, but platinum was in a different league. Rare. Precious. *Expensive.*

She felt her pulse stumbling. What was she supposed to make of a gift like this? What to think? *How* to think even when his gaze was tight on hers, warm, deep, making her heart drum and drum. Was this Raff holding himself back? Because pearls set in platinum didn't say holding back. The question was, what were they saying? He'd called it a whim, but it was obvious he'd chosen it with care, matching it to what he knew about her, what she—

'So, you like it…?' He was looking anxious again. 'Really? You're not just saying it?'

She felt tenderness blooming, tears prickling. How could he be so insecure when he'd chosen the most perfect gift imaginable?

'No, I'm not just saying it.' She put a hand to his face. 'I love it.'

And I love you.

Could he see it in her, feel it pulsing through her palm, all the things she wasn't saying? Maybe she ought to tell him, but then again, wouldn't that be hijacking this sweet moment, the moment he'd designed for her, held close to his chest while she'd been rambling on about her downward spiral, letting it out—*admit it*—as much for herself as for him, because she'd *wanted* to share, felt safe enough to?

She ran her eyes over his face. Open. Kind. No guile hiding in his corners. That was the thing about Raff. He was safety. Sanctuary. Talking to him was so easy because he

was good, strong, anchored in all the right places. That was
how it felt. But he'd said he wasn't strong, that he wasn't
whole. Where was he, emotionally, right at this moment?
Was losing the beard a sign that he was finding his feet, a
sign that Brianne was fading from view?

Her heart dipped. And what about the necklace? Was
that a sign too? Was she closer than she knew, winning?
Her heart dipped again. Oh, God! If Raff was emerging
from his sadness, coming back into himself, then she *had*
to tell him the truth about herself. Only…maybe not now
because the car was waiting, wasn't it, had been for a while?
She inhaled a slow breath. Later, then.

Soon.

She blinked him back into focus, felt warmth surging
through her veins. What mattered right now was showing him her delight, every scrap of the love she was feeling inside.

'I really *do* love it, Raff. Thank you.'

'I'm pleased.' His eyes held her, a deep considering look,
and then he was undoing the clasp, smiling. 'Shall we see
if it fits?'

CHAPTER TWELVE

'RAFFIEL TELLS ME you're a ceramicist...'

Arlo was sliding into Raff's empty seat, setting his wine glass down.

Kind brown eyes, warmth in his smile, so why were her nerves suddenly chiming, and why was her tongue thickening, sticking fast? She'd felt calm and confident earlier, walking in on Raff's arm, appropriate, pretty, happy. Happy to stop and smile for the conference photographer—laughing, actually, because of Raff crooning nonsense into her ear the whole time.

'Chin up, darling...that's it...work it now...more...that's it...fabulous!'

As for the venue: perfect ballroom, perfect royal-blue walls and gleaming parquet, perfect glittering chandeliers and tables dressed in white linen, laid with silver and crystal, candles glowing in tall candelabras. And the dinner had been perfect too, every morsel delicious, not that she'd managed much. Too busy staring at Raff, drinking him in, the easy way he had of talking to the people at their table, not just Arlo, who was his friend, but the others too. No trace of that inner sadness, just smiling eyes and keen interest in whatever it was they were saying.

Raff had stayed close, kept everything rolling along, made her feel as if she belonged, but now he was gone—

where?—and it was like being back at school again, feeling eyes she couldn't bring herself to meet burning her skin. She touched Raff's necklace. His eyes had been burning too when she'd turned round to show him how it looked but she liked that burn, the way it melted her in all the right places. It didn't sting like this.

She swallowed. Maybe the trick was to copy Raff, simply show the face she wanted everyone to see, like at Parc Güell. She'd pulled the wool there all right, hadn't she? And probably it was just her imagination anyway, dragging her back into the old dark tunnels, imagining slights, vicious whispers. *Silly!* Because these people were grown-ups, not stupid teenagers with petty agendas. The glances she'd caught earlier had been admiring, so why would they be different now? She *was* dressed to the nines, and she *was* with the hottest guy in the room, even if right now he was mysteriously absent, so if she was feeling the heat of curious eyes then no wonder. She needed to pull herself together and get on with it. Also, she needed to reply to Arlo.

She drew him back into focus, smiled. 'That's right.'

'You haven't thought about exhibiting here?'

'Erm…no.' It was impossible not to laugh. 'I'm afraid I'm a long way away from being international calibre.'

Arlo raised disbelieving eyebrows. 'Raffiel says you're very talented, and believe me, when it comes to art and design, he knows what he's talking about, so if you change your mind, you could submit for next year…'

She felt a little tingle. So Raff had talked about her work to Arlo Ferranti, praising it. Rating it. Wonky vessels that for her always fell short, that didn't quite express the wonk-iness inside, or whatever intangible thing it was that kept her at it, battling, questing, trying to pin herself down—

'Raffiel's such a powerhouse.' Arlo was talking on, his eyes alive with obvious affection. 'He has so many interests. Passions! And of course, he wants all of them represented, so he's grown the conference year on year, so now it's this behemoth...'

She felt a frown coming. 'What do you mean, *he's* grown it?'

Arlo picked up his glass. 'Well, when he started it—'

'*He* started it?'

'Yes.' Arlo's eyebrows twitched up. 'Didn't he say?'

'No.' She felt a hollow beat thumping.

'Ah...' For a piece of a second, he looked uncomfortable, and then he smiled, shaking his head indulgently. 'Well, that's Raff all over. Mr Modesty.' He took a sip from his glass. 'What did he tell you, let me guess, that he straightens the tables, puts out the chairs...?'

'I'm one of the many backstage minions.'

'Something like that.'

Arlo laughed and set down his glass. 'Well, the truth is, it's his gig.' And then his expression altered, clouding a little. 'When he put the first one together it was here.' His eyes lifted, circling the room. 'Can you imagine?'

Right now it was hard to even think straight. Why on earth hadn't Raff told her that it was *his* conference, *his* baby? Modesty was one thing, but it didn't make sense, unless for some unfathomable reason he'd thought she wouldn't be interested...

'I mean, this space is a fair size, but when you consider how big it's got...' His eyes came back to hers. 'Raff moved us to the World Trade Centre three years ago so he could add an interior design exhibition, a partner event to offset the tedious—' he comedy slapped his head '—oops! Did I really say that? I mean the *fascinating* debate about the future direction of architecture and—buzzword alert!—sustainability.' A smile filled his cheeks. 'In case you haven't noticed, Raff is passionate about sustainability...'

Just yesterday, that fire in his eyes at the World Trade Centre:

'We have to step up, take responsibility, right?'

And she'd said it wasn't all on him, said he should cut himself some slack and he'd got a bit defensive then, hadn't he, told her he wasn't trying to save the world...? Her heart clenched. Had she inadvertently offended him? Surely not, because he'd been fine afterwards, excited for Parc Güell. She bit her lips together.

But who knew what was really going on inside him? Easy imagining that she *knew* him because she could *feel* him, because of the connection that felt real, because of the love that was exploding inside, but the truth was, she didn't know Raff at all. How could she? They were barely three days old. How could she know all the things that made him tick? The only thing she knew for sure was that she wanted to. More than ever now.

She lifted her glass, shooting Arlo a smile. 'I think I might have picked up on that.'

Arlo's lips pressed into a knowing grin and then his focus suddenly shifted to a point beyond her left shoulder. He flashed his eyebrows in that direction and then he was pushing his chair back. 'If you'll excuse me, I'm being summoned...'

'Of course.' She felt panic fluttering. First Raff and now Arlo! What was with all the disappearing? She swallowed hard, painted on a smile. 'Erm...before you go, do you know where Raff is?'

'Yes.' He nodded to the same spot behind her. 'He's over there.' And then he split a grin. 'He's the one doing the summoning.'

Dulcie was twisting round, looking over, her chin tilting up in that quizzical way she had. He shot her a smile then looked down at the mic in his hand, riding out the swell of faint guilt. Maybe it had been a poor decision not to tell her about the speech, but mentioning it in the limo would only have spoiled the joy of sitting beside her, breathing in her perfume, drinking in her excitement, her astonishing beauty.

And it would have led to questions, opened doors into rooms he couldn't enter yet. But when he'd been writing it—short and sweet because who wanted to listen to him droning on when the stage belonged to Arlo now?—it had seemed like an opportunity to lay a few bricks, drop some hints, to prime her. That was the thinking, anyway, thinking that had felt sound at the time.

'Hey!' Arlo was arriving, beaming warmth. 'I like your Dulcie very much. *È molto carina, proprio bella.*'

Raff glanced at Dulcie again, felt his heart filling. She was still looking over, one slender arm draped over the back of the chair, a small smile playing over her lips. She most certainly was a beauty, and so much more.

He met Arlo's gaze. 'Tell me something I don't know.'

Arlo leaned in. 'So what are you going to do about *you know what*?'

The truth, Arlo meant.

He felt a knot pulling tight. 'I'm going to tell her tonight. After we leave.'

Arlo's gaze faltered, then the light inside it intensified. 'It'll be fine. You'll see. The way she looks at you… I mean, you've got to be feeling it, Raff.'

He could, the warmth pouring out of her, making his heart sing, but whether it was love or just—

'It looks like the real thing, my friend.' Arlo was smiling. 'That's what I'm seeing anyway, and the real thing doesn't care about royalty. You're still you at the end of the day, whatever it says on the label, and it's *you* she's crazy for.'

Arlo, *Italian*, the eternal romantic.

Could *he* believe it though? He wanted to, but how were things really going to play out? In this place, right now, he was a free man, but that was about to change and it wasn't as if he and Dulcie had had time to establish roots. The root-growing part was still to come, that was, if she was even interested in trying, because dating him wouldn't be easy.

Spontaneity was out for a start. And outside the confines of the palace and the various other crown properties in Brostovenia and Switzerland he was always going to have a security detail at his shoulder. Discreet perhaps but nevertheless there. And in the public eye, in the public mind, dating translated as *courting*. Fine by him, because that was his intention anyway, but for Dulcie it could feel like ridiculous pressure, and if things didn't work out, then she'd be trailing him behind her everywhere she went. *The Prince's ex*.

It was a lot to ask of anyone, never mind someone he'd only just met, someone whose life was determinedly insular, someone who was looking at him right now with a sweet, perplexed gaze. The knot inside pulled tighter. *Dulcibella*. She didn't know it, but it was thanks to her that he was turning himself around. She'd lit his candle, kindled him back to life, given him a view that went beyond the bars of his cage.

And now it was starting, the process of opening up the view for her in return.

Baby steps.

He looked at Arlo. 'Are you ready?'

Arlo grimaced. 'As I'll ever be.'

'Right then.' He switched on the mic, tapping it to quieten the room, and then he drew in a breath. 'Good evening, ladies and gentleman...'

'So you were never *just* a minion...?' Dulcie was frowning a little, a glimmer of hurt behind her gaze. 'Why didn't you tell me?'

'Because…' Getting into the intricacies would have been sailing too close to the royal patronage thing and he hadn't wanted to get into all that with her on day one. God help him, he'd just wanted to be Raff Munoz, the lift guy, the guy she'd liked well enough to have coffee with. But *baby steps…*

He drew in a breath. 'Because it didn't seem that important given that I'm stepping down—'

'Because of new challenges.' Her mouth tightened a little. 'New horizons.'

Quoting his own speech back at him. He hadn't been specific. The people closest to him knew where he was bound. The rest didn't care. They were here for charity, for a good night out or, being cynical, they were here to be seen doing the right thing for charity, to be snapped at the doors in their finery. It didn't matter. They'd paid handsomely for their tickets, pledged further donations as well as extravagant auction prizes for next year. The money, every cent of it, would go to building villages for the homeless, providing them with support services to help them get their lives back on track. That's what mattered, and that the charity ball was now an annual fixture in Barcelona. Year after year, the money would keep rolling in, and if, from the lofty heights of the Brostovenian throne, he could keep pushing for—

'Are you at least going to tell me about your new challenges?'

Dulcie's clear blue gaze came back into focus, reaching in, pleading almost.

His lungs locked. God, she was lovely, and he hadn't even kissed her yet, had barely dared to touch her. Too scared at the hotel in case he'd unravelled but somehow they'd got here intact, were still intact. Pristine in fact.

Enough! His speech was delivered. The crown was Arlo's now, the responsibility, the work. Meanwhile the orchestra was striking up, and the girl he loved was looking at him, her gaze softening, registering the music, the changing vibe in the room.

He felt his heart dipping then lifting again, a smile coming. 'I'm going to tell you all about it later, I promise, but right now I want to dance with you...'

Warm light filled her eyes, warming him right back.

He pushed up out of his seat, holding out his hand. 'Will you do me the honour?'

'You know I will...' She was laughing now, taking his hand, rising. 'It's what I came for.'

CHAPTER THIRTEEN

SO MAYBE RAFF hadn't filled her in about his exact conference role but right now it was impossible to care because she was in his arms, being whirled around the floor, and his dark eyes were locked on hers, full of warm, brimming light. Such a feeling, dancing under sparkling chandeliers, dress swirling exactly as Georgie had said it would. She felt a smile curving. Georgie would *so* love to be in *these* pink silk shoes, dipping and gliding with such an exquisite partner, feeling these warm fingers at her back, moving, caressing…

Her breath hitched. There they went again, shooting electric tingles along her spine, and here he was, pulling her closer, leaning in.

'Have I told you how much I like this dress?'

She breathed him in, savouring his deep, musky warmth. 'Only about a hundred times.'

'Apologies for the repetition.' His fingers moved lower, a lingering stroke, bolder. 'But I just can't stop thinking it.'

Thinking *it*, and what else? Because if his talking hands were telling the truth, and the dark glow in his eyes was real, then his mind was on the same track as hers. And yet, he hadn't so much as kissed her. He'd given her an exquisite, thoughtful gift, but no kiss. Not in the suite, nor in the limo.

She felt her heart sinking. Was it Brianne, still—in spite

of the gift—wielding her invisible strings? How could that even be possible when every nuance of his body language was sending tremors through *her*, making *her* pulse drum? How could a part of him still be possessed by Brianne when she was feeling his possessiveness flowing around *her*, feeling it in the firmness of his hold, in his unswerving gaze? And what about that gaze…? So adoring. So tender. Tender for *her*. Adoring *her*.

Crinkling. Smiling. Leaning in.

'You dance beautifully, Dulcie.'

She felt a blush tingling. 'Right back at you.'

He laughed, then spun her hard, and suddenly she was laughing too. She could feel her heart soaring, all her doubts vaporising. Raff was filling her to the brim, to the tips of her senses. She was so high she didn't even know if there were any other dancers on the floor. All she could see was his handsome face, all she could feel was…

Everything.

But what was the use of feeling everything if she couldn't give it, make him feel it? Her heart clenched. In three days she was leaving. Would she be leaving empty-handed? Was she going to be forced to rebrand whatever this was as her 'little Barcelona fling'? How could she do that when it was less than a fling but felt like more?

She tore her eyes away from his, fixing on the impeccable bow at his throat. In a million years she couldn't have foreseen this, imagined that this could happen to her. A hen week in Barcelona and now, somehow, she was head over heels with this man, this extraordinary man who was confusing her every which way. Saying he was crazy for her but holding himself back out of, what, respect? Uncertainty? Her heart clenched. She was tired of aching and wanting, tired of not being able to do anything about it because she'd resolved not to push him, determined that it was for him to take the lead…

But then, actually, what was he doing now if *not* taking the lead? His fingers were sliding under the silk cowl at the base of her back, stroking circles, stirring that ache. She felt a tug, her focus skewing. Oh, God, his touch was sublime, assured, definitely *not* ballroom, and definitely *not* ambiguous. This was her signal, the very one she'd been waiting for! He was making moves on her, as far as was possible mid-waltz, and what was she doing? Not signalling back was what, just staring dumbly at his tie.

Stupid, Dulcie!

She swallowed the smile that was rising and lifted her eyes, sliding her hand from his biceps to the back of his neck, nice and slow so he'd know she was reading him down to the small print. 'By the way, have I told you how hot you look in this suit?'

'Hot?' He seemed surprised, a little abashed. 'I thought I looked fitting. Smart.'

She felt her heart melting. Did he really have no sense of how imposing a figure he cut, no sense of how handsome he was, how sexy? It was endearing, made him even more attractive.

'Well, you *do* look smart, of course…' She stroked his nape, circling her fingers, smiling inside as a satisfying little glitch interrupted his gaze. 'But also, you *are* hot. If we were to unbutton this—' she gave his collar a tug, enjoying the sudden flare of his nostrils that betrayed his sharp intake of breath '—loosen the tie, you'd graduate to full-blown smoking hot.'

His chin dipped. 'If you unbuttoned me, people would notice.'

Three days left… Nothing to lose.

She loaded her gaze with every iota of intent she possessed. 'Not if we were somewhere private…'

His lips parted, moving silently, and then suddenly she was being pulled in tight against him, his voice in her ear torn black velvet. 'Do you have any idea what you're doing to me?'

The raw emotion in it stopped her breath. He was holding her so close now that it was verging on the indecent, but he didn't seem to care. He was waltzing on, turning her deftly, every powerful movement of his thighs making her weak, giddy. She could feel wetness gathering between her legs, the ache inside building and building.

She turned her head to catch his eye and her belly clenched. He was burning up with it too, openly, feeling the same hurtling desire, the tantalising crush of their bodies, the heat, and the swirl, feeling the ache of the music, the flow of silk, the soft rub of wool, the warmth in the room, the scorch of their skin, his fingers, her back, her fingers, that damp softness at his nape, and then the tempo was slowing, and the music was ending.

Ended.

For a heart-thumping moment his eyes held her fast, and then he leaned in, lips grazing her ear. 'Let's go.'

'Wait…'

Her heart lurched. *Wait?*

He was pulling away, raising himself onto his elbows, his hair falling forwards over his forehead. 'I need to tell you something…'

She felt her cells screaming. He couldn't be doing this, not now that they were actually alone in his stateroom, not after that blistering kiss in the lobby of The Imperial, that wild, hungry kiss that the concierge had interrupted none too politely with a loud, disapproving cough; not after asking the driver to raise the privacy screen in the car so they could keep kissing all the way back, kissing and touching, hands sliding… Raff's hand sliding under her skirt, driving her pulse into the red zone.

All this foreplay, days of it, it felt like, and now they were tumbled on his miles-wide bed, blissfully private with the lights down low, and his tie was hanging loose, those top buttons finally undone, and he was beyond super-smoking hot and now—*now!*—he was putting the brakes on!

'Can't it wait?' She could hear the whimpering frustration in her own voice. 'I mean, it isn't that I'm not interested…' She put a hand to his cheek, catching the soft ripple in his gaze. 'But I don't want to talk, Raff, not now. I just…' She looked at his lips, imagining where they could go, and suddenly there was a flood crashing through, breaking her voice to pieces. 'I just want what I want. All of you.'

His gaze held her, burning, and then the burn mellowed to a deep, soft glow. 'You can have all of me, Dulcibella, everything…' And then he smiled. 'Just not all at once.' His smile became a chuckle. 'If you'd had your way, we'd have been naked on the back seat of the limo.'

She felt a smile twitching. 'Are you telling me off?'

'No.' The corner of his mouth ticked up, acknowledging the familiar line, and then he was leaning in, brushing his lips over hers. 'But I need to tell you that I'm not in a hurry, and you shouldn't be either.' His mouth came to hers again, warm, brief, teasing. 'I want to slow things down, give you the attention you deserve…'

Those eyes…that velvet voice…full of promise. She felt her insides melting and aching at the same time.

'Come…' He was sitting up, pulling her up too.

Electricity arced up her spine. He was in control now. It was there in the confident set of his shoulders, in his darkening eyes. She felt a delicious weakness threading through her veins. He'd demonstrated his physical strength in the hall of columns, in the easy way he'd lifted her up, and she'd felt it in him while they were dancing too, but this was a different kind of power, a different side of him, a side that was making her senses sit up, making her blood quiver.

He leaned in. Another kiss. Slow, sensuous, electrifying and then his fingers went to the loose lock of hair that was tickling her cheek. He tucked it behind her ear. 'I love your hair like this…' His eyes came to hers, crinkling. 'Little plaits.'

Her insides went limp. Surely on no planet whatsoever had 'little plaits' ever sounded so sensual.

'My cousin Tilly's idea.'

'She has good ideas…' His focus drifted to her hair again. 'But I want your hair loose now.' His eyes snapped back. 'Is that all right?'

'Of course…' Anything for him, especially when his gaze was taking her apart like this.

She reached up to take out the pins but immediately his hands were on hers.

'No. Let me.' He was smiling a hazy smile. 'I want to do it.' He released her, shifting back a little. 'Turn round.'

She turned, feeling the nakedness of her own back, the weight of his eyes and then it was his hand she was feeling, on her shoulder, and his lips on her neck, trailing kisses into her nape. She felt her nipples hardening, hot darts arrowing to her core.

How could he stand to string things out like this? He'd been rock-hard on the yacht, rock-hard at Parc Güell, and rock-hard in the limo. His body had to have been on fire but still he was putting her first, taking his time for her. *Loving her.*

She felt tears welling behind her lids, the love inside surging, and then it was his breath she was feeling, and warm lips behind her ear, and his deft fingers unclasping her necklace. It clacked softly as he set it down, and then his fingers were back, tracing a warm path up her spine to her shoulders. She closed her eyes, leaning into the tingle, the quiver, the ache of his touch.

And then his hands were moving over her head, searching for pins, pulling them out with excess gentleness. She felt section after section falling down, his unhurried fingers combing through it.

'I'm not going to attempt the plaits…' She felt his smiling breath in her hair, the press of his shirt against her back, insane heat punching through it, and then his hands were on her shoulders again, sliding her straps off. She lifted her arms free, felt the silk bodice falling into her lap.

A burning silence. Just her heart drumming and then that voice.

'Look at me, Dulcie.'

Her core tightened and pulsed, wetness soaking into her underwear. How could an accent do that, stroke her in places that fingers couldn't reach?

She licked her lips and turned.

His breath caught audibly and then his eyes were sliding down. She felt her nipples hardening more, craving his fingers, his mouth, his tongue and then suddenly he was moving, easing her backwards, fire in his eyes, and something else that triggered a heart skip.

'God, you're beautiful…'

Hands in her hair, lips scorching hers, and then he was moving down, trailing kisses along her collarbone, nipping and sucking, lower and lower, his breath warm on her skin, and then his hands were sliding over her breasts, caressing, his fingers teasing her nipples until the sharp pulsing darts were firing in volleys. She arched her back, wanting his mouth, and he was right there, reading her need. For an instant the wet caress of his tongue felt like balm, but then the low-down yearning was back, stronger than ever, relentless, overpowering…

'Raff, please…' It came out cracked and dry, but it was all she could do to get it out at all.

'What do you want, baby?' His head lifted. 'Tell me what you want…'

Her pulse spiked. That accent, those words, smoky eyes burning into hers. Dishevelled Raff. Suddenly her favourite ever view. How to tell him she wanted everything he was, all of him, not just this, but how could she tell him that when he didn't even know who she was? She'd planned to tell him, and maybe she could have in the car, but the moment they'd got in he'd asked the driver to raise the screen, and his eyes had been full and deep, still burning with the dance and that lobby kiss and she simply hadn't been able to stop herself from sliding onto his lap—

'Dulce…' His lips grazed her nipple again, sending a fresh spike pulsing through and then he was shifting himself back up, his eyes searching, his gaze deep and full. 'What do you want…?'

Those eyes, blue as the ocean. No wonder he was drowning…

So much for noble intentions. Could a dress be held to account? Because Dulcie in *that* dress had been his undoing. He simply hadn't been able to stop his fingers from caressing her skin while they were dancing, hadn't been able to resist sliding them lower and lower, and then the wheels had been coming off, and all the wheels within the wheels. Impossible not to pull her close, to feel that close wasn't nearly close enough. Like in the hall of columns, fever taking over…

Close dancing, *ultra-dancing*, blood pumping, the slightness and lightness of her, her hands in his hair, and her smooth skin, and the warm floral pulse of her perfume. When the music stopped there'd been no logic operating, no saying the things he needed to say, only desperate hunger for the softness of her mouth, that strawberry heat inside it, and then the concierge had coughed, and the lobby he hadn't even noticed walking into had snapped into focus, people going by remarking with their eyebrows, and all he'd been able to think then was that he *needed* to be alone with her, to tell her who he was before the fire consumed them both.

And then it was getting into the car, asking the driver to put the screen up, barely drawing breath before Dulcie was on his lap, kissing him, pulling at his tie, pulling him to pieces, shredding his resolve. She felt so right in his hands, so right in his heart, and God help him he'd tried to tell her, but she'd overturned him, slayed him with her open desire, that fatal crack in her voice. And now he was all split open, ready to be her slave, and he wanted to hear it from her lips, what she wanted him to do.

He drew her back into focus, felt his pulse ramping. He knew what *he* wanted. He wanted to tear off the rest of that dress, explore every inch of her skin, make her whimper, moan, climax with his name on her lips, and then he wanted to sink himself inside her, bring her to ecstasy again, and himself. God, how much he wanted that sweet release, an end to this torment of hard pulsing desire that had been his basic state from the moment she'd opened her hotel door. But he needed to hear it, needed—

'I want *you*, Raff…' Her gaze was deep, full, making the love inside surge and froth, and then there was playfulness surfacing, that little spark at the edge of her gaze. 'I want you on your back first and then, after that, I want you every which way, all night long, so please—' she wriggled sideways '—roll over.'

He rolled, obeying, liking the gleam in her eye, the way the light from the bedside lamp was bathing her firm little breasts. She rose up onto her knees, pushing the dress over her hips. Pale underwear came into view, tiny, see-through. He swallowed hard. A smile touched her lips, and then she was coming for him, straddling him, going for his last three shirt buttons, lifting the fabric away.

Silence.

'And there I was thinking you couldn't look any better.' Her eyes came to his, a tiny, perplexing glisten in their corners and then her hands were moving over his skin, caressing, stroking, fingers running warm tingling trails, lower and lower.

He felt his breath coming in patches, his eyes wanting to close. His hardness was insistent, throbbing, and definitely not lost on her because she was moving back, undoing his button, unzipping him. He felt a gasp arriving, hissing through his teeth. *Sweet heaven*, she was all over him, fingers moving, thumb sliding over his tip, teasing him, shuffling backwards. He felt his fingers curling into his palms, anticipation beating. He was desperate for her to do what she was setting herself up to do, but…no… *No!* What he wanted more was to be the one in control, to go down, then go inside. He wanted to watch her face, kiss her mouth, feel every beat of her heart, her heart beating close to his. *That* was making love…

'Dulce…' He rolled up, so they were face to face. 'I don't want you to do that.'

She blinked. 'Ever?'

Ever?

His heart pulsed. Did 'ever' mean that she *was* thinking beyond Barcelona, thinking that there could be other nights, days, weeks, beyond this one? A relationship…? He felt his heart speeding up. That glisten in her eyes before, that extra layer hovering in her gaze, the magical, compelling, irresistible layer. *Was* it love…for *him*? She wasn't saying it, but he was feeling… Oh, God, and he wasn't saying it either, was he? Because when he declared it, it had to come from the lips of Prince Raffiel Munoz, not Raff Munoz, architect. His heart creased. But he couldn't tell her now, not when her eyes were taking him apart like this, not when all the love inside was pleading for release.

He put his hands to her face. 'No, I'm not saying *ever*…'

A slow smile curved on her lips. 'Good.'

CHAPTER FOURTEEN

A LOW, insistent buzzing noise filtered in, then grainy light, then the sound of gentle breathing. She turned her head. *Raff!* Sprawled on his front, sleeping, his features soft, his lips slightly parted, his hair a sort of dark nest. She felt a smile tugging. Her fault! His hair was longer than it looked when it was combed back, too irresistibly soft not to touch, to bury her fingers into at critical moments.

She suppressed a giggle. So many critical moments. A whole night of them! A whole night of loving, of feeling loved, of feeling her own love pouring out, wanting to say it but not saying it because first she had to tell him who she was, so that the truth could be true from every angle. Her chest went tight. Would he be upset that she'd lied not twenty minutes after telling him that she didn't approve of dishonesty…and what about her title? Would that bother him? It didn't seem likely somehow, not after seeing him in action at the conference, the way he could talk to people, the confident way he'd delivered his speech. He'd fit right in at Fendlesham, that was for sure. Better than she did.

She felt a frown coming. There it was again, that weird buzzing—

Phone!

On the low drawer unit by the door.

Bound to be Georgie, checking up, wanting all the luscious details. As if she'd even go there! As if she even could. The words hadn't been invented yet to describe how she was feeling inside, what she was feeling for Raff, but she couldn't leave the phone buzzing. It was going to wake him, and after the glorious, toe-tingling night he'd given her, Raffiel deserved to sleep!

She slipped out of bed, snatched up his shirt from the floor then tiptoed out.

Ten missed calls from Georgie!

Ten!

Her heart slipped sideways. Had something terrible happened…an accident…someone hurt? She forced her feet along the corridor, heart pounding, pulling on the shirt, fumbling with the buttons. *Oh, God!* Tilly's nut allergy! The sunset cruise people had been informed but that didn't mean—

She slammed through the door that led to the upper decks, taking the steps two at a time until she was on the third. At the rail, she drew in a deep breath, and tapped dial. The thing was to sound calm and reassuring. If Tilly was in the Emergency Room, then Georgie needed her to be—

'Dul—cee—bella—lella…'

She felt her heart righting itself. What was that law about the simplest explanation being the most likely…?

'Morning, Georgie.' Trying to lure Georgie away from her teasing wouldn't work but trying was reflexive. 'How was the cruise?'

'It's almost afternoon, sweetie. And the cruise was delightful. Meanwhile, what *I* want to know is exactly *when* you were going to tell me about Raffiel.'

'I sent you a text…' From Raff's hot lap in the limo, admittedly, so there might well have been typos, but still, the scramble of words should have made sense.

'I'm not talking about that.'

'What, then?'

'God, Dulce, this is *me* you're talking to! Please, don't be disingenuous.'

Disingenuous?

She felt a vague flutter of panic. 'I'm not; I don't know what you're getting at.'

'Really?' Georgie's voice was dripping with a sort of affectionate sarcasm. 'So there's nothing *massive* you want to tell me about the waltzing architect, no extra tiny thing about him that a cousin might have wanted to know first-hand instead of discovering it on social media—*trending*, by the way—along with some interesting pictures and a frenzy of speculation?'

Her chest went tight. *Pictures? Speculation? Trending!* She felt a queasy sensation lodging in her stomach, old ghosts stirring, grey shades of school morphing into full colour.

'Georgie, please. I don't know what you're talking about...'

Silence.

'You *are* joking, right?' Georgie's tone was darkening, making the jumping panic inside jump higher.

'No...'

'So you're telling me you don't know that Raffiel is a prince...'

Prince? For a beat the word came into focus, solidifying, and then quickly it was turning to liquid, vaporising. Georgie was pulling her leg, winding her up because she hadn't gone back last night. Raff wasn't a prince! He was an architect. A regular person, moving through the world in a regular way, doing regular things... If he was a prince, he'd have an entourage. A bodyguard! If he was a prince, he would have told—

'You're deafening me with your silence, Dulce...'

'Oh, I'm sorry.' She felt a smile tugging. 'That must be just the sound of me not falling for it.'

'I'm serious, Dulcie. Your Raffiel is Prince Raffiel Munoz of Brostovenia!'

Her heart clutched. She hadn't told Georgie Raff's surname, or where he came from—

'And soon he'll be the King of Brostovenia because of that horrific accident at Dralk racing circuit...'

Prince... King... Dralk...

Dots were dancing, peppering her vision.

'It was all over social media a few months back, and there was a big spread in *Hello!* magazine as well because Prince Gustav was a bit of a celebrity, being a handsome prince *and* a racing driver.'

Racing driver?

'It was awful. He spun out on the track, flipped his car over into the royal stand. The explosion killed him and the King and his younger brother. Surely you saw it...?'

Words tumbled.

Surely...surely...surely...?

No! She hadn't seen it because she didn't look at social media, didn't follow the news. And now she couldn't even breathe but Georgie wouldn't stop talking—

'Raffiel's father is King just now, but his health isn't good, so it's expected that Raffiel is going to be taking the throne within the year. That's why the pictures of you and him are going viral. You're hashtag royal romance. Also, it doesn't hurt that the two of you look beautiful together...'

Beautiful...?

Her throat closed. There was nothing beautiful here. Raff was a liar! Not noble, not gentlemanly but secretive, conniving. *Cruel!* How could he *not* have told her who he was? How could he have sat blithely listening to her pouring out all her pain over Charlie, listening to how Charlie had taken her in, pretending to be the golden boy, pretending to be courteous, and decent, and responsible, when the whole time *he* was doing the exact same thing? How the hell could he have sat there *pretending* to be moved, acting all concerned when he was hiding behind a great big lie?

'Dulcie…' Georgie's voice came in like an echo bouncing. 'You mean to say that Raffiel hasn't told you any of this?'

'No.' The word crept out, tearing a hole. Saying it out loud, admitting it out loud hurt so much. Her ignorance. Her stupid gullibility. She felt wetness scalding, seeping, the hot messy clog of it in her lashes, the thick ache of it swelling in her throat. She couldn't talk, couldn't bear to, not here. She squeezed her lids shut, swallowing hard. 'George, I can't do this now, I'm sorry.' She killed the call. Powered off.

What kind of fool was she? Falling for the wrong man a*gain*, falling for lies. Sad Dulcie. Droopy Dulcie. *Stupid Dulcie!*

'Dulcie!'

Her heart pulsed. And now he was here, faltering at the top of the steps, his face taut. From the look of him, he'd just got the news too. He seemed to gather himself, and then he was moving, coming over.

She felt her stomach hardening. So what was he about now, coming to lie to her a bit more, break her heart a little bit more?

He stopped a pace away, his eyes reaching in. 'I'm so sorry, Dulce…'

That voice, shredded velvet. Those stricken eyes, tugging at her even now, even when he was the cause, even though he'd lied, even though because of him she was now *trending* on social media, a prime target for a bit of shooting practice, sniping. Pulling her to pieces, pulling pieces right off when all she'd done was fall in love. She felt a sudden searing stab of anger. She'd never got the chance to tell Charlie Prentice his fortune, but she sure as hell was going to tell Raff his.

She lifted her chin. 'Is this what you call a *royal* apology?' He blinked, recoiling a little. 'When were you going to tell me, Raff, or maybe you weren't going to bother?' She offered up a shrug. 'It's a minor detail after all.'

His mouth tightened visibly, a sudden flash of steel at the edge of his gaze. 'Well, *Lady* Dulcibella *Davenport*-Brown, if we're talking about minor details…'

Her heart seized, then burst into angry flames. 'Don't you dare do that! What I did doesn't even come close to what you did. I *told* you about Fendlesham, that I lived there. The only thing I didn't tell you was that it belongs to my family.' His mouth was opening, forming a *'why'* but she wasn't finished—not nearly.

'I told you about Charlie, how he pretended to be nice—decent—and you didn't think to tell me then, didn't *think* to yourself that pretending to be a normal person when you're actually a prince would be a *huge* deal to me; didn't *think* that, after all the nastiness I went through at school, the possibility of being photographed with you—quite likely in view of your being a *prince* and everything—being splashed all over social media for even more people to laugh at would be a fricking *huge* deal…' And then a fresh thought was pulsing, ripening in her mouth. 'Or maybe you don't care. Maybe your head's so full of Brianne that you can't see beyond—'

'Dulcie, stop!' This was insane. Last night he'd poured himself into her, body, and soul, and now she was dredging up Brianne! 'This has got *nothing* to do with Brianne.'

Her lips clamped shut, but her eyes were still blazing,

wild hurt pulsing behind them, tearing his heart out. He needed to dowse this quickly, then explain. Try to.

'I was going to tell you everything after the ball last night.'

Her chin lifted. 'Easy to say now.'

For the love of God!

'I'm not just saying it. It's why I asked the driver to raise the privacy screen, but then you were all over me, didn't give me a chance...'

Her eyes registered the truth of it, and then her chin was lifting again, defiant. 'Raff, you're six foot two if you're an inch, and I'm...' she frowned '...much smaller. You could have stopped me!'

'Maybe but...' Hands under his shirt, her lips scorching, tongue snagging, drawing heat through, sending heat pulsing... He felt a tight breath leaving, caught a flicker of acknowledgement travelling through her gaze.

'I tried again when we were downstairs—'

She blinked, and then the mask she was wearing slipped, relenting a little. 'I remember, and I didn't want to hear it, but, Raff, it wasn't exactly a choice moment.' Her lips tightened again. 'The choice moment would have been day one. You could have told me then.'

'Could I?' His heart pulsed and then suddenly a torrent was rising, pushing up all the pain and bitterness. 'What if I couldn't find the words? What if it seemed too big to talk about, too damn hard?'

She blinked again, and then suddenly there was that familiar gentleness filtering in. He felt a tentative seed of hope germinating.

'Dulce, I haven't been straight with you about who I'm going to be, and, God help me, I'm not trying to defend that, but I've been completely straight with you about who I am, because *this* is me.'

Her gaze opened into his more, warming him, inviting his hand to reach for hers, making his heart leap when she didn't pull away.

'I'm an architect, spent seven years training to become one, loving every second because I live and breathe architecture, and art, and design. It's why I founded the conference here in Barcelona, because Papa brought me here when I was fourteen to inspire me, to show me Gaudí's work. *This* is where it all started for me and...' His heart clenched. 'And it's where it all ends too, not because *I* want it to, but because Gustav—'

He swallowed hard, trying to push it all down, so he could keep speaking, explaining, so she'd understand, so she wouldn't hate him. 'For months I've been stacked high with grief...anger...bitterness and... I just didn't want to get into that with you. I didn't want to talk about what was coming because I don't know what's coming. My whole life, I've been free, Dulce. I carved out a niche, doing the thing I love, and now I'm next in line, where *next* means *soon*, because Papa isn't strong, and I don't know how to be what I have to be now, but I have no choice.'

Her eyes were full, glistening, which had to mean she understood. Would she forgive him though?

He squeezed her hand, loading his gaze. 'Thing is, I never expected you to come along, but you did. I was moping because I'd just handed *my* conference over to Arlo, and you jumped into that lift laughing, and you seemed like sunshine to me. I was praying that the lift wouldn't get fixed, but when it started moving I realised that, because of who I am, asking you out was impossible, so I forced myself to walk away.'

'Oh, Raff.' Her eyes were soft on his, glistening more.

'But then there you were again at the basilica, and it felt like, I don't know, fate or something. I couldn't not come over, but I didn't have a plan, or any expectations. I simply wanted to *be* with you, bathing in your sunshine. I told myself that as long as I didn't let things go too far, as long as I didn't hurt you, then it would be okay.'

Her gaze slipped for a beat. 'That explains why that first night you wouldn't—'

'It isn't that I didn't want to.'

'I kind of got that at Parc Güell…'

'Not my finest hour.'

'And Brianne was what…?' Her eyebrows flickered towards a frown. 'An excuse…?'

'A plausible reason, in lieu of the real one…'

Her eyes clouded. 'But you could have told me then, surely…?'

'What, and have you look at me differently, treat me differently?'

'I wouldn't have…'

'But I didn't want to take that risk because you seemed to like Raffiel the architect, the normal guy. I was scared that if I told you the truth then you'd disappear on me, and I didn't want that to happen.'

'But if you'd told me, then I'd never have had to…' she faltered, and then her eyes came back to his, glistening all over again '…then I'd never have had to lie to you about who I was.'

'You thought it would bother me?'

Weariness in his gaze. Gentleness.

'I don't know.' She felt her thoughts jostling, pushing, and pulling. 'You'd just been telling me about Brianne, about how you didn't feel like a whole person, and I panicked. I thought my title would intimidate you…'

A smile touched his lips. 'It doesn't.'

Of course not. He was a prince. She was a Lady. It was almost poetic. So why wasn't there relief tingling, a sweet lightening sensation happening?

'Dulce…?' His eyes clouded and then his fingers tightened around hers. 'What's wrong?'

'I'm just…' She felt her words fading. Last night, he *had* been going to tell her who he was. Undeniably. At the dance, promising to tell her later about the new *challenges* he'd mentioned in his speech, and there'd been that urgent edge on his voice when he'd asked the driver to raise the privacy screen, urgency she'd interpreted as…and then he'd pulled away from her in the stateroom, trying again. *And* he'd given her the necklace, chosen with obvious care. Pearls.

Platinum!

After all the sidestepping, last night he'd been set on telling her the truth, but why? Why then?

She drew him back into focus. Concern in his gaze, but behind it, something burning, something that had been burning all night long, something she'd felt in his touch, in the way he'd made love to her. *Oh, God!* She felt a sob wanting to rise. Was Raffiel in love with her? Was that why he'd suddenly felt compelled to tell her the truth?

She felt her heart twisting out of its socket. It was what she'd wanted, wasn't it? Because she was in love with *him*, had been from the first moment, but now he was somehow a prince, a prince who was soon going to be a king, a king who was going to need someone confident and poised by his side, sure of who she was, and maybe that was where he was going with all this, where this was all leading, but she wasn't confident and poised, was she? She was a girl with a title she couldn't use, hiding in Devon, making her wonky vessels, stamping *Dulcie Brown* on the bases because she was too scared to be Lady Dulcibella, to take the good and bad that came with it.

Her heart seized. And that was the truth right there, the real reason why she hadn't told Raff who she was. Maybe five per cent not wanting to spook him, but a hefty ninety-five per cent because Fendlesham wasn't all tea with Amy Madison and playing dress up with Georgie and Tilly. It was whispering at school and burning cheeks. Having. To. Endure. And it was weaponising Tommy. Causing. Pain. It was Pandora's box, a stuck genie festering in the bottle, impossible to open, impossible to talk about.

'Dulce…?' His hands were suddenly on her shoulders, his gaze deep and full. 'Look, I know it's been a hell of a day so far, but we're still here, aren't we, still standing? And maybe this isn't the best time, but I want to know…' He swallowed. 'I *need* to know if you can see—'

'Camisa bonica, Senyoreta Dulcibella!'

Raff flinched just as her own heart jumped. And then there were more voices, and a rattling whirr of camera shutters from the quayside, flashes blinding her, and Raff's strong arm going around her, her feet barely touching the deck as he bundled her inside.

'Are you okay?' He was breathing hard, searching her face, fury dancing behind his gaze. Protectiveness. That whole irresistible noble thing he had going on.

And then her heart was buckling, hurting. He'd been about to ask her if she could see a future for them. It had been there in his eyes, the hope unwinding, but how would it be, dating him, continuing? Would it be like this, lenses aimed all the time, taking her apart, even on a private yacht?

Yes…

Because it happened all the time, celebrities caught unawares for the gossip mags. And now she was 'it' for the second time in twenty-four hours, on the way to going viral in nothing but Raff's dress shirt, and, just like with Charlie, she couldn't hit back, couldn't *do* anything, except… Her heart pulsed. She *could* go home. Not to Devon—no security there—but to Fendlesham. The family wing was private. Private garden. Nice high walls. Georgie would understand…

'I'm so sorry, Dulcie.' Raff's hand came up, stroking the hair away from her face, tenderness in his touch. 'I'm not used to this…' And then his face darkened into a study of self-admonishment. 'But I *should* have seen it coming. Gus always had the press on his tail, and I know it wore him down sometimes…'

Blaming himself when it wasn't his fault, when he'd been so quick getting her inside, shielding her, protecting her, but he couldn't protect her from everything, from the fear and turmoil mounting inside. His touch was soothing, stirring a familiar ache. With her whole heart she wanted to lean into it, go with it, but if she did…

'Raff, I want to go home.'

His hand stilled. 'To England?'

She nodded.

And then the light was draining from his eyes. She closed hers so she didn't have to watch, so she could string some words together.

'I'm not what you need.' She felt tears burning behind her lids, an ache filling her throat. Maybe she was overreacting, but she couldn't help the way she was feeling, couldn't switch off the impulse to hide. 'I'm sorry. I care for you so much…' *more than you'll ever know* '…but I can't do this.'

There was a long, deep silence, and then he was removing his hand, stepping back. 'I understand.'

She felt her heart collapsing. Did he though? Could he see the tangle inside her, the fear and the anger, the hopelessness, and the love?

He breathed in audibly. 'The royal helicopter's your best bet if you want to avoid the press. It'll take you to the helipad at the Regal, or to the airport if you want. Barcelona, or Girona or Reus…' His voice was cracking now, putting cracks in her heart. 'I'll go prime the pilot.'

CHAPTER FIFTEEN

Six weeks later...

'MORE CHAMPAGNE?'

Dulcie glanced at the bottle. She *wanted* more, yes, but she'd already had two top-ups, and getting any tipsier wouldn't do. She was on team bridesmaid, after all.

'No, thank you.' She smiled at the waiter, taking the opportunity to detach herself from the little group of guests she was with.

Mingling wasn't hard, nodding and smiling, framing the occasional interested exclamation, but it was dull. Even dissing those awful people from the past had felt pointless and boring. She looked over the lawn to where Georgie was standing, resplendent in ivory silk, looking every inch the perfect bride. Laughing with Peter, in love, glowing with it. Happiest day and all that. Georgie deserved nothing less.

She swallowed hard and headed for the shade. It was tempting to sit down, but in spite of the warm sunshine there was a faint moisture clinging to the grass that would undoubtedly mark silk, and damp splotches were not a good look for a girl who'd already blotted her copybook by being photographed in only a dress shirt on the third deck of the Brostovenian royal yacht. So it was standing, nursing a half-empty glass, trying not to think about Raffiel, trying not to let the ache inside show.

She drew in a long breath. If only she could stop seeing that hope in his eyes, hope that there could be a future... Her stomach tightened. There couldn't be, of course, but it was still a torment, remembering. Those eyes. And his kiss. His touch. His smile. All the things she loved, missed, but the price was too high. She couldn't pay it, couldn't bear the scrutiny that would come if they were together. Just...*couldn't*!

She shook herself, lifted her glass to her lips. At least there was Fendlesham!

The sudden compulsion to return had come as a surprise. Maybe telling Raff about it had thrown it up her charts somehow, but, whatever, she was glad. Of course, because of the photographs she'd had some explaining to do to her parents, admitting the obvious, that she and Raff had had a thing, but she'd downplayed it, pretended it hadn't meant anything.

Maybe it had made her seem a bit wanton, but that was better than letting them conjure any fanciful notions. And then somehow, one explanation had led to another, and suddenly she'd been telling them all about Charlie, and it hadn't felt so hard because she'd already been through it with Raff. They'd been shocked, of course, horrified, angry, but she'd smoothed their fury down, then gone on to explain about Tommy. More horror, more sadness, but she'd told them she was fine, and she'd felt fine inside saying it, so it had to be true.

She looked up into the canopy. Leafy air. She breathed it in, pulling it all the way into her lungs. Yes, she *was* fine. Motivated actually. Brimming with energy. She felt a smile coming. She was Lady Dulcibella Davenport-Brown and she was making changes at Fendlesham. As she'd walked round the house and grounds, ideas for improvement had kept popping out. Pop, pop, pop! The counter in the café was in the wrong place. Moving it down would allow for six more covers. And the old stables were a total dead space, piled high with junk, coated in dust and dangling cobwebs. Clearing out the rubbish and removing some of the stalls would create an exhibition space, perfect for artists and makers. And the hayloft above could be converted into a mezzanine, which could be used for workshops...creative writing maybe, or felting. Whatever she could pull together. Because that was another thing she was going to do: create a programme of events that could provide extra year-round income, not a vast income, like the film location fees brought in, but enough to pay for bits of maintenance. For a start, the chimneys at the gate lodge were woefully in need of repointing!

Georgie seemed bemused by her schemes, but then Georgie could afford to be bemused. She wasn't inheriting a problem. Creighton Manor, and all the work that went with it, was going to her older brother, Jonathan. Meanwhile Georgie was waltzing off into the sunset with Peter Harrington of the Harrington Bank group, waltzing off to an impeccable six-bedroom mansion in Kensington.

Waltzing...

Her heart dipped. That night, waltzing at The Imperial, the warmth of Raff's hand on her back, the way he'd held her, turned her, that heat in his gaze, desire pulsing through, the way his lips had found hers in the hotel lobby. She closed her eyes for a beat, fighting temptation, but it was no good. She set her glass down on the grass and took out her phone.

She couldn't be with Raffiel, couldn't share his public life, but at least his public life afforded her a glimpse. Hashtag Raffiel Munoz was the place, the place she went in private, to torture herself. There were always new pictures trending. Raff at charity events, looking drop-dead gorgeous. Raff playing polo, managing somehow to look handsome in the helmet and—posted four hours ago—Raff boarding the royal jet, a burly bodyguard at his heels. Off on some royal business, no doubt, probably hating it but smiling through anyway, for duty.

It was what she was doing too, smiling through for Georgie, mingling for Georgie, being the model bridesmaid for Georgie, not hating it, to be fair, but not exactly loving it either. She slipped her phone back and picked up her glass. *Enough.* Time for some cool sparkling water and more mind-numbing conversation with another group of total strangers!

'Ten minutes to landing, sir.'

'Thanks, Jed.'

He waited for his bodyguard to disappear then met his own eyes in the mirror, levelling the tails of his bow tie for the third time. Ridiculous how long it was taking to tie the damn thing.

Come on, Raff, focus!

Not so easy when his nerves were chiming, when the hopes he'd put through the shredder after Barcelona were busy gluing themselves back together.

He let his hands fall. What if Georgie was wrong? What if Dulcie wasn't obsessing over the management of Fendlesham to fill her miserable, heartbroken hours but was doing it for the love of home, a love he'd felt coming through from the moment she'd started describing it to him? And what if her sudden willingness to participate in social events, her willingness to talk and mingle with strangers, had nothing to do with proving herself worthy of her title, and of *him*, but was simply her finding her feet again, building on the experience of Barcelona with the 'hens' who became 'girls' and then friends…?

It wasn't as if keeping a busy schedule himself had anything to do with Dulcie, or, at least, anything to do with framing a future for the two of them. Yes, successive royal duties did help to keep his mind from sliding backwards, and the evening hours he was putting in compiling a dossier about his country—GDP, resources, taxation, debt, infrastructure, population distribution—did help to keep the pain ghosts at bay, but if he was getting on with life, trying to do his best, trying to take the weight off Papa, then why couldn't it be that Dulcie was doing the same thing, helping to take the weight off her own parents, coming into her own, for herself?

But Georgie was adamant and…determined!

God knows how she'd acquired his secretary's number, but somehow she had, and then Karolina had been putting through the call, and Georgie had been berating him roundly for not being straight with Dulcie from the start, for putting her poor cousin through hell, and then her tone had suddenly shaded into concern, her love for Dulcie shining through.

'Do you love her, Raff?'

He'd felt the pain surfacing then, catching him in the chest and throat.

'Yes, I do, but she wants to live a private life, Georgie, and I must respect that, because I know how precious it is. I was free and now I'm not. I had no choice, but Dulcie does, and I won't try to persuade her to a life I don't even want myself.'

'That's very noble, I must say, but here's the thing: my shy, introvert cousin is on fire right now. She's drowning in schemes, refits, and renovations. She's planning a ceramics exhibition, workshops. "You know, Georgie, we've

got outbuildings to spare so why not use them, create new streams of revenue...?" She's relishing it all so hard, Raff, that I can't help thinking that what's really going on is that she's compensating, or she's on a mission to prove herself somehow, and the only reason that comes to mind is that deep down, subconsciously, it's all for you.'

Georgie had paused then.

'She's in love with you, Raff. I knew it in Barcelona, and I know it now. So the way I see it, if you love her and she loves you, then you can work it out. Come to my wedding, see her, talk to her. Please, Raff...'

He'd said no, told Georgie it wouldn't be fair.

God, even on the yacht, when his heart had been breaking, screaming at him to tell Dulcie he was in love with her, use his feelings to stop her from leaving, he'd resisted because she'd looked so small and broken standing there with the past surfacing in her eyes, everything she'd been through with Charlie, the cruel exposure, that frustrated helplessness. In that moment he'd known categorically that whatever he was feeling, he couldn't use love as a weapon, so instead he'd pushed his pain down and steeled himself to be strong for her, organising the helicopter so she could escape.

But Georgie must have steeled herself too, for victory. For the past two weeks she'd been the voice in his ear, feeding him hope, stirring his feelings so hard that now he couldn't even get his fingers to work, working on him so relentlessly that now, somehow, he was on the royal jet, on his way to her Oxfordshire wedding reception, the plus one Dulcie didn't know she had. His stomach roiled. What was waiting for him? Happiness or heartbreak?

'Sir...?'

Jed again. All one hundred and seventy pounds of him.

'The pilot says you need to take your seat for landing.'

'Thanks.' He sucked in a breath and attacked the tie again, working it into a passable bow, giving it a final tug. 'I'm coming.'

Dulcie scanned the seating plan, felt her heart sinking. Why on earth had Georgie marooned her on a table with a collection of Peter's elderly relatives? Nancy, Edward, Posey, Crispin, Henry, Harriet, and JJ. She hadn't come across JJ yet, but she'd attempted a conversation with Posey in the garden earlier. It had been a bit of a comedy show since Posey was hard of hearing. Come to think of it, so were Great-Uncle Crispin and Great-Aunt Harriet. As for Great-Uncle Henry, he was likely to spend the entire dinner asleep because he'd been sozzled and swaying when he'd passed her not twenty minutes ago. She eyed a passing tray of champagne. Maybe getting sozzled was the right idea!

'Excuse me, Lady Davenport-Brown…?'

'Yes…' She turned. It was Felix, Lord Rayner's butler.

Felix inclined his head, leaning in. 'I'm sorry to disturb you but Jasper Júlio has arrived…?'

'Jasper Jú—'

Her breath stopped. And then her limbs were turning to rubber. JJ! *Raffiel!* Here? But how? Why? And then an unexpected sob arrived, thickening in her throat, straining at her chest. *Georgie!* She was behind this. It had *her* fingerprints all over it. That extra little twinkle going on in Georgie's eyes every time she'd looked over. She'd put it down to their reclaimed closeness, to wedding-day sparkle, but it wasn't. It was this…this plan hatched in secret… Oh, God! And Raff had colluded, was here. *Here!*

'Are you all right, madam?'

No. She most definitely wasn't *all right*. What to think? What to feel? How to pin a single thought down when her blood was rushing, and her heart was thrashing, and tears were burning. She swallowed hard. But she *must* think. Because Raff was here and it had to mean he wanted them to try, wanted *her* to try. Could she? Could she let go of her fear—for him—so she could *be* with him instead of missing him every second of every day? Oh, God, just the thought of him, those eyes, those lips, those strong arms, the safety inside them…

She felt her breath slowing. Because that was how he'd always made her feel, wasn't it? Safe. Protected. It was why she'd been able to open herself up to him, letting out all the hurt that had been dragging her down, cramping her style, and she was stronger for it, steadier. And that steadiness had given her the courage to open up to her parents, let them in again, and it had cleared space in her head and in her heart, space she'd been able to devote to her beloved Fendlesham. She was pulling her weight, doing her bit, and she'd been doing her bit at this wedding too, circulating, mingling, not loving it, but the thing was she *could* do it, was *doing* it, and, with Raff by her side, maybe she could do it better, come not to dread it, and maybe having *her* by his side would help him too, help him face what was coming.

Could… It was a word full of possibilities, the key to a world of possibilities. She felt a little lightness coming. And the thing was, she was wiser now, and so was Raff. No more forgetting that the press could be lurking. Knowing the enemy was half the battle. The other half was knowing…

She drew in a breath, refocusing. 'Yes Felix, I'm absolutely fine, thank you, maybe even better than fine.' She felt a smile loosening, a tingle winding through. 'So, tell me, where will I find Jasper Júlio?'

'He's in the library, madam.'

Raffiel ran his finger around his collar. It wasn't tight, just felt tight, as did his throat, and his chest for that matter. *Nerves!*

He turned away from the window, ran his eyes over the polished furniture and the leatherbound volumes lining the walls, only half taking them in. Maybe *Jasper Júlio* would make her smile. It had seemed like a good way to forewarn her, because no way had he been going to just walk up to her in front of everyone. She'd have hated that, being on display *again*. Because of him, she'd been on display quite enough already, in the hall of columns, in the lobby of The Imperial and—he felt his stomach shrinking—worst of all, on the royal yacht.

No, there'd be no public sighting of the two of them at this wedding or anywhere else until…his heart quivered… *unless* it was what she wanted. He felt sweat breaking along his hairline. Would it be what she wanted? Georgie thought so but that didn't mean—

The door creaked, yanking him round, yanking his breath away.

'Jasper Julio, I presume…?'

Blue eyes gleaming, a smile tucked into the corners of her luscious mouth. Her dress was pale green silk, and… she was wearing his necklace.

He felt his heart filling, a smile rising. 'The one and only.'

'How fortuitous.' She closed the door then stepped into the room, smiling that mischievous smile of hers.

'How so?'

She was coming nearer, sighing. 'Well, the thing is I have an ache that won't go away.'

'A spinal thing?' He took two tingling steps, stopping in front of her.

'No.' And then suddenly tears were mounting from her lower lids, glistening. 'It's more of a heart thing.'

He held his breath, or maybe it was that he didn't dare to breathe.

'It's a full-on love thing, to be honest. Been going on for ages.'

So Georgie was right.

He felt a hot ache filling his throat. 'Ages...?'

How was it possible to be feeling so many things in the space of a single heartbeat? Joy, relief, and this huge vibrating ball of pure, bright, overwhelming love.

He had to touch her, take her face into his hands. 'Ages, as in from the very first moment? Because that's how long I've had it...'

Her eyes closed as if she was savouring the words, and then she was looking at him again, stealing his breath, his heart, his soul. 'You love me?'

'Oh, Dulce, why else would I be here? I love you with every breath in my body.' Tears were escaping from her eyes now, rolling down her cheeks. He caught them with his thumbs, feeling a scald behind his own lids. 'I wanted to tell you that day on the yacht, but I didn't because I didn't want it to feel like pressure...'

'Oh, Raff, are you for real?' And then she was smiling, wet-eyed. 'I wanted to say it too, so many times, but I was too scared, because love at first sight is mad, right, like a total fairy tale?' And then her smile faded a little. 'So, what happens now?'

Eyes to drown in, that sweet mouth he needed to claim, taste, explore.

'I think we kiss, and then...' He brushed his lips over hers, feeling the familiar pulse spike and a swell of pure, overwhelming happiness. 'Then in true fairy-tale tradition, I think we live happily ever after.'

'Mmm...' He felt her lips curving under his, her cheeks lifting. 'I like the sound of that...'

EPILOGUE

*Breaking: King Raffiel Munoz marries Barcelona lover
Lady Dulcibella Davenport-Brown!*

AFTER CAUSING A *stir with their passionate antics in the
lobby of The Imperial Hotel, at the Architects Against
Homelessness Charity Ball in Barcelona last year, King
Raffiel Munoz of Brostovenia and Lady Dulcibella Davenport-Brown tied the knot today in a lavish ceremony at
the English bride's family seat, Fendlesham Hall.*

*For a Brostovenian king to marry outside his own coun-
try is a significant break with tradition, but in a press
statement issued two days before the wedding, King Raffiel was determinedly unapologetic.*

*He said, 'Fendlesham is dear to my fiancée, and my
fiancée is dear to me. I don't care where I marry her, as
long as I marry her.'*

*King Raffiel has been quick to establish his own style
of monarchy, so this particular departure from tradition
is very much in keeping.*

*The marriage ceremony was not broadcast live, but has
been recorded for future release. There will, however, be
some official photographs released later today.*

The bride's dress, designed by Lady Dulcibella's cousin, Lady Georgina Rayner Harrington, is rumoured to be breathtaking.

* * * * *

BILLIONAIRE'S SNOWBOUND MARRIAGE REUNION

JUSTINE LEWIS

MILLS & BOON

For my dad, who took us to Yosemite,
even though we got snowed in.

CHAPTER ONE

SNOW IN OCTOBER around Yosemite National Park was not uncommon, but snow in September was almost unheard of. It hadn't even occurred to Lily Watson to pack her snow chains, let alone put them on her tyres as she drove along Route 41.

The snow had begun falling softly as she'd headed towards the national park. By the time she'd driven through Wawona heavy clouds had blocked out the sun, bringing an early evening across the mountains. The car windows were freezing to the touch, and there was no chance of taking a detour down to Tunnel View to catch a glimpse of spectacular El Capitan. When she reached the turn-off to Yosemite West she couldn't see much further than the reach of her headlights, let alone the famous view.

Lily drove the last twenty minutes at a cautious five miles per hour and reached the cabin just as she began to feel her tyres losing their grip on the road. But she had arrived safely and had no intention of leaving the cabin for at least a week. Maybe longer.

As she turned carefully off the trail and into the drive she looked up at the familiar wooden cabin, a well-known, well-loved refuge from the pressures and cares of the rest of the world. A glint of light in a window caught her eye, and she squinted to focus properly. The mirage—for it must be one—gave the impression a light was on inside the house.

No, it was just her eyes playing tricks. Or a reflection from a nearby cabin. Even if the closest house *was* a hundred yards away.

Lily searched her handbag for the garage-opener Meredith had given her with the house keys. Then she looked up and saw the light again. There was definitely one on inside.

Her heart hitched. Who would be in the cabin? Meredith was in LA, and Bradley was in New York. No one was meant to be here but her. She sighed at her own foolishness. Meredith or Bradley must have left a light on the last time one of them was here. Or maybe the caretaker. That was all.

The simplest explanations were usually the correct ones, and she shouldn't let her overactive imagination get the better of her. She wrote crime novels for a living, and over the years had trained her mind to jump to the worst, most dangerous conclusions.

There was no one else here. More importantly, no one else in the world knew *she* was here.

The cabin belonged to Lily's long-time friend and agent Meredith, and Meredith's soon-to-be ex-husband, Bradley. Two days ago Meredith had pressed the keys into Lily's hand and told her to come here, out of phone signal, to escape the public announcement of her separation from David. It would also give her the mental space she needed to finish her latest novel, which was woefully behind schedule and due to her editor in only four weeks.

Unlike Lily's divorce from Jack, all those years ago, which had been sudden and rushed and confusing, her separation from David had been calm and orderly—the result of decisions made by two rational adults. She and David still cared for one another, but in the past few months they'd come to realise they wanted different things in life. David wasn't prepared to give Lily the one thing she wanted and, after much soul-searching, Lily had decided that was one dream she wasn't prepared to give up.

The announcement of their separation would be made by their respective publicists via carefully drafted press releases. On their own terms.

A week or two at the cabin, free from distractions, free from the internet was precisely what she needed.

Lily had been to Meredith's cabin in the mountains many times, to write, relax and to escape. When the intrusion had been too much…when she, him, *they* had been all anyone wanted to talk about.

She pressed the button to open the garage. Nothing happened. She shook the opener and pressed it again. This time she heard a faint click in the stillness of the snow and the door began to rise. *Finally.* In mere moments she would be warm inside, with a cup of tea in one hand and soup on the stove.

She closed her eyes and stretched her arms, tilted her neck from side to side. Her neck clicked; she felt older than her thirty-two years.

When Lily opened her eyes her headlights flashed across the shape of a vehicle already in the garage. A black sports car, parked slap-bang in the middle of it. Like it owned the place. An Aston Martin.

A chill slid down her spine. Aston Martins always reminded her of *him*. Never mind the obvious James Bond reference, they were her ex-husband's car of choice. At least they had been ten years ago. It would be foolish to think he hadn't changed since then. Either way, who cared? Because the car could *not* belong to him. Last she'd heard, Jack was still living safely far away on the other side of the country in his Manhattan penthouse.

Though it was strange that Meredith hadn't mentioned there would be a car in the garage...

Bradley. It must be something to do with Bradley, Meredith's soon-to-be ex-husband.

But even that was strange. Why would Bradley leave a car all the way up here? It wasn't as though there was any public transport in this part of the world. It was the wilderness. With no phone signal. It wasn't as though he could've called an Uber to take him to the airport.

And as far as Lily knew neither Meredith nor Bradley owned an Aston Martin.

Lily lifted her foot from the brake and carefully manoeuvred her car into the narrow space the rude owner of the sports car had left between the car and the wall. Maybe Bradley had let some local friend leave a car here? Or he'd bought a new car in his efforts to spend more money while his divorce was being finalised.

Or a murderer had used the vehicle to abduct someone and stored it here to frame Bradley...

Lily giggled to herself. Yes, she had a novel to finish— but it wasn't that one.

The internal door between the garage and the house was suddenly flung wide open and a large golden retriever jumped through. It stopped in Lily's headlights and started barking frantically. Lily slammed her foot on the brakes with such force that even at the slow speed she was travelling her head hit the headrest with a thump.

Her heart pounded in her throat.

So the murderer was still inside, hiding the body or...

Before she could think of any more scenarios for her next book, or even reverse her car and save herself from whoever—or whatever—was going to emerge from the house, a tall, solid figure followed the dog out of the house and into the garage.

The light from the next room—the laundry—only half lit the man's face, but sadly she'd have known his silhouette anywhere.

He gripped a long solid object in his hand. Maybe a torch or a hammer? In the shadows, Lily couldn't quite tell. He held it at chest height, not threatening her with it, but protecting himself nonetheless.

He wouldn't know who she was. She had the advantage of the angle of the light at least. She could see him, though it was unlikely he could see her beyond her headlights. And Lily had another advantage. While Jack Thorpe was many things—billionaire, CEO, heir to one of America's largest media fortunes and the ultimate disappointment as a husband—he was not a psychopathic serial killer.

She took a deep breath in a futile attempt to calm her racing heart. It was a mix-up. Possibly the world's most awkward one, but still just a mix-up. Not a potential hostage situation.

But that didn't explain why on earth he was here.

Not that it mattered; he'd be leaving in a moment.

She couldn't leave. The snow was too deep and she didn't have chains.

The dog continued to bark, but Jack grabbed its collar and held it next to him. Lily kept her headlights on and even turned them to high beam, to make absolutely sure he wouldn't catch a glimpse of her before she was ready.

Jack shielded his eyes when the brightness increased as she drove her car fully into the garage. He pulled the dog closer. It was a healthy golden dog, with a shiny coat. He'd had a dog just like it all those years ago, but with a sudden stab of pain in her chest she realised this couldn't be Rosie. This dog was far too young, too sprightly.

Rosie had been seven or eight years old ten years ago: she must have crossed the Rainbow Bridge by now. A memory Lily hadn't revisited in years jumped back into her mind—that of walking with Jack and Rosie through the Rambles in Central Park.

He'd loved that dog.

He'd loved that dog more than anyone.

This dog, New Rosie, was rising off her front paws as Jack held her collar. Lily shut off the engine. The man and his dog slunk slowly backwards to the internal door, and he raised the object in his hand.

She might have turned off the engine, but she wasn't ready to dim the lights.

Lily took a moment to put herself in the other person's shoes—a skill she'd practised all her life, first as an actor, then as an author.

If I were in a cabin in the middle of a snowstorm and a strange car with an unidentified occupant opened my garage and drove their car into it, I would probably grab the nearest blunt object too.

Or run.

Or...

The sight of Jack made her thoughts wander. Hair, thick and dark, made for running your fingers through. Shoulders a swimmer would train years for. Cheekbones so chiselled they must be illegal in some states. But she could handle all that. It was his clear blue eyes and the way she felt his gaze in every cell of her body that was more problematic.

She wished he would run—get into his car and drive away and never return.

Jack Thorpe was lots of things, but she'd never known him to back away from a fight.

She flicked off her lights.

Jack steadied his heart rate with deep, slow breaths.

Whoever had an automatic opener to Bradley's garage

probably *wasn't* a serial killer, even though Daisy was carrying on as though they were.

It was a mix-up. That was all. It wasn't as though Meredith and Bradley were speaking to one another. It was probably just Meredith. Furious about the messy divorce, she'd taken it upon herself to visit the cabin one last time before she lost it in the settlement.

Jack had some sympathy for her; he knew all about bitter divorces. His own had been acrimonious, though it hadn't been messy. Lily had left with only a suitcase and made no further claims on him or his family. Despite all her entitlements agreed in their prenuptial agreement. Lily had hardly been poor, she'd earnt a pretty penny from her acting, and now, as far as he knew, she'd made a success of her writing career, but her fortune back then had been nothing compared to his own. Let alone the Thorpe family's. If Lily had engaged a lawyer to write just one letter of demand his father would have offered her a settlement larger than ten years' worth of movie fees.

But she never had.

Guilt, he told himself. The only reason someone relinquished a fortune like that was a guilty conscience.

Jack's stomach dropped. Meredith was meant to be in New York tomorrow. She had a face-to-face settlement conference with Bradley.

It couldn't be Meredith.

In all likelihood it was simply a holiday rental Meredith had neglected to tell Bradley about. A misunderstanding that would soon be fixed.

Jack reached across to the nearby wall and flicked on the overhead lights just as the car's headlights dimmed. At first he thought his eyes were tricking him—that all those memories of divorce had brought Lily to mind. But even *his* imagination wasn't strong enough to make her actually materialise in this garage. No, it was just someone who looked a bit like her.

The driver's door of the tiny hatchback opened, and slowly a figure uncurled itself from the car. The woman stood behind the open door and smiled at him. An enigmatic, closed-mouth smile. It was either a sick joke or a nightmare and he wasn't sure which. Maybe both.

She looked familiar, yet strange. Older, yet more beautiful. Her face was thinner, her skin finer, her eyes deeper. It had been a decade since he'd seen her in person, though he'd seen her image in the media more often than he would have liked. Sometimes he'd catch her being interviewed on television if she had a new book out. Too often he'd notice her face on the cover of a magazine or in his social media feed. There would even sometimes be a badly Photoshopped image of her face with his own, and a headline announcing, yet again, that they were back together.

It was beyond absurd, but the tabloids of America seemed to share a bizarre delusion that he and Lily Watson still had feelings for one another.

A fantasy that was not grounded in fact or logic.

A fantasy even he had given up on a decade ago.

Jack realised he still held the torch aloft, like a threat, and dropped his arm to his side. Lily Watson was a lot of things—fiercely intelligent, funny and determined—but she wasn't physically strong enough to threaten him. He placed the torch on the nearest shelf. Once he'd done that, she nudged her car door shut and, with one hand on a jaunty hip, ran her eyes up and down his body.

His muscles tensed. Well, if she was going to check him out from tip to toe, he'd do the same to her. She was wearing brown leather boots…tight black jeans that clung to her toned but shapely legs. An oversized cream sweater covered her torso, but through the loose fabric he could just make out the outline of her curves. Her dark hair was pulled off her face in a messy ponytail.

Even in those clothes, and after her long drive up here, she was gorgeous.

His mouth went dry, and his pulse quickened.

Which was more than a little inconvenient.

He focused instead on her car. The ridiculously tiny hatchback. Totally unsuitable for these conditions. And no snow chains.

He frowned. 'Where are your snow chains?'

'It's lovely to see you too, Jack.'

'How could you be so silly as to drive in a blizzard with no snow chains?'

He regretted his tone even as the words were leaving his mouth, shocked by how worried he sounded.

'You flatter me, really, and your concern is so sweet. Misplaced, but sweet.'

She smiled at him, as if to disarm him, and she almost did. There was a pain in his gut as though someone had pressed a thick dagger up against it. But he steeled himself, held firm, and the blade didn't penetrate.

'I'm thinking about the search and rescue workers who'd be forced to risk their own necks to come out in this weather and look for someone too reckless to put on chains. I'm thinking of the poor person who'll find the wreckage of your car and your mangled, decomposing body after it's fallen over the edge of one of Yosemite's impressive vertical drops.'

That was all. He didn't wish Lily dead—of course not. But the shiver running up and down his spine at the thought of her being injured was surely just the cold.

'Oh, you're such a softie. And here I was thinking you didn't care about me.'

She fluttered her eyelids. He was sure she hadn't been

this sarcastic all those years ago, but maybe he just didn't remember.

No. He remembered everything about Lily Watson and the two years, six weeks and one day they'd been together.

She walked around the back of the car and opened the back. Seriously, the car was hardly bigger than one of the ride-on lawnmowers at his father's Long Island estate. It was a miracle she'd made it here safely at all.

'It wasn't snowing when I left, and the forecast was for rain. It's only September, for crying out loud.'

A flurry of snow blew into the garage behind her. For a moment they both looked out into the darkness. He could only see as far as the lights from the house stretched. The cold air reached right through the garage, where he stood with only thin socks covering his feet.

Lily turned from the snow and walked to the wall where the internal garage control was located. If she was familiar enough with this place to know where that button was she'd been here before. That didn't mean she was staying now.

'Wait!' he called.

'You want more snow to come in? Or are you about to get into your car and leave? I assume you have chains, given the dressing down you've just given me?'

'I'm not going anywhere—but you will be.'

She laughed—a musical laugh that reminded him of a song he hadn't heard in years. And, like a song that had once been his favourite, the melodic sound transported him instantly back over the years, to a simpler, happier time.

No. Just because he'd been oblivious to life's complications and obstacles back then, it didn't make it a 'simpler' time. Besides, any happiness he might have thought was his had been just an illusion. And any trust he'd placed in anyone had been naïve.

'As you kindly pointed out, I don't have any chains—and

I wouldn't want to risk anyone's neck. You, since you're so concerned for the search and rescue workers, presumably do have chains, so you can drive right on out of here.'

Damn. Why had he made such a big deal of her lack of snow chains? The danger she'd put herself in? The danger she'd just escaped? It wasn't as though he had chains either.

But you didn't drive in a blizzard and you weren't planning to. You still aren't. You're both stranded.

He groaned. He didn't want to show his hand—but, really, could the week get any worse? First his father and those stupid papers. And now this: stuck in the middle of a blizzard with his ex.

Lily left the garage door open and walked around to her open car. Her tight black jeans stretched over her bottom as her hips swayed.

Jack dragged a deep breath of cold air into his lungs and his chest stung. Of all the places, in all the world, why was Lily Watson here? Now? It couldn't be a coincidence. This week of all weeks.

'What are you doing here?' he demanded.

'Meredith suggested it,' Lily said as she pulled out a small suitcase.

Meredith and Bradley owned the house.

A few weeks ago Bradley had told Jack, 'I'd rather stab my own eyeballs out than ever speak to that woman again.'

Jack could easily believe that Meredith had no idea Bradley had lent the cabin to Jack. And when Jack had asked Bradley if he could use the place Bradley would likewise have had no idea Lily would be here.

It was plausible.

But not exactly probable.

'Is she still your agent?' Jack asked.

'Yes—and she ordered me to come. I'm getting close to

my deadline, and she thought a change of scenery would help me finish the book.'

Lily was an author now. Jack hadn't followed her career closely—he had to maintain his sanity somehow—and he certainly hadn't read any of her books. He'd rather, as Bradley had so eloquently put it, stab his own eyeballs out.

Lily lifted a cool box out of the car and placed it on the ground. Then she reached in for a black backpack and shut the rear door. Daisy had stopped barking and sat on her hind legs obediently as he watched Lily unpack. Some guard dog she was. Lily slung the backpack over her shoulder and wheeled the case towards the door.

A large gust of wind blew a burst of cold air in through the wide-open door. Lily's shoulders clenched in a shiver. She kept moving towards the door. And him.

'Why here?' he asked.

'Why not? This is Meredith's house too. She's as much right to lend it out as Bradley.' Lily stopped a few feet from him. 'I could ask you the same thing. Why are *you* here?'

'Shoulder surgery. I've come up here to recover. Doctors' orders.'

'You've come to the middle of nowhere, away from all medical help, to recover from surgery and—what? Go climbing?'

The left side of her face cocked into a smirk. Okay, maybe he hadn't come up with the world's best excuse, but it was plausible.

Not probable, but plausible.

'Besides, don't you have half a dozen weekend places of your own?'

She was right, but he couldn't argue with her without revealing the real reason he was here. Off the grid. Somewhere he wouldn't be found.

Dropping the handle of her suitcase, Lily crouched down

to dog height. She held out her small hand. Daisy sniffed Lily's fingers, then moved in quickly for a cuddle. Not only was Daisy not a guard dog, she was also a traitor.

Lily stroked the pup's head and whispered something that sounded like, 'You beautiful girl…you good girl.' Lily cooed and Daisy basked in the adoration as though *he* hadn't been telling her how beautiful she was just ten minutes ago.

He'd never been jealous of his dog before, but the way Lily was stroking Daisy, rubbing her cheek in the dog's fur, stirred something in him. Or maybe it was the look of unguarded pleasure on Lily's face. A look he hadn't seen in years. A look he now realised he'd purposefully forgotten.

'I need rest, that's all. I want peace and privacy. I have my doctor's blessing.' He mirrored her smirk back at her, but she was too busy petting Daisy to notice. 'Besides, I was here first. You could go anywhere.'

'No, I can't. Unlike you, I don't exactly have half a dozen houses to choose from. What's her name? What's your name, beautiful girl?' Lily asked Daisy.

'How do you know she's a she?'

'She is, isn't she? You've always had girls. Rosie… Holly.'

At the sound of his old dogs' names the dagger that had been pushing against his stomach pressed in sharp. 'Daisy,' he muttered. 'Her name's Daisy.'

Lily stood and brushed her hands on her jeans. 'Daisy? I sense a botanical theme. Including me!' She laughed, that same musical tune of cascading notes, and ruffled the fur on Daisy's head again. 'Hey, sister. Either he likes girls with flowers for names or I reminded him of one of his dogs.'

Holly, Rosie, Daisy… He knew he named his dogs after flowers—his mother had named Holly, his first retriever, and it had gone from there. But it had never occurred to him that Lily was part of that theme.

He'd been four when his mother had given him Holly. The same week she'd told him she was leaving to go and live in Paris. The unexpected memory of his now long-dead actress mother further added to the feeling of unease that had taken up position in his stomach.

It was a coincidence.

He'd sought Lily out because she had been impossibly pretty and he had been a shallow twenty-two-year-old.

Nothing more.

'Hang on—'

But before he could protest about likening Lily to one of his dogs, or even tell her his dogs were far more loyal than she would ever be, she grasped the handle of her suitcase and moved towards the door. And him.

When she was a foot away, she stopped. He was wide enough to block her passage through the doorway unless she was prepared to brush her supple body past his. And he was reasonably confident she wasn't. He looked her up and down. He felt himself stir slightly. If she were anyone else in the world he wouldn't mind those curves brushing up against him. But this was Lily Watson, and he definitely didn't need or want her curves anywhere near him.

He couldn't leave. Even if he wanted to. He'd come here for a good reason and that hadn't changed. There were very few places in the world these days without an internet signal. Even planes had Wi-Fi now. The landline out of this cabin was his only link to the rest of the world. No television, no internet. He was utterly uncontactable. The only person who knew he was here was Bradley.

She made to walk through the door, but he spread his legs and she halted her forward motion just in time to avoid bumping into him. His feet were numb from standing on the freezing concrete floor. He didn't care.

'I told Meredith not to tell anyone I was coming here,' she said.

There was no love lost between Jack and Bradley's soon-to-be ex-wife, Meredith. Jack didn't dislike her personally, but he associated her too closely with Lily. Even though his best friend was still raw with anger and pain over the breakdown of his marriage, a tiny, guilty part of Jack was relieved that Meredith was out of Bradley's life and therefore out of Jack's. It meant his final connection with Lily was gone.

Meredith had been instrumental in helping him meet Lily. She'd been Lily's agent, and a good friend even then. When Jack and Lily had separated he'd made an unspoken pact with Meredith: Jack would never ask about Lily and Meredith would never mention her in front of him. However, he had never been able to shake the feeling that Meredith still held a grudge.

As though he was the one in the wrong and not Lily.

And anyone who knew anything about Jack and Lily's divorce knew *that* wasn't true.

Lily being at the cabin today was a stupid mix-up, that was all. It was a coincidence. Even if it felt a little like the universe was trying to tell him something.

Jack didn't want anyone to know he was in Yosemite and Bradley had honoured his trust by not telling anyone. But, Jeez, couldn't Bradley have at least emailed his wife to tell her that the cabin was to be occupied?

'And I told Bradley the same thing.'

'I figured… Look, it's obviously a mix-up, and since I can't leave until the snow clears you'll have to. Since you have snow chains…' She raised a perfect eyebrow in challenge. 'You *do* have chains, don't you?'

Jack looked out into the darkness at the pile of snow that had fallen on the driveway in the time they'd been talking. He stepped over to the control on the wall and pressed it. The door began to slide down and shut the night out.

Of course Lily took that opportunity to slip past him and into the house.

She shouted over her shoulder. 'Don't take too long to pack. If you leave soon you'll make it to the lodge by nine. They probably have rooms available.'

It didn't matter if the lodge had rooms or not. Neither of them could leave without risking their lives.

'You're not going anywhere tonight,' he admitted.

'But you are? Good.'

It had been over a decade. And though it didn't appear as though she was any less stubborn, he would show her that he had grown up. He'd be the bigger person.

'Neither of us are going anywhere. It's snowing and dark. And for crying out loud, Lily, I don't have chains either. We're both stuck here.'

CHAPTER TWO

STUCK.

It's probably just for the night. You can handle this.

In the meantime, her stomach felt as though it was eating itself and her bladder was stretched to its limit. Dinner with Jack was the only option that wouldn't result in her keeling over from hunger and wetting herself. Talk about an impossible choice.

The first thing that hit her when she struggled through the door with her heavy bags was the warmth. The second was the smell. Onions and garlic frying. It smelt better than any of the frozen meals she'd brought with her.

'I'm in the main bedroom—you'll have to take another room,' he said as she wheeled her suitcase in through the door and to the right. Lily paused. She usually took the main room, but if Jack had slept in those sheets then it was the last place she wanted to lie.

Never mind; the lower wing would be fine. It had two bedrooms, both small, but she'd manage. As long as she had her own space.

'I usually sleep down there anyway,' she said, turning to look at him.

Jack had strong, definitive brows. He raised one of them in response. In contrast to the darkness of his hair, below his brows were two familiar piercing blue eyes. Eyes she'd used to lose herself in…eyes she couldn't even look at now.

Instead, she turned, breathed in deeply, and took in her surroundings.

Bradley called the cabin his 'shack', which was an attempt at humility. Or humour. It was a luxurious house, larger than Lily's own, fitted out with every convenience anyone wanting to escape the rat race could possibly want.

The main wing, now occupied by Jack, was up half a flight of stairs at the top of the slope. It had a bedroom and bathroom and opened out to a deck with a hot tub and views over the tree line. In the centre of the house were the living area and a large country kitchen with a dining table. The main room had a tall, raked ceiling with wooden beams. At the front of the room an enormous window overlooked a spectacular view of the valley. The room had always reminded her of the inside of an old church, a place to look out over the magnificent valley and worship nature. On the other side of the room was an imposing brick fireplace that faced comfortable, oversized leather sofas.

She loved this place. But it wasn't the same with Jack's presence looming next to her.

One night. You can get through one night.

As she stepped down to her rooms, the cool air of the lower wing chilled her.

'I just turned on the heat down there, but it may take a while,' Jack called after her.

Lily heard the gentle hum of the furnace and the warm air circulating through the rooms began to warm her bones, relax her, and yet…

She should have thrown her car into reverse as soon as she'd seen Jack's car in the garage. She could have driven back to Wawona slowly.

No, you couldn't. You'd just driven four hours from Mon-terey. There's a blizzard. And you need the bathroom.

Lily dropped her suitcase at the bottom of the short flight of stairs leading to the lower wing. These rooms looked out into a peaceful wall of green—not that she could see any-thing through the early darkness and the blizzard. She'd be happy here. Even happier tomorrow, once Jack left. She chose a bedroom and pulled the curtains shut to keep in the warmth.

Suitcase deposited, Lily went back to the garage to get the cool box full of the food she'd need for the next week. Jack was standing in the doorway to the kitchen as she passed, his arms crossed over his ridiculously broad chest. He worked in an office, for goodness' sake. What business did he have with pecs like that?

He eyed her as she carried the box in, but she refused to meet his gaze. 'There's room in the laundry freezer.'

The laundry and mud room were next to the garage. As she unpacked the meals into the large deep freeze, she sensed someone behind her and jumped.

'Gourmet?' he said, spying her stack of frozen meals.

'I've come to write, not entertain.'

He shrugged. 'Fair enough, but I've cooked some din-ner and you're welcome to share. It'll be ready in fifteen minutes or so.'

As much as she wanted to tell him she'd wait and have frozen soup later, she was dizzy with hunger. Not eating as soon as possible was likely to be a worse mistake than eating with Jack.

Lily looked up, but unfortunately, squatting on the ground as she was, her eyes came to just below Jack's crotch level. He wore a thick plaid shirt and grey track pants—more mountain man than CEO. She didn't like seeing track pants on a man like Jack. They revealed too much, and

Jack was the last man on earth she wanted to look at from this angle.

He was larger than she remembered. Not overweight— far from it. His stomach was still tighter than most men of his age. But his shoulders seemed broader, his chest squarer.

And, in the absence of any disfiguring accident, he was still—unhappily—as handsome as ever. The open-eyed, eager boy of a decade and a half ago was now a cooler, expressionless man. His feet were planted on the floor with determination and resolve. Twenty-two-year-old Jack had never frightened her. This Jack was unknowable. Unreachable. And so far unpersuadable.

Lily made a mental note: the ex-husband in her novel would suffer a horrible, painful accident. She grinned. Writing thrillers was the best fun.

'What's so funny?'

She hadn't realised she was smiling. 'Nothing.'

She closed the freezer and went back to the lower wing.

After using the bathroom and washing her face, she opened her suitcase. She'd packed several pairs of track pants and some old sweatshirts. The perfect clothes to wear while finishing a novel and escaping the press. Entirely unsuited to appearing effortlessly fabulous while having dinner with her ex-husband.

She looked down at the jeans and soft white sweater she'd driven up in. They were the most glamorous clothes she had with her.

Not that she either wanted or needed to look glamorous for Jack Thorpe, of course. Still, her appearance should at least say, *I'm happy, I'm gorgeous, and I'm having a marvellous life without you.*

Lily rifled through her suitcase for her make-up bag,

and her heart dropped as she remembered. Back in Monterey she'd decided she'd be on her own and busy writing, so it would be pointless to pack make-up.

Lily flopped face-first on the bed.

He's already seen you like this, and you don't care what he thinks, remember? This is just an unfortunate misunderstanding. Just pretend he's any other friend of Meredith and Bradley's.

If he were any other friend she'd simply accept his invitation for dinner and not stress about it. If he were anyone else in the world she'd tell herself how she'd laugh about it when she got back home. She might even write it into a story. And she certainly wouldn't worry that her face was bare and her eyes bloodshot with exhaustion and stress.

Jack might as well be a stranger. She hadn't seen him for ten years—most of her adult life.

But Jack wasn't anyone else.

Jack-an'-Lil. She'd always thought it sounded like a type of flower. Or a nursery rhyme. Either way, 'Jack-an'-Lil' was an entity entirely separate from her. It was the portmanteau the tabloids had christened them with when they'd first started dating.

*Jack-an'-Lil went up the hill
To get stuck in the snow...*

Even after all these years she was still a punchline.

She'd had boyfriends since Jack, and even believed once she was on the cusp of marrying one of them, but people still rolled her name together with Jack's as if they were the same person. *Jack-an'-Lil.* The trashy mags still put photos of them on their front covers, touting exclusives about alleged reunions.

Lily groaned into her pillow. What would the tabloids make of *this* fiasco?

Thank God they'd never find out.

She was still the most beautiful woman in the world. Even with her face bare and heavy with exhaustion, she still had the power to stop his heart. And make other parts of his anatomy surge.

And she still couldn't stand him. It was obvious how uncomfortable she was around him. Her shoulders bristled every time they came within a few feet of each other, and her eyes were wide and on the lookout for danger.

Not that it was a problem; he didn't want her either. Not seriously, not sanely. But how could she possibly be angry with him? It wasn't his fault they were both at the cabin, and he was open-minded enough to believe it wasn't her fault either, but she seemed determined not to spend a second longer in his company than was absolutely necessary.

If anyone had a right to still be angry about what had happened all those years ago it was him. Despite that, he would show her he could put the past behind him—show her he had moved on. That would be the best way of proving that his life was wonderful and fulfilling without her. That their marriage had been a brief and unimportant blip in the story of his life.

Jack had made spaghetti carbonara—just the type of quick, simple and filling dish he specialised in. With a green salad, there would be more than enough to feed both of them. He never made small portions. He poured two glasses of Shiraz and waited.

He'd come up here for some peace and space to think. He had some big decisions to make. Probably the biggest he'd ever had to make in his life. And having Lily here, even safely tucked away in the other wing of the house, wasn't going to help at all. In fact, she was just about the last person he needed up here, looking over his shoulder, passing judgement, however silently and unknowingly.

Daisy jumped up and wagged her tail. Jack looked up to see Lily enter the room. She greeted Daisy with a smile and a rub on the head. Jack received a glare that morphed into a look of suspicion as he passed her a glass of wine.

'Shiraz. The perfect accompaniment to getting stuck in a blizzard with your ex,' he joked.

Her lips tugged up. She was trying not to smile, and she accepted the drink. 'Thank you. And thank you for dinner. You didn't have to share.'

'I know, but I'm sure we can have a pleasant meal together. We haven't seen each other for a long time.'

So much water had passed under the bridge of life for both of them. He wasn't overjoyed to see Lily, but he didn't feel the need to run off into the blizzard to avoid spending even a minute in her company.

At barely twenty, Lily had not only been pretty, but undeniably one of the most magnetic women in the world. America's sweetheart.

At thirty-two she was still beautiful, but also deeply, intensely sexy, in a way that twenty-year-olds simply didn't have enough life experience to be.

Of course he'd loved that type of sweet allure at that age; he'd only been twenty-two himself. But there was something stronger about Lily today—something that told him he wouldn't stand a chance of winning her now, even if they hadn't shared the past they had.

Jack carried two steaming bowls of pasta to the table. Lily sat and Daisy, his traitorous dog, sat by Lily.

'Here, girl,' he said coaxingly to his dog as he took a seat.

Daisy looked to him, and then to Lily, and back again. She moved slowly to Jack's side.

Lily tried to suppress another grin, this time with less success. She twirled some pasta onto her fork, lifted it slowly to her red lips, smelt it, and flicked her pink tongue cautiously across the food. Assured it was edible, she opened her lips and devoured it, before going quickly back for another, larger forkful.

Lily tilted her head to one side. 'This is great. When did you learn to cook?'

'I took some cooking classes once.'

'You? Why on earth…?'

The implication being, why should he, heir to one of the largest fortunes in the United States and all-round spoilt brat, ever need to learn to cook?

He judged it best not to tell her it had been the idea of a woman he'd been seeing for a while, although he wasn't exactly sure why that was something he didn't want to mention to Lily.

'Because I don't like frozen meals,' he replied. She raised a dark eyebrow, and he realised with a jolt that if he expected her to lay off the sarcasm he probably should as well. 'I like to be able to fend for myself, that's all.'

If you'd asked him a decade ago who the practical one of them was, it would have been Lily—no contest. She'd been able to cook, clean, iron… She'd once even teased him for not doing his own laundry.

They'd come from different worlds. She'd worked in one job or another since she was fourteen, supporting and looking after herself. His early years had been spent surrounded by servants who even picked up his underwear after him, followed by the sanctuary of boarding school where, likewise, everything had been served up to him—literally and metaphorically. Even at Harvard there'd been someone to pick up after him wherever he'd gone.

'Sure, but don't you ever just want to be by yourself?' Lily had asked him once, when he'd first taken her to his house in LA and she'd seen how many household staff he had. 'I'd hate to be surrounded by people all the time.'

Not long after, he'd realised how right she'd been. He'd liked people to do things for him, and he had been dependent upon and quite fond of his household staff in Manhattan and LA. But as he'd grown older he'd also liked to know that he could do things for himself. So if everything in his life fell apart—as it had now—he could take himself off to the middle of nowhere and be alone. Not have to depend on anyone else.

Because when it came down to it, the only person you could ever truly count on was yourself.

Jack took another sip of wine and felt warmer. He tried not to think too much about his time with Lily. If he dwelled on the end of their very short marriage he'd get very bitter, very quickly. It would be best if he understood that the woman sitting across the table from him now was very different from the one he'd known a decade ago. Just as he was a different person, it was safe to assume Lily was too. That way he could get through this evening and night politely and be able to convince her to leave first thing in the morning.

'What did you do to your shoulder?' she asked.

He put a mouthful of pasta in his mouth to allow himself time to think of a plausible story. 'It's an old injury, but the doctor said it was time to do something about it before it got worse.'

'Sensible. What was wrong?'

Suddenly everything he'd ever known about anatomy—which, he had to face it, wasn't that much—deserted him.

He took another mouthful. He could tell Lily it was none of her business, but who got coy discussing shoulder injuries?

'Torn rotator cuff,' he said.

He was pretty sure that was something in the shoulder, but whether it was a muscle or a tendon or even something that could be operated on he had no idea, and he hoped she didn't either.

'Oh,' she said.

Better get in with his own question rather than wait for another of hers. 'So, you're an author now?'

'Yes.' She kept eating and didn't expand.

'Thrillers? Crime? Right?'

She nodded.

'Why?'

He thought it was a reasonable question, but the look she gave him was as frosty as the air outside.

'Why not?'

'I mean, you starred in sitcoms, then rom coms.' When he'd first met Lily she'd been the star of the biggest sitcom of the moment—a role that had launched her into a hugely successful though very short movie career. She'd been the highest-paid female actor in the world two years running, but then shortly after their divorce she'd stopped acting for good.

Lily placed her fork down and, maybe he was imagining it, it felt as though her stare was accusing him of something.

'I may have starred in them, but I didn't write them. I've always liked reading and watching crime. It's where my ideas come from. I can think up a dozen ideas for the motivation of a murderer, but none for a romance.'

Her dark blue eyes, the colour of midnight, watched him as she waited for his return shot.

But he didn't have one. He understood what she meant. Since Lily had left him he hadn't been in the mood for romance either. There had been other women, but it was never the same. *He* wasn't the same. He'd never found a woman he could trust since Lily. And, of course, he hadn't been able to trust her in the end, either.

Just as his father had always warned him.

Reminded of his father—the father who had raised him after his mother had left them both—Jack remembered the files on his laptop and the information on the USB stick in his pocket, which he now fancied he could feel burning through his jeans. Uneasiness grew in his gut and he washed it away with another sip of Shiraz.

'Better not let David hear you say that,' he said.

'What?'

'David Parks. You're seeing him, aren't you?'

Parks was a tech billionaire. Jack understood that he and Lily had been dating for quite a while now.

'He wouldn't get touchy about something like that. He's a very practical man.'

'Sounds romantic.'

She cleared her throat. 'I don't want to talk about David.'

'Trouble in paradise?'

'I just don't want to talk about him with you. It doesn't seem right.' She studied the base of her wine glass, spun it carefully on the tablecloth.

He studied her more closely now. She'd pressed her full lips together. Lily was right. And she was right to be discreet. He knew from bitter experience what could happen if you weren't.

So Jack asked after Lily's mother, and her sister, Ruby, and she gave polite, perfunctory answers. They were well, she said. They both still lived in San Jose.

The only time her face came to life was when she spoke about her baby niece. Her eyes sparkled and her nose crinkled as she told him how Georgia was six months old and smiling and giggling. Seeing Lily let down her guard like that made something in Jack's chest loosen. He smiled as she told him a story about watching her niece try solid food for the first time. Then, as though she'd suddenly remembered who she was talking to, the wall came back up.

Jack noticed she didn't ask him about his father.

'Do you miss acting?' he asked.

She looked down, took another sip of wine, and shrugged.

That wasn't an answer; it was a rebuff. Acting had been her passion, her life, and he'd never understood why she'd given it up so abruptly. A small, niggly part of him wondered if it had had anything to do with him, but he didn't allow himself to dwell too long on that. Lily was a grown intelligent woman, in charge of her own choices. He hadn't been able to influence her ten years ago, and he figured he had even less of a chance of doing so now.

But he wanted to know the answer to his question.

'Do you ever regret giving it up?'

'I don't think regret is a very useful emotion.'

Her words were heavy with ambiguity. Was she talking about her acting career or their marriage? And if it was the latter did she not regret being with him? Or not regret the way their marriage ended?

'I'm not sure what you mean,' he said, regretting his curiosity before she'd even answered him.

'I made a decision that seemed like the best one at the time. I wouldn't be who I am today if it hadn't happened.' She waved her hand around, as though suggesting that what she really meant was, *I wouldn't be who I am today if we hadn't happened.*

'I decided to put it all behind me years ago,' she continued.

Jack's chest tightened. What did *that* mean? It had never occurred to him that Lily's career-change had been anything other than her decision, but now guilt clawed at him.

She stood and picked up her plate, then his. He watched her as she carried them to the sink.

The dip from her bust to her waist to her hip was more pronounced than it had been the last time he'd seen her. She wasn't larger—not at all. Just softer. Squeezable, not breakable. As an actor, she'd had to control her weight very strictly, losing it or gaining it—usually losing it—for whatever role she was playing.

Now she had settled into her natural weight and she seemed much more comfortable, more confident than she had ever been as a toned but slightly tense woman in her early twenties.

What had happened to her over the years? What had her life been like after him? Had she been happy? Was she happy with David? Did he treat her well? Why had she come all this way without him? Why couldn't she stay and work in Monterey?

Watching the woman in front of him move around the kitchen, stacking the dishwasher, doing simple everyday things, he suddenly missed her. Missed her more than he had in years—nearly as much as he'd missed her in the weeks and months after they'd separated.

He missed not knowing her all these years. Not knowing the things she'd done, the people she'd known, the things that had happened in her life. The stresses, the victories. The small, happy moments.

Just then, Lily turned and looked at him. She clutched a dishcloth in her hands and twisted it slightly. She opened her mouth and he waited for her to speak, but no words came out. Then he noticed she'd cleaned up the whole meal while he'd just sat there and gawked at her.

Lily couldn't remember ever having a more awkward meal in her life. First there had been that weird small talk, though she supposed she should've been grateful that Jack had been able to think of things to say to her as there was nothing she wanted to say to him. Well, nothing polite anyway.

And then he'd asked about David, and she hadn't known what to say. She didn't want to talk about her relationship with David—or rather their break-up. But she hadn't meant to lie about it. Tomorrow, when Jack went back to civilisation and a phone signal, he'd find out that she and David were no longer a couple and he'd know that she hadn't told him the truth.

Did it matter if he did? She wasn't sure.

And now there was the odd way he was watching her as she cleared away the dishes. If she hadn't known better she might have thought he was eyeing her up, even though his tone and the questions he'd peppered her with all through dinner had made it perfectly clear he was still clinging to a grudge as big as his family fortune.

As ever, he couldn't acknowledge that *he* might have something to apologise for himself.

Maybe you were checking him out a little as well?

Maybe…but only to see if the passage of time had ravaged his features beyond description.

Sadly, no, it hadn't.

His straight dark hair was cut shorter at the back and sides and left longer on the top. His cleanly shaven chin was still bisected by the same crease that had once mesmerised her.

She closed the dishwasher and pressed the start button. She had to get him out of this cabin before she started reminiscing too much.

'The snow will probably stop overnight, so I'm sure you will be able to leave in the morning,' he said.

'It won't be me leaving,' she replied firmly.

What was his problem? Why was he being so stubborn?

Clearly he found this whole situation as uncomfortable as she did. She *had* to stay—though she wasn't about to tell him why.

Yet another one of my relationships has bitten the dust, and I want to avoid the media fallout. No, thank you.

Shoulder surgery? He could go anywhere to recuperate from that. Why didn't he just go to his father's place on Martinique? The Thorpes had holiday homes on every continent. He could go anywhere on earth.

'I was here first.' He grinned.

Spoken like a true Neanderthal. 'That tactic might work in business, but it won't work on me.'

Jack's nostrils flared. 'What do you mean?'

'Stubbornness…inability to compromise. Threats. This isn't a business transaction. It's a deeply awkward social situation.'

The whites of Jack's eyes reddened. 'That isn't how I do business,' he muttered through clenched teeth.

'Whatever… Why can't you just be the one to give?'

He pushed his chair back and stood, glared at her through narrowed eyes. His jaw tensed so hard it looked as if he might crack a tooth.

'Maybe the same reason you can't?'

She threw the dishcloth down. 'Thank you again for dinner. Goodnight.'

She could make herself perfectly comfortable in her part of the house. If he didn't want to be around her, he could be the one to leave. She knew from previous bitter experience that Jack didn't like to be told he was wrong.

Lily left without a further glance and rushed back to her room. Only once the door was closed behind her did she realise her heart was racing. She fell, face-first, onto the bed and punched the pillow. She'd thought she knew how she felt about Jack.

No, you made a decision to stop thinking about Jack. It's not the same thing. You made that decision for the sake of getting on with the rest of your life. You made that decision because if you hadn't you'd still be obsessing about what happened in those few short weeks after the wedding. You made that decision so you'd stop blaming Jack. And, most of all, so you'd stop blaming yourself.

One thing she did know, even if Jack didn't, was that they were both to blame for the break-up of their short marriage. And something else she knew, beyond the shadow of a doubt, was that Jack still blamed her. Entirely.

They were different people now—they might as well be strangers—and they had to deal with this situation. He'd leave the cabin when he realised she wasn't going to. And he'd have to put up with her in the meantime.

But first a shower. To wash the journey away. And the smell that seemed to have settled on her after arriving in the mountains. The cabin smelt different with Jack here. And what was worse it wasn't a bad smell. Not remotely.

It was the same scent he'd had all those years ago. It was like visiting her mother's house and being transported back to her childhood. Smelling Jack, being in the same room as him, was like going back half a lifetime. All her memories of him slammed back into her consciousness. The places they'd gone…the things they'd done. The things they'd planned to do.

As she showered and slipped on her pyjamas, an uncomfortable ache started to grow inside her. It curled from her belly and began to claw at her chest. Bitter and sad. It was the adventures they'd never been on, the trips they'd never taken, the house they'd never built. The children they'd never had.

The ache grew, and she clutched her hands to her stomach. This morning she'd been mourning the loss of one relationship. Now she felt as if she was mourning two. And all it took was a few quick thoughts and she was suddenly questioning all the choices she'd made over her life: the jobs she'd taken and the ones she hadn't. The men she'd dated. The ones she hadn't.

She was stuck in a remote cabin with her ex-husband. Somewhere along the way she'd taken a wrong turn—but when?

Had it been when she gave up acting? No. Maybe… At the time it had felt like she didn't have a choice. Jack—or rather his father—controlled the biggest media and entertainment companies in the world. The rumours that had swirled about her and why she'd broken up with Jack had been suffocating. Producers had become wary of working with the woman who had been shunned by John Thorpe and his son. Not all of them, but enough.

If the rumours and lies had simply been in the papers she might have been able to cope. But her colleagues and co-stars had whispered about her. Speculated about what had happened right in front of her. Most days it had felt as though no one was on her side. The emotional strain had led to physical pain. Stomach ailments. Persistent insomnia. Too much weight loss. Even her hair had begun to fall out.

It had been easier just to walk away from it all. Yes, she sometimes regretted her decision, because some days it still felt like the Thorpes had won. But whenever that happened she reminded herself to go easy on her twenty-two-year-old self. The pressure of being in the public eye was hard enough when one of the richest families in America was on your side. But when they were against you…? Lily hadn't stood a chance.

Of course she'd been sad about giving up acting: she'd loved telling stories, expressing herself. But when it had become too hard to get dressed or to leave the house she had tried writing, and had been eternally grateful to find she was actually good at it. Slowly and surely she had found her niche, and a new place in the world.

Was dating David where it had all gone wrong? David was a nice, interesting, successful man, who'd turned out to be a commitment-phobe. Had David made a mistake? Or had the error been hers, for not asking sooner what he wanted from their relationship? For not telling him sooner that, for her, children were non-negotiable?

Had the mistake been in her twenties, when she'd dated a string of men she didn't love—had known she could never love—because then she couldn't get hurt?

Or had Jack been her big mistake all along? If the conversation they'd had that day in Beverly Hills had gone another way would everything have been different? What if she'd been more persuasive? Managed to get him to see her point of view? What if he hadn't found her with Drake?

But she hadn't, and he had, and it had all played out the way it had.

There was no point dwelling on the 'what ifs' because it was done. It wasn't like one of her books. There was no misplaced letter that might resurface and explain away their separation as a misunderstanding. There was no long-lost relative ready to appear and reveal some secret about the past that could have saved their marriage.

No. There was nothing that could transform their break-up into anything else. They had both made mistakes. They had both done the wrong thing. They had both hurt each other.

Their marriage had ended because of what he'd said. And because of what she'd done next.

The life they'd planned remained unlived, and Jack Thorpe still smelt like expensive aftershave and freshly baked bread. Every one of her pores seemed to open up in an effort to suck in all that glorious scent. And the only air that could fill her lungs was the same air he breathed.

She *should* hate him.

She *should* loathe him.

But when it came down to it Lily knew exactly how she felt about Jack Thorpe. She just didn't like it.

Lily unpacked her computer and her papers. She was there for a reason—she hadn't lied about that—and she needed to finish her book. She would just have to do what she'd been doing with her thoughts of Jack Thorpe for the past ten years: push them to one side. Even if he was less than fifty feet away, she would bury her feelings underground and then build a wall around her heart for good measure.

Unfortunately there was no desk in this room. She'd planned on just setting herself up across the kitchen table, but her lap would have to do. She pulled the curtains wide open, to see if the snow was easing. Outside, the wood was pitch-black. An ambient light, no doubt coming from one of the rooms on the other side of the house, cast an eerie pale glow that was mostly swallowed by the vast blackness of the trees and the snow.

Sometime later the light went out, but Lily didn't notice. She typed and typed until her fingers could no longer type. She typed about a woman suspected of murdering her ex-husband.

CHAPTER THREE

SLEEP WAS NEVER going to come easy. Jack had one of the most important decisions in his life to make. And that was even without his gorgeous ex-movie-star ex-wife in the other wing.

He wouldn't think about Lily—she'd be gone soon—but his other problem was going to take more than a set of snow chains to fix.

Most decisions came easily to Jack—which was fortunate, since he spent his days making hundreds of decisions, some big, some small. But never quite like the one he had to make now.

It was still dark when he gave up trying to sleep and switched on his laptop. Daisy lifted her head and looked at him with half-open eyes, before exhaling and laying her head back down to sleep.

He had a few years' worth of deals to look at and he might as well start now. He scrolled through the files, the transactions, but nothing struck him as out of the ordinary. It might be because everything was above board. Or it might just mean that someone had done a very good job of covering their tracks.

Just after dawn, Daisy started whimpering by his bed. The sun was barely up, but they were both still on New York time. Daisy needed to go out.

Jack looked out of the window and made a quick assessment of the temperature. It was not snowing at present, but it might be about to. He grabbed his coat and put on his big boots.

He had hoped to find a chance to have some long hikes around Wawona meadow with Daisy and thinking space—not to be cooped up in the cabin for days. He did his best thinking on his feet, while moving. He walked everywhere he could in New York; he wasn't a fan of driving and absolutely eschewed limos.

Still, you couldn't get up a really good pace on New York's sidewalks, and there was only so many times you could walk around Central Park. LA was worse—the least walker-friendly city in the world—but here you could walk for ever with eye-wateringly beautiful scenery to boot.

As soon as he opened the door Daisy took off down the drive. The trails were covered in a few inches of clean snow and the road hadn't been ploughed. He decided to walk the two miles to the next junction, to see how that road was looking and whether a plough had come through yet.

The snow wasn't deep, but it had frozen into ice overnight. Neither of them could drive out with the road like this. But the alternative was spending a whole day trapped in that cabin with Lily and her judgemental stares.

Jack tilted his head up to the clouds. They were still thick and dark, and the sun was struggling to push its rays through them. There was more snow to come; he could smell it. Even if it didn't snow again, with temperatures this low the snow already blanketing the ground wasn't going anywhere fast.

He made slow but steady progress along the trail that connected the cabin with the road. Once he reached it he saw with dismay that the ploughs hadn't been through. He hadn't expected them to come down the trail, but there were a few other cabins out along this loop.

Maybe later today.

You could get your car out of here if you really wanted to. It's a high-performance car.

Yeah, but not on ice.

Was he really going to risk his own neck just to avoid spending a day or two alone with Lily? He sighed. No. She'd already destroyed his heart; he wasn't letting her get the rest of him just out of stubbornness.

The air was still, and he couldn't remember the last time he had known such silence. He could be the only person in the world. The rest of the world could drop away and he wouldn't know. Jack Thorpe, alone. Physically and metaphorically.

How had he not seen what his father was doing earlier on? How much damage had he done? Was the business salvageable? Was *anything* salvageable? Or was it all merely a terrible mistake?

He had tried to convince himself that it was the latter. A misunderstanding. But then he remembered his father's words.

'Things are bad right now; life is tougher than it used to be. We have to adapt, Jack. Sometimes it's okay to take a shortcut or two.'

The cold air stung his lungs. To the west, the sky was dark—and not because it was barely dawn.

'There's more snow on the way, girl,' he said to Daisy, who wagged her tail and danced through the snow as she explored and foraged.

He smiled. He loved this dog. He'd loved all his dogs, but Daisy was special. He'd never had to share Daisy and her affections with anyone. Daisy was loyal. Well, dogs *were* loyal. People—not men, and definitely not women— were not.

Soft, cold, white flakes started to flutter before his eyes. One landed on his cheek.

Three days ago the air in Manhattan had still been heavy with humidity, the summer still refusing to depart. His office window looked out from the fiftieth floor over Central Park and beyond to the East River. He'd been looking over the financial records for a newspaper group his father was trying to convince the board to buy. In Jack's opinion, Western State Media was a dud: it was barely turning a profit. Even if John Thorpe had negotiated to purchase it for a steal, it would still be a retrograde step.

Jack and his father agreed to disagree on the subject of traditional media—or 'legacy media', as Jack called it. Thorpe Media had made its money from newspapers, then television. Jack knew they should be looking at new and emerging opportunities in the digital world. His father was still wedded to paper, radio and television.

John Thorpe was planning on presenting the purchase of Western State Media—a legacy media group covering three western states—to the board at the next meeting. As Jack had looked through the papers that day, he'd wondered again how his father had negotiated the low purchase price.

Jack's assistant had brought him his signing mail and his second cup of coffee of the day. There had been some deeds he had to sign, and under those papers a cheque for his signature. Jack had picked it up and turned it over. It had had a name on it: John Thorpe.

Jack was really John Thorpe. His father was John Thorpe. His grandfather and his great-grandfather before that had also been John Thorpe. But Jack had always been Jack. 'John Thorpe the Fourth' sounded ridiculous, so he was only ever John on property deeds. And his marriage certificate. And cheques.

The cheque had been made out to Luc Harmon, a notorious paparazzo who often took big money shots. Jack had been about to call his assistant back but then had thought better of it. Clearly he was not meant to have seen this cheque. Someone at Thorpe Media had made a mistake. And it wasn't his assistant...

Daisy barked. He should get back to the cabin. And Lily. Hopefully she'd be awake by now, so he could give her the bad news that it was unsafe to drive. The house, as large as it was, was not big enough for both of them, but somehow they'd have to manage.

The Lily he'd known had been chatty and vibrant; this Lily was quiet, and had learned the trick of shutting up and waiting for someone else to say something stupid first.

Maybe she was entitled to.

Maybe she had been right about one thing all along.

Back at the cabin, there was no sign of her. He took off his boots and in socked feet, as quietly as he could, walked to the door to the lower wing. He leant his ear against it. Nothing.

He shouldn't care. She was probably writing, and he had things to do himself.

Jack made himself a coffee and pulled out his laptop to continue going over the major acquisitions made by Thorpe Media over the past five years.

Would five years be enough? Or did he have to go back even further?

Even as he perused the financial records, he kept one ear out for any sound in the lower wing of the cabin.

There was nothing.

Jack shut his laptop lid and stood. He checked the time. Two-thirty. He flicked the clock on the oven with his index finger and glanced outside. The snow was falling heavily now, and Lily still hadn't emerged.

Not that he was in a hurry to see her, but was she seriously going to hide in her room until the snow melted or she starved to death? If something did happen to Lily, and she was found dead in a remote cabin with her ex-husband— well, it wouldn't look good for him, would it? Who would believe Lily had died of natural causes?

It would certainly take the focus away from the scandal his father was about to face. Yeah, that would be right. His father would get away with everything and Jack would find himself wrongly accused of murder.

He laughed cynically, a deeply wicked cackle rippling up his throat. That would be typical. Bloody typical.

'What's so funny?'

Jack jumped. Lily stood at the kitchen door and rubbed her eyebrows with her fingers. Her long dark hair was tousled and one cheek was redder than the other. He'd bet if he touched her she would still be warm from bed. A loose T-shirt hid her shape, but he could tell by the way it hung off her bare shoulder she wasn't wearing a bra underneath.

'I'm going to get some breakfast,' she said.

'Bit late for that, isn't it?'

He wasn't sure why he'd snapped like that—probably because he'd been sitting in this kitchen ever since he'd got back from his walk, waiting for her to come out of her room.

'Yes, Mom. I worked late. Or early. I only just got up.' She spied the coffee machine. 'Mind if I get some coffee?'

Without waiting for an answer, she stepped past him into the kitchen and the air around him shifted as she moved to the coffee machine. Summer. She smelt like peaches. Or cherries. Or both.

'Can I make you one too?' she offered, but when she

touched the handle he knew she would feel it was warm to the touch. 'Oh, you've made some.'

Yeah, about four hours ago.

'Help yourself; there's plenty.'

Lily poured her coffee and took it over to the table with her laptop under one arm. She sat on the opposite end of the table to where his identical-looking computer sat and set hers down, opening the lid. Lily started to type and Jack could only stare at her.

She was just going to wander in, help herself to coffee and then set herself up at the kitchen table like she owned the place?

Her skin was bare, her cheeks a shade paler than the day before. Her eyes were free from make-up and she looked... younger. Prettier. A memory of her on their brief honeymoon in Paris flashed back into his consciousness. She was standing by the Seine, hair blowing in the breeze. He was realising he was the luckiest man who had ever lived.

He shook the memory away.

Knowing what he did now, he had some regrets about how their marriage had ended. Not that his behaviour had *caused* the break-up, only that maybe he shouldn't have been so quick to disagree with her about his father. *She* was still the one responsible for ending their marriage.

But, even so, he wondered for one crazy second if he could talk to Lily about what his father appeared to have done. If he could ask her advice.

No, that wouldn't help. Jack knew exactly what she would say, and the answer would not be helpful. He might also open himself up to recriminations about the past. After their conversation last night, it was clear she still blamed him for their break-up. Entirely. And, while he could now accept that he might have played a part in it by not going to her sooner, he was certainly not going to accept the blame entirely, as she seemed to expect him to.

This problem with his father was something he had to figure out all by himself.

Alone.

Not with Lily sitting at the kitchen table wearing a thin T-shirt and baring the soft skin of her shoulder. Reminding him of the past. Of the way their bodies had fitted together as if they were designed specifically for that purpose. The magical sensation of her skin rubbing against his. Of how, whenever they'd looked at one another, the rest of the world had fallen away.

Jack had no intention of leaving Yosemite for at least another week. Without his presence at the vote it was possible the board would delay voting on the purchase of Western State Media until he got back. The problem wouldn't go away in the meantime, but as long as he was here he couldn't be contacted. He would have time to figure out what to do next. His father might also use the time to reconsider his position and do the right thing.

Lily stood and brushed past Jack, going back into the kitchen proper. The pores of his skin burned as though she'd touched him as she passed. But she hadn't.

She went to the laundry fridge and returned with bread, butter and jam, and started fixing herself some toast. He was relieved she wasn't about to starve to death, but she was making herself quite at home.

'It's snowing again. I don't think either of us are going anywhere today. Or tomorrow.'

The smile she gave him was classic Lily, designed to melt hearts and minds. But he told himself he was long immune to it.

'How's the shoulder?' she asked.

'It's fine,' he mumbled.

What did someone who was recovering from rotator cuff surgery do? What *couldn't* they do? If this place had the internet, he could look it up. But one of the reasons he came here was to be uncontactable.

Lily leaned her backside against the bench and lifted a slice of toast to her mouth. She rested it on her plump lower lip and her blue eyes regarded him, wide but steely. He knew he shouldn't watch her perfect lips as she chewed, but he couldn't help himself.

As she swallowed, the tip of her tongue flicked over her red lips. She walked back to the kitchen table with her toast and put the plate next to her laptop. 'I'd like to work in here today. At the table.'

'I'm already working here.' Jack moved to his computer and stood behind it.

'Oh? Doing what? I thought you were resting. Doctor's orders.'

He couldn't tell her exactly what he was doing. He couldn't tell her what his father had done. Not when he hadn't even decided what he was going to do about it himself.

'I need the table. You can work downstairs. I think it's the least you owe me.'

Lily nearly choked on her toast. When she'd regained her breath, she said savagely, 'I owe you *nothing*.' She said the last word as if intending to cut him.

He just shrugged. On this, they would never agree.

'Do you seriously not remember how our marriage ended?' she asked.

He instantly regretted bringing their divorce up, breaking the promise he'd made to himself not to.

Now, as much as he'd tried to forget it, the memory of that night flooded his thoughts. The sight of Lily with her arms and lips wrapped around those of her co-star—Drake

Johnson—a man whose sex appeal wasn't just legendary, it was iconic.

Jack wondered for an instant what 'Drake the Rake' was up to these days, and then realised with an inward smirk that he didn't care. The main thing was, he wasn't with Lily. She'd thrown away a marriage she'd claimed was the most important thing in the world to her for a brief affair with a co-star. It was clichéd and it was pathetic.

But what had he expected? His father was right; actresses could not be trusted.

'I remember everything.' His voice was lower than he'd intended, and the air in the room suddenly became thick.

'I'm sure you think you do.'

Her eyes were rimmed with red, but he couldn't tell if it was from fury or sadness. They faced each other over the table, behind their respective computers.

She leant forward, just a fraction. 'I don't know if you're lucky or unfortunate to just see things in black and white, but my world is made up of shades of grey. I don't think our marriage ended because of one thing. I know it was more complicated than that. We were different people, from different backgrounds, with very different expectations.'

The calmer and more rational she pretended to be, the angrier he became. 'Expectations? Yeah, I didn't *expect* my wife to sleep with another man six weeks into our marriage.'

Lily sucked in a sharp breath. 'I didn't sleep with him,' she said in a whisper.

'So you say.'

'I'm not even going to respond to that. Maybe one day you'll realise that *this* is the reason our marriage ended. Not because of Drake, but because you never listened to me. And you certainly didn't trust me. Oh, and the fact that you announced our divorce before you'd even listened to my side of the story didn't help either.'

He'd found his wife of six weeks with another man; of course he was going to divorce her.

The tension in the room was crushing his ribcage. He couldn't get enough air into his lungs and his head was light. He knew what he'd seen and that was enough for him. Did it matter how far they'd gone? One glance at that kiss had been more than enough to tell him their clothes would have been off within the minute if he hadn't walked in. Lily wanted to argue over details, when the main point was that she had cheated on him.

Lily was leaning over the table now, placing her hands palm-down on it as she spoke. 'You never listened to me,' she repeated.

'I did.'

'So listen now.'

'No. It's ancient history.'

'So it won't matter if you listen to me then, will it?'

'I don't want to go over it again. The past is the past.'

Even if the past *had* just jumped up and slapped him across the face now, Lily and their marriage belonged to another life.

'What are you afraid of hearing, Jack?'

Afraid? He didn't *want* to hear the allegations he knew she was going to make about his father—the man he idolised, who'd taught him everything—but he wasn't afraid.

'I'm already set up here.' He pointed at his things on the table.

Lily let out one of her musical laughs, notes of glee cascading down several scales. Anger and humiliation coursed through his veins, and yet something in his chest softened. Lily had the most remarkable laugh. Still.

'Forget the table for a moment. I want you to listen to me. Hear me out.'

He couldn't give her that. He stood with his arms crossed.

'I have an idea,' he said instead.

'Oh, yeah?'

'Yeah. A competition. For the table.'

Her left eye twitched. 'I have an even better idea. A competition. You win, you get the kitchen table. I win, I get the table *and* you have to listen to me. Finally listen to why our marriage really ended.'

CHAPTER FOUR

'Deal,' he said.

Lily sipped her coffee slowly. Finally she would get Jack to listen to her side of the story. Finally he'd have to sit down, shut up, and hear what had really gone on all those years ago. Who cared if he believed her? She'd at least have the chance to have her say. The opportunity he'd denied her all those years ago.

What sort of competition? she wondered. If it was a battle of strength then of course he'd win; she was no match for his broad chest, tight abdomen, and thighs that were probably still strong enough to lift her and hold her against the wall behind her. But those days were far behind them. He would never again lift her effortlessly and press her against a wall as he caressed her with kisses...

Aware her gaze was stuck on his still-magnificent thighs, she lifted her eyes to his face. The smooth skin of his chin was this morning rugged with stubble. The soft lines of his jaw at twenty-something had hardened into powerful angles. Jack had always had good posture, and still did. He held his head perfectly upright, the muscles in his neck and arms clearly visible.

No, definitely not a battle of strength.

'You're supposed to be recovering from shoulder surgery. Or is that not true?'

She strongly suspected his excuse for needing to stay in the cabin was about as genuine as the one she'd given him, but she hadn't gathered enough evidence to confront him about it yet.

'Of course it's true, and I think my shoulder can withstand a little battle of wits with you.'

His eyes fixed on hers, and the longer he looked at her, the more exposed she felt. Her cheeks warmed, and heat travelled from her face into her chest. She crossed her arms and let her gaze fall on the table in front of her. If she couldn't win a staring contest with him, how was she supposed to beat him at anything else?

'What did you have in mind? Toss a coin? Rock, paper, scissors?'

'Tempting…but I think we could make it more interesting than that.'

'They're quick games; this could all be resolved in minutes.'

'Yes, but…where's the challenge in that? Wouldn't you prefer to beat me? Actually best me with your skill, not just with dumb luck?'

He was annoyingly right. Rock, paper, scissors was barely better than a coin-toss.

Like all good holiday cabins, this one had a well-stocked games shelf. Board games, cards… Jack caught her looking at it.

'I do have work to do. I don't have time for games,' she protested.

'I told you—it's snowing again and as of four hours ago the ploughs hadn't come through. You're stuck with me for a while yet.'

She was trying not to think about that. Being stuck with Jack. With his strong arms and that delicious fragrance that made her mouth water.

Battle of wits? Lily stood and moved to the games shelf to get a better look.

'Scrabble?' she asked.

'Against a bestselling author? I don't think so.'

'Chicken,' she jeered.

'Monopoly, then?' he said.

'Oh, please… If Scrabble against the author is out, so is Monopoly against the billionaire mogul.'

He clutched his chest in faux pain. It was a vulnerable gesture, one he'd used to make when they were dating and which was still strangely adorable. She pushed the memory aside. He was a different person now. *She* was a different person now.

'It should be something we both agree on.'

Jack joined her at the shelf. His scent made her nose twitch. She didn't want to breathe him in, but apparently her nose did. He wasn't wearing aftershave today, and smelt somehow of the fresh woods outside.

He picked up a deck of cards, shook them out of the box and flicked his thumb across them. The sound of the cards flipping against each other vibrated in her stomach. He looked at the cards intently, then looked down at her. His pale blue stare pricked her chest. They'd played cards a few times. Early on in their relationship. A game of strip poker might have led to one of their first times in the bedroom… If she remembered correctly, they'd both played to lose.

'Not cards,' she whispered, and he placed them back on the shelf without a word. 'What about Trivial Pursuit?' she asked, mostly to distract herself from memories of *that* game of strip poker. Of her unbuttoning his shirt and running her tongue over his hard nipples. Of him pulling down her panties with his teeth. Of the way their satiated bodies had tangled together afterwards, still pulsating, gasping with pleasure.

Lily watched Jack's long index finger hover over the box that held a chess board. 'How about chess? I was school champion,' she lied. She couldn't play chess to save her life and hoped her bluff would pay off.

It did.

'All right, then. Trivial Pursuit. You weren't the school champion of that, I assume?' He pulled the game off the shelf.

As far as she could remember they'd never played it together, so there was no baggage on that account. But, more importantly, she was a whizz at Trivial Pursuit. She'd always loved trivia—and you didn't write fifteen novels without picking up lots of pieces of semi-useless information. Jack, to the best of her admittedly outdated knowledge, was not a trivia buff at all.

'I haven't played it in ages.' *Not since last month anyway.* 'It's not really my thing.' A total lie.

'It's not my thing either, so we'll be as bad as each other.'

He smiled his goofy smile and her stomach did a backflip. What was it about Jack that made him all ruthless billionaire one moment but with one lopsided grin turn back into the kid who'd stolen her heart?

If he was a stranger she'd step towards him right now and see how he reacted. If he didn't step back, she'd take another step forward, and so on and so on, and then she might lift her heels to stand on her toes and press her yearning lips against his.

The hair on his head was dark brown—the colour of the trunks of the sequoia trees outside—but the stubble appearing on his cheeks was golden as it caught the light. His square jaw was perfectly straight, but for the dimple in the middle.

His cheeks had been smooth when they'd got married…
A lifetime ago, when she was another girl.

If only they could meet as strangers. If only she had yet
to learn how perfectly her hand fitted in his. How perfectly
her head rested against his shoulder and how perfectly their
bodies fitted together in every respect.

Her body clenched at the memory.

They *weren't* strangers—and not even a decade apart
could change that.

She wasn't made of stone. Or even wood. She was a living, breathing woman with needs and wants—and apparently an awkward overreaction to Jack Thorpe's presence.
That he was good-looking was hardly up for debate. But
she'd been around good-looking men before. Heck, she'd
acted with some of Hollywood's hottest men and met many
more besides. But none of them had managed to inspire the
same rush of hormones, the same disorientating, crazy-
making, can't-control-her-own-limbs response that Jack
Thorpe had always aroused in her.

It was latent memories—that was all. Of when they'd
first met. Of their two years together. Two years when they
hadn't been able to keep their hands off each other. Two
years when her body had ached every moment she wasn't
with him.

That time belonged to the life of another person. Even
though, according to the rest of the world, they were the
two years that still defined her.

'Let's play, then.'

She would beat him. Thrash him. Make him wish he'd
never heard of Yosemite. Or Trivial Pursuit. But she had
to play it cool.

'You get some work done,' he said. 'I'll cook an early
dinner and then we'll play. Since I'm a gentleman, I'll let

you use the table first. It'll be the last time you use it.' He grinned.

'How generous of you.'

From this evening the table would be all hers. And Jack would understand, once and for all, how wrong he'd been about her and what he'd thrown away because of his pride.

Jack waited until he was in his room before releasing the smile he'd been containing for the past five minutes.

Trivial Pursuit. *Ha!*

He couldn't remember the last time he'd lost a game. Maybe never? His veins pumped with excitement. But the satisfaction he felt at tricking Lily into playing a game she was sure to lose faded when he remembered the rest of their conversation.

How could she imply that he was the villain? That he was somehow to blame for their divorce? She was the one who'd traded saliva with Drake Johnson. He hadn't made her do it. Sure, there were some things about his marriage to Lily that he regretted. Some things that now, with hindsight, seemed like a mistake.

But she was the one in the wrong, wasn't she? What she'd done was unforgivable, wasn't it?

He punched one of the large pillows on his bed, but that did nothing to release the frustration pumping through his veins. There was a scratching at the door, and he opened it to let Daisy join him. He rubbed her head, but the walls still moved in on him.

He hadn't come here to stay inside all day. He'd come to hike until his legs ached and breathe fresh air until he'd blown the smog and dust from New York out of his lungs. Instead snow a foot deep was banked up at the door.

'So, Daisy, girl, what are we going to do?'

Daisy nuzzled him. At least he wasn't talking to himself. And Daisy's response made more sense than his father's.

John Thorpe's response to Jack's questions had been inadequate, to say the least.

The cheque to Luc Harmon had been strange, but Jack might not have even mentioned it to his father if the chairman of Western State Media hadn't suddenly died.

CHAPTER FIVE

LILY OPENED HER laptop and read over the last scene she'd written before she'd passed out at some point after six a.m. *Argh!* It hardly made any sense all. What had she been thinking when she wrote it?

She sighed. She knew exactly what she'd been thinking about.

Or rather, *who.*

The Jack she'd once known had been little more than a boy, with a boy's openness and a straightforward sweetness that was mostly missing now. Now he was guarded, cynical and darkly suspicious. His features had hardened, just like his heart. His lean shoulders had filled out somehow. His legs, while never weak, now seemed more strongly rooted to the ground, demonstrating his stubbornness.

Why was he still denying her a chance to tell him what had happened, even now?

But even though he was different, somehow he still smelt the same. He wore the same aftershave—a classic. The last word in Fifth Avenue luxury. Sandalwood, ylang-ylang and fresh citrus. That aftershave and a secret dash of what made Jack uniquely Jack. Smell was the most evocative of the senses, and it transported her back to a time like no other.

It had been a meet cuter than fifty golden retriever puppies.

Her career had been going better than she'd ever allowed herself to dream. Not that she'd had very long to think about how it might develop. She'd only been seventeen when she'd been picked up for the sitcom *My Crazy Life*, and that show's runaway success had surprised everyone—not least its young star, who had gone from Hollywood hopeful to household name within a year.

The show had been running for three years and she'd been getting used to living in LA. It had been a world away from her upbringing in San Jose with her mother and sister. They hadn't been poor—her mother said they were 'established working class'—but they were still a totally different species to the Jack Thorpes of the world.

Things had been good, but the day she'd met Jack it had felt like someone had pressed fast-forward on her life and in the space of two hours changed it for ever.

Meredith Baker had been Lily's agent for about a year back then. Meredith was a confident, extremely well-groomed, and slightly jaded woman. She'd only had a little experience as a celebrity agent when she'd first met Lily. But Lily had trusted her. Meredith hadn't been patronising, like her last agent, and she hadn't tried to mother her like the one before that. Meredith had understood instinctively who Lily wanted to be and the career she was looking for. And Meredith had made it her mission to help Lily get it.

Over lunch one day at the swankiest restaurant *du jour*, Soleil, Meredith had told Lily she'd been offered a three-movie deal for a sum that was so large it had been almost meaningless to Lily. With her head still spinning from that meeting, Lily had walked out to the car park of the Beverly Hills restaurant. A silver Aston Martin had been parked next to her Ford, which was not unusual. What *was* unusual was that leaning against the car, wearing shorts, flip-flops, a loose white shirt and dark glasses, was Jack Thorpe.

She'd never met him before, but his silhouette was familiar to every woman in the world with a pulse. He'd lifted his sunglasses when she'd approached and hesitated a moment before approaching her with supplicating hands.

'Hi, I'm so sorry to bother you, but I was wondering if I could ask a favour.'

'Oh?'

Even though it happened regularly these days, Lily was still not used to strangers approaching her for selfies and autographs. And this was Jack Thorpe—a man more famous than her ten times over. A man who, with hindsight, probably should have been using the valet parking service.

'I've done something stupid,' he confessed.

Lily laughed. He wasn't after an autograph after all. 'I'm sure you haven't,' she replied.

'No, I have—really. It's pretty embarrassing.'

He twisted one side of his mouth into a half-smile. The same look he'd go on to give her many times over the next two years. A look she'd never seen him give another person.

'I managed to lock my keys in my car. And my phone. See—they're sitting just there.' He waved her over to his car window and pointed in.

Lily peered into the tinted glass and saw his phone sitting on the black leather seat. Standing next to him, she caught her first smell of the scent that would always remind her of Jack. Her stomach somersaulted.

'Would you like to use my phone to make a call?' she'd offered.

'Only if that's okay? I was about to go into Soleil, but I just left an awkward business meeting telling a person to take it or leave it, so it might spoil the effect if I walk back in now.'

She smiled again. It was physically impossible not to.

Jack was so charming her insides were beginning to turn to mush.

He held out his hand. 'Hi, I'm Jack.'

She appreciated he hadn't assumed she knew who he was, his entire life story or approximate net worth. Even though there was hardly a woman alive who didn't.

'Nice to meet you, Jack, I'm Lily—Lily Watson.' She extended her own hand and warmth slid from her shoulders to her toes as his large hand gently enveloped hers.

'I know,' he said, and grinned at her again.

When he smiled at her, his gorgeous face came into sharp focus and the rest of the world blurred into the background.

He made his call and handed back her phone. Then he kicked at the ground and asked, 'I don't suppose you'd like to have a drink with me while I wait for my friend to get here?'

Lily had supposed she would, and the drink had turned into dinner, and then another dinner, and then that strip poker game.

His self-deprecating demeanour had charmed her. She'd expected him to be more...alpha. But with her he'd just been a sweet guy, and he'd opened himself right up to her.

He was different around others, she'd observed. He'd used a completely different tone on the phone to his friend who had brought over the spare keys to his car, a different tone when speaking to his good friend Bradley. And a completely different tone altogether with his father.

Which was fine, Lily had told herself. She was special. Jack loved her like no other. So when he proposed it was the most natural thing in the world to accept. As far as she was concerned it was already settled that they would spend the rest of their lives together. There was no other option. Her fate had been sealed that day in the car park.

The sound of footsteps made her look up. Daisy walked in first, followed by her master. Heaven help her... How could his mere presence still make her body temperature rise like that? Despite her plans to write a couple of thousand words she'd just been staring out of the window into the snow, thinking of Jack.

She tried to concentrate while he moved around in the kitchen. Couldn't. She hadn't managed to write any new words; she'd only deleted some. This wasn't going to work. She didn't want to surrender the table, but she couldn't concentrate and be in the same room as him.

She looked down at herself. She was still in the clothes she'd been wearing when she'd woken up: a T-shirt and a comfy pair of track pants.

'I'm going to get changed for dinner,' she said.

'Take your time. It will be at least an hour.'

Back in her room, she set the computer on her lap and typed away. Not her best words, but she did start to lose track of time.

A knock at the door startled her.

The door opened slowly and there was Jack, carrying a tray. And on the tray was a steaming cup of coffee and some cookies.

'Sustenance,' he said, and placed it on the bedside table without another word.

She hadn't been wrong. Jack had been good once. Maybe a part of him still was.

A short time later Lily showered and then assessed her limited clothing choices. Track pants, yoga pants, or the jeans she'd worn yesterday.

It had to be the jeans again. She paired them with a plain black T-shirt and looked at herself in the mirror. Her dark hair was clean, but un-styled. It fell around her shoulders in limp, uneven waves. She twisted it into a loose bun, but that made her bare skin look too stark. She undid the elastic and ran her fingers through her hair.

With the limited supplies in her small suitcase there was nothing much she could do about it. Ditto her bare skin. She found a lipstick in her handbag and applied a little of that, but that was the extent of her preparations.

He's seen you, remember? And he's seen you worse. He's seen you after your grandmother died. He's seen you hunched over a toilet bowl with food poisoning. A face bare of foundation and mascara isn't going to scare him away. Besides, you don't care what he thinks, do you? Your relationship with Jack is beyond irredeemable. It's terminal. Fatal. Unrecoverable.

He'd even come right out and told her he hadn't forgiven her for the incident with Drake. She'd seen by the way he'd clenched his fists and ground his jaw he was still furious about it. The fact that she'd kissed another man had struck him at his very core.

And it had been no more than a kiss, despite what Jack had thought and clearly did still think. Drake had been her co-star. Her friend. He had been so understanding about what she'd been going through with Jack's father and her career.

Yes, it had been wrong. Yes, a better, stronger person would not have kissed another man.

But she hadn't been a better, stronger person that night. She had been badly hurt and extremely vulnerable. And Jack hadn't been there for her. He hadn't even listened to her, let alone contemplated the fact that his father was deliberately trying to sabotage her career. But Drake had listened to her, and held her, and brushed her tears away when she'd cried.

Drake was not the reason her marriage had broken down.

He had been a symptom, but not the cause. So it didn't matter what she wore tonight, or whether or not she was wearing make-up. And it certainly didn't matter that her pulse raced and her most private parts tingled when Jack was around. It didn't matter that the scent of him made her head light and her heart soar.

With one last glance in the mirror and a shake of her head she went up to the kitchen. As she climbed the steps she made a mental list of no-go topics of conversation during dinner:

> *When they could leave the cabin.*
> *Their previous relationship.*
> *Their break-up.*

That didn't leave much else beyond the polite small talk they had already covered last night.

Lily glanced around the enormous room. The table was set, the kitchen clean. Jack Thorpe, billionaire, wasn't a slob. The remnants of her late breakfast were all gone.

He's playing house, that's all. This is just another game for him.

Her nostrils twitched. He'd showered and changed. He wore a fine wool sweater, knitted in a blue that made his eyes dazzle. It looked soft to the touch, and she'd bet it would feel sublime beneath her fingertips.

'Glass of wine?'

The man could give a boy scout a run for his money. She'd packed half a bottle of Scotch for shifting writer's block and a bottle of champagne for the day her separation from David was announced. Jack seemed to have a brought a generous supply of Russian River's best.

'That'd be lovely. You really came prepared.'

He shrugged. 'It's hard to get good food and wine up here. I always make sure I've got more than enough.'

She accepted the wine and touched her fine glass lightly to his.

'To shades of grey,' he muttered.

She paused with her glass halfway to her mouth. Was that an apology? Or was it a dig at her earlier comment? He smiled and she felt it in her chest. She supposed it was as close to an apology she was ever going to get from Jack Thorpe.

Lily took her seat and realised she was starving. Jack presented her with a plump and perfectly seared fillet steak. On the table in front of her was a generous colourful salad and a perfectly baked potato. It was simple, good, well-cooked food.

The steak fell apart in her mouth. She tried not to groan in pleasure.

'How's the book going? Tell me to shut up if you'd rather not answer,' he said.

When her writing wasn't going well she hated that question, but after a surprisingly productive twenty-four hours she didn't mind. 'It's going okay—better than it was. I still have a bit to go, and I'm struggling to figure out the final twist, but I'm feeling better about it than I was this time last week.'

Even if she *was* stuck in a cabin with her obstinate ex-husband.

'Did you always want to write? I don't remember that you did, but then maybe our memories aren't as reliable as we like to think they are.'

Jack's cutlery lay on the edge of his plate, and his palms were flat on the table as he waited for her answer. She looked at his eyes, brilliant blue against his sweater, and something inside her clenched. She looked quickly down to his jaw, but the sight of the dimple in the middle of his chin made her clench some more. Her gaze dropped to the defiant jut of his collarbone, pressed against the soft fabric of his sweater. She remembered that collarbone…remembered tracing it with her fingertips. And her lips.

She clenched again. This was *very* inconvenient.

'I always made up stories, but acting was what I fell into. When I couldn't do that any more…'

She wasn't sure she wanted to tell him the real reason why she'd started writing. At least not yet.

He won't believe you anyway…

When her pause dragged on for a second mouthful he prompted her. 'Why did you stop acting?'

She narrowed her eyes and looked at him. His question had been so loaded she expected it to blow up in their faces, but he clearly wasn't going to give up until she answered him.

'I decided I didn't want to handle all the rubbish any more. The attention…the fuss. The constant scrutiny.'

This was absolutely true. Not the whole truth, but she wasn't lying. And later tonight, after she'd beaten him at Trivial Pursuit, he'd have to listen to everything anyway.

'LD Watson is pretty famous.'

LD Watson was her pen name. Everyone knew it was *her*, of course, but initials were much more impersonal. LD Watson was her brand, leaving her free to just be Lily.

'Writing is different. I work alone, wearing what I want, and I don't need to worry about how I look.' She waved her hands over her face. 'Once a year I put on some proper clothes, do a book tour and face the cameras.'

'That's still publicity.'

She shook her head. 'No. Maybe… It's easier to handle for shorter periods, and it's nowhere near as intrusive as acting. Besides, you know as well as I do I'm never going to be anonymous. I expect even on my deathbed someone will shove a camera in my face and ask me if I'm getting back with you.'

She worried that she'd said too much, but only for a second.

Jack laughed. 'God, yes. Even death won't stop the tabloids speculating about our reunion.'

'They'll have a "source" in heaven who will claim to have seen us together.' She motioned inverted commas as she said 'source.'

'Jack-an'-Lil in Secret Heavenly Tryst!' he added.

She laughed. Hard. The force of it loosened something in her chest and she laughed again. It felt good.

'Can you imagine the frenzy if anyone found out we were both here? Alone? They'd never believe we're not back together.'

The thought made her laugh again, and loudly. So loudly she wasn't aware at first that Jack wasn't laughing with her.

She caught her breath and explained, 'Seriously, it would be ridiculous.'

'Well, you're with David, for starters.'

Lily paused for a moment too long before mumbling, 'Yes, of course.'

She'd lied again. It shouldn't feel wrong, but somehow it did. She didn't owe Jack anything, much less honesty. When he'd refused to believe that his father had been trying to destroy her career he'd lost her trust. Completely.

Jack took another mouthful of steak and chewed it slowly and carefully. The look he gave her across the table was cold, and perhaps a bit hurt. What the heck was *that* about? She'd thought they were laughing about the constant speculation about their break-up. Someone had to. They'd cry otherwise.

There should be a rule that all ex-husbands were exiled

to a distant planet to live out the rest of their days annoying each other. They shouldn't be allowed to wander back into their ex-wives' lives looking tall and handsome and rugged and delicious, getting grumpy when anyone laughed at the idea of them getting back together.

A moment later Daisy appeared at the table. She looked up at Jack, but Lily took a small piece of steak from her plate and held it out for the dog without Jack noticing. Daisy ate the steak gratefully and made herself comfortable at Lily's feet.

'She's not the most loyal dog I've ever had,' Jack muttered.

'She can sit by me and still be loyal to you.'

Jack lifted both eyebrows in doubt.

'A dog can be loyal to two people at once. A person can be too, for that matter,' Lily said.

Most people could. But not Jack.

He looked to the living room and she followed his gaze. Trivial Pursuit had been set up on the coffee table by the fire.

The scene gave at least the appearance of being cosy.

'You've been here before, haven't you?' he said.

'You mean the cabin?' she asked.

He nodded.

'I started coming not long after Meredith and Bradley bought it,' she told him.

Not long after we divorced.

'You did? Me too.'

The air in the room was warm, and smelt of burning wood. 'Bradley suggested it when…well, you know…'

Jack looked away. 'It's been my sanctuary from time to time too,' he said.

It was like a part of her soul had been exposed. This had been *her* escape from the world. But they'd slept in the same bed, maybe only days or weeks apart. How could her haven be his too?

'Up here it's like another world…another planet. You can get away from everything, and you can also see what's really important,' he said.

'Another universe…' She sighed. 'I've been up here many times to get away too. To be just me. Without pressures or expectations.'

'Maybe it's not so remarkable that we met each other here this time. Maybe it's more remarkable that we didn't run into each other until now.' He smiled.

'Maybe,' she replied.

'Maybe the time was finally right?'

What on earth was she meant to make of a remark like that?

She didn't realise her eyes were wide with shock until she saw Jack's expression harden into dismay, as though he hadn't meant to make the last remark.

He cleared his throat and sipped his wine. 'We should get this game started.'

She shouldn't let Jack's good qualities—and he did have some—outweigh out the bad. She exhaled with a pang in her chest. There had been good times. But that didn't mean they needed to be friends now.

CHAPTER SIX

LILY TOOK A fortifying sip of wine. Just the one. She had to keep her wits about her, but one more sip wouldn't hurt and it would settle her nerves.

She shouldn't be nervous, yet little bubbles of anxiety simmered in her belly. She could beat Jack Thorpe at a game of Trivial Pursuit, no matter how confident he was pretending to be.

Jack has no idea about me, the life I've lived since he left me, the things I've learnt...

A fire smouldered in the fireplace, giving the vast room a comfy feel. She assessed the table where he'd set the game up. On which side did he plan to sit? Had he rigged the cards with the questions on them?

'Take either side,' he said. 'And feel free to shuffle the deck of cards if you don't trust me.'

She studied him closely. His eyes were open and honest. If she shuffled the cards, she'd show him she didn't trust him. She'd also show him she was worried about winning. *Ha!* Even if Jack had spent the afternoon trying to memorise the questions in both packs, she would still beat him.

Lily sat on the floor by the table and curled her legs underneath her. Then she took another sip of wine. One more wouldn't hurt.

He handed her the dice. She held her hand out to take

it, but instead of dropping the dice, as she'd expected, he pressed it gently to her palm and held his fingers on her skin for a moment too long. His touch was warm, and obviously designed to unsettle her. *Piffle.* It was going to take more than a lingering touch and an intense stare to put her off her game.

But her hand still tingled as she shook the dice. Stupid, tingly sensations were moving up her arm, up her neck. Across the table Jack's pink lips curled into a seductive grin. Even though she knew what he was doing, and even though she knew he was only doing it to unsettle her, her stomach flipped in anticipation.

Seriously? Was he so worried about losing this game of Trivial Pursuit that he'd bring out the famous Thorpe smile? Well, if he was going to play dirty, she could too. She pushed at her messy bun and then twirled her index finger around a loose strand of hair as she considered the board. Then she pouted.

It was the sexy stare she'd perfected when she'd still been acting. She hadn't used it in years and hoped she wasn't too rusty. Full lips, opened just wide enough to allow her to slide the tip of her tongue quickly over her teeth. She hoped she still had it. Hoped she was making him wonder what else she could do with her lips, not making him think she was slightly deranged.

She noticed Jack's eyes dart from her face to the board, to the wall behind her and to his wine glass. Then, finally, reluctantly, they fell back on to her. His attention caught, she rolled the dice. A five.

Jack grabbed the dice and tossed it without delay. The dice rocked back and forth before landing with the six facing up. This time he looked at her without hesitation and gave her another one of his famous smiles. Expensive. Cocky. And full of the belief that he ruled the world.

Oh, she was going to enjoy winning this game very, very much.

The room was warm and the fire heated her skin. She kicked herself for not wearing the tank top she'd packed. Was it too late to go back to her room and change, so she could show more distracting skin?

Don't be silly, Watson. You can thrash this man fair and square. You don't need to resort to underhand tactics. Just because he's so insecure he feels he needs to distract you by brushing his hand against yours, it doesn't mean you need to undress.

Jack rolled a one and landed on a sports question. Her heart dropped, but she smiled as she took the card with the first question. Jack wasn't just a sports nut he *owned* sports teams, for crying out loud.

And you've written bestsellers and stared in Oscar-winning movies. What's your point, Watson?

"'In which year did the Boston Red Sox break their eighty-six-year World Cup drought?'" She sighed as she completed the question. Even *she* knew the answer to that.

Jack scratched his chin and looked at the ceiling. 'Hmm…let me see,' he murmured.

'Give it up, Thorpe, you're no actor.'

He clutched his chest in faux outrage.

'You know the answer to this—just get it over with.'

'2004.'

'That wasn't too hard, was it?'

Jack rolled again. A six this time, and a chance to try for a general knowledge token.

"'What are the four main ingredients of cake?'" she asked.

Jack's eyes flicked to the ceiling, contemplated it for a few moments, then turned back to the table and met Lily's.

His generous lips didn't break into a smile, but his eyes sparkled.

'Flour…'

Lily nodded.

'Sugar…'

Good guess.

'Butter, of course.'

'Of course.'

'And…'

Jack rubbed his chin and looked around the room for effect. But Lily wasn't fooled for a second. Her heart dropped as he answered.

'Eggs.'

Eggs was right. All over her face.

She had completely underestimated him and would have to dial her distraction game up a notch, but it was hard to look diverting in her comfiest jeans and a nondescript T-shirt.

Luckily, some of her long-neglected acting techniques were not completely forgotten. She tipped back her head and ran her fingers through her hair. When that didn't even make him blink, she tilted her face down and then looked up at him through her lashes. She threw in another pout for good measure. Then she let out a little sigh. The kind of sigh she might make involuntarily in the bedroom.

Jack's eyes flicked over her, but he quickly grabbed the dice and rolled again. That was something. He'd landed on a neutral space and it was her turn.

She reached for the dice and he did at the same time. Her hand came to rest next to his. Their eyes met and she thought she saw a spark in his. When his thumb slid over the side of hers, she snatched her hand away. A pout and a sigh were one thing, but a second finger-graze in as many minutes…?

If that was how he wanted to play it, then fine. It would be at his risk. Because she was completely and utterly immune to Jack and his pathetic tricks.

Trivial Pursuit. *Ha!* Maybe he shouldn't have lied to her and told her that it wasn't his thing, but all was fair in trivia contests and war. Especially now she was twirling her hair, puffing her lips and giving him doe eyes. Did she really think he was going to fall for long soap opera gazes or romcom pouts? He might have tricked her into the game, but he'd win fair and square and get control of the kitchen table. And, most of all, he wouldn't have to listen to Lily and whatever pathetic excuse she had for cheating on him.

It was funny that he'd never told her about the bar trivia nights he'd gone to when he was at Harvard. Tuesday Night Trivia at O'Connell's. He smiled at the memory.

Although Lily was pretty good too. She wasn't stupid—of course he knew that. But he was surprised. Still, he was currently leading four tokens to two.

'"What did the Roman emperor Caligula order his soldiers to do instead of invading England?"' he asked.

'Collect seashells,' she said, and rolled the dice without even waiting for him to tell her she was correct. She landed on a neutral space and the turn was back to him.

'More wine?' she asked.

They had drained their second glasses and he was feeling relaxed and confident, but not yet hazy. Lily, however, was smaller than he was, and a third glass might prove the difference for her.

'Okay.'

He moved to get it, but she stood and waved him back down. Then she stretched her arms wide and unnecessarily high. As she did so her T-shirt rode up, giving him a long glimpse of the white skin of her taut stomach. She let out another one of her bedroom sighs.

As if he didn't know what she was up to.

As if he didn't recognise that sweet, lazy, contented sigh.

She was a fool if she thought he was going to somehow react to it. Even if it did remind him of long nights and lazy days spent wrapped around her glorious body, exploring her skin, breathing her in. That had been years ago. He was over Lily Watson. He had no intention of revisiting that particular place...even if he could feel familiar stirrings in his pants.

Not even then.

They were history.

And she had a boyfriend.

Do you think something might happen if she didn't *have a boyfriend? Thorpe, you're a fool.*

Lily bent over more deeply than necessary to pick up his wine glass. The coffee table was low to the ground, but still... He meant to look away—he didn't intend to give her the satisfaction—but at the last minute his gaze was dragged towards her and he glanced down the front of her T-shirt. He saw a flash of red lace and the smooth, creamy flesh of her upper breasts.

His muscles tightened. *That was a cheap shot, Watson.*

When she turned to pick up her own glass she made sure her perfect bottom was facing him. When she bent, her jeans rode down, giving him a perfect view of her narrow waist, the velvety skin of her lower back, and another flash of red lace.

Low move, Lily, really low.

If those were the rules she wanted to play by, maybe there would be time to play a different game before she left in the morning? One where the participants ended up with no clothes on. Like the strip poker they'd played on their third date.

What had she said about this cabin being in another universe? Maybe they really could pretend the rest of the world didn't exist. That there was no past, no future. Only now.

He exhaled. *Don't be ridiculous, Thorpe. Not Lily. How could you even contemplate it after what she did? You know you can't trust her, a woman who ran into the arms of another man only six weeks after your wedding.*

What had Drake given her that he hadn't?

He didn't necessarily want to blow his own horn, but all the feedback he'd received from past relationships had been overwhelmingly positive. Except from the woman refilling his wine glass in the kitchen now.

Lily came back with two wine glasses, both overly full. He smiled to himself. He'd let his glass sit there, but she was welcome to finish hers. She passed a glass to him, and as he took it he was careful to let his fingers linger over hers. Sparks rushed through his fingers, up his arm, and the blood in his veins fizzed. He found her eyes again, hoping to see that the touch had at least affected her the same way, but her smile was light. Nonchalant. As if she was completely unmoved. As if she wasn't using every ounce of her self-control to keep her hands off him.

Jack took a sip of wine and forced himself to concentrate on the game.

His bladder was aching, but he wasn't going to leave the board. He only needed two more tokens, and they were in his strongest categories: sport and entertainment.

Lily was two behind, so he shouldn't stress. She'd given him a fright early on, when she'd correctly guessed the smallest bone in the body. But since then the game had stalled, with neither of them landing on another token square.

Lily rolled a two and landed on a square to win a sports token. She sighed audibly, high and squeaky, part-relief, part-trepidation. She'd lost her last go at a sports question. It was clearly her weak spot.

Jack picked up a card. "'Name the NFL player with the record for most touchdowns in a season.'"

'Oh, I know!' she blurted with spontaneous, unchecked glee. 'It's Trent Davison.'

Jack turned the card over. It said 'Trent Davison'.

Lily squealed and grabbed the sports token with undisguised delight.

'You're correct, by the way,' he said.

'I know. I dated him,' she added, by way of explanation.

Jack clenched his fists. He had met Davison once. He was a foot taller than Jack and quite a bit broader. Big. Big enough and talented enough to make even the most confident billionaire feel slightly inferior.

Jack might have been her only husband, but Lily had dated many men after him: movie stars, footballers and even a rock star. Not that he'd been paying attention. Okay, maybe he had. But only to enjoy the schadenfreude that inevitably followed when those relationships had ended.

Now she was dating David Parks, a tech entrepreneur from Silicon Valley. He was self-made, scarily smart, and well regarded. Though he hadn't yet overtaken Jack on the *Forbes List*.

Jack hated himself for the thought. Lily was the last woman on earth who would compare men by where they were placed on the rich list. David was probably a better man than he. Attentive, reliable. Dependable.

Was David a keeper? Was she going to walk down the aisle again?

Somehow it had been a source of perverse pride to him that Lily had never remarried. But would David be the man?

How different would his own life have been if he was a better man? If he'd gone to her when he should have after her accusations about his father instead of hesitating? If they'd stayed together his life would have been more stable. Fuller. They'd probably have a family by now, of beautiful, precocious children. They would…

'Earth to Jack?' Lily waved a hand in front of his eyes. 'Entertainment for a token.'

Entertainment was, not surprisingly, one of her strongest categories, but still he hoped the next question would be a doozy. It was, but for the wrong reasons.

He groaned. '"Name the three main stars of *Some Like It Hot*."'

She chuckled to herself. 'Monroe, Curtis and Lemmon.'

Jack didn't even turn the card over to check the answer, but slipped it back in the box. Lily rolled again and found herself on a square for the geography token. Her third token attempt this round. If she got this right she'd overtake him.

'"What is the largest living thing on earth?"'

He held his breath. He knew this. He thought Lily would too. They had once spent a week on a small island on the Great Barrier Reef. He had proposed to her on the perfect white sand as they'd watched the sunset.

For some reason he willed her to answer the question correctly. Even if it meant she'd be one step closer to winning.

'The Great Barrier Reef,' she said softly.

It was four tokens to five now, and she was on a roll. She tossed her hair and gave another faux stretch, this one coupled with a soft little sigh.

Jack reached for his wine glass.

Half an hour later, their fourth glasses were drained and they were both locked at the finish line in a sudden death contest. The first to get two correct answers in a row would win. Which also meant that the first to miss a question would probably lose.

Lily hadn't missed a question—but neither had he.

The room was getting very warm. He'd thrown a new log on the fire and it had burst back into life. He had removed his sweater, leaving on only his white undershirt. He hadn't removed it to show her his pecs, though he did admit that was a fortunate side effect of the heat in the room. Lily was trying hard not to look, but it was difficult for her to give him her 'come hither' eyes without actually looking at him.

Lily was fanning herself by pulling at the neckline of her T-shirt, being careful to stretch it lower and show him more flesh each time she did so. With each glimpse of the soft white skin of her chest his sweat pants tightened. Her body was as beautiful as it had been a decade ago, and he'd bet it felt just as good. His body also remembered her. His muscles shifted and braced with each move she made... each look she gave him through her eyelashes.

Stupid libido.

Being with Lily had been amazing, in the way love was when it was new and when you thought it would last for ever. The way it was when you took everything for granted a little. Even though you never quite meant to.

Jack landed on a science question and correctly named the symbol for carbon.

'Why can't you trust atoms?' she asked.

He shrugged.

'Because they make up everything,' she quipped, with a smile that made his chest swell.

He realised with a jolt that he was having fun. Actual, good old-fashioned fun. He'd forgotten where he was, who he was with and what he was competing for.

If he lost he'd have to listen to Lily telling him what she

thought his father had done to her. Listen to her saying what an awful husband he'd been to her.

What are you afraid of hearing, Jack?

He wasn't even sure any more, with the red wine having numbed him, the fire making him sleepy.

What exactly *was* he afraid of hearing?

That Lily loathed him?

Well, that was clear; she wasn't even bothering trying to hide it. And she was still maintaining that she was somehow the injured party.

Ten years ago Jack had gone to LA to talk to her about what she thought his father had done. Maybe he hadn't gone as quickly as he could have…maybe he shouldn't have waited a week to do so…but he'd been sure it was just a misunderstanding they could sort out.

Instead he'd found her locking tongues with Drake Johnson.

Lily picked up the dice, rolled a two. Entertainment.

Jack picked up the next card and read it to himself. *Name the actor John Thorpe the Fourth was married to for six weeks.*

Jack placed the card down. 'Not this one.'

'You don't get to pick and choose.' She put her hands on her gently curvaceous hips.

'Not this one,' he said again.

'Cheat!'

She grabbed at the card, but he held it to his chest. If she wanted it that much, she'd have to come and get it.

'You can have the point,' he said.

'Then why not just ask me the question? I want to know what it says.'

Her face was glowing with indignation. Her cheeks were flushed and her eyes were wide. Her offended face looked a lot like her aroused face if memory served…

He dismissed that particular memory and pushed the card across to her, face-up. Then he watched as the look on her face melted from outrage to something else. She stood quickly. Without all the stretching and posturing.

'I need...' She looked around the room. 'Water.'

She went to the kitchen. Jack looked at the board. He could cheat and read the next card...or he could follow her into the kitchen and check she was okay.

He fell onto his back and looked up at the beams in the ceiling. Damn it all. Damn this stupid game. Damn the whole world and its inability to stay out of their lives. Even here, after all the steps they'd taken, the distance they'd travelled to get some space and some peace, the world still poked its nose back into their lives. It was jarring...intrusive.

Jack rolled over and pulled himself up. He could do with some water too.

He found Lily in the kitchen, her hands pressed against the edge of the sink, staring out into the dark void of the forest beyond.

'I'm sorry,' he said.

'Why? It's not your fault I'm a Trivial Pursuit answer.'

She turned and shrugged. Her face was pale, she looked exhausted. Drained. Beaten.

'Would you rather be a Trivial Pursuit question?'

She smiled, and some of the life returned to her face. 'When you put it like that, I suppose not.'

He took two glasses from the cupboard and filled them with ice-cold water from the faucet. He passed her one.

'Stuff 'em,' he said.

She took the glass. 'I know you're right. And most of the time it wouldn't bother me. Except...' She turned away and looked back out through the window.

When she didn't go on he said, 'Except it's weird being

here with your ex, in your sanctuary? In the place where you're meant to be able to forget him and everything associated with him and your crazy life?'

She smiled again, and something started to unravel inside him.

'Yes, exactly that.'

She was blindsided—that was all. As if the whole past twenty-four hours hadn't been strange enough, here she was now, trying not to look at the way Jack's pecs perfectly filled out his tight white T-shirt, or at the seductive jut of his collarbone and the faint outline of a nipple she could see straining through the thin fabric.

And the fact that the more she ruffled her hair and ran her tongue over her teeth, the more she thought about running it somewhere else...

The crazy thing was, she was having fun. Her blood was pumping faster than it had in ages—and not just because of Jack's T-shirt, but because she was having to stretch herself to beat him. He pushed her. Challenged her. And she had laughed more tonight than she had in months.

And as for the way her insides tingled when he brushed his fingers against hers... Which he was doing often...

Jack moved past her again to refill his water glass and she watched the way his shoulders twisted, caught a glimpse of the tendons in his smooth forearms. Seeing her watching him, he paused. She inhaled. There it was again. That smell. Of wood and clean air. And man.

'We don't have to finish the game, you know,' he whispered.

'Of course we do. Otherwise how do we know who wins?'

He didn't reply, he just moved closer and looked down at her.

'What if no one won? Does it really matter?'

It did matter. She hated it that it mattered, but it did. He hadn't really listened to her before; he hadn't believed her. He'd betrayed her trust. He'd thrown away their marriage, and her.

She shook her head. She thought he was going to reach out and touch her arm, but he didn't. Instead he looked down at her and smiled. Not a sarcastic smile, but a genuine, caring one. The sparkle in his blue eyes sent soft ripples up and down her body.

Now they weren't arguing about who should leave, or why their marriage had ended, they were having fun.

Granted, the way their marriage had ended was still a pretty big problem...

She gulped her water and it was so cold her throat stung. Though her head wasn't any clearer.

Had the sex been as good as she remembered? Or had she just been too naive as a twenty-year-old? Not in touch enough with her own body and feelings. So overwhelmed by the fact that Jack Thorpe had wanted her that she'd failed to notice he lacked any actual skill?

Curiosity gnawed at her now. She yearned to know... to remember what had it been like to be in bed with Jack.

Could she be twenty again and know everything she knew now?

She gulped down more water. It gave her energy, but did nothing to quell the heat inside her that was growing hotter, even away from the fire.

When she'd finished the glass Jack took it from her. When his fingers touched hers it wasn't a surprise. Her heart was already hammering, and the heat emanating from his body, mere inches from hers, was more distracting than any brush from his fingers could be.

This was crazy. Why was he standing so close to her?

'What if no one won?' he repeated.

'If no one won…?' she whispered.

What if they could both just put it all behind them? Agree that the past didn't matter? For the first time she didn't dismiss the idea outright, but let it sit for a moment in her mind.

They could both pretend, at least while they were stuck here. They could pretend they didn't have a past. Or a future. Only the present. And at present things were looking pretty good.

She stared straight ahead and all she saw was his chest. A wall of hard defined muscle and soft skin.

He moved forward again. She had to step away, tell him that it would be a mistake. But before she knew what she was going to say, she lifted her gaze. Big mistake. As soon as she looked into his pale blue eyes nothing else seemed to matter.

He lifted his hand and his thumb brushed the underside of her chin, gently lifting it up. He lowered his mouth to hers.

Just a test couldn't hurt, could it? To remind her that memory could be fickle and Jack Thorpe was not as good a kisser as she remembered? Just a taste, a little nibble, that was all…

But it turned out Jack Thorpe was made of wicked appetite stimulants. The second his lips brushed against hers she needed more, needed to taste him. To devour and be devoured. There was no tentative exploration, no careful evaluation. Just everything, all at once.

His open mouth caught hers and their tongues collided in a frantic tangle. He tasted of wine, heat and male. He tasted like her memories, like her innocence.

Though there was nothing innocent about the way he cupped her bottom and pulled her tightly to him. Moisture started pooling inside her, molten and urgent. She clawed at his shirt, sighed when her fingers connected with the smooth skin of his waist. She slipped her hands around his waist and grasped him with needy fingers. His fingers slid up into her hair and he tilted her face to his at just the perfect angle for their mouths. Every cell in her body was reacting to him, tingling, moving, or anticipating.

Jack lifted her with one movement onto the nearby bench. She spread her legs, wrapped her feet around his backside and pulled him even closer. They were groin to groin, their lips at the same height. His hand slid up her T-shirt over her bra. Into her bra.

Don't forget to breathe. No, do. Die right here. Let them find our bodies years from now, entwined in each other's.

Lily groaned. Jack did too: a sweet, frustrated sound that echoed the pitch of her own heart.

This wasn't just a test any more, nor an innocent taste. This kiss had just become adults only. This kiss wasn't even a prelude to something more. When she pressed her groin to his all her muscles contracted and it *was* something more.

She pushed him away, panting.

He looked lost, confused. His eyebrows dipped together in question.

The room swayed around her.

'I'm sorry,' he said. 'I shouldn't have.'

His face was red. Creased with guilt.

He thinks you're with David. He thinks you've cheated again.

'It's not what you think—' she started.

'You don't need to explain.'

'I'm not a cheater. I don't…'

Jack's face opened with curiosity. She didn't know what to say next. She wanted him to know that she wasn't a cheater. That she was single, free to kiss whomever she chose.

But she didn't owe Jack an explanation. And if she told him she wasn't with David then maybe they would kiss again and…

She wasn't sure she wanted that either.

That's really why you lied about David, isn't it? Because if he knows the truth then there will be one less thing stopping you from sleeping with Jack Thorpe.

She could just grab him again and resume what they'd been doing. It would be easier to avoid the conversation they had to have and as an added bonus her clitoris would be eternally grateful. It wasn't going to forgive her for what she had to do next.

'You win.' She pressed her hands to his chest and pushed him back. She hopped off the bench and away from his heat and temptation.

'Lily—'

'I can't.'

She slipped past him, but he reached for her arm. Her muscles froze under his hand.

Why on earth had she kissed him back? Had she lost control of her body to such an extent that she couldn't keep her hands or her lips to herself?

It was foolish. Too much wine. Not enough oxygen to the brain.

You have to get out of here right away.

Her temples throbbed. Her judgement was if not impaired then definitely compromised if she was thinking about ripping Jack's clothes off and climbing on top of him. Right here in the kitchen.

'Goodnight.'

She shook his hand away and fled to her room.

CHAPTER SEVEN

IF ONLY SHE'D thought to sneak back upstairs for some food during the night.

She supposed that late last night, when she'd fled down here, she'd hoped the weather would have eased and that she'd be able to sneak away in the morning. But no. Outside her window the tree branches were still heavy with snow and the sun was nowhere to be seen.

She would wait until he left the house to walk Daisy. Or wait until he went to bed. Then she'd get more food. But that was hours away. And her stomach was tight with hunger. She'd love a cup of tea… Maybe she could bring the kettle down with her.

One thing was for certain: she couldn't face him. That decision had been made for her the moment she'd surrendered to his kiss. The moment she'd made him think she was an unfaithful feckless woman after all.

They'd played to win and she'd lost. Not the unfinished game of Trivial Pursuit, but the unspoken game of psychological warfare they had waged at the same time.

They'd flirted and teased and danced around each other. It had all been a ruse. Her head had known that. But her body hadn't. And she'd lost. She was the one who hadn't been able to keep her hands off him. The one who had started to rip his clothes off him.

Her skin burnt with embarrassment just thinking about it. All that effort to keep Jack Thorpe out of her mind, all those walls built to keep out the pain—all undone in a single moment of weakness.

But now she was stuck here. With him. The only positive thing she could see was that it had all happened in private. No one knew but the two of them, and she was sure Jack wanted to forget about the whole business just as much as she did.

She tried to type, but intrusive thoughts about Jack kept distracting her from her characters.

It wasn't fair. It wasn't meant to snow in September and stupid Jack Thorpe wasn't meant to be at the cabin. *Her* cabin! And he wasn't meant to be sexy and intoxicating and eternally unattainable. And still blind to all the reasons why their marriage had been a short but comprehensive disaster.

She wasn't meant to turn her back on everything she believed in. She wasn't meant to forget that the last decade of her life had ever happened and kiss him.

When would he decide to leave?

How long could she last without eating?

What would it feel like to die of hunger?

She knew from researching for one of her books that the first stages were tiredness and loss of reason. She cackled. Tiredness and loss of reason were what had made her kiss Jack in the first place.

This probably wasn't the worst moment in her life, but right now it felt like it.

You know exactly what the worst moment was, she reminded herself.

John Thorpe the Third had never bothered to make a secret of the fact that he thought Lily Watson was beneath his son. An *actress*. From the wrong side of the metaphorical tracks. That was two strikes as far as John had been concerned. Lily was simply not good enough for his son and never would be.

John had liked to make sly, sarcastic references about her career and her co-stars, asking her if she was attracted to them. Asking her if she liked kissing them. It had been creepy in the extreme. But, not wanting to come between Jack and his father, Lily had never told Jack the full extent of his father's comments. Apart from anything she'd been just twenty, and in awe of Jack and his family.

John's campaign against Lily had become more intense after Jack had proposed. In the lead-up to their wedding, John's comments about Lily's career, and the fact that she kissed other men for a living, had become more frequent—to the point where Lily had tried to talk to Jack about them.

Jack had dismissed her concerns with excuses like, 'You must have heard him wrong.' Or, 'No, he told me he loves you; he must just have been joking.'

Since she hadn't told Jack any of the things his father had said earlier, he didn't believe her when she finally wanted to.

By the time of the wedding Lily had been a mess, but had told herself that once they were married John would give up his campaign of hatred against her and become resigned to their relationship, if not accepting.

He hadn't.

After their honeymoon in Paris, Lily had gone back to work: she'd been contracted to two more movies, and Meredith had been negotiating a role for her in a new trilogy based on a bestselling series of young adult books. Shortly after she'd returned, the executive producer of the trilogy, Mark Allen, had dropped by the set and asked her to join him for lunch.

She'd thought he was going to tell her personally that she'd been given the role.

He hadn't.

Instead he'd told her that he'd received a call from John Thorpe. What he'd gone on to say had shocked her to her core.

'So…am I not getting the role?' Lily had asked shakily at the end of his revelations.

'It hasn't been decided yet,' Mark had said evasively.

She hadn't believed him.

Jack had been in New York, Lily in LA. When she'd phoned him and tried to tell him about the conversation he had dismissed her concerns again, and she'd been able to tell he hadn't really heard what she'd said.

'Allen's just trying to come up with an excuse not to give you the role,' Jack had said.

'But why would he bother to do that? He could just give the role to someone else.'

Even successful actors didn't get every role they wanted. And Lily had never been the sort of prima donna to make anyone believe she needed to be placated when she missed out on a role.

The stress of the conversation, her separation from Jack, and a gruelling filming schedule all took their toll. A week later Jack still hadn't come to LA, like he'd promised, and she'd been a wreck.

It had been obvious to her colleagues that she was upset. One night she'd poured it all out to Drake, who had listened, and refilled her wine glass several times, and that was when Jack had arrived and found Drake comforting her.

She hadn't meant to let Drake kiss her, and she certainly hadn't made the first move, but for the first time in many, many months someone had actually listened to her about John's behaviour towards her. Someone had believed her.

But Jack had believed she was the unfaithful Jezebel his father had always thought she was.

Sometimes you could ignore a kiss. Write it off as being the result of too much alcohol. Or an experiment that didn't work.

This was not one of those kisses.

Jack looked hopefully out of the kitchen window, but the sun wasn't even trying to peek through the clouds. The temperature was firmly stuck in the sub-zero range. Even if the snow stopped falling it would need a day or two above freezing before it started to melt.

Jack had considered kissing Lily, his thoughts having taken a detour in that direction on several occasions in the past twenty-four hours. Lily was beautiful—even more beautiful than she'd been a decade ago. She was confident, self-assured, and maybe more attractive because she neither wanted nor needed him now.

So, yes, in several idle moments he'd thought about kissing her—and more—but he'd never intended to act on it. It would have been foolish in the extreme. Lily Watson was the last person in the world he should be kissing. She was with someone else, and his life was already messed up enough without throwing an ex-wife into the horrendously complicated mix.

But his lips still tingled…his skin still burnt. Two cold showers and a fitful night's sleep hadn't stopped the dull, throbbing ache.

A throbbing ache that couldn't be acted upon.

He'd kissed her.

He'd kissed *her.*

She'd kissed him back. Enthusiastically. But he'd made the first move.

A sickening realisation kept pushing to the front of his thoughts and he couldn't ignore it any longer. *He* was the other man.

He was no better than Drake the Rake.

'I'm not a cheater. I don't...'

He hadn't let her finish her sentence. Or had she just stopped talking? What had she been about to say?

She'd been about to defend herself. Accuse him of kissing her. Accuse him of starting it.

Just like she'd always said Drake had.

A chill froze his neck and shoulders. She'd been the one to pull away. She'd been the one to walk away. If Lily hadn't left, he might have made love to her on the kitchen floor.

He searched the kitchen for the coffee beans, forgetting where he'd put them.

She's the one with the partner, so she shouldn't have kissed me back.

He tried to tell himself that...tried to tell himself he was less to blame than she was.

But he didn't believe himself.

He'd kissed her. He'd made the first move. If it was anyone's fault, it was his.

Jack wanted to vomit. This was one of those shades of grey she'd been talking about.

He found the coffee and started the machine.

This time he couldn't sneak out. He'd done that the last time. Like a coward, he'd left the apartment without a word, refused to speak to her until... Until now, he realised. And while leaving her without a backward glance had worked when he was twenty-four, it wouldn't work now. He wasn't that man any more.

It would be wrong. Just as it had been wrong then. Only he'd been an immature twenty-four-year-old then, and nothing in his privileged life until that point had prepared him for how to react when his wife accused his father of sabotaging her career and then was caught kissing another man.

Leaving the coffee machine dripping away, he moved towards the lower wing. Not sure what he was going say, he turned the handle of her door. It didn't budge. Locked.

That was understandable. After what he'd done.

He knocked. 'Lily? Lily, do you want some coffee?'

No response.

'Lily?' His words bounced off the closed door. There was only silence.

A terrible thought gripped him and he spun and raced to open the garage door.

Her car was there. At least she hadn't driven away. She had just locked herself in her room.

Daisy looked up at him. Then looked to the door.

'Not right now, girl. When Lily comes out.'

Daisy walked over to her bed, stepped in, curled up and went to sleep. Jack sighed. The dog was probably right. Lily would take her time. Best to make himself comfortable.

The day dragged on. With hardly any sunlight it was difficult to tell how fast time was passing. A part of him knew he was being melodramatic. But it had been all day. She had water from the faucet in her en suite bathroom, but did she have any food in there? He had no way of knowing.

What if she died because he'd kissed her?

That was a crazy thought. She wasn't going to die. But she couldn't be comfortable. It was five p.m., and as far as he knew she hadn't eaten anything since last night's steak.

That's her own fault. You haven't locked her in there.

Maybe not physically, but if something happened to her Jack knew he'd be far from blameless.

Why on earth hadn't he just listened to her properly?

He remembered how upset Lily had been leading up the wedding, how unlike herself. She'd told him she didn't think his father liked her, and Jack had told her she was being paranoid. After all, anyone who knew Lily at all knew that Jack was the lucky one—he was the one who was 'marrying up'. So he'd dismissed her fears without properly listening to her because surely Lily could see that Jack adored her? That his world revolved around her? That there was nothing he wouldn't do for her?

Then she'd told him something about his father interfering with her getting a role. He couldn't remember the details, he realised now, hot with mortification. Because he'd been so sure she'd misinterpreted something she'd heard that he hadn't listened to her properly. Instead, he'd told her she must be mistaken, and when she'd become really upset with him, he'd thought she was just pouting about the director wanting someone else for the role.

A week later, frustrated with what he'd thought was rather a petulant ongoing silence from her, he'd flown to LA to sort the whole thing out.

He'd thought it was all just a misunderstanding.

But he'd arrived too late. If he had come even an hour earlier would Drake have been at her apartment?

He shouldn't have suggested the stupid competition yesterday; he should have just listened to her in the first place.

Especially now his own doubts about his father's true character had been creeping in recently.

You should have listened to her ten years ago.

Jack looked around the cabin. There wasn't much to work with. But he had to give it a try.

CHAPTER EIGHT

I'LL JUST HAVE a nap, Lily thought. *I'll set an alarm for eleven p.m. and wake when I know he'll be asleep. Then I'll go upstairs and have toast. And pasta.*

She began to salivate.

Pizza. Hot, fresh pizza. Dripping with cheese. Lasagne. Fried chicken. French fries.

Her stomach groaned and her head felt light. She had to stop thinking of food. She had to stop thinking, full-stop. Especially as most of the food she longed for she hadn't even brought with her!

She let her head rest on the pillow. She'd sleep now, eat later.

Just as she was drifting off into sleep a sound ripped through the house. Blaring, high-pitched. She immediately awoke.

Smoke alarm? Was the house on fire? What the hell was Jack up to?

Lily grabbed her jacket and looked around for her shoes. Damn, they were in the laundry. She rushed up the stairs and into the living room.

The noise stopped.

She looked around the big room, searching for signs of smoke…chaos. Found none. Instead there, standing in the middle of the room, wearing sunglasses, flip-flops, shorts and a white shirt that barely fitted him, was Jack.

'What on earth's going on?' she asked.

He lifted his sunglasses onto the top of his head. Grinned.

There was no smoke. No fire. Just a madman standing in front of her, looking pleased with himself. He'd tricked her out of her room.

Damn.

She looked around the room again, and the things that caught her eye were the letters, cut out of white paper, taped to the brick wall behind him, spelling the word *Hollywood*.

'What are you wearing? What is going on? Have you totally lost your mind?'

'Possibly...' she heard him mumble. Then he spoke louder. 'I'm trying to turn back time. I want to pretend that it's ten years ago and this is LA and I've come to listen to what you want to tell me about my father.'

'Oh, Jack...' Lily's body sagged.

'Are you hungry?'

'Maybe a little.' She didn't want to admit that she was so ravenous she was approaching delirium.

He led her to the table, where a plate of pancakes was sitting. She could smell the sticky maple syrup they were drenched in from several feet away. This wasn't a coincidence; she'd used to make pancakes for him for breakfast every other day.

He pulled a chair out for her and she sat. He nudged a glass of orange juice in her direction and she took it, her grateful body devouring the sugar. Then she ate the pancakes steadily, giving her body time to adjust. Slowly, her blood sugar levels returned to normal.

Finally, he said, 'Tell me. Please. I'm ready to listen properly this time.'

'Really? Are you?'

'I'd say so. I think I'm about ten years too late. So I ought to be ready. What happened, exactly, the week we broke up?'

The clothes were way too small for him, he thought. The shorts rubbed awkwardly against his groin and one of the buttons on the shirt had actually popped. But he deserved the discomfort. It was worth it as Lily was now out of her room and she had eaten.

'Are they your clothes?' she asked.

'These? No, I found them in the closet. But they look like something I might have worn ten years ago. Give me a break. I'm improvising. And you're delaying. I thought you wanted to tell me.'

He hoped he looked ridiculous enough that she'd at least stay upstairs and not hide away down in her room again. Wearing too-tight clothes and listening to what she had to say was a small price to pay for peace of mind.

She sighed and began, 'Your father never liked me—'

'He did. He just had a thing about actresses.'

Lily held up her hand. 'If you aren't prepared to listen to what I have to say, then what are we even doing here?'

Jack made a zipping motion across his lips and sat still.

'He really didn't like me, Jack. From the moment he met me. And he constantly tried to scare me away from you. When that didn't work, and once we were married, he tried to get me to give up my career.'

And Lily *had* given up her acting career. Although by then she and Jack were over.

'It wasn't long after our honeymoon, as you know, and I was back at work in LA and you were in New York. Your dad wanted you there, but I had commitments in California. One of my executive producers, Mark Allen, called me to lunch one day.'

Jack remembered that.

'He told me that they'd wanted to give me the lead in a trilogy they were developing, but your father had called them and told them that it was the Thorpe family's preference that I didn't act any longer. I don't know exactly what your father said to them—only that the studio believed they would be risking some sort of retaliation, probably withdrawal of funding, if they chose me. Mark had no choice but to cast someone else.'

Jack flinched. He didn't recall that.

'I called you,' she went on. 'I remember the phone line wasn't great, or you were somewhere noisy. And I remember you didn't listen to me properly or believe me. You said he was just coming up with an excuse not to give me the role.'

He remembered that. But what about the rest of it? What about when he'd come to LA?

'I was upset,' she told him. 'I was really upset about all of it. I wasn't sleeping beyond maybe a broken hour or two each night. And I was losing too much weight…my skin was a mess. You were in New York and we weren't talking. We were both busy, and the time difference didn't help. And I was having trouble keeping it together on set. Everyone knew there was something up and there was a lot of gossip. I was a newlywed; I should've been glowing. Instead I looked wretched. Drake noticed, but he wasn't the only one. He came over that night because he was worried about me. I didn't invite him. I know what you think of him, but he's a good man. He's never breathed a word about any of this to the press. I told him what Mark had told me.'

Lily looked up at the fake Hollywood sign and drew a long breath.

'And I told him what you'd told me about him just looking for an excuse for not giving me the part. Drake didn't agree with you. He said that didn't sound right.'

They were silent. So silent that he heard a crow squawk from across the valley.

Jack's muscles had turned to stone and he was filled with rage—mainly at the thought of Drake comforting Lily like that. He was ready to punch him all over again.

'He listened to me because he was a friend and then, yes, he kissed me, and I kissed him back. Jack, you didn't believe me when I told you that your father was actively against me, and I was going out of my mind. And that was when you came. I didn't sleep with Drake. Not then, not ever. But when you wouldn't listen to me…when you filed for divorce a week later without even speaking to me again. Well…' She shrugged.

The way she said it made it sound like the whole thing was his fault. But it couldn't be, could it?

'You did kiss another man while you were married to me,' he pointed out through gritted teeth.

'Yes Jack, I kissed him—that was all. I don't deny it. But you have to understand that I was right at the edge of my emotional limits, exhausted and more than a little tipsy. And I was totally devasted that you hadn't really listened to me, and what you had heard you didn't believe. You certainly didn't support me. You sided with your father. And you never stopped for a second to consider whether any of it was true. You believed your father wholeheartedly instead of me.'

Jack sat there, his eyes not focused on anything. Certainly not on her.

What did you expect, Lily? What did you think was going to happen when you kissed another man?

Then a memory hit him.

'Women are fickle creatures. And actresses are the worst...'

Those were his father's words. And he had once thought his father was always right.

Until this last week, that was.

'They didn't give me the part—you probably figured that out. Mark Allen didn't offer me any more roles. Nor did any of the other big studios. Oh, I was still offered parts by the independents, and I tried a few, but eventually I couldn't do it any more. I hated being on set. I hated the way everyone would gossip about me, speculate about us. There were comments about how awful I was looking. About my weight, my hair...' She stopped as the words seemed to get stuck in her throat.

He looked at her hair now, dark and long and as lustrous as he'd always known it. But a memory of that time crept back into his consciousness. Of their honeymoon. How she had already been looking thinner then. Bordering on too thin. And there had been dark circles growing around her eyes.

The stupid thing was that now he'd properly listened none of this was a huge surprise. He'd known in his heart that what she was going to tell him about his father would shake the last of his faith in the man, but hearing the effect his father's actions had had on her...that made him ashamed to his core. Because this was the first time he had taken on board what she was saying and now he believed her. Not his father. He'd heard her side of the story, which was not what he'd wanted to hear, and he knew it was true.

His father did not trust women. He didn't even particularly *like* them all that much. And he couldn't stand actresses—not since Jack's mother had betrayed him. Could Jack have picked up on his father's bias more than he'd realised?

Lily had been not much more than a kid. His father had behaved appallingly towards her, and Jack had let him do it by disregarding her concerns.

You didn't believe her at the time...you thought she was overreacting.

Only now, with hindsight and a new clarity over his father's character in the last week, was he able to see that John Thorpe was capable of doing such a thing.

'I see now that my father isn't the person I thought he was. I'm so sorry, Lily. I should have listened to you, and I should have believed you.'

'I think, looking back, we were both far too young for such an intense relationship,' she said.

He shook his head. 'That doesn't make it right.'

'No, it doesn't. But it's at least something. Things probably turned out for the best in the end. I have a career I really love.'

Something inside him twisted uncomfortably and a bitter taste appeared in his mouth. He was glad she didn't seem to hate him or his father for ending her acting career; she had every right to. But she was also saying that she was happy they'd broken up.

And why shouldn't she be happy? They were over, weren't they?

Jack's voice was gruff as he spoke, and he made no effort to look at her. He stared at the darkness outside the window to hide his eyes.

'I'm truly sorry,' he said again, his voice full of devastation. 'I just didn't believe he would do such a thing to you.'

'I know you didn't.'

She'd had longer to digest the fact that his father wasn't perfect. That he was capable, in fact, of cruel things. Jack hadn't been prepared to believe that at the time, so he'd chosen not to hear it.

'Look, Jack, it's ancient history now.'

As she'd told him just the night before, regret wasn't helpful. She'd forged a new career. On her own terms. And she wasn't going to let anyone take this one from her. Not this time.

Lily got up from the table with her plate and took it to the sink. Jack followed and Lily realised they were both standing just where they had been last night. At the sink, framed by the kitchen window.

'Let me,' Jack said, and reached for her plate.

As he did, two buttons on the too-small shirt popped. Lily laughed.

Jack regarded his torso, shrugged, and slipped the shirt off, revealing his perfectly broad muscular chest. 'Thank goodness! That was cutting off my blood supply.'

Lily would have laughed again if she'd had control over her muscles. As it was, her mouth flooded with saliva. He was less than a foot away from her. She had to lift her head to meet his eyes and she found him staring down at her, his eyes full of concern and something else. Something that made her heart contract and her core tighten.

She had to look away from his face. But when she did her vision was blocked by wall-to-wall smooth skin, tight over evident muscles. Her fingers tingled, longing to connect with his flesh. She flexed her fingers, but the sensation only became stronger. As she tried to breathe, all she could smell was him.

It was more than a little surreal to be back here again, where they'd kissed, only a few hours later, but it was as though days had passed. Being trapped in the cabin together seemed to have had the effect of warping time.

'I acted inappropriately last night.'

It took her a moment to understand his meaning. 'Jack—'

'I shouldn't have kissed you.'

'Jack—'

'I know you're a grown woman and make your own decisions, but you have a partner and I shouldn't have kissed you. It's my fault.'

The tightness and remorse in his voice made her heart ache, and before she could think better of it she said, 'David and I have broken up.'

Jack's mouth dropped. He looked horrified. 'Because we kissed?'

'No. No! Relax. Before… Months ago.'

'But you… I thought…'

Lily drew in a deep breath. 'We didn't tell anyone except our families and the lawyers. And Meredith, of course. It hasn't been announced yet.' She took a moment to calculate the date. She'd lost track of time since being here with Jack. 'Actually, it's today, I think. Meredith is announcing it today.'

'I'm sorry,' he said awkwardly.

'I'm sorry too. For not telling you the truth.'

Jack shook his head. 'It was none of my business.' He looked her directly in the eyes and asked, 'That's why you're really here, isn't it?'

She nodded. 'I wanted to be alone. Away from everyone and most of all away from social media.'

'But instead you found the last person you wanted to see.'

She was about to agree with him, but stopped herself. Was he really the last person she wanted to see? Maybe he had been at first, but there was something comforting about his familiarity. And now he'd let her talk about the past something very honest was happening between them.

'I'm sorry about David. I really am. And I'm sorry for being here when you needed peace and quiet.'

Jack picked up her hand but didn't take his eyes from her. His grip was soft, warm. Familiar.

But his apology, while welcome, brought a new complication to the mood. The air grew heavy with a growing sense of anticipation and she was struck by the need to brush it away.

'You should be sorry for these clothes,' she told him. 'For luring me out of my room.'

'No, I'm not at all sorry about that. You've eaten, haven't you? I was really worried.'

She froze, stunned at the significance of his admission. Jack Thorpe? Worried about her?

Her hand was still in his, and that small area of contact was suddenly not enough. She imagined his hand sliding up the bare skin of her forearm. Under her shirt, over her shoulders, across her back. She shivered. She had to get a grip.

His feet were too big for the flip-flops. His body was too big for the old shorts.

'You cannot be comfortable in those.'

'I'm really not.' He adjusted the tight shorts and his face creased with pain.

'Oh, just take them off.'

'Here?'

'I… That is…' Oh, heavens, had she really just told him to take his shorts off?

Thankfully, Jack left the kitchen and went into his room.

Last night's game was still spread out on the coffee table. Untouched. Unfinished.

The board game wasn't the only thing unfinished. Last night she had wanted to kiss him out of curiosity, because of their flirtation, because of the wine.

Now she wanted to kiss him again, but for more basic reasons…more indefinable…yet simpler.

Just because you've spoken about his father and he's apologised for not believing you, that doesn't mean you should pick up where you left off, said a little voice.

She glanced at the Hollywood sign and chuckled.

'I wanted us to pretend that it was ten years ago.'

She followed him to his room. He'd left the door ajar. She couldn't see anything without walking in. Should she knock?

You should go back to your room, that's what you should do, said the little voice.

A louder one said, *But wouldn't it be better to knock on the door?*

She knocked lightly and pushed.

'Lily?'

His voice was inquisitive, but not at all annoyed, so she pushed further on the door and walked in. He was standing in the middle of the room, wearing only his boxers, the too-tight shorts discarded.

Her limbs felt heavy and slow, giving her eyes time to take him all in. She couldn't help comparing the sight of him to the last time she'd seen him undressed. His shoulders were as broad as ever, his collarbone as well defined as always and his stomach as flat. But his chest seemed more muscular, covered in a smattering of dark hair. More hair than she remembered and not at all unappealing. In fact, the sight of thirty-four-year-old Jack was every bit as gorgeous as the sight of the twenty-four-year-old version had been.

He didn't look unhappy to see her. In fact, part of him looked quite happy about it.

He took a step towards her.

What was she doing in here?

He took another step.

You know exactly what you're doing in here, said the little voice.

He picked up her hand, like he'd done in the kitchen, and turned hers over in his.

'We can't go back ten years,' she said.

Her voice was a whisper. Almost as if she didn't mean it. But how to explain? She wanted Jack. She wanted his arms around her and his skin against hers. But she could never trust his family. She could never risk being drawn into their sphere again after what John Thorpe had done to her. He'd nearly destroyed her.

'I know.'

He slid his warm hand up her forearm, just as she'd imagined him doing.

'I wouldn't want to. You're more beautiful than ever before.'

His words washed through her, sweet, delicious. He slipped his smooth fingers beneath the fabric of her shirt and over her shoulder. Her body came alive beneath his touch, bursts of warmth spreading through her limbs. And the skin that wasn't lucky enough to be brushing against his fingers yearned for it.

Touch me! Hold me!

Every pore in her body wanted to feel his touch. He didn't touch her again, but he didn't move away either. She held her breath. Kept holding it. Forget starving to death— she was going to die right here from lack of oxygen.

She watched the top of his dark head as he stroked her hands and her forearms. Her fingers itched to slide through his thick hair and her nose ached to bend down and smell his head, but she was too scared to touch him. Scared of how he would react.

What if he stopped this wonderful caressing?

She was too terrified of what touching him might unleash in her and at the same time too terrified of what her body would do if she didn't.

'You're wearing more clothes than I am,' he said, and it sounded as if his voice scratched along his throat.

'It doesn't seem fair, does it?' Her voice was just as hoarse.

Jack hooked his fingers under the hem of her T-shirt and lifted it up over her head. Cold air hit her torso, but he slid his arms around her and pulled her close. Warm skin hit warm skin. The breath she'd been holding escaped in a long sigh. One by one the muscles in her body softened, then melted.

Jack leant his face close to hers. His mouth was so close she could see the pores in his skin, the fine lines in his pink lips.

She had told the truth earlier; she didn't regret their relationship. Her biggest regrets were the things she hadn't done. She wished that ten years ago she had confronted him about filing for divorce before they'd even spoken properly about what had happened. She wished that last night she had kissed Jack senseless until her lips were numb. Until she had nothing more to give...until he'd shaken her very core.

Jack's eyes found hers and held her gaze. Behind his eyes she could see he was tossing this moment around in his thoughts, going over all the reasons why he should step back, get dressed. Yet he stayed where he was.

Lily didn't budge either. There were reasons why she should move away—some good ones too—but the reason for staying was even simpler. Life was precious.

She didn't take her eyes from his and saw the moment he broke. His lids lowered slowly and he moved his face the last inch to hers. He brushed his lips to hers again. Unlike last night, when they had fallen straight into the deepest, fervent kiss, this was slow, light and cautious, but it made her core melt just the same.

Lily held her breath, waiting for Jack to pull back and tell her that it was still a mistake. He didn't. His tongue explored her mouth with great care, but when he lifted his hand to her breast and rubbed his thumb against the sensitive skin just above her bra, heat erupted inside her. She felt herself unravelling, unfolding, opening up.

She kissed him as though it was her last day on earth. She kissed him in case it *was* her last day on earth. And he kept kissing her back, his lips fused with hers. She would breathe later. She didn't need air…she only needed him.

Jack's lips traced down her neck, over her collarbone. Her fingers reached for his head and slid through his perfect thick locks. Jack ran his palm over her bra strap and Lily spread her hands over the warm bare skin of his arms, his shoulders, then down his torso, marvelling at the sensations under her fingertips, the way his muscles turned taut under her touch. She slid her hands down his torso, over his abs and lower, to the soft fabric of his track pants. A frustrated sigh escaped from his mouth.

'Are you sure?' His voice was ragged.

'Yes.'

She would unravel the consequences later, but she and Jack had always been…unfinished. Their arguments never complete, their conflicts unresolved. Physically, they had needed each other as much as ever. Being newly married and separated for weeks had left her with an exquisite tension as she'd waited see him again. But of course that release had never arrived. Perhaps if their relationship had fizzled out, instead of exploding, she wouldn't feel like this now.

'There are things I've always wished we had a chance to do.'

Jack's eyes widened and a knowing smile stretched his lips. He cupped her face in his hands. Slowly, reverently, he pushed the hair away from her face. He stroked her cheeks, kissed her forehead. There was no point holding back; life was short, and precious, and she wanted this, dammit. She didn't want Jack back, and she didn't want to be married to him again—heaven knew she didn't want that. Just his body against hers, warm skin on warm skin, to breathe the same air as he did.

He slid her bra strap off her left shoulder and planted a kiss where it had been. Then he repeated the action on the other shoulder, before reaching behind her to undo the clasp. Lily shook the bra away and stood before him, memories stirring, awakening. Jack had always known exactly what to do with her breasts, but now he stroked the skin on her back, as if not wanting to be too eager. Or had he changed?

Her nipples were hard and expectant. She wanted him to touch her so much she could hardly get air into her lungs. When he lifted his hand to cup her left breast she sighed. When he took her nipple into his mouth she moaned.

Her knees buckled, but he caught her, and they half fell, half crawled onto the bed.

'There are things I always wanted to do to you too, you know,' he said in muffled tones as he kissed his way down her belly to her waistband.

'Oh, yeah…?' She sighed.

'Oh, yeah. But ladies first.'

Lily giggled, and pushed him aside and onto his back. She straddled him and he grinned. Lily looked down at him and for a moment she froze. Now Jack Thorpe was under her, at her mercy, what would she do with him? He was gorgeous, chiselled, vulnerable, and so handsome her heart sang and her loins wept.

He raised a knowing eyebrow. 'I could stare at you all night, you know?'

'Good, because that way I can look at you too.'

She trailed her fingers softly down his chest, over his hard stomach, and loved the way his eyelids flickered. She drew small circles lightly over the bulge in his boxers and he inhaled a sharp breath. She didn't have a lifetime to do all the things she wanted to do with him—she only had tonight.

With that thought, she leant forward and kissed his lips. The flame that had been smouldering inside her ignited.

The rest of their clothes soon lay as discarded as their worries as they found old pleasures and discovered new desires. Their bodies were warm and breathless, their hearts open and free, their skin aflame. Tingles were followed by tremors, followed by a few tears.

Discovering, remembering, twisting, curling, climbing, then finally falling together.

Lily's breathing was gradually slowing. Jack felt as though he'd gone through a hundred emotions in the past couple of hours: fear, shame, sorrow, and now exhilaration, relief, wonder.

And he was spent.

Lily lay warm next to him. Her limbs were tangled in his. Her soft breasts nestled perfectly against his chest. Her breath came out in short, sweet gasps. He shifted slightly, only to feel her skin slide against his again. He couldn't get enough of the sensation of her naked body moving against his.

Each moment was a precious gift.

That worry he'd felt about her earlier hadn't subsided entirely. It was muted as he held her beautiful body in his arms at this very moment, so his world was complete, but a few drops of fear still circulated in his blood.

Jack untangled his limbs from hers. This type of fear wasn't good. It was the type of fear that came from caring.

But the feelings he was having couldn't be real. They were only because of the moment, being stuck together like this. They were confused, misguided emotions that swirled within them both, and those emotions had bamboozled them down onto this bed and into each other's arms.

Lily was single.

Separated.

That's a good thing, isn't it, Thorpe? You didn't help her cheat on her partner.

It *was* good. And yet…

'Dinner?' she said, and pulled her body from his. She grabbed the throw off the bed and pulled it around herself.

She's self-conscious. Does she regret this?

Did he?

His body was still humming in the aftermath, and he didn't regret it yet, but he wondered whether he would at some point. She'd just broken up with someone, after all. That was it, wasn't it?

Lily looked at him properly. He saw her face register the look on his and her mouth opened slightly.

'It doesn't have to mean anything,' she whispered.

It doesn't have to mean anything.

She'd said it as though they'd just shared a cup of coffee, not earth-shifting sex.

'I didn't mean to suggest it did, only that—'

Before he could mangle his words further, she wrapped her palm around his forearm. She knew better than he did that this was the point when he should just stop talking. Neither of them needed to be bound by the words they spoke at this moment.

He looked around for her clothes, gathered her jeans and undershirt. 'Where are your panties?'

She laughed.

'I was going to do some laundry. I thought, since we're stuck here for the foreseeable future, you might appreciate it.'

She had the decency to look contrite. Then her pretty lips pouted into the sexiest grin he'd seen in years.

Jack picked up their clothes and carried them away to the laundry. Lily watched him with her mouth open.

If he thought sex with her was a mistake, why was he laundering her clothes?

She flopped back on the bed.

Jack was freaking out. Since when did he offer to do anyone's laundry?

Did she care if he was freaking out? She wasn't sure yet. She wasn't sure she wasn't also freaking out. The sex had been good. The sex had been fantastic. But rather than satisfying her curiosity, or releasing all her pent-up tension, she felt…well, *not* released. *Not* satisfied.

Because Jack had *lied*.

She had no idea why he would lie about such a thing as shoulder surgery, but he had. So why was he really here?

She stretched out on the bed and looked out of the window into the snow.

He lied to me, and he's still lying to me.

Mind-altering, body-transforming sex with Jack was all good and well, but he was keeping something from her. There was nothing wrong with his shoulder. The skin there was as perfectly toned, tanned and unscarred as it had been when she'd last seen it, when he was twenty-four. Now that she thought about it, she should have realised earlier, when he'd first slipped his T-shirt off those perfectly intact, perfectly perfect shoulders, unscarred by a surgeon's knife.

Does it matter? This was just sex. You both know it can't lead to anything else. You both know that it was simply due to the conversation you'd just had and the forced proximity. Being stuck together. He's entitled to have secrets from you. You're not together. You never could be.

Lily sighed. She had told Jack her real reason for being here. He should come clean too. It was only fair.

She rolled over and pulled herself up. She heard Jack in the kitchen, the sound of frying, and then the unmistakable smell of bacon.

And if they'd been caught up in the moment, in the heightened emotion, if they'd had sex, then so what? Plenty of couples had sex after they broke up, for all sorts of reasons—just as she had said. It didn't have to mean anything.

Even if she couldn't shake the memory of the way his tongue had explored her body in focused circles...the way his face had crumpled when he'd climaxed.

Her stomach tightened, but not with arousal. With simple animal hunger.

She pulled herself up and went to the kitchen. The pancakes earlier had been good, but she hadn't eaten anything else all day. Now, delicious smells found her salivating.

Jack stood in the middle of the kitchen, dressed again in his track pants and another torso-loving white tee. He stood scrambling eggs, next to freshly toasted sourdough and crispy bacon.

'Breakfast for dinner?' she asked.

'This was meant to follow the pancakes. I didn't realise we'd get so...distracted. Do you want something else?'

'No way. It smells great. Will it go with wine?'

He smiled and laughed. 'Red or white?'

Could this really be Jack Thorpe, media entrepreneur? Privileged billionaire?

She tugged the blanket around herself. 'I should get dressed.'

His gaze slid from her head to her toes.

'Or not…'

He grinned again and his smile hit her right in the chest. Desire and longing curled down through her body. What was a day or two more stuck here alone with Jack? She'd already passed the point of no return.

'How's the shoulder?' she asked.

CHAPTER NINE

JACK RUBBED HIS left shoulder. 'It's all right.'

'You didn't strain it? Putting up the Hollywood sign? Making love?'

'The sign was hardly difficult. And the sex was great, but it wasn't exactly acrobatic.'

'Maybe, but still... You've been doing pretty well for someone recovering from recent surgery.'

'You're not that heavy.'

He dished up creamy eggs, bacon and toast dripping with butter. He wanted to eat, relax, think about how great the last hour had been. Not to have *this* conversation with Lily.

'Thanks. You'll have to give me the name of your surgeon.'

'Why? You've torn your rotator cuff too?'

He took his plate to the table and motioned for her to sit, but she planted her feet firmly where she stood.

'No. Because they must be a magician. There's not a mark on you.'

She gave him her sweetest smile. She obviously knew. She should just come right out and say it.

He looked at the food. 'It's getting cold.'

She eyed the plate and he saw her indecision. He heard her stomach growl, but she still didn't move. 'Fine,' he said. 'Get dressed and I'll tell you.'

Lily returned to the kitchen a few minutes later, looking bright and refreshed. She approached the breakfast he'd cooked for her with gusto. 'Your talents are wasted on media mogul-ship. You're an amazing cook.'

It sounded like she was letting the topic drop, but Jack knew her better than that. They had shared something. And she'd come clean with him about her break-up with David.

'I found out something about my father,' he said slowly.

And as soon as the words had left his lips he felt lighter. There was no turning back now.

Lily regarded him and chewed her mouthful carefully. 'Something else?' she asked slowly, as though she were unsure whether he would consider confiding in her.

He nodded.

'What?'

'I'm not exactly sure yet.' Jack reached for a bottle of wine and the opener.

She didn't prompt him, but waited for him to open the bottle and pour out two glasses.

'I don't know if my father's business practices have always been completely above board. I think he's been using threats and stand-over tactics to get deals done.'

'Oh.'

After what his father had done to her, Jack knew it wouldn't surprise Lily to learn that John Thorpe wasn't above using manipulation and intimidation. Not one little bit. But it did surprise Jack. He'd worked closely with his father for years...learnt from him. And this—the deal with such an underhanded paparazzo like Luc Harmon—was unlike anything Jack had seen him do before.

Had his father always been involved in shady deals and threats? Had Jack been too blind to see?

'In an immoral way or an illegal way?' Lily asked.

'Both, I think.'

'Oh, Jack…'

While the revelation might not shock her, even a week later it still shocked him. Not only did he love his father, he also idolised him. When his mother had abandoned them to live in Paris his father had been everything to him—father, mother, mentor, boss… Now business partner.

'In the past few years I've noticed him going after deals that are on the risky side, or making decisions that are just downright short-sighted. I put it down to the fact that he's getting older, the world is changing and he's a little reluctant to change with it. But something happened recently and…'

Jack rubbed his hand over the stubble on his chin. There were so many reasons why he shouldn't tell Lily any of this.

'You don't have to tell me, but if you want to talk I'll listen. And I won't tell a soul.'

'No one would believe I'd told you anyway.'

'That's probably true.' Her face opened into that famous smile. All white teeth and eyes that sparkled with humour.

'He was trying to acquire a group of television stations in Europe. I didn't agree with the purchase. Dad and I often disagree on the role legacy media should play in the Thorpe group.'

'Not a good investment?'

'Not these days. I don't think it's the direction the company should be going in. I'm trying to branch into digital media and mediums. Dad doesn't get it, though.'

Lily nodded.

'He's stuck in the last century, and the board are happy to go along with him because he's John Thorpe. But lately they've been pushing back too. Dad's been getting angry. Frustrated. Annoying people he shouldn't.'

'Oh, dear.'

'But he managed to negotiate a deal for Western State Media that was astounding. Not much more than a steal.

I could tell the board was going to agree to buy it, despite their reservations. And then the majority shareholder of Western State Media died.'

'I don't understand...'

'At first I hoped it was just a coincidence.'

'But?'

'I found out that Dad's been paying Luc Harmon, a particularly nasty paparazzo, large sums of money.'

Lily openly shivered. He knew she would be well aware of exactly what kind of scum Luc Harmon was.

'I asked him why he was paying Harmon and he said Luc had offered to do him a favour. Just to help "lubricate" the deal.'

Lily screwed up her face. 'Did you ask your father about the deal? The dead man?'

Jack pushed his plate away and nodded. 'He said the death had nothing to do with the deal. That it was just a coincidence.'

'Maybe it was?'

'I hope so. But why get involved with someone like Luc Harmon? There's a big difference between playing hard and blackmail, and right now I don't know which category my father falls into.'

Lily pressed her palm to her chest. 'How did the man die?'

'It's unclear, but it seems like suicide.'

Lily's jaw hung open.

Jack noticed his hands were shaking. He grasped his coffee mug. 'Dad didn't deny that he'd played hard, or that Luke was helping him win the deal.'

'How so?'

'Dad said that he'd let the man know he had photos of him he wouldn't want anyone else to see. I'm still trying to figure it out, but at the same time I'm not sure I want to know. Lily, it isn't how I do business.'

'Of course not... I'm just trying to understand. What happens next?'

Jack sighed. 'Yeah, good question. Dad pretty much confessed that he'd used Harmon before, to blackmail other purchasers who wouldn't sell. Or who wouldn't sell at a price acceptable to the Thorpe board. I have no idea how long it's been going on and Dad wouldn't say. I don't know if I've just been naïve, or if the whole business is built on a lie. And maybe I don't really know anything about business at all.'

Lily laughed. 'You're joking, right? You built E-Quinox Media from scratch yourself.'

E-Quinox was Jack's 'side hustle'. It was a billion-dollar side hustle, but still dwarfed by Thorpe Media.

Jack shrugged.

'You're not serious? Jack, you built your own company into the success it is now because you're an amazing businessman. Bullying people into selling their businesses for next to nothing isn't business—it's blackmail, coercion and God knows what else. It's a crime. Picking trends, getting in early and developing ideas—that's good business, Jack.'

'My father is still the face of Thorpe Media. The President takes *his* calls, not mine.'

The remains of their breakfast/dinner lay on the table in front of them. Lily stood and started to clear up.

What Jack hadn't admitted to Lily—what he could barely acknowledge even to himself right now—was that *she* had known all along that his father was capable of this. She had known John Thorpe could manipulate people, intimidate them, tell lies to get what he wanted. She'd tried to tell him, her husband, who should have believed her, and he'd refused to listen.

And there was another question he didn't dare ask himself—one that had been hovering at the back of his thoughts and gnawing its way into his consciousness ever since he'd found out. How had he not seen it? He was close to his father—so close. For the last thirty years John Thorpe had been everything to him. How had he not even suspected that his father could do something like this?

Should he have seen?

The answer to those questions, he feared, were: *Because you chose not to.* And: *Yes.*

He loved his father, and he was so proud of being his son, of being Jack Thorpe, that believing there were cracks behind the successful, powerful façade of the man had been unthinkable. His father might be getting older, and was noticeably frailer, but he was as driven as ever.

What had Jack missed?

He should have started looking into those cracks when Lily had first flagged that his father had tried to derail her acting career. He should've at least asked some questions. He shouldn't have dismissed her claims outright.

'So what are you going to do?' she asked now.

'I don't know. That's why I came up here. To think. And avoid the board meeting.'

'What meeting?'

'The board was due to meet...' Jack looked at his watch '...today, actually. Before I left I opposed the acquisition and took it off the agenda. Dad was furious.'

'I'll bet.'

'I don't expect the problem to just go away, but I'm hoping to buy some time.'

'And if he brings it to the meeting anyway?'

'It's a possibility. But if they do try to hold a vote without me and approve the purchase, at least I won't have been there. I'll be able to distance myself from the actions of the board and the company will at least stand a fighting chance of survival.' Jack sipped the last of his coffee. 'It's cowardly, I know.'

'It's not cowardly to stand up to a bully,' she said.

'But I'm avoiding it—standing up to him, that is.'

'But you will when you're ready.'

Lily said it as if she was sure. She said it as if it was simple.

Jack grimaced. 'I always knew he was a hard negotiator, but I never believed he could sink to this level.'

I didn't believe you and I'm sorry.

The words formed once again in his brain but he left them unsaid, afraid of where they would lead. To recriminations? More accusations? Or possibly forgiveness? What if she told him she understood why he hadn't believed what his father was like when she'd told him? What if she said that she knew how much he loved and idolised his father? What if she said she forgave him?

It wouldn't matter if he did receive Lily's forgiveness—because he couldn't forgive himself. He was as undeserving of Lily's forgiveness as John Thorpe was of his fortune.

'Do you know how long this has been going on? The extent of it?' she asked.

'No. I'm looking over the records of all the deals Dad's been involved in, but nothing untoward has jumped out at me so far. I'm trying to dig deeper.'

'Maybe you need to go to the police? If you don't and it all comes out, and they find out you knew all along, you'll be an accessory.'

'And if I go to the police and Dad goes to jail and Thorpe Media is dissolved then thousands of people will lose their jobs. And I'll be responsible.'

'You won't be responsible. Your father will,' Lily whispered. 'I know that it's difficult, but you know what you have to do. You're a good man.'

He heard her words but didn't let himself absorb them. She was just being nice. Just trying to convince him to go to the police. She didn't mean what she said.

Jack sighed. 'It isn't just my fortune: it's my aunt's, my cousins', our staff's, all the shareholders'... Not to mention I could be sending my elderly father to jail.'

'But if you don't say anything you could make it even worse.'

'I can't destroy the whole company. It isn't just the Thorpe family that depends on Thorpe Media.'

'You don't know what's going to happen—you don't know the extent of the problem. You said so yourself. And even if some people do lose their jobs, what's worse? Some highly paid professionals being made redundant or more people getting hurt? More people being blackmailed? More crooked deals?'

Lily made good points, but he could counter every one of them. It wasn't as simple as she wanted to believe—especially as he didn't know what he would expose if he went to the police. What worried him, and what he couldn't confess to Lily, was his own naivety.

Why hadn't he noticed? Why hadn't he seen what was going on? He could explain his own blindness by the loyalty he owed his father. But what about the rest of the board? The rest of their staff? Had no one else noticed? What was the extent of his father's cover-up and who else would Jack expose?

And if it all came out, what could he possibly do to fix it? His father might be able to live with the death of a man on his conscience, but Jack wasn't sure he could. He wasn't sure that Thorpe Media could.

'Your business, E-Quinox Media, is separate to the rest of the group. It could still survive,' said Lily.

Despite the fact that she feigned nonchalance, and claimed not to know what he'd been up to since their divorce, she must have been paying some attention to know these things. It made his heart a fraction lighter. But not light enough.

'Lily, I started E-Quinox with Thorpe money. Everything I have…everything I've worked for…is tainted.'

'You don't know that the corruption even goes back that far.'

He didn't know how badly stained the reputation of Thorpe Media would be if it came out, but it would certainly be damaged. 'I don't know that it doesn't either. Are you really asking me to turn my father in to the police?'

Lily pressed her palm to her chest. '*I'm* not asking you to do anything. I'm just saying I believe you know right from wrong.'

How was she so confident? How, after everything, could she still believe the best of him?

He gave a sigh, deep and frustrated. 'It isn't as simple as you think it is.'

'I'm not naïve. I do know that someone like your father didn't get where he is by being a really nice guy. Business is ruthless. And I know you didn't become successful by—'

'By being a nice guy?' he offered.

She pulled a face. Despite what she might think, he tried to be a good guy, and he tried to make fair deals. He treated people with respect. But if his life, his fortune, everything he believed about himself and his family, was all based on a lie…? Then he didn't know anything any more.

'You don't understand what the fallout could be…the scandal. We'll all be ruined.'

'Don't patronise me. I know exactly what it's like to be in

the eye of a scandal. But I also know that scandals do pass. One day the only people who care about them are the gossip mags, and even they start to look ridiculous after a while.'

'This isn't like our divorce, you know.'

Lily's jaw dropped, and her face couldn't have turned redder if he'd slapped her with his palm, not his words. Shame flooded his veins. Lily had been so calm and measured as he'd told her his story. She had every right to say, *I told you so* about his father's iniquities. But she hadn't. Not once. She understood how close he was to his father. She understood why this was so hard for him. She'd only encouraged him to be a good man, and he'd responded with words that had wounded her.

Before he could say anything else, she turned and left the room.

CHAPTER TEN

HE'D RATHER HAVE been sleeping in the same bed as Lily, curled around her, knowing that no matter what else was going on in the world at least she was safe in his arms. Instead, he had to be content with Daisy snoring in the corner.

Jack woke before dawn again, his body clock still resolutely set to New York time. He opened his laptop and resumed the task of going through the business files. All the transactions seemed fair, everything was properly documented, the paper trails complete. Everything had been approved by the board and double-checked by the lawyers.

Jack sighed and rubbed his eyes. He could spend his whole life looking for something that wasn't even there.

The next file he chose was regarding the sale of a regional Australian newspaper group to an Australian media company. The price was right, and the deal made sense, but it jogged a memory for Jack. The week the deal had been completed, the Australian chairman, Damien Masters, had joined them in New York to finalise matters and meet them for dinner. They had entertained the man at his father's penthouse and the evening had been pleasant.

Except that his father had kept calling the man Douglas. Jack had corrected him, but John had just laughed it off. He had kept getting it wrong, and Jack had given up correcting him after Damien had told him to forget it. Jack had apologised, but Damien had insisted it wasn't a problem.

Jack had forgotten the incident until this moment. In a random or isolated social occasion such a thing might have been nothing, but they had been working on that deal for a while, and Jack thought now, looking back on it, that perhaps it hadn't been the small matter he'd brushed it off as being.

Or was he reading too much into it? Maybe he should just forget the whole thing. Let the board approve the Western State Media deal and get on with his life.

Yeah, Lily wouldn't like that.

Since when do you care so much about what Lily thinks?

Jack shut his laptop with a little too much force and stood.

'Daisy, let's go.'

The snow had stopped momentarily, but there was little warmth in the sun as they made their way to the main road and the meadow.

Lily.

He shouldn't have told her. He had known all along what her response would be: go to the police. Simple, yet naïve.

He bit down on nothing as he remembered snapping at her. Insinuating that his current predicament was worse than their divorce. The two things were different, but no less devastating than one another. Though time had dulled the pain, his divorce had been far worse than what he was going through now. But what if the business scandal broke? What if it ripped through the entire Thorpe empire, taking innocent people down with it?

Lily wanted to bring things out into the open, yet Jack's instinct was to hide things. Not to confront them. He'd done it with their divorce—never giving her a chance to explain—and he wanted to do it now. Stick his head in the sand and forget anything had ever happened.

Why was he like that?

You know why. It's easier that way. You're less likely to get hurt.

Was he really *that* gutless?

Maybe so.

Maybe Lily's kiss with Drake had been as insignificant as she insisted it was.

Maybe it hadn't just been insignificant, maybe it had also been understandable.

Maybe Lily's kiss with Drake hadn't been the unforgiveable crime he'd thought it was.

And maybe, just maybe, Jack had let his father and his attitudes towards women influence him on this as well.

Jack's mother had cheated on his father—a fact John constantly reminded his son of. Helena Thorpe had left for Paris when Jack was young, and Jack had never seen her again. She had died two years later, when Jack was six.

It was Jack's own attitude that needed a reset.

Could he change?

Could he start with Lily?

Lily had been surprised by Jack's story about his father, but not shocked. She knew John Thorpe was a bully, but had figured he restricted his threats to women he didn't want to marry his son. It hadn't crossed her mind that he would use those tactics in the business world.

And yet, logically, there was no reason why he wouldn't threaten people indiscriminately. The strategy had got Lily out of Jack's life—why wouldn't someone who was bereft of a moral compass use tactics like that in his professional life as well? In all likelihood his behaviour towards Lily was typical of the way he usually conducted business.

She felt sorry for Jack—and yet she didn't at the same time. She was glad not to be in his shoes, and she didn't envy the decision he had to make. But she was also proud of herself for not saying the four little words that were still screaming in her brain: *I. Told. You. So.*

It brought her too little joy, far too late, to have this sort of vindication.

She knew Jack was torn. Torn between loyalty to his father and loyalty to his employees and shareholders. Torn between his love for his father and breaking the law.

Torn between his father and her.

For the first time ever, in all the years they'd known each other, she sensed Jack was contemplating choosing her over his father.

Are you really asking me to turn my father in to the police?

She *did* want that, but she would never—*could* never—ask him to report his own father to the authorities. She wanted Jack to find a path out of this mess legally and morally—but because *he* wanted to, not because she was asking him to.

She resolved not to bring any of it up again; it was none of her business. She was not part of his life and could never be again. Far too much water had passed under that rickety old bridge.

Lily opened her laptop and started to type. She might as well keep busy. Going over her conversation with Jack wasn't going to help her or him. She'd wait until he was ready to talk. Until he was ready to apologise for what he'd said to her.

Lily typed and typed. The sky went black and the house went cold. Lily fell asleep with her laptop still open.

When she woke it was light outside, but only just. She was momentarily disorientated, with no idea of what day or time it was. The events of the day before came in chunks. Some happy, some painful. Many confused.

She wrapped a blanket around herself and went towards the kitchen. The house was eerily quiet. She should be hearing Jack moving around in the kitchen by now, talking to Daisy.

She checked his room. As empty as the whole house felt.

She even called out. 'Jack? Daisy?'

No response.

All the lights in the main room were out and the fire was barely glowing embers. It looked as though he hadn't been in here for hours. She tossed a small log on the fire and poked, but the embers glowed for only an instant before turning black.

'Damn it.'

Jack was usually so good at keeping the fire going. She found some newspaper and pressed it gently to the embers. It smouldered. She sat close to the fire, gently tending it for the next little while.

He wasn't here; she'd have heard if he was. As much as she tried to block his presence out when she was in her half of the cabin, working, she was always aware of his movements. Her body was always aware of him—her skin, her muscles, her heart—even if she willed her brain not to think about him.

She went back to her room and tried to write, but the words wouldn't come and those that did made no sense. She shivered and her eyes were drawn to the window. It was snowing again.

Where was he? How long had he been gone? Sure, he was angry—they both were—but he should be back by now, to sulk in front of her or maybe argue with her some more.

What if he was injured? Lying somewhere unable to get up? She was the only one who knew he was here. If he had disappeared, she'd have to tell someone. Could she go looking for him on her own? She didn't have the appropriate clothes or footwear, and visibility was low. She'd be likely to get herself lost. Or worse.

Eventually she abandoned her writing, went back to the kitchen and looked in the fridge. She should cook something. Not that she was hungry—heavens, her stomach felt as if it had shrunk to a tenth of its normal size—but Jack would be hungry when he got back.

She chopped. And when she'd chopped enough vegetables to feed a soup kitchen she searched for something to tidy.

When there was no more cleaning or cooking to be done she got to work biting her nails.

To her, there was no decision for him to wrestle with: Jack should go to the police, tell them what his father had done.

But if it was your mother or your sister? Would it be so easy?

Lily sighed. No, it wasn't easy. But a man had died, so surely Jack had to tell someone what he knew? Surely covering it up was worse?

Lily had begun pacing by the front door when she heard a bark and her heart leapt. She threw open the front door and Daisy bounded up to her, damp but hot. Jack emerged slowly from the darkness. When he stepped into the light he stopped and regarded Lily.

'How did you know we were here?'

'I heard Daisy.'

He twisted his mouth but said nothing more as he walked past her into the foyer and took off his sodden boots.

'I'm making soup. It won't be long.'

Fifteen minutes later they were eating the soup in silence. It wasn't exactly a Jack Thorpe feast, but she thought she hadn't done too badly. He ate it without stopping to speak, which either meant he liked it or he was simply starving. After he was finished, she could tell the exact second he relaxed. The air in the room shifted. Even Daisy looked up from her bowl at him, with a curious look on her face.

'It's snowing again. I was worried about you,' she confessed.

He sighed. 'I'm sorry for snapping at you last night. You listened to me. I sought your advice and then I was angry about it. I'm sorry. I truly don't think our divorce was nothing.'

'Apology accepted. I'm sorry if I was too blunt about your father.'

He shook his head and picked up her hand. Then he leant forward and looked at her—really looked at her.

'I know I said it yesterday, but I'm going to say it again now. I am so sorry, Lily. I'm sorry I didn't believe you when you told me what my father had done. I just couldn't believe he was like that. I'm still having trouble processing it. I know it isn't much of an excuse, and I know that being young isn't an excuse either, but I didn't *want* to believe that my father could be like that. I loved him. I idolised him. But you were my wife—I loved you too. And I should have treated you with respect. It's a mistake I'm going to regret for the rest of my life.'

Now, *that* was an apology. Lily's throat constricted. For a moment she feared a tear might escape from her tear ducts, but she swallowed it back.

'Thank you for saying that,' she said softly. 'Jack, I do know it was hard for you. I understand the pressure he put you under... I understand that I was asking you to choose between him and me.'

Jack shook his head. 'No excuse.'

In all the years she'd known him she'd never seen him so vulnerable, so open with her—not even last night. He'd always shown her more of himself than she'd seen him give the world, but that was understandable. They'd been in love...they'd been married. But this was something else. This was a true acknowledgement of what had happened between them and his part in it. It was more of an apology than she'd ever hoped to have.

And at the same time her heart broke for him. Poor Jack, who was only now learning what his father was. John Thorpe was Jack's hero, and Jack had just seen his hero unmasked.

'He's your father and you love him. It may not excuse everything, but it is something.'

Lily's words reached into Jack's chest, through his ribs, and cracked his heart wide open. He hadn't expected her forgiveness, and he still didn't, but neither had he expected her understanding. to have that was like a gift...like a ray of hope.

Lily stood and started to clear the table.

'Leave it. You cooked. Go and sit by the fire.'

Lily's eyes darted back and forth with indecision.

'Sit down and I'll bring you a cup of coffee.'

Her face cracked into a smile and she moved to the fire.

If you'd asked him a week ago what were the things in the world he could trust the most he'd have said his father, his own self, and the power of money to influence human behaviour. Now he realised that only the most cynical of those points was true.

He cleared up the food, made two cups of coffee and joined her on the couch.

'Can you promise me something?' she asked.

He nodded. 'Anything.'

'You don't know what I'm going to ask.'

She smiled again, this time flirty and, he thought, slightly suggestive.

'It doesn't matter.' He'd do anything for her if she gave him the chance. 'You can ask me anything.'

He held her azure gaze. Held those eyes that the camera had adored and the screen had worshipped, still as blue and magnificent as they'd been when she was twenty.

'Promise me not to leave the cabin again without telling me.'

Had she really been that worried about him? It hadn't been his intention to worry her. But he realised now he'd been unkind to stay out for all that time without telling her where he'd gone. He'd just needed space, air, time to think. He hadn't solved all his problems, but he had realised anew how badly he'd treated Lily.

She had a point about his going to the police—he knew her well enough to know that that was what she'd say all along. And deep down he knew that was the right thing to do. But that didn't make it any easier. What he had figured out on his walk was that he wanted to forget about his father for a few hours—for the next while. There was only one thing he wanted to think about. One person.

'I think I can commit to that,' he said. 'There's nowhere in the world I'd rather be than inside.'

She moved across the couch and snuggled into him.

'Everything that's happened these past few days can't

go outside—it has to stay within these walls. I can't go through all that again,' she said.

Jack didn't even think it needed saying. He knew what she was referring to, and he knew he couldn't go through it again either: the intense public speculation, the rancorous judgement—all of it.

In some ways it was as if his marriage to Lily had never actually ended. The rest of the world still seemed fascinated by it and, while no one besides the two of them and Drake knew the exact reasons why it had ended, the tabloids still speculated endlessly about a possible reunion. They both knew that the last thing they needed was anyone finding out about them being here together. The press, his friends— the whole world, it seemed—were relentless in their quest to see he and Lily back together.

'Of course it will.'

And yet…

For the first time since he'd found Drake Johnson with his arms wrapped around his wife Jack began to wonder. It was as if a world of possibilities had opened up—an alternative universe, as it were—where it might be possible for them to be together again.

He no longer burnt with anger, but with something else. The sight of Lily sitting in the firelight, the highlights in her dark hair catching the flickering rays and her shirt skimming over her perfect curves, made him wonder if it was such a ridiculous idea. He remembered the way his body had pressed against hers yesterday evening. And the memory of her face, her sighs as they'd lain in his bed together, was nearly enough to bring him undone then and there.

It was certainly enough to make him move closer to her on the sofa.

When she smiled at him the rest of the world, all doubts

and worries, everything else, dropped away. He took her hand, unsure if she would push him away. She didn't. Her fingers relaxed in his, pliant and soft. He turned her hand slowly over between his. She had short, clean, unmanicured fingers, silky skin. He saw one or two sunspots that had not been there when she'd been younger. Ten years had passed since he'd held these beautiful hands in his. He didn't want to wait another ten until he held them again.

Her face was bare, her eyes unadorned, unlike her face on the big screen or the inside of a book's dust jacket. She looked as she had when they'd been together. When she'd trusted him. It was as if they had never broken up, as though they were still together...

'Can we play a game?' he asked hoarsely.

'Trivial Pursuit?'

'No, a game where for one night we don't talk about the past. Or the future.'

'I like that game. I'm very good at it. I reckon I can beat you.'

He smiled. He reckoned *he* would win this contest.

His first move was to bring his face close to hers. She countered, her movements mirroring his, and their lips met halfway. Just like they always had. In a perfect compromise of soft and hard, push and pull. Her lips parted for his. She let him in and his heart unfurled. Sparks spread from his lips to his chest and lower. Her tongue teased his and waves of pleasure rushed through him.

He kissed her behind her ear, down her throat, softly but definitively. She would stay in the cabin because she wanted to. She would stay because she couldn't bear to leave. Not because she was stranded. She would stay because she wanted to feel his body against hers as much as he wanted to feel her move in his arms.

She tugged at his shirt, searching for the skin of his

stomach, seeming to need his touch as much as he needed hers. He unbuttoned the top two buttons of her shirt and slid his hand inside. When his fingers touched the soft naked skin of her breasts, his fingers froze. She wasn't wearing a bra. With that thought, every muscle in his body was hardened. His blood grew heavier, pushing, straining him nearly to his limit.

Her moans were the sexiest damn sound he'd ever heard in his life. All his senses were running in overdrive, and he knew he needed to pull them back or risk losing control completely. The smell of Lily's skin made him more excited still, the scent of her own excitement almost too much for him to take. Each kiss was more exquisite than the last, sweetness and agony swirling in equal quantities in an amazing, exhilarating concoction.

He'd adored her when he was twenty-two, without the perspective on life of a true connoisseur. Now he knew she was magnificent.

The next morning Jack opened the curtains to his room. The snow had stopped falling and the temperature was above zero for the first time in days. Hints of blue peeked out from the clouds.

'I have to take Daisy for a walk,' he told Lily.

At the sound of her name, Daisy ran into the room.

'What size shoe are you?' he asked Lily.

'I don't think your boots will fit me.'

Lily lay sprawled out on his bed, limbs tangled in the sheets and a relaxed, satiated expression on her face.

He smiled. The sight of her on his bed was far more spectacular than the UNESCO-protected view from the window.

'Meredith's might. There's a couple of pairs in the mud

room. I thought you might want to come for a walk too. The snow's melting.'

'I'd love to. I've been cooped up here since I arrived.'

She rolled out of bed and Jack had to stop himself from staring too long at her sensuous curves.

There were boots of various sizes in the mud room. She found a pair that fitted her well enough, as well as a thick jacket, and they headed out into the snow and the sunshine with Daisy.

Something had definitely shifted between them. A crack had opened—just a crack, but Jack had glimpsed through it to a life where he and Lily could potentially work through their differences.

In a welcome change from yesterday's greyness, the world this morning was full of colour. The green of the evergreen trees and the reds and browns of the tree trunks contrasted with the perfectly white snow, and everything was overlaid with the clear light from a dense blue sky.

They had considered last night's game a draw, neither having mentioned the past or the future. But he wasn't sure if they were still playing this morning.

She cheated on you. Are you just going to forget it?

The voice came from over his shoulder. He recognised the voice. It wasn't his own subconscious, or a bad fairy on his shoulder. It was someone else.

Twenty-four-year-old Jack might have listened to that voice, but thirty-four-year-old Jack knew life was far more complicated than the voice would have him believe. Thirty-four-year-old Jack had to stop listening to that voice and start trusting.

The three of them walked in single file along the path, letting the sun soak into their faces, the fresh air fill their lungs. Lily chatted to Daisy about the wildflowers and the trees, as if they were old friends. Lily was happy, and Jack couldn't help but smile like a fool.

She turned back to face him now. Her dark hair blew behind her in the breeze. Her eyes sparkled and her cheeks were flushed with colour. She smiled at him and his chest constricted. He reached out and took her hand in his, spun her back to him and wrapped her in his embrace.

Looking down at her, he said, 'I wish I could go back.'

She shook her head. 'Jack, there's no going back.'

No, but they could move forward. That was what he was trying to tell her.

'I've apologised.'

He'd told her he was sorry, and he had listened to what she'd told him about what had really happened between her and Drake.

'I know you have—yesterday. But you can't go back and change what happened any more than I can.'

'I know what I did was wrong. I know I need to start by trusting you. Do you think you could ever trust me again?'

She strode off along the narrow path. He caught up with her, but she didn't slow.

'Why does it matter if I trust you?' she asked. 'Can't we just leave things as they are?'

Because I want to see you again.

'Because I want to put this behind us.'

'We have, Jack.'

'I want us to be able to move on. Move forward.'

He wanted them to forgive one another so they could move on. And he wanted to move on with her. With them together. He wanted her in his life again.

But he realised the way he'd said it sounded like something he'd tell a boardroom full of executives. Not a lover.

Lily halted, and Jack nearly slipped over as he pulled up short to stop himself barrelling into her. She still hadn't responded to what he'd said. She was just standing there, looking around the meadow. As if she was looking for something.

'Where's Daisy?'

Jack spun around, searching for a dash of gold amongst the white.

He couldn't see her.

CHAPTER ELEVEN

'DAISY!' THEY CALLED, their voices echoing around the valley.

'She can't have gone far,' Lily said.

'There are bears…'

A chill slid through Lily's body.

'We would surely have heard if…' She didn't want to finish that sentence.

'We were too busy talking,' he said shortly.

You were too busy hinting that you want to see me again. Is it any wonder we forgot to watch Daisy?

'You go ahead. I'll go back,' Lily suggested.

Jack took two determined strides forward then stopped. 'No, we should stay together.'

'It'll be better if we go in opposite directions.'

'And more dangerous. What if…?'

'What if what? I'll stick to the path.'

Lily kept her voice as calm as she could, but inside she was shaking. She knew she had to be the calm one; Daisy was Jack's dog and he was clearly distressed by her sudden disappearance. His face had become several shades paler and his voice quivered. He stood frozen in the middle of the path.

She pointed ahead. 'You walk that way for ten minutes. I'll go this way, then we'll meet back here. She can't have gone further than that.'

Unless she's wandered off into the snow...then we may never find her.

Lily didn't give voice to those thoughts, and before Jack could argue she turned and followed the path back the way they had come.

'I want to move forward.'

What did he mean, exactly? Was that management speak for something? Or did he actually mean he wanted to see her again?

The thought made the ground shift underneath her. For one second a fissure opened in her heart and she glimpsed a new world, another life. But that crack closed again as quickly as it had appeared. Jack was living in a fantasy world if he thought they could take their relationship out of the cabin and back to their proper lives. He was deluding himself. He might have apologised for what he'd done in the past, but if his fragile trust of her was tested in the future would he choose her? Or his father again?

You know why he didn't believe you, and you've always known that the loyalty he owes his father is far older and deeper than any he owes you. He might love you, but the Thorpe family is his identity.

She couldn't entangle herself with them again. Jack might think *he'd* changed, but his father certainly hadn't. If anything, John Thorpe might be even more manipulative than ever. Who knew what attempts he'd make to ruin her life if she got back together with Jack?

'Daisy! Here, girl! I've got treats!' she yelled into the groves of ponderosa.

But there was no sign of Daisy's golden fur and wagging tail.

She couldn't expect Jack to believe her over his father if it came to it again. He still couldn't do it fully now—not even when he had seen the evidence of his father's treachery with his own eyes. Even now, with everything he knew about the Western State Media deal, even with his father's confession that he'd been blackmailing people, Jack was still having trouble believing John Thorpe could not be trusted.

Lily looked at her watch. It had been five minutes. Her heart was pounding and her face was sweaty, yet her feet were icy. There were holes in the soles of the boots she was wearing that she hadn't noticed when she'd tried them on at the cabin. The snow was seeping in and soaking her socks with each step.

She pressed on. Another minute. Another three. When her ten minutes were up she turned back, and hoped with every bend in the path that she'd see Jack and Daisy.

She didn't.

Eventually she rounded the last curve and saw Jack standing alone in the middle of the path.

'So we go off track—one in each direction from this point,' she announced.

'No, *we* don't,' Jack said.

They stood for a while longer. Lily stamped her feet to get the sensation back in her feet. She rubbed her hands together.

'What's the matter?' he asked.

'Nothing.'

'You're cold.'

'I'm fine.'

Jack stepped over to her and took her bare hands in his gloved ones. He blew warm air onto them. 'I'm sorry, I didn't think of gloves.'

I'm sorry.

Jack had apologised to her for the past, but had she truly forgiven him? Could she? It would mean letting go of the anger and resentment she'd clung to for the past decade. It would mean genuinely forgiving him. And that was about so much more than regret. It would be saying it was okay that she'd been hounded out of her career, left to fend off the paparazzi, the media, the gossip all alone.

Could she really move forward after that?

Her chest was tight and her head light. She wanted to be with Jack; she longed for him, ached for him. Felt truly alive when she was with him. But that was only how she felt here, at the cabin. The cabin was not the real world and she and Jack eventually had to go back and live and work in that real world. A life with him beyond the cabin was surely a fantasy only.

Jack bit his gloves off with his teeth and handed them to her. She hesitated before accepting them and slipping them on. She didn't want to tell him about the leaky boots. And then she sneezed.

'You're going to get sick if you don't go back to the cabin.'

'How about I go ahead on the path and you go towards that meadow?'

'No, we're going back,' he said.

'What? No!'

'We stay together. Anything else is madness.'

Lily remembered how worried she'd been when he hadn't returned for so long the other day. It didn't make sense for them to keep risking being separate. If one of them got into trouble the other would have no way of getting help.

'Then let's both go ahead,' she suggested.

Jack regarded her with a thoughtful stare, then nodded.

They set off in a forward direction, calling as they went. The trees were no longer beautiful, just ominous in their sameness. Tall, green. Monotonous. They walked and walked, then backtracked. They must have done five laps of that stretch of path, but still they didn't see Daisy.

The sun had reached the top of its path and was inching steadily downwards when Lily tripped over her own frozen feet.

Jack looked at the ground where she'd tripped. 'How are the boots?' she asked.

'Okay,' she said.

'Are they too big?'

She shook her head.

'They're leaking, aren't they?'

'Just a little, but it's fine.'

'Hell, Lily.' He turned and pulled at her elbow as he passed her. 'Let's go.'

'But Daisy…?'

'She'll find her own way back. She was the one who ran away.'

'Jack, you can't mean that.'

'I do. I love her—don't get me wrong. But she's not…'

He didn't finish the sentence and dragged Lily behind him, making her trip again on the frozen blocks that had once been her feet.

She's not… Not what? My favourite dog? What had he been about to say?

Lily kept calling for Daisy as they trudged back, though Jack was mostly silent.

She's not my biggest problem?

Soon the path looked familiar again, and then they saw the turn-off to the cabin in the distance. Even though she had lost all feeling in her feet, and her shoulders shivered with each breath she took, the sight was not a welcome one.

'She'll find her way home…she knows this place,' Lily said, trying to reassure herself.

Unless she did happen to meet a bear. Or a coyote.

Jack shrugged. His face was hard. As cold as Lily's frozen feet.

They walked slowly up to the front door.

'Jack, I'm sorry…'

'No need to be. I lost her—not you.'

'No! I mean, of course I'm sorry about Daisy. But I mean I'm sorry I don't know if we can see one another again. After this.'

Jack's mouth hung open and she could see his heart breaking in his blue eyes.

'I like being with you here, but I just can't go through all that again. Any of it.'

There was a bark, and seconds later Daisy bounded up to them. Jack's arms still hung at his sides, and he didn't reach for his dog when she jumped up at his chest. But then it was as if something snapped, and he returned to the world and hugged his dog, who was hot and sweaty after running goodness knew how far.

He let Daisy down and she gave Lily a bark in greeting.

'Daisy, where did you get to? We were so worried.'

Lily rubbed the dog's head. Then she looked up at Jack. He opened the door and Daisy ran inside. Jack followed, but Lily stayed outside. Frozen feet and all. Wasn't he even going to acknowledge what she'd just said?

Realising she hadn't followed them in, Jack turned. 'You're freezing. Come in.'

'I'm sorry,' she repeated.

She didn't know what else to say.

'No, you're right, Lily. There's no going back. Get inside and have a warm shower,' Jack said, and nodded towards the lower wing of the house.

She knew she was right. It was for the best. So why did she have a sick feeling deep in her stomach?

Lily showered and then climbed into her bed. She covered her head with the blankets and slept.

CHAPTER TWELVE

LILY WOKE A few hours later. She made herself some lunch and didn't see Jack. Maybe he was sleeping too, or going through more business records in his room.

She went back to her room and tried to edit a few chapters, but the pages moved slowly and her mind was elsewhere. She'd written thousands of words in the past few days, so it was understandable that she was drained. But it wasn't exhaustion that was keeping her fingers off the keyboard and her ears on the rest of the house.

When it was dark, she shut her laptop with a sigh and stood. They had to talk again at some point. Well, maybe they didn't have to talk, but they did have to eat.

Because I want to move forward.

Jack was insane. They were not getting back together. Never. So apologising to each other gracefully was not something they needed to perfect.

Jack was in the kitchen, chopping.

'Can I help?' she offered.

He passed her some potatoes to peel, wiped his hands, and took out his phone. Moments later lazy jazz music filled the room. The casserole he had prepared was simmering and releasing all sorts of comforting smells into the room.

He poured her some wine and they sat and sipped it while they waited for the dinner to finish cooking.

'Thanks again for the food,' she said. Jack's meals were far more nourishing than the frozen meals she'd planned to eat. Speaking of which… 'If we eat all your food we'll have to start on my frozen stuff,' Lily said.

'It won't come to that. I brought a lot. And I can go and top up at Wawona if need be, once the roads are passable.'

He smiled at her and her stomach flipped, but her head jolted. Her plans were open-ended, as were his, but was he really suggesting—even after their discussion today—that they should stay here even once the snow had melted? Together? For how long?

'Jack—'

He lifted his hand. 'I know what you're going to ask, and the answer is I don't know. I want to take it a day at a time. An hour at a time. I want to enjoy this dinner with you. I want to enjoy this evening with you. I don't want to think about the past and I don't want to think about the future. Can we just keep doing that for a little longer?'

She swallowed and nodded. 'I'd like that.'

They ate dinner, talked about movies they'd seen and common acquaintances, and laughed over current affairs. They covered all sorts of topics—everything apart from his father and their past. Two things that faded into the background once more for a few pleasant hours.

'It's the perfect evening for a hot tub, don't you think?' Jack said.

'I don't have a swimsuit.'

Jack grinned. 'I don't think that's going to be a problem.'

Jack sat in the tub, arms spread wide, his head lolling back as he looked up at the sky. The sky was perfectly clear, and a million stars were visible in a way you would never see even in Monterey. Let alone LA. Forget Manhattan.

Lily laid her head on one of his comfortable shoulders

and drew absent-minded circles on the other. The steam rose around them, cocooning them in their own bubble and blocking out the night and the rest of the world.

She didn't want to leave. She was aware that the world existed beyond them, beyond this point in time, but she had no interest in it. She'd stay here until they were down to the last stale bread and frozen meals. But she didn't tell Jack that. She imagined the look on his face if she confessed that she thought they should just abandon their lives and stay here for eternity.

The scary thing was she thought there was a good chance he would agree.

Just because you've talked about the past, and just because you've both apologised, that doesn't mean anything for the future. You're still different people, with different lives.

Jack Thorpe was as infuriating as ever. As unpredictable and unfathomable…and yet so heartbreakingly vulnerable and addictively tempting.

And the Thorpe dynasty was as big and powerful as ever. It had come close to destroying her once. Giving up acting had been hard—it had broken her heart nearly as much as losing Jack—but she'd been young enough to bounce back, build another career. If John Thorpe went for her career again, and she couldn't earn a living from writing, what would be left for her? There was nothing else she knew how to do. If she went back to Jack and it all went wrong again, she wouldn't survive taking on the Thorpes a second time.

It was best just to enjoy this moment: the relaxing warmth of the water, Jack's secure embrace, and the million stars watching over them.

'I planned it, you know,' he murmured.

'The hot tub? I figured.'

'No, not that. Meeting you. I knew you were having lunch with Meredith that day at Soleil.' When Lily's mouth remained open, he explained, 'Bradley told me you'd be there.'

Lily had always assumed it had been a coincidence that her agent and Jack's best friend were a couple. And a coincidence that Jack had been in the car park of Beverly Hills' most popular restaurant that day.

'That's why you didn't use the valet parking,' she whispered.

'What?'

'Never mind. Bradley told you I was there?'

'Not on purpose. He let it slip that Meredith was going to be meeting you, and I couldn't resist the chance to be there.'

'Stalker, much?'

She pulled herself off his shoulder and smiled at him. Ambient light from the house shone out through one of the windows, and the stars twinkled like fairy lights above them. In the half-light she saw him smile back.

'I wanted to meet you. As part-owner of the company that owned the studio you'd just signed with, I could have insisted on it.'

'Exactly. So why go to all the trouble of locking your keys in your car?'

'If I'd asked you to a business meeting it would have been clear that I was the boss and you were an employee.'

'That's more your father's style.'

Jack grimaced. 'Well, I suppose so. I thought about getting Meredith and Bradley to arrange a date, but a set-up would have been too forced. And, honestly, if we'd met at a party and I'd asked you out, what would you have said?'

She didn't answer. She truly didn't know. 'Why are you telling me this now?' she asked.

'You don't think I'm a creep or a bully?'

'Oh, Jack, no.'

'After everything with Dad...everything you've said to me these past few days... I'm questioning a lot of things about myself right now.'

'Jack, I don't think it's creepy. It's funny, actually.'

Jack pulled her closer, and she nuzzled her face into his chest.

'Are you worried you're like your father?'

'I'm worried that I don't know if I am or not. I'm worried that my fortune has been based on threats and lies. I'm worried I didn't treat you well. I'm worried that I don't deserve your forgiveness.'

She was so close to forgiving him. She understood why he'd done what he'd done—she'd always understood the predicament he'd been in. But forgiveness...? He was genuinely remorseful. And it was a fact that he had been so worried about her earlier he'd been prepared to leave Daisy in the snow. That was something she couldn't reflect on without her chest constricting.

'I don't think you're like him,' she said honestly, and pressed her face harder into his chest.

She breathed him in, committing his scent to memory. Lingering cologne mixed with the salt water of the hot tub, the gentle steam from the water. Even if they did manage to put the past behind them, their path forward together would inevitably end when they left the cabin. Besides, they'd made a deal not to talk about the past. Or the future.

The hum of the motor was soporific; the vibration of the warm water was lulling Lily into sleep. She hardly heard Jack say, 'Do you want to talk about David?'

Lily pressed her cheek against his lovely chest once more before she pulled back and looked at him.

'You don't have to,' he said. 'I don't mean to pry. But it seems like a pretty big thing you've just gone through, and

I feel like an insensitive jerk for not asking. So I figure I can't win either way.'

Jack shrugged and lifted half his face into a lopsided grin. Lily was reminded instantly of the boy outside Soleil all those years ago.

'It was mutual, I guess…as much as these things ever are. We talked about it…prevaricated. But eventually I realised it wasn't going to work.'

'Different schedules? Lifestyles?'

'No, we're actually pretty similar, and from similar backgrounds. He grew up in Oakland with a single mother, and he's earnt every penny he has. We think alike on most things.' Lily felt the muscles of Jack's body stiffen against hers. 'We just didn't think alike on the one thing that really matters to me.'

Lily could sense Jack was holding his breath. He didn't dare ask what that one thing was. She wasn't sure if she should tell him. David was an ex, but a recent, decent ex. She still owed him a certain amount of loyalty and would expect it in return.

But she was here with Jack now. And, while they had agreed not to discuss the past or the future, no promises had been made so none could be broken. But Lily owed it to him to be truthful. And she owed it to herself. To Past Lily and Future Lily.

'My sister had a baby in March.'

'Yes, you told me. Georgia.'

A burst of warmth rushed through her: he'd remembered.

'I just adore her. More than I thought it was possible to love anyone. I'd do anything for her.'

Jack nodded, but let her keep on speaking.

'I always thought I'd have kids—at least I never believed I wouldn't. I guess I assumed that David and I would…

Eventually. But it turned out he didn't want them. He said he loved me, but…'

Lily had spent the past few months discussing David's reservations about children with him. She didn't need to rehash them with Jack.

'He has his reasons, and so there we are.'

Lily placed her hands on her knees and the water sloshed around the tub. She waited for Jack to say something like *That's understandable*. Or, *Well I don't want kids either*. But he didn't. Instead, he reached for her hand. He pulled her across him and lifted her onto his lap. He took her face in his hands and brushed his lips gently against hers.

He hasn't run.

With that realisation Lily let her body relax into his kiss. Jack ran his hand up her back and slipped his fingers through her hair. His kisses became deeper, more resolute. Her muscles melted as her blood pumped faster.

But before she lost herself entirely in the kiss she pulled her lips back. 'What about you?'

'What about me?'

She looked up at the stars.

You have to ask him. You know that.

She drew a deep breath. 'Kids. Do you want to have kids?'

They both exhaled at the same time.

'I can't really answer that now.'

'So it's a no.'

She waved the air to brush her question away. What did it matter anyway? It wasn't as if he'd be having kids with *her*.

'No, it's an *I don't know*. I don't know what's going on in my life right now.'

'I get it,' she said, but her voice cracked.

It's okay that he's not sure, because you don't have a future together, remember?

'Lily, it's complicated.'

'I know. I understand. With everything that's going on with your father.'

Jack shifted his position in the tub and looked at her directly. 'It's not just that. It's my mother too.'

Jack's mother had died when he was young. She knew he'd always been sad about it, but John Thorpe seemed to have filled any gap left by her absence. Helena Thorpe had been an actress, but that was just about all Lily had ever known about her.

'I don't think I've ever told you everything about her.'

'I know she died when you were young.'

'Yes, but she and my father were already separated by then.'

Lily had a vague recollection of knowing that too. 'So you weren't living with her when she died?'

'No, I hadn't seen her for a while. A couple of years.'

'Oh, Jack, that's awful. I didn't realise.'

'I don't think I ever talked about it. I think it's because I was always told not to. It was always a secret, but Mum cheated on my father. She had an affair with one of her co-stars.'

Everything around Lily stopped for a moment. *Jack's mother had had an affair?* 'I don't think I ever knew that.'

'No, it was kept very quiet. Dad managed to keep it quiet. You couldn't manage it these days. My mother left acting, the States, and me. Dad was furious, but that fury masked his devastation. I don't think he ever got over her.'

John Thorpe had never remarried. That only now struck her as strange. Most of his contemporaries were on their third wife. At least.

'Oh, my goodness. You're serious?' The significance

of what he was telling was dawning on her bit by bit. 'No wonder he hated me.'

'He didn't hate you. He just…'

'No wonder he tried to get me out of your life. And when that didn't work he forced me to stop acting.'

'We've been over this, Lily. And I've apologised on his behalf.'

'Except you never told me this. It explains things, doesn't it?'

'What does it explain?'

'Maybe he didn't do it out of spite, but out of love? Maybe he genuinely wanted to protect you from the kind of hurt he went through with your mother?'

Jack moved across the hot tub, away from her.

'You must have thought about that?' she said.

He shook his head. 'Lily, I'm ashamed to say I didn't even believe that he'd tried to sabotage your career in the first place. I didn't think about his motivations.'

It was hard for Lily to reassess John Thorpe with this new information. 'How did I not know this about your parents?' she asked.

'Like I said, the story was buried.'

'How?'

'You tell me. No one but us and Drake knows why *we* really broke up,' Jack said.

And sometimes I don't know either, thought Lily.

'My mother moved to Paris. Never looked back. I don't know what went on between her and my father. I was too young. I only know that one day she brought me Holly, kissed me, and said goodbye. Apparently she was diagnosed with breast cancer six months later. I wasn't told anything, really. I was told we were going to visit her, and then I was told that she had died. I think Dad was trying to protect me. I've just never been sure form what.'

'Oh, Jack, that's just awful. And you were—what? Five? Six when she died?'

He nodded. 'Six. So that's what I mean by complicated.'

She slid across the seat to him. She couldn't help but hug him. Four-year-old Jack, given a dog and left behind for ever by his mother.

And that was why Jack was not certain if he wanted a family. The scars from his childhood were deeper, more painful, and more complicated than she'd ever realised.

A cool breeze slid over them and she shivered. They'd never spoken about kids back then, being so young and full of optimism. Maybe if they had stayed together the children issue would have been the one to break them up in the end anyway?

She wasn't sure how to feel, but Jack pulled her close to him again and she looked back up at the endless sky.

She exhaled. She didn't need to think about the future— only this moment. Whatever else happened, she would now be able to look back on the past with far less pain. They had shared some very happy times and she had some wonderful memories. Over the past few days Lily had felt able to open up those memories and look at them again.

'How long were you waiting there?' Lily asked.

'Where?'

'Outside Soleil,' she said.

'I don't remember. But however long it was, I would have waited longer.'

Lily smiled.

CHAPTER THIRTEEN

FOR THE FIRST time since she'd arrived, Lily heard the birds singing outside. The drip-drip-drip of melting snow echoed over the valley. The kitchen curtains were wide open, revealing the morning sunshine and the full beauty of the landscape. She sipped her coffee and looked out. Her laptop was open in front of her, but her eyes kept being drawn upwards and outside, her mind less on her writing and more on what had passed between the two of them last night.

After all these years it felt as though she and Jack had reached a point of understanding, of closure. The burning anger she'd felt after their divorce had long faded, although confusion and uncertainty had persisted. Now maybe they could be friends. Discreetly, at any rate. They wouldn't have to avoid each other if their paths happened to cross.

It was unlikely that they would see each other, though—especially now Meredith and Bradley had separated.

'How's the book coming?' Jack opened his laptop across the table from hers and sat down.

'Getting there. I still have some work to do, but I'll have something to give my editor when I get back and I'll make my deadline.'

It was strange how productive she'd been in the past few days. So much had happened in her life, but being up here with Jack had unlocked something in her and the words had flowed faster than they had in years.

Jack had inspired something in her.

Either that or she had purposely focused her thoughts and energy on the book because it was easier than focusing them on Jack.

'What's the book about?' he asked.

'It's about a woman who's been falsely accused of the murder of her ex-husband. She doesn't have an alibi, and of course she's wished him dead in a thousand ways and made no secret of it. The only way she can defend herself is to track her ex-husband down and prove he's not dead.'

Jack leant forward. 'But *is* he dead?'

Lily smiled. 'You'll have to read it to find out.'

'Does it work out? Does it have a happy ending?'

'That would be giving it away, wouldn't it?' She grinned, and when he grinned back her stomach turned cartwheels.

'So, it's like a romance?'

She snorted. 'Hardly. It's a thriller, Jack. They don't get back together in the end, if that's what you're wondering. He's a complete jerk.'

'Oh.' Jack turned from her and back to his screen and lowered his head. He seemed disappointed.

'I told you—I don't write romance,' she said softly.

Putting the past behind them and resolving their differences was one thing, but they'd agreed not to talk about the future. As far as Lily was concerned there was nothing to be gained by thinking about a future with Jack. They both knew that couldn't happen. Jack's life was in turmoil. Even if she understood why he'd acted the way he had in the past, she didn't trust him not to abandon her again on the basis of some lie John Thorpe might spin against her in the future. Besides, even if he managed to resolve things with his father, he might still decide he didn't want children.

She went back to her screen, he to his. It was nice, working at the kitchen table, near the fire. Daisy lay at Jack's feet, lifting her head every now and then for a scratch.

It was good being here together. Comfortable. Until he looked up and smiled at her and her stomach went off cartwheeling again.

She didn't know what Jack was going to do about his father, but she did know one thing: it was a decision he had to make alone, and she couldn't help. As much as she might want to offer advice, she was the last person in the world who should. Her opinion of John Thorpe was too low to be unbiased. And her feelings for Jack were too complicated to be objective.

'Tea?' she asked, and stood to boil the kettle.

'That would be great, thanks.'

'How's your research going?'

Jack shrugged. 'I don't know. I've found a few deals that I'm trying to look at more closely, but nothing is leaping out at me.'

'Maybe your father was very good at covering his tracks.'

'Or else Western State Media is an anomaly.'

Lily filled the kettle and rummaged in the cupboard for the tea bags. She felt his eyes on her and smiled across the kitchen at him.

'Is it really such a bad idea? Seeing each other again after we leave here?' he asked.

Lily's fingers hovered over the teacups. She wasn't sure if she'd heard him correctly. She looked back at him. He was staring at her, earnest, pale with uncertainty.

'Jack, you know as well as I do it won't work,' she whispered.

Surely he saw that? The barriers that had been in their

way a decade ago still existed—his father's low opinion of her for starters.

'Why?' Jack jumped up and moved towards her. The kettle started to hum. 'You're single. I'm single. We've sorted out our differences, haven't we?'

'Well, yes, but it took us a decade to resolve one disagreement—that hardly means we'll work well together.'

'I'd say it was a once-in-a-lifetime disagreement, wouldn't you?'

He smiled at her again, and her stupid stomach didn't just cartwheel, it back-flipped and somersaulted in mid-air. If only she could look at that smile every day...

The kettle started to boil and she found she had to raise her voice slightly to hear herself speak. 'It's not that simple. The press would... They'd crucify us.'

'Crucify?'

'Well, maybe not. But they'd never leave us alone. I can't do that again.'

She'd barely survived the first time.

Jack picked up her hands and wrapped his around them. He moved his face close to hers and the room started to spin. She closed her eyes and dropped her head to make it stop.

She was falling for him again. If she had ever fallen out of love with him in the first place. The truth was she'd never stopped loving him. Sure, at times she'd hated him, but the love had always been there too. Just overshadowed by feelings of hurt and frustration. But the closer they became now, the more she was aware of how far apart they really were. Being here, away from the world, was one thing. But back in the real world it would be impossible.

Jack-an'-Lil. The intrusion into their lives would be immense, her mother would never recover from the shock, and Meredith would never forgive her. What about all the people who'd helped her pull her life back together after the break-up? All the people who'd protected her from the fallout? All the people who had been her loyal friends and confidantes over the years? She couldn't do it to them.

The kettle reached boiling point, hissed and screeched. They both turned and looked at it. She wondered if the automatic switch was going to turn it off or whether the damn thing was broken. Finally it clicked off and the noise dropped away.

'Is it really about the rest of the world, Lily? Or is it about us?'

'I'd be risking everything.'

'It's my father, isn't it?'

'Your father has already taken one career from me.' *And it seems he's as ruthless as he ever was.*

'I can't risk my second career…my reputation.' *My heart.*

She didn't have that strength in her. Her first break-up with Jack had taken every ounce of resilience she'd ever possessed.

'I can't get over you again.'

'I'm not asking you to.'

He squeezed her hands in his, but as his grip tightened she only felt the need to run away.

She pulled her hands out of his. 'Jack, you know it's not that simple.'

'I'll make it that simple. We'll forget about the rest of the world. Pretend it doesn't exist.'

'But it *does* exist,' she said. 'Maybe not up here. We can pretend here for a few more days. But eventually we'll run out of food. Eventually we'll have to return to the real world and you will have to make your choices.'

She couldn't even tell him what those choices were, because that would mean interfering between him and his father. He had to make those decisions himself. And he couldn't do it with her because she was biased against his father. And if he couldn't make such a momentous life decision with her at his side, then what was the point of them being together?

'Choices? You're still asking me to turn my own father in to the police? That's what this is about, isn't it?'

'Jack, I'm not asking you to do anything. I've told you— it's not my business, not my place.'

'You still think I should tell them.'

She sighed deeply. 'If you must know, the Jack I know... the Jack I...'

The words were left unspoken. Sensibly so. She couldn't ask him to turn his father in. But she couldn't be with him unless he did. And he'd never forgive her either way.

'Jack, you don't want me involved. You said so two days ago.'

Jack frowned, but didn't argue.

'I don't want to see you caught up in his mess. I don't want to see you getting into trouble for something *he* did,' she said.

'I'm already in trouble. What if my life, my own business, is built on a lie? I've always believed that my father is the most remarkable, talented man in the world. I respected him professionally. I admired him for raising me alone after my mother left.'

A decade ago Jack had had to choose between his father and Lily. Now it seemed he had to do the same thing again. But this time Lily knew better than to demand his choice. She knew from bitter experience that there was no right answer here. There were no winners.

'Jack, when we broke up my life changed for ever. I won't go through that again.'

Lily shook her head, her throat too tight to speak any more.

Jack's face turned from brightly hopeful to dark. Then he shook his head.

'Daisy!' he called. 'We're going for a walk.'

Without Jack and Daisy the house was quiet. But her heart was screaming and her soul was whimpering.

He'd put her in an impossible position. His father was still between them and would be for a long time. Lily couldn't be with Jack while he was still loyal to his father—and yet she couldn't imagine being with him if he was not. Jack had an impossible decision to make, and either way Lily would have to deal with the consequences.

But even if John Thorpe hadn't blackmailed his way into a dozen business deals, so what?

Lily's chest tightened.

Suggesting they see each other again was not only delaying the inevitable, it would also make the situation so much worse. Up here, in the privacy of the mountains, no one knew what was going on between them. But outside this bubble...? The chance of keeping even a platonic friendship a secret was non-existent.

The stress of their wedding and their marriage had almost broken her. Their divorce had. She'd lost her career and very nearly her sanity. But she'd managed to pick up the pieces and make a new, happier life for herself. It was happiness and security hard fought-for and won, and she couldn't risk that.

But you're older now. Stronger too. You're no longer beholden to a studio—you're your own boss. It's completely different.

Maybe. But maybe not. The Thorpes were still so powerful in the entertainment industry. If John Thorpe decided he wanted to buy her publisher and cut her from the list there would be nothing stopping him from doing so.

Lily pressed her hand to her chest. More than anything she'd be risking her heart. She had never stopped loving Jack—not completely. There had always been a secret pocket of love for him, hidden away in a corner of her heart. How could there not be? They'd been together for two mostly wonderful years. They'd got married. Of course she'd loved him with everything that was in her—and did love like that ever really completely stop?

But sharing a history and a few days of passion didn't mean you simply threw caution to the wind and exposed your soul to the universe. And that was what she'd be doing. She thought once again of her mother and sister and Meredith, and everyone else who'd stood by her and supported her through her break-up with Jack. If she started seeing him again, it would be a slap in the face to all of them.

She attempted some work, but it was useless. Every single one of her senses was alert to each wind gust or bird call outside. Was it Jack coming back? She longed for his tall, broad silhouette to come into view, but what would he say when he returned? What would *she* say? Would he tell her it was time to leave now the snow was melting? Or would he just get into his car and drive away without a word?

If only he'd waited a few more days to ask her, maybe she would have had a better handle on whatever it was between them. It was as if she was being lashed by waves and wasn't sure which way was up. If only she'd had more time to think.

Her life was full of 'if-onlys'.

If only it was simple.

If only they could love each other as if the rest of the world didn't exist.

A shrill noise made Lily nearly jump out of her seat. The sound of the phone ringing was as strange as it was unexpected, and it made her heart freeze. The only people who knew she was here were Meredith and her sister, Ruby, and neither would call except in an emergency.

It would just be Ruby checking in, that was all. And the sudden desire to hear a friendly voice hit her like a giant wave.

She raced to the phone and lifted the receiver. 'Hello?'

'Um…hello?'

The voice was deep, unfamiliar. Masculine. She froze.

'Can I help you?'

She put on her most formal voice. It was a wrong number—it had to be. The only possible alternative, she supposed, was that it was someone calling for Jack. And if someone was calling for Jack then they mustn't know she was here.

'I'm calling for Jack.'

The various risks of every response flashed through her brain. If she said Jack was here, she'd be acknowledging she was here with him. Jack was wanting to hide, wasn't he? But what if the caller was calling about something important?

'He's not here right now. May I take a message?' She hoped she sounded like an efficient secretary, not a secret lover.

'Lily?' the caller said.

Her throat seized. 'I don't know what you mean.'

'Lily? It is you, isn't it?'

'Of course not.'

She tried to make her voice sound different, but it only sounded shaky and nervous. So much for being an actor.

'Who may I tell him has called?'

'It's Bradley—Bradley Jackson.'

Her pulse hammered in her throat.

'And he has your number, Bradley?'

'Of course he has it, Lily.'

'It's not…'

She shouldn't lie to Bradley Jackson, of all people. Bradley, even with all his faults, was a loyal friend to Jack. Surely he wouldn't expose them?

But this was just the beginning. The beginning of what would await her if people found out that she'd spent the past few days stuck in a remote cabin with Jack.

She put the handpiece back into the cradle.

Lily was standing at the door when Jack pushed it open. For an instant his heart leapt. She'd changed her mind. She was sorry. She wanted to give them another chance.

'Bradley called,' she said, and his heart instantly felt several pounds heavier.

Daisy bounded past him and greeted Lily like an old friend, but Jack stood still by the door.

He understood on an intellectual level that Lily had reservations about them seeing each other again. Heck, he wasn't sure it was the most sensible, most cautious thing to do. Especially now. But he also knew that, as awkward as rekindling their relationship might be, not seeing her again would be far worse.

After a long walk along the ridge, he had begrudgingly accepted her point—figuring out what to do about his father was his dilemma, not hers. It wouldn't be fair to pull her into it. Let alone to drag her along in whatever fall-out eventuated.

That didn't mean he had to be happy about it.

'What did he say?'

'He asked that you call him. And, Jack, he guessed it was me.'

Her voice was fast and panicked.

He shrugged off his coat.

'It's not such a leap; he knows that Meredith has lent you the place in the past.'

'But he knows I'm here with you *now*.'

'You didn't think he'd find out?'

'No! Of course not. I didn't think anyone would know. *Ever*.'

'It's his house. Meredith may have already told him you're here.'

'Jack, what if he tells someone?'

'He's not going to tell anyone. He's one of my oldest friends—he's kept bigger secrets than this.'

Jack walked over to her, and as he did he finally understood what she'd been trying to tell him.

'That's what you're really worried about, isn't it?'

'What?'

'People finding out. About us.'

'Of *course* I'm worried about that. Aren't you?'

Jack grunted. 'Funnily enough, it isn't my biggest worry right now, no.'

If Lily was worried about people finding out about them, then she really didn't trust him. And if she didn't trust him they couldn't ever move forward.

'This isn't nothing for me,' she said. 'You have protection…the Thorpe name, the Thorpe fortune.'

'The Thorpe reputation may not turn out to be as strong as you think.'

The world finding out that he had slept with Lily wasn't his biggest worry. It wasn't even in the top ten. His biggest worries were so big and all-consuming that every other worry in the world felt petty in comparison.

In no particular order, his three biggest concerns were: his father might be going to jail. His family company might be going down the tubes, taking the livelihoods of all his staff with it. Lily didn't love him.

Maybe the last one was in fact his number one worry, because on his walk he'd realised something for the first time. He might be able to survive worries One and Two if he wasn't also burdened with Three. If Lily loved him she would be by his side, and then he would be able to handle anything that followed from everything else.

And now…

But he couldn't dwell on that. It was strange that Bradley had called. He probably just wanted a whinge about Meredith. Or to check in. And yet…

He dialled Bradley's number, and as he did so he noticed Lily disappear with her computer off to the other end of the house.

Bradley was quick and to the point. Jack would have expected no less. Yes, of course Jack would leave right away. Yes, Bradley would ask his PA to get Jack on the next commercial flight back east. LAX? No, on second thoughts better make it San Francisco.

He knocked on Lily's door and she opened it an instant later.

'I need to leave. Ten minutes ago.'

He turned and walked back to the kitchen.

She rushed after him. 'Wait—what's happened?'

'You can stay. You don't need to leave.'

'But, Jack…the roads.'

'The ploughs have come through. I saw them on my walk with Daisy just now. Once I get to the main road I'll be fine.'

'Jack, what's happened?' There was a tremor in her voice.

'Dad's had a stroke,' he said, and he pushed past her out through the door to the garage.

'Oh, Jack, I'm so sorry. How is he?'

'Conscious, but not speaking.'

Jack opened his car boot. Looked in. Realised he didn't have his suitcase to put in it.

She crossed her arms and blocked his path. 'Jack, please. Wait a moment.'

'I need to leave.'

'Then, I'm coming with you.'

'And what if we're seen together?'

She shook her head. 'We'll be in the car, no one will see us. Besides, at this point I'm more worried I'll never see you again. You're upset, you shouldn't be driving alone, especially when the roads are like they are.'

For a second, hope bloomed in his chest. He ignored it.

'So we'll both go over the cliff together?'

'If that's what it takes.'

He walked past her to go and get his suitcase, but she grabbed his arm and stopped him. Her hand was warm and soft on his arm; she wasn't gripping him hard, but he didn't seem to be able to pull away.

'Why?'

'Because I care.'

'You don't care about my father.'

Let's hear her deny that.

'Don't be like that, Jack. I care about *you.*'

It would be madness for her to come. He couldn't put her at risk from her fears about the world's press. But he also didn't want to be alone just now. And he wasn't ready to say goodbye to her just yet.

'I'll drive you to the airport,' she said.

'I'll be fine.'

'Don't be stubborn. You've had a shock. I'll drive.'

Ten minutes later Lily was reversing carefully down the drive. All their bags were squeezed in her boot, and Daisy was sitting happily across the back seat.

Once they were safely on the cleared main road, she said, 'There may be no need to panic. Many strokes are very mild, and I'm sure he has the best possible care.'

'Bradley called all the way down here to tell me, and he said I have to get back before there's an announcement to the stock exchange. Does that sound serious enough for you?'

She flinched. 'Jack, I didn't mean to imply it isn't serious. I was only trying to make you feel better.'

'Well, you don't need to.'

He didn't want to be unkind, but every time he felt her sympathy he wondered if he might cry. And he wasn't about to do that. Especially not after she'd told him she didn't want to see him again.

Everything was a mess.

How long did his father have?

What had to happen now?

What if the Western State stuff didn't come out until after he was dead? Then Jack would probably never be able to clear his name.

But what if his father had to face a criminal prosecution on his deathbed?

Each scenario was worse than the one before.

'I'm very sorry,' said Lily. 'And I'm sorry if you thought my comment was insensitive—'

'It *was* insensitive, whether I thought so or not.'

Maybe his remarks were insensitive too, but if anyone in this car had a right to be upset right now it was him. He'd just been rejected by the woman he loved and barely an hour later had been told his father had suffered a stroke serious enough to make him lose his ability to speak. If that wasn't an excuse for a few sharp comments then he wasn't sure what was.

The woman he loved?

He looked across at her, but she was focusing intently on the road. Of course he loved Lily—he'd never stopped. He'd tried so hard to, but now it was impossible. His feelings for Lily had always been there, kept hidden but secure in a special compartment of his heart.

He loved her. But there was no joy in the realisation, only pain. Because she didn't love him back.

The truth was he had no idea how serious his father's stroke was. There hadn't been time for any discussion. All Bradley had said was that the hospital had urgently been trying to locate Jack.

'The board's going to make an announcement later today and you need to get back yesterday.'

That was what Bradley had added, just before Jack had hung up.

'I understand,' Lily said softly.

'Do you?' he snapped.

There was no way anyone in the world could understand all the thoughts and emotions that were going through Jack's mind right now. For all Jack knew his father might not even be alive by the time he got there...

The skin on Jack's chest started to burn. He glanced over at Lily and saw her face was etched with concern. He looked the other way. He pushed his broken heart back into the compartment he'd been keeping it in for the last decade and firmly closed the lid.

CHAPTER FOURTEEN

THE SPECTACULAR SCENERY was a surreal backdrop to the uncomfortable silence in the small car as Lily drove along narrow, winding roads, gradually getting back to civilisation and the rest of the world.

When they were two miles out of Oakdale she said, 'We should stop for a quick break.'

She half expected him to argue, but he didn't speak. She drove up to a diner and pulled in.

'Coffee? Something to eat?' she asked, but he shook his head.

He was out of the car and on the phone before she could unbuckle her seatbelt.

Lily went into the diner, used the bathroom, then ordered two coffees to go. As an afterthought she grabbed some doughnuts as well. She didn't feel like eating, and doubted Jack did either, but they had both skipped lunch and she had no idea where her next meal was coming from.

As she waited for the coffee she looked out through the diner window. Jack had his phone to his ear and was pacing by the car. Daisy sat at his feet and looked up at him.

Lily watched as Jack repeatedly ran his hand through his thick hair. Her chest tightened. She wanted to go to him. To wrap her arms around him and hold him tight. To absorb some of his pain.

He's not your responsibility...you can't fix this.

Had it only been a few hours ago that she'd woken up entangled in his arms, happy, content, complete? Was it only this morning she'd looked at him across the kitchen and willed the moment not to end? Had she really felt those things, or had she just been dreaming? Their conversation, the phone call, the drive down here—it was all nightmarish. And this, here and now, waiting at the counter in a dodgy diner in Oakdale was real. What had happened between them at the cabin had been the dream.

No amount of passion, no matter how addictive, could mend this. No amount of attraction, no matter how strong, could bind them back together.

She carried the coffee and doughnuts back to the car and climbed in. Jack continued his conversation a few minutes longer, then climbed back into the passenger seat.

'Coffee?'

'Thanks,' he muttered as she started the car.

'There are some doughnuts too,' she added, but didn't receive a reply.

They were still a couple of hours away from San Francisco International, but she knew it would be the last few hours she ever spend with him. She didn't want to waste them arguing, and yet she didn't want him getting on a plane feeling like this. His pain spread, somehow, to her.

For better or for worse. In sickness and in health...

She had no right to know what was going on—not since she'd told him they couldn't see each other again. But she needed to at least ask.

'How is he?'

'The board are going to make an announcement publicly this evening, just after the markets close.'

'Before you get back?'

To make an announcement so soon, even before Jack

was back, must mean John Thorpe's condition was serious. Or there was another explanation, but Lily didn't dare give voice to it.

Jack nodded. 'They can't really keep it a secret.'

There were all sorts of explanations for that as well, though Lily didn't want to speculate.

'Jack, I'm so sorry. What are you going to do?'

'He's in hospital. I'm hardly going to turn him in to the police now, am I?'

'That's not what I meant.'

She placed her hand tentatively on his knee. When he didn't shake her away she squeezed.

Lily drove into a multi-storey car park and chose a spot in a quiet, out-of-the-way corner.

'Since privacy matters so much to you, you may want to wait until I've left before driving away,' Jack said.

'Jack, please just hear me out.'

'You said you didn't want to see me again once we left the cabin.'

'I didn't say that. I said we *couldn't* see each other again.'

'It's the same thing.'

It wasn't, and she hoped that one day he'd realise why and agree that this was for the best.

'Jack, you're about to get on a plane and walk into one of the most stressful periods of your life. Possibly the biggest scandal. Do you really think my presence is going to help? At the very least your father would flip if he thought you were seeing me again.'

Jack's expression softened, although he didn't look at her.

'Do you want to layer scandal on scandal?'

'Do *I* want?' He laughed scornfully. 'That's a good one.'

He was acting like a kid, though she'd forgive him that.

He'd just had some awful news, on top of what he was already dealing with. Still, it hurt to have it directed at her.

And after that what else was there for him to say? *Thanks for driving me? Thanks for nothing?*

Maybe one day she would feel grateful for the last few days, for that precious time with Jack, for the circumstances that got her book pretty much finished.

Maybe one day she'd look back on this week with some positivity.

But not now. Now there was only one more thing to say.

'Goodbye, Jack.'

CHAPTER FIFTEEN

THE NEWS OF his father's stroke had broken by the time he arrived in New York. Everyone was extremely shocked, and desperate to tell Jack how sorry they were, but Jack was almost numb, and he walked through the airport in a daze.

If only Lily had stayed by his side.

But that, as she had made very clear, was impossible. And who could blame her?

Every eye in the place was on him, even with a special escort through the back corridors of the airport. He couldn't have dragged Lily into the storm that was currently swirling around him.

Bradley was waiting for him.

'Lily Watson, hey?'

'That's what you open with? How's Dad?'

The smirk fell away from Bradley's face and they started to walk towards Bradley's waiting car.

'Not great, but he's breathing on his own and conscious.'

'What does that mean? How is he really?'

Bradly shook his head. 'I can't tell you anything else. You'll have to speak to the doctors. Why didn't you tell me he had dementia?'

Jack stopped walking, feeling the earth rock under her feet. 'He has *what*?'

'Dementia. That's what one of the doctors said. He wouldn't tell me much, but I wondered what you knew.'

What Jack knew? *Nothing.* It was all news to him. And yet at the same time he wanted to kick himself. He'd noticed his father getting frailer physically. He was in his seventies after all. But he hadn't dreamed that his father's cognitive abilities were anything less than they had ever been.

Now it all made sense. His father's actions over Western State Media, when Jack would have sworn he'd never do anything like that.

Jack didn't know much about dementia, but he did know it was more complex than just memory loss. It could cause personality changes as well. And sufferers sometimes tried to hide or deny what was happening. They were also at increased risk of other health issues. Like heart disease and stroke.

'Damn.'

'I know,' said Bradley. 'I'm so sorry. I hope it goes without saying that I'm here for you.'

Jack closed his eyes and rubbed his temples. Where to even start?

When he opened his eyes he noticed for the first time that it was dark already on the East Coast. A wave of exhaustion washed over him.

'What do you need?' Bradley asked. 'A stiff drink? Something to eat?'

'I need to get to the hospital, but I also need to speak to our lawyers as soon as possible.'

Bradley's face creased.

'I'll explain at some stage, I promise.'

'Whatever you need.'

The two men began to walk again.

'So, Lily Watson...' Bradley said again.

CHAPTER SIXTEEN

THERE HAD BEEN no need for Lily to park in such a far-flung corner of the San Francisco Airport multi-storey car park to say goodbye to Jack. There had been no need for Lily to keep what had happened between them a secret from everyone, including her sister.

It was the stop at the Oakdale diner she should have worried about.

After dropping Jack at the airport Lily had driven straight back to Monterey. She'd stayed inside, finishing her book for the deadline, and only ventured out of the house properly for the first time about a week later.

She'd gone out one morning to the supermarket and seen the photos.

Jack-an'-Lil in Secret Mountain Tryst! the headline screamed.

Lily's heart had stopped beating for several moments before her veins had flooded with adrenaline and fear. She'd climbed straight back into her car and driven home without her groceries.

At home, she'd done something she hadn't done in years—she'd searched online for her name and Jack's together.

Sure enough, there were the photos on a popular gossip website. A photo of Lily standing inside the diner, waiting for her coffee. She was looking out of the window with a wistful look on her face. The caption read: *Lily's concern for Jack.*

Lily's skin turned hot. She had been worried. She remembered that moment perfectly—the way she'd been thinking about Jack and what news he might be hearing on the phone at that moment. The way she'd worried about whether he would confide in her or not. The way her heart had been breaking, both for him and for her.

Following her recent break-up with long-time partner David Parks, Lily Watson escaped into the wilderness with ex-husband and current flame Jack Thorpe. News of John Thorpe's serious illness sent the couple back to New York to be with him.

It can only be a matter of time before the pair announce their plans to remarry, say sources close to the couple...

There was a small shot of her climbing into the car, and a larger one of Jack on the phone, raking his hand through his hair and looking gorgeously tormented.

She touched her fingers to the screen, then quickly pulled them away as if she'd been burnt.

It was ten a.m. in California, one p.m. in New York. Would he have seen the photos? Someone surely would have told him about them by now.

Lily sat at her computer and tried to write, but it was useless. She was waiting for the phone to start ringing, for her emails to start going crazy. With every moment that passed she felt sicker.

Jack would call, wouldn't he? He'd have to. They'd need a plan.

The idea of talking to him terrified and excited her all at

once. But the phone didn't ring. She had to shut down her computer, because instead of working she was scanning every website she could think of, but there was nothing else. Was she the only person in the world who had seen the photos? Why wasn't anyone *doing* anything?

When nervous energy threatened to rip her apart she went for a walk and left her phone behind. For a few precious hours she walked along the beach and the cliff-edge, not jumping at each noise expecting it to be a phone call.

What was Jack going to say? What would she say? Why, when she knew that she'd done the right thing back at Yosemite, was it still ripping her insides apart? Why was she still waking up in the night and reaching for him, only to feel bereft when her limbs found only empty space beside her?

I could handle it if only he was with me. If only he'd call and let me know we're in this together.

But he didn't and they weren't. She had chosen her life and sent him back to his.

Back at her house, she tapped her phone cautiously.

Nothing.

No missed calls. No messages. Not even any emails.

She dialled her sister.

'Hey—' Lily began.

'It's Aunt Lily!' Ruby cried.

Lily heard Georgia gurgling in the background and her heart clenched.

'How's it going?' asked her sister.

'Did you see the photos?' Lily asked, her heart in her throat.

'What photos?' Ruby wasn't talking directly into the phone and Lily heard her moving around.

'*The* photos.' Lily didn't think it needed more explanation.

'Sorry, sweetheart, I'm in a baby haze. I'm getting no more than two hours' sleep at a stretch.'

'There were photos today…'

'What sort of photos?'

'Of Jack and me,' Lily whispered.

'Who? Sorry—I missed that.'

'Jack and me!' Lily shouted.

'Jack Thorpe?'

'Of course Jack Thorpe. Who else?'

'So, what are you doing in the photos? Are you topless? Naked? Pregnant? Abducted by aliens?'

'No, nothing like that. He's standing by my car. I'm inside a diner.'

'So?'

'So, don't you see? Everyone will think it's on between us again.'

'Hang on.'

Lily heard shuffling, Georgia screeching, the phone being dropped.

After what felt like an hour Ruby picked up the phone again. 'I see them, but I don't understand the problem. It's a couple of random photos of someone who looks like you and a random photo of someone who could be Jack. I suppose… If you squint. They're obviously not real.'

'I guess so…'

'You guess so? Wait, Lily.' Ruby's voice was loaded with warning. 'They aren't genuine, are they?'

Lily couldn't answer. This was why no one had called. Everyone assumed the photos were fake. No one believed for even a moment that she and Jack had been together at a roadside diner halfway to the middle of nowhere.

'Why don't you come and stay for a few days?' Ruby said.

Later that evening, over a bottle of wine, Lily told her sister everything. Well almost everything. She left out the part about wishing she could stay in Yosemite for ever with Jack, and she certainly left out the part where Jack had said he wanted to see her again.

She didn't get the reaction she'd expected. Ruby laughed.

'Six years ago every second person asked me when the baby was due after an obviously doctored photo was published of you with one hand in Jack's and another on a fake pregnant belly. Now, even though they're real photos, no one believes it. That's fantastic!'

Ruby laughed again. Loudly and long.

'I'm glad you find my misfortune amusing.'

'It's not misfortune—it's good fortune. You've had a few days of string-free sex with your ex and also managed to escape the attention of the paps. All that and your book is nearly done. Seems like a win-win to me.'

The next day Lily noticed, during her forensic and obsessive searching online that Meredith had released a one-line statement denying the photo was Lily. Someone from Thorpe Media had done the same for Jack.

Meredith hadn't even come to her for a statement.

Of course not. As Ruby said, no one believes the photos are real.

If she hadn't been so tense she might have laughed, just like Ruby. It was an enormous relief.

'You seem flat. Disappointed,' Ruby said to her.

'I often get this way when I finish a book.'

'Rubbish. You're usually elated.'

Lily held Georgia in her arms and stroked the soft hair on her head as she rocked her hips to lull the baby to sleep. 'I guess it's everything. The book. Yosemite. And I have just broken up with David.'

'How exactly did you leave things with Jack?' Ruby probed.

Badly? Awkwardly? Excruciatingly?

'It was rushed. He had to get back for his dad.'

'Did you agree to see each other again?'

Lily looked away and shook her head.

'Do you want to see him again?'

Lily didn't answer.

'I'll take that as a yes.'

'No, it's not a yes.'

'But he wants to see you?'

Lily didn't reply.

'So he wants to see you. Of course he does—he has good taste. We've always known that.' Ruby grinned.

'It doesn't matter what he wants.'

'It does, to a point. But you need to worry about what *you* want.'

Lily shrugged. 'I don't think that matters much either.'

'What? Sweetheart, no. Of course what you want matters. At this point it's all that *should* matter.'

'I can't go through it again.' Lily could barely get the words out.

Ruby took her hand. 'You're older this time. And John Thorpe probably won't have the influence he had before—especially after his stroke.'

What Ruby said made sense. But even though she was older, was she truly stronger? Lily didn't feel stronger. She felt as vulnerable as ever. She was in her thirties and she couldn't play around any more; her next relationship had to be The One.

Besides, Jack didn't seem to want kids as badly as she did, so why was she even still thinking of him at all?

'It's not just that. He's dealing with his dad. The last thing he needs now is—'

'Maybe what he needs is you.'

It was far more complicated than Ruby knew, but Lily

couldn't tell her about the whole mess. Lily had been searching obsessively for news of John Thorpe and Thorpe Media, and even Western State Media, and reading everything she found.

If Jack did expose his father, what then?

Would she finally fully forgive him? Would it make it right?

It was a crisp and dry December day when Lily and Meredith met at Soleil for lunch.

'They love the latest book,' said Meredith. 'They're talking film options.'

'Film options? Are you kidding?'

Lily's throat constricted. None of her novels had ever been adapted for the screen, despite many of them being bestsellers. She'd put that down to the fact that 'Lily Watson' was still on most producers' blacklists.

'It's about time, don't you think?' added Meredith.

Lily's elation was muted. She was glad her publishers loved the book. She did too. But her memories of finishing it would always be mixed. Getting a movie deal would be bittersweet.

'Have you spoken to Bradley?' Lily asked.

'Only through the lawyers.'

Lily had known this was probably the case, but was disappointed nonetheless. Meredith and Bradley were her only real link to the Thorpe enclave.

'Have *you* spoken to Jack?'

Meredith's question surprised her, but she said, 'No, why would I?'

'I know he was at the cabin with you.'

'Oh.' Lily's heart paused. 'Who else knows?'

'Just Bradley. As far as I know. So?'

'So what?'

'So what happened?'

'So there was a mix-up, wasn't there? You lent me the cabin the same week Bradley lent it to Jack.'

Meredith smirked. 'I'm so sorry. It was completely unintentional, I swear. So what happened? Who left?'

'We... Well, we both ended up staying.'

'Together?'

'There was snow, we were stuck without chains, so we both stayed.'

'Even when the snow melted?' Meredith's lips twitched.

'You know something, don't you?' said Lily. 'There's something you're just itching to tell me.'

'Not exactly. I have a theory, though. Can I try it out on you?'

Lily poured them both another glass of wine. 'Sure. And make it good.'

'So, you arrive at the cabin and you're both surprised the other is there, but you're stuck and neither can leave. However, you haven't seen each other in years, and have all sorts of unresolved feelings for each other. It's probably not pleasant to begin with, but you're forced to speak to one another and have conversations you should have had years ago. Am I warm?'

'You're in the ballpark.'

'I don't know what happened next—Jack's obviously in a world of pain with his father, and he's been busy with the business and giving half the family money away.'

'It's not quite half their money.'

'He's given billions away—not just to the people his father has been dealing with recently. But to charities too. All sorts of people. Did you know about that?'

Lily nodded. At first she'd tried to avoid all the news about John Thorpe's declining health, the allegations against him and the entire restructuring of Thorpe Media that Jack had implemented. But not knowing had been somehow worse, so she had been following the case as closely as Meredith. She had learnt that even though he was recovering from his stroke, John Thorpe had also been diagnosed with Alzheimer's disease.

'So it seems that Jack has finally taken over the business,' Meredith said.

'But he had to.'

'Yes and no. Despite his health issues John dug in pretty hard, and it took a lot of work on Jack's part to get his father to stand aside. Did you know that?'

Lily shook her head. The backroom goings-on at Thorpe Media were not public knowledge, though Meredith obviously still had an inside source.

All Lily knew was that John Thorpe had retired permanently and was 'assisting the FBI with their enquiries', although under the circumstances he'd never be charged. Luc Harmon was apparently being equally helpful. Jack was now firmly in charge of Thorpe Media, and had marked the new regime by giving a large portion of their holdings away—including returning some newspapers and television stations to their previous owners. Thorpe Media had also recently made significant donations to the various communities involved.

The share price had suffered at first, but was steadily growing again under Jack's tighter, more focused leadership.

Lily had watched it all unfold with mixed feelings, glad that John Thorpe was no longer controlling such a powerful company, but still sad about everything he'd done to her in the past. She was glad for Jack too, but sometimes the realisation of what they'd both lost swept over her and almost felled her. They might have lived a wonderful and happy life together if John Thorpe hadn't been so broken. If he'd been more open and honest with everyone.

'I'm celebrating something else,' Meredith said. now 'Bradley and I reached a settlement yesterday.'

Lily lifted her glass and tapped it gently against Meredith's. 'That's great. Of course none of it's great…but at least it's not hanging over you any longer.'

Meredith smiled, but Lily noticed her eyes were glistening.

'Who's getting the cabin?' Lily asked, not knowing if she hoped it was Meredith, so she could continue to visit it, or Bradley so that it would be closed to her for ever.

'Neither of us. It's been sold.'

'Sold? Already?'

'Yep, months ago. Why? Did you want to buy it?' Meredith grinned.

'Maybe…yes. No. I don't… It doesn't matter anyway.'

It was just as well the cabin was sold. She couldn't go back there—not now…not after everything that had happened.

'So what are you going to do about you-know-who?' Meredith asked quietly.

Lily gave a long sigh. She had thought about reaching out to Jack, but each time something different had held her back. They hadn't parted on good terms—they had both agreed that they didn't have a future together—so why torture one another? It would be best to keep the break clean.

'Nothing.'

'Really?' Meredith asked.

'You're not seriously suggesting I call him? You of all people. You had to pick me up after what happened last time and listen to my endless ranting and raving. I thought you'd be telling me to run a mile from him.'

Now it was Meredith's turn to shrug. 'You were both

young and under a huge amount of pressure. Honestly? I've sometimes blamed myself.'

'What?' This was crazy talk.

'I should have stood up to John Thorpe. Called him out. Defended you more. You were just a baby dropped in a shark tank.'

'Meredith, it was not your fault.'

'But was it really Jack's? I mean, yes, to some extent, but he was young too. In awe of his father...forging his way in the world.'

'Are you seriously suggesting I get back together with him?'

Meredith gave a sad smile. 'I'm only saying that you shouldn't hang on to tightly to the past. Because the past tends to fade to dust and one day you might find you're holding on to nothing.'

Meredith was probably just feeling sentimental now her divorce from Bradley was being finalised, Lily thought. It was possible she wasn't the best person to be taking advice from right now.

I want to move forward.

As much as she wanted to see Jack again, she knew that it would only lead to more pain. More pain than she would not be able to withstand.

CHAPTER SEVENTEEN

LILY STEPPED OUT of Soleil into the crisp December air. Although this was LA, not Monterey, and certainly not New York, so 'crisp' was more like 'pleasantly mild' to most people.

She handed her valet parking ticket to the man at the lectern and pulled her blue blazer around her. The valet drove her car around the corner. She sighed. Even though they'd only shared one ride in it, every time she saw it she thought of Jack. For weeks, every time she'd climbed into it, she'd imagined she could smell Jack, and mostly Daisy. The smell had faded, but the memories had not.

The car stopped next to her, but the valet did not get out. She knocked lightly on the window and it slid down.

Her heart slammed into her throat. Despite the valet's hat obscuring the top of his head, those were the blue eyes she saw in her dreams. He nodded to the passenger side and Lily glanced around. No one was looking, or else they were in on the game and pretending not to be.

Did Meredith know? Probably. Either way, this was Beverly Hills and Jack Thorpe was sitting in her car. The safest option was simply to get in. And get out of there as quickly as possible.

Around the corner Jack flipped the cap off and threw it into the back seat. If the car had smelt faintly of Jack before, the effect now was…devastating. Discombobulating. Delicious…

'You knew I was there today?'

'Meredith might have mentioned it.'

'I planned it, you know… That day at Soleil.'

She was overwhelmed to see him. Surprised, certainly. Confused, definitely. But she wasn't sure yet if she was happy.

'Why are you here? You could have called me,' she said.

She'd thought about contacting Jack almost every day in the three months since they'd left the cabin but, terrified he wouldn't want to speak to her, had managed to talk herself out of it every time.

It's best left in the past. For all the reasons you told him. And then some.

But the ache hadn't gone away. Nor had the desire.

'I wasn't sure you'd want to see me,' he said.

Lily's heart hammered away in her chest like a ticking bomb. She didn't know how to calm it.

'How are you, anyway?' she asked.

'I'm okay. How are you?'

'I'm fine…well. Jack, I'm sorry. I wanted to call you… to see how you're doing. It was only…'

There was no excuse except for fear. And self-preservation.

'No, *I'm* sorry. I should have called you. I shouldn't have left things as they were. But I was hurt.'

'That was understandable. How is your father?'

Jack grimaced. 'He's doing okay. Physically, anyway. Mentally…he's been better.'

Jack pulled up at a red light and looked over to her.

'He'd been noticing a decline in his cognitive function for a while, but didn't tell anyone. About six months before the stroke his doctor made him have some tests. It's likely he's been suffering from the early stages of Alzheimer's for the past few years.'

'Oh, Jack, I'm so sorry.'

'It explains the Western State Media deal—but it doesn't excuse it. I should have noticed. If I'd been paying better attention to Dad it would never have happened.'

Lily reached over and squeezed his arm. She wanted to wrap herself around him, to comfort and console him.

'No, no…these things are insidious. And I'm sure he was doing everything he could to hide it.'

'Yeah—like trying to prove he could still put significant deals together.'

They sat in silence for a few moments. It was easy to hate John Thorpe; it was harder to accept that he was simply a person who had made some bad decisions through ill health.

There was a loud beep behind them. She looked up and noticed the lights had turned green.

'It must have been a difficult few months,' she said. 'With your father and sorting out the business and everything.'

Jack nodded. 'But that hasn't been the hardest thing.'

'It hasn't?'

He pulled over abruptly outside a shopping mall. She had no idea where they were. He turned off the engine and faced her.

'Lily, do you think there's any chance you could forgive me? I'm dying here. I love you with every ounce of my being. I'm sorry I didn't tell you that back at Yosemite. I wanted to tell you everything—promise you everything. A life together…children. Everything you want. I love you so much, and I'm so sorry, and I would do anything to make it right.'

She touched his arm. 'I love you too,' she blurted, and

the declaration took them both by surprise. 'I've never stopped loving you. Granted, sometimes I loathed you a lot too. But I never, *never* stopped loving you. I thought you must hate me. I thought…'

Jack took her face in his hands. 'My love is not delicate. It has withstood more than a few frank words from you.'

'It didn't withstand seeing me with Drake,' she pointed out.

'I was seriously hurt, Lily. I was more hurt than I could even articulate. And I was an idiot. I was hurt, but also confused. I didn't know who to trust—you or my father— and… Well, I've told you before. I should have come to LA sooner. I should have believed you immediately and stood up to my father, called him out on his behaviour. But I'm older now. And I know that's no guarantee I'll get things right in future, but I promise you I will try as hard as I can.'

'I was a fool too. I shouldn't have let Drake kiss me.'

'That's behind us now. I shouldn't have snapped at you back at Yosemite, but everything was so up in the air. I know you don't trust the Thorpes to look after you, that you don't trust us not to betray you again. I know that. But I want you to know that I will never hurt you again and I'll stand up to anyone who tries to. Do you think you could even just think about giving me a second chance?'

It was a risk. But Jack had changed and so had she. She had far more to lose by not letting him back into her life.

She smiled. Jack leant across and brushed his lips over hers. She didn't feel greedy, or rushed. She knew they had all the time in the world. The rest of their lives. She leant in, deepened the kiss.

It was only when she felt herself falling irrevocably into it that she pulled back. 'Where are you driving to?'

'I don't know. I didn't think that far ahead. I only wanted

to see you. Tell you how sorry I am and beg you to love me again.'

She giggled. 'Where even are we?'

'I have no idea. All I care about is being with you. I don't want to go back, only forward. And only with you.'

He leant over the centre console and took her into his arms.

It wasn't like their first kiss, or even their last. They had both changed and grown.

It was a kiss that promised her the future.

EPILOGUE

'CAN I TAKE the blindfold off?'

'Impatient, much?' he replied.

'It's been three hours, Jack, and it's itching.'

'Not much further. You trust me, don't you?'

Of course she trusted him. More than anyone. But it had been a long drive and her bladder was bursting. It had been doing that a lot these days. Just as she'd been told to expect. When you were expecting.

She was impatient. Jack, though, was not. But then he wasn't three months pregnant.

She couldn't quite remember if he'd been this patient when he was younger, but now he was calm, reassuring. Lily knew he'd wait for ever for her. Not that he had to— they had got married yesterday.

'Of course I trust you. But is there a bathroom where we're going?'

He laughed. 'Yes, I'm sure you'll be quite comfortable. Besides, the honeymoon is meant to be the groom's surprise.'

Lily wasn't exactly sure about that, but it was too late to argue now.

They had left her house in Monterey that morning, after a quiet and low-key day yesterday. A million miles from their first, gala-style wedding, their second had been small, intimate, and so much less stressful. Which might have had something to do with the fact that they'd got married again before anyone had even got wind of the fact they were dating.

It had been a small ceremony, with only her mother, her sister, her brother-in-law, Georgia and Meredith for her, and Bradley for Jack. His father had even flown in from New York, assisted by his nurse. He'd sat quietly through the ceremony and been overly polite to Lily. She wasn't sure that had been out of manners or remorse, but she'd decided not to let it worry her.

John Thorpe couldn't hurt her any more.

The President returned Jack's calls now—not John's.

The car slowed and Jack turned off the engine.

'Now?' she begged.

'Yes, now.'

Lily pushed the blindfold off her face and laughed.

'You guessed?' he said.

They were parked in the driveway of Meredith and Bradley's cabin. The high sky was bright blue and the view of the valley that had been largely obscured by snow on their last visit was now wide and open, and the rocks were glowing in the sunlight.

'I've been thinking of all the places we might be driving within three hours of Monterey, and I admit Yosemite was on my shortlist. But not here… Jack, I don't understand. It was sold ages ago.'

'Yes, to me.'

'When?'

'The day we left.'

Lily rubbed her temple. He would have had to have called Bradley pretty much as soon as he'd arrived back in New York.

'But…' She couldn't find the words.

'As soon as I left you that day I knew I'd made a mistake. And not just about that day—about everything. I always planned to give it to you, but I was pretty sure you wouldn't accept it.'

She nodded.

'But now it's my wedding present to you. I know you've always loved it. It's been your special place for over ten years…your refuge.'

'Yes, but…'

'Don't get all principled on me now. You know I can afford it. Thorpe Media might have taken a bit of a hit in the past few months, but they aren't kicking me off the rich list any time soon.'

He ran his hand through his thick hair. Attempted to look modest. But his eyes still sparkled.

Before she could think better of it, Lily reached out and grabbed his arm. 'Jack, no. We've talked about this. I'm sorry, and I know you are too. You don't have to keep on making gestures like this. The only thing I want from you is…you.'

He smiled and her insides somersaulted.

'You *and* a bathroom,' she added.

'You romantic, you.'

After they had unlocked the door Lily freshened up and Jack carried in their bags. Then he made them both a warm drink.

It was early March, but the sky was blue and the winter snow had all melted. Although it was warmer than it had been in September, Jack lit a fire while Lily read on the couch.

When it was lit, Jack joined her, and Daisy sat at Lily's feet with her nose resting on Lily's foot.

'Why does she like you best?' Jack asked a little grumpily.

Lily laughed. 'She knows who's boss, I guess.'

'Hmm…' Jack said. 'She might be right.'

'You don't really mind, do you?'

'Of course not. I told her to look after you.'

'Right…'

'I said, "Daisy, you have to look after Lily and the baby." So she knows.'

'But we agreed not to tell anyone until twelve weeks!' Lily feigned outrage.

'I don't care if Daisy never comes to me again as long as all three of you are with me.'

All three of them. They were a family. It was a strange and wonderful thought.

'What'll we do now?' Jack brushed a lock of her hair to one side and kissed her neck.

She sighed.

'Monopoly?' he suggested as his lips trailed their way up her neck to her jawbone.

'You're kidding, right? How about Scrabble?' Lily said.

Jack's lips found hers, firm and loving, and she yielded to his kiss. The sensation of his tongue against hers, his hand cupped her chin, made her stir inside.

He drew back just far enough to ask, 'Poker?'

'Now, there's an idea…'

If Lily wrote a hundred books she would never imagine a better man than Jack.

* * * * *

COMING SOON!

We really hope you enjoyed reading this book.
If you're looking for more romance, be sure to
head to the shops when new books are
available on

Thursday 2nd March

MILLS & BOON

OUT NOW!

3
BOOKS
IN ONE

Postcards
from
Paradise
— BRAZIL —

CHANTELLE
SHAW

CHARLOTTE
HAWKES

ANN
McINTOSH

Available at
millsandboon.co.uk

MILLS & BOON

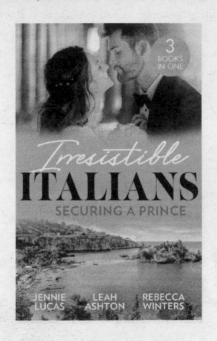